The Lion's Share of the Air Time

GAIL HULNICK

Sirocco Press

Sirocco Press, an imprint of WindWord Communications
#509, 4438 West 10th Avenue
Vancouver, BC, Canada V6R 4R8

www.siroccopress.com

ISBN-10:0987727486
ISBN-13:978-0-9877274-8-0

Copyright © 2015 Gail Hulnick
All rights reserved.

This is a work of fiction. Names, characters, businesses, places, events and incidents are either the products of the author's imagination or used in a fictitious manner. Any resemblance to actual persons, living or dead, or actual events is purely coincidental.

THE LION'S SHARE OF THE AIR TIME

For David, on the bright side of the road

GAIL HULNICK

THE LION'S SHARE OF THE AIR TIME

1

Envy at first sight. Definitely. Chelan took one look at Tess Cunningham, sitting at the head of the cedar boardroom table, then experienced such a craving to stand in the woman's thousand-dollar shoes that she was almost paralyzed. She wanted Tess's job title—Vice President, News, Programming and Operations, Lions View Television, Channel Two. She wanted a family like Tess's, her parents and brother owning half of the city. But more than anything, she wanted Tess's confidence.

The Executive Floor was not Chelan's usual turf, but when Matthew Dixon, the news director, asked for a volunteer to deliver a box to the president's office, she seized the opportunity. As a newcomer to the Vancouver TV station, her place on the ladder was precarious, and as a research assistant, her view of the upper echelon was usually blocked. She needed anything that could give her a better grip or vault her up to a less slippery perch. In her three months at the station, she had not even seen, much less met any of the movers and shakers.

She hovered outside the partially open door.

"Item One. The team. As you know, we've been planning to create a new position, Executive Vice-President, and to ask Tess to take it on." The president cleared his throat. "Circumstances dictate that we have to postpone that change."

Interesting. Chelan leaned in to catch a glimpse of

Tess's face. Not a sign of any reaction.

"Chelan Montgomery! What do you think you're doing?"

The words came in a hiss. Chelan turned to look. Uh-oh. Bad enough to be caught snooping, but what rotten luck that it had to be her boss.

"Matthew," she whispered. "I didn't want to interrupt them, but I wasn't sure where to leave the box you sent up."

Matthew Dixon looked at her as though she'd been unable to find a seagull at Ambleside Beach. "Go and ask my assistant." Reaching past her, he pulled the door shut.

Bad, bad luck.

Ξ

When the monsoons were howling and the Vancouver rain was horizontal, there was no better place to be than The Scribbler. It was a home away from home for every reporter, producer and editor in the city. Chelan dodged a friendly hug as she picked her way across the crowded room, two sudsy mugs of beer in hand.

Keith Papineau watched her every step until the drinks arrived, intact, at their table.

"Next time, you go," Chelan planted the mugs on the vinyl tabletop.

"Glad to. "Keith was giving all his attention to her, not the beer, but maybe that was just good manners. That Shaughnessy private school upbringing showed up at odd moments. Or maybe it was his age—guys over forty sometimes seemed to looked at women as if they were some unusual other species, while guys her own age seemed to just take them totally for granted.

"What is this, our third? Have we washed all the LV-TV dust off yet?" Chelan took a gulp.

"Naw, we'll need at least two more," Keith grinned at her as he pointed at a bit of foam on her upper lip. She could just imagine how geeky she looked. It was tough enough to be taken seriously, when she seemed barely old enough to vote. Even with her serious-journalist clothes and her long, red hair pulled back, she knew she didn't look the part. Her grandmother told her that the skirts needed to be longer, the hair shorter, and the necklines higher before she'd be treated like an equal. Chelan could just guess what she'd say if she saw her with beer suds on her face.

But this was the 21st century, not 1945, and solutions weren't so simple. If it weren't for Keith, she thought she'd go berserk in that newsroom. He was the best digger in the place, the reporter who hammered away at a lead until it cracked open and offered up its secrets to him or shriveled into dust. Once he took hold of a story he didn't let it go. He was very generous with his time and his skills, too, helping her to figure out a problem more than once. Little problems, nothing career-destroying—at least, not until today.

"Don't worry about Matthew. He'll forget all about this boardroom door thing." Keith smiled as the music changed from soul to rock 'n' roll. "Now, let's cut to the chase. What was it you were listening in on?"

"I wasn't there very long. The president was just announcing that they're postponing Tess Cunningham's promotion to executive vice-president."

"No surprise. Latest ratings weren't great."

"She needs another brilliant Keith Papineau exposé to draw those viewers in. What are you working on right now?"

"Can't say." Keith drummed his fingertips on the table and scanned the room.

Where was his usual blast of excitement for talking about his work?

"But it's good, right?"

"Yeah, it's good." Keith leaned back from the table. "I can't tell you much but it has to do with the marijuana grow-ops."

"And the money behind them?" Chelan guessed.

"Yeah."

Either he had no enthusiasm for the story or he was

distracted by something else.

"Connections? Surprising connections?" Chelan persisted.

Keith nodded. "Yeah. Long-time associates who want to let sleeping dogs lie." He leaned back in his chair, and then drained the rest of his mug of beer. "As maybe they should."

"That doesn't sound like you." Chelan tried to make eye contact.

"I think the police will have it nailed down in the next month or two."

Chelan couldn't believe he was talking about just following the herd and turning up at a police news conference to get the story. "You told me never to wait for the police, if I wanted to know what was going on."

As a group of half-drunk reporters, with their assorted friends and acquaintances, roared through the door, Keith stiffened.

"The atmosphere has definitely taken a turn for the worse." He stood and pulled on his jacket. "Come on. I'll walk you to your car."

A bit bossy, Chelan thought, but it was probably time to call it a night. She swallowed the last of her beer, then hustled to catch up to Keith at the door. He held it open for her to pass, then opened a black umbrella to shelter her from the rain.

"Whoa, what's this? It's like date treatment or something." It was a joke, but he didn't laugh. He steered her around the corner of the building to a sidewalk and tilted the umbrella so that they couldn't be seen from the street.

"Chelan, there's something I want to talk to you about." His eyes were beaming some sort of message but she couldn't decode it. Was he going to tell her a juicy piece of office gossip that couldn't be spoken in a room full of professional snoopers? Or ask her to work with him on the grow-op story—or on some other important research piece?

He winced. "Funny. I can blather on in front of a

THE LION'S SHARE OF THE AIR TIME

camera with no effort at all, but this kind of stuff is still hell."

Chelan stared at him, waiting. He moved his face toward hers. Unbelievable—was he going to try to kiss her? She took a step back and pulled her purse across the front of her body, opened the zipper and groped for her car keys.

With most men, that would be enough. But either Keith didn't get the 'this is a dead end' signal or just chose to ignore it.

"Chelan, there's some chemistry here. We both know it."

She raised her eyes to his and shook her head. He shook his in response, raising an eyebrow.

"No?" He smiled and she almost had a change of heart. But—"No."

"We could go as slow as you want. Maybe go out, somewhere other than this dive. Talk about something other than work."

"Keith, I can't."

"Do I get a reason?"

"You get at least three. You've only been separated from your wife for three months. We work together. And I'm seeing somebody else."

Chelan often felt moods rising from people. Call them auras, vibrations. Maybe just thoughts so powerful they had to be read. Whatever. The strong flash from Keith right now was pain.

She wished she could say yes to one date, but that would be wrong. Too easily misinterpreted as a come-on. And she was as sure as she was ever sure of anything that going out with any of her coworkers would be the wrong thing to do if she ever wanted to be taken seriously as a reporter at LV-TV.

If she even had a job left at LV-TV.

"You're seeing somebody?" Keith's eyes came back into focus and a hint of that gorgeous smile returned.

"His name is Twain."

"Twain?" Keith snorted.

"Yeah, I know, a bit unusual. It's a family thing. His mother loved Tom Sawyer or something." The atmosphere definitely seemed lighter. "Keith, I hope we're okay. I really like you. I respect you as a journalist... and I like being pals. I hope we can... I hope this won't..."

She studied his face. The age difference between them seemed very obvious at this moment.

"No, of course it won't." There was something phony in his tone but she had to be satisfied with what she could get. She tried to give him a hug but he pulled back. "Let's keep it no contact, okay?" The words were a bit abrupt but he softened them with a smile.

She smiled back. "Absolutely. And thanks."

He walked her to her car, parked at a meter about a block away, then went off down the sidewalk without a backward glance. Chelan watched him until he turned west on Georgia Street.

What a rotten day.

She couldn't face the rest of the evening alone in her apartment. It would be even worse if Layla, her roommate, came home. She decided to go back down to the station, chat with any of the reporters still working on stories for the late news, and watch the broadcast in Master Control.

Ξ

When Chelan pulled open one of the double glass doors leading to the newsroom, no one paid any attention to her arrival. She tried to slink into the corner, to the desk she shared with the night line-up editor, but Elliot noticed her.

"Chelan, there you are. Matthew's still here and he wants a word."

The all-purpose Assignment Editor. Elliot Dahl was an import from Fleet Street. He had spent his formative years in London, learning to pursue the news and write it in as colorful a style as possible. He said that one day he woke up

THE LION'S SHARE OF THE AIR TIME

and discovered he'd become a drone, an underpaid slave to the comings and goings of a small group of elected politicians. He packed up wife and three sullen children, moving them all to Canada's west coast, where he might still be just as miserable, but at least he was toiling in a city with a lower cost of living.

"And by the way, when am I going to see that list of property developers you're supposed to be researching?" Elliot had raised his lanky frame from his chair to skitter across the room and stand beside her desk. He moved faster than any human Chelan had ever seen, away from a track or an athletic field. The well-worn running shoes that he wore every day probably helped with that. Today they were accessories to a fashion crime of camouflage pants, vintage orange heavy metal rocker T-shirt, and leather wrist cuffs. His sandy brown hair had been finger-combed, which in a younger guy might mean he was up to date on style, but in Elliot's case meant he'd left the house in too much of a rush.

"Elliot, I've almost got it done. Just a couple of issues I want to be absolutely sure of." Chelan smiled into his eyes with what she hoped looked like confidence and professionalism.

"What issues would we be speaking of? It's a list of addresses and phone numbers." Elliot usually got the last word before dashing back to his own desk at the hub of the grid of nine television sets, set high on the south wall of the room. "Go see Matthew in his office upstairs."

Chelan sighed. When was he going to give her something substantial to work on? Something that would put her in the club with the others in this newsroom. LV-TV News had a reputation as an aggressive operation. Elliot and Matthew handed out tough assignments and expected their reporters to go after the facts, grab hold and hang on. They backed up their journalists, particularly the three senior investigative reporters. Every day they urged Keith, Wayne and Sam to go deeper, uncover more secrets, chase down the story, and bring the bad guys out into the open. Take no prisoners.

They had no interest in government news conferences or school board politics. That was not to say that they didn't assign and air many stories like that—millions of stories, actually. But those stories were given to the two reporters lowest in the pack, Amanda and Leonard, and they were processed like sardines on a canning line. Chelan hadn't yet even worked her way up to that level. She was usually assigned to the "light, bright, and trite" items. Who knew how long she'd have to wait before she got the chance to show Matthew that she knew how to attack a real story?

Chelan stood in front of the elevator, looking at her shoes when the doors opened and she almost took a step forward before she realized that the news director was right in front of her.

He was the best-dressed male in the building, except for George Stratton-Porter, the company president. Matthew didn't look much like a newsman, with his preppy ties and well-cut suits—more like an investment banker. Or a hockey coach behind the bench during a game. He was in perfect shape, a noteworthy achievement for a man who was a gourmet cook and a wizard in the kitchen, according to rumor.

"I want to speak with you," he said, stepping off the elevator.

He veered toward the wall near the window, leaving her to follow. Probably wasn't anything particularly heavy, since he hadn't suggested they go to his office.

He glared at her. "If you pull something like that again, you'll be fired."

Called that one wrong.

"Matthew, I'm very sorry." She kept her tone as sincere and matter-of-fact as possible.

"Could you not have predicted how bad that would look, if anyone had seen you? Skulking there, like some third-rate spy, eavesdropping on a corporate board meeting?"

THE LION'S SHARE OF THE AIR TIME

"I wasn't eavesdropping, Matthew, I was just… listening." Even Chelan could hear how lame that sounded.

"It looked like you were eavesdropping. You're lucky I spotted you, and not the president. Or Tess Cunningham." He glared at her and she had a déjà vu sense of being back in grade school, when a scolding closed off every avenue of apology or explanation, and the only thing you could do was wait it out. Then, just like when she was ten, the resignation gave way to rebellion.

Was this the same man who praised the investigative team for their stakeouts, their film shot through office windows, and their ability to read documents left lying around by a naïve source? Guess it all depended who the target was. And who had the job with the big pay check.

Whatever. He was the boss and he was her ticket to a better job. Chelan fought for self-control. "Of course, Matthew. I'm very sorry and it won't happen again."

He wasn't finished. "Do you understand me, that you are on probation now? If you take a step in the wrong direction, you'll be out that door so fast you won't know what happened."

Chelan wished there were a place to sit down. She could only nod, silently, and resist the urge to press her hands against her cheeks, which were burning now. Matthew stared at her for another second or two, then walked back to the elevator.

Ξ

Chelan usually ignored the constant talk on the police monitor in the newsroom. It was the desk editor's job to keep one ear on it, not the reporter's. When she was in her first news job at a small radio station, the police dispatcher's nasal voice, announcing "Code this" and "Code that", street addresses from the Downtown East Side, and cryptic references to various events "in progress" put her curiosity into overdrive. After a while, though, she got used to it, and like everyone else, relied on the assignment editor to pick up on anything important. It was easier just to tune it out, rather than forever wonder what had happened with the "domestic dispute on Victoria" or the "armed robbery in progress on Hastings."

But this one was unusual. Very unusual.

"A stabbing in Stanley Park, the scanner said. I'm going to go take a look."

The only other person left in the newsroom that night, Nevada Leacock, shook her head, typing faster. Nevada was one of Chelan's heroes, a veteran of every beat and every major story of the past 20 years. "Knock yourself out, Chelan. I'm going home, as soon as I file this. I haven't seen my boyfriend in three days."

So lame. Had Nevada always been this uninspired? Why be a reporter, if you didn't want to go and check things out? If she ever married anybody, she would make sure they understood that point. She grabbed her jacket and headed for the door.

As she passed the last desk she picked up the telephone and tapped in the two-digit local for the camera department. Twelve rings, no answer. That might foil some people, but she had another idea. She checked the staff directory and found Thomas's home telephone number under the Photography Department listings. A sleepy woman's voice answered. "Yeah?"

"Hello, this is Chelan Montgomery from the TV station. May I speak to Thomas, please?" Chelan could hear a baby begin to wail in the background, and then the cameraman came on the line.

"What?"

"Thomas, it's Chelan. There's been a killing in Stanley Park, and I wondered if you wanted to meet me there to check it out."

"Nah, I'd rather sit home and let somebody else get the stuff. Duh. Whereabouts in the park?"

"No idea. Have you got your camera with you?"

Chelan could hear the sounds of doors and drawers opening and closing. "And again—duh. I'll try to meet you at Prospect Point in half an hour."

"Okay, but if we miss connections and you don't see me by... oh, say, eleven, you go on your own and look for the exact location. Try to get some pictures, anything, even just a few pan shots of the totem poles if you can't find anything else. I'll call you if I get any more details. I'd like to have something on the late news, if we can."

"Gotcha. See ya later, maybe."

Chelan's Mini was not built for speed, but the traffic through downtown slowed everybody down anyway. She maneuvered around an SUV the size of a small bungalow and headed for Stanley Park, the heavily forested heart of the city. It was not far from the station's downtown location, but Thomas lived out in one of the suburbs in the valley, and it would take him at least three-quarters of an hour to drive in. Chelan was not counting on getting the visuals in time for the late news, although that certainly would be a bonus. But if she could get some facts from the cops at the scene, pick up some atmosphere, and even write a short script for the late-night news, then surely Matthew would let her continue with the story tomorrow.

And let her keep her job.

Ten minutes later, she was stopped in her tracks. Three police cruisers were lined up, cutting off the West Georgia Street lane that veered east into Stanley Park, forcing all of the traffic to carry on along the Causeway through to the Lions Gate Bridge and over to the North Shore. A fleet of huge, white, movie trucks was edging its way out of the park onto Georgia. Chelan pulled way over and parked her car. In an instant, a police officer was at her window.

"Move along, please," he said. "The park is closed."

"I'm a reporter from LV-TV News," Chelan fumbled in her jacket pocket, looking for an identification card.

"Call Media Relations. We'll probably have information at the regular morning news conference."

Chelan smiled and looked directly into his eyes. "What's happening, that you would close off the entire park? Is it somebody on the bridge?"

The officer smiled back. "Not a suicide. You'll get the details at the news conference." He turned away, then came back. "The ambulance will be coming through in a few minutes."

Chelan looked out through her windshield into the darkness. "Was it near the Aquarium over there?"

"No, on the other side, just past Second Beach."

"Dead? Or wounded?" Chelan persisted.

The policeman considered for a second. "Homicide."

Chelan smiled. "Thanks."

"Now come on, you have to move along." The officer stepped back from Chelan's window. She started the ignition and looked over helplessly at the stream of cars trickling along the three-lane road that cut through the heart of the park. The helpful officer walked over and held up a hand, directing Chelan into the flow. She drove through and rode the traffic tide onto the bridge, reaching for her cell phone as she went. She punched eight, her speed dial code for Thomas's phone.

"Somebody's been killed on the seawall over near Second Beach. I saw a lot of movie trucks around—I wonder if it something happened on some set? The police have closed off the park—get some shots of the traffic jam, and the cop cars parked across the entrance. And try to do it without anyone seeing you."

"Gotcha."

"You could park a few blocks away and go over on foot. Try going in off one of those little streets in the West End."

"I got it covered. What are you going to do?"

"Go back and file something for the late night, then try to get back over there and talk to somebody."

Chelan drove through North Vancouver and reconnected with the highway that led back to downtown,

THE LION'S SHARE OF THE AIR TIME

crossing the inlet over Second Narrows Bridge. It was late and traffic was light—she was back at her desk in half an hour, pounding out a script on her keyboard. She found some stock footage of the west side of Stanley Park—the seawall, the pool, the beach—and a few cutaway shots of Lost Lagoon and of the causeway. It would do for illustration on her short script tonight, and again tomorrow for her longer piece on the early evening news, when far more people would be watching.

She kept her eye on the computer and one ear on the radio news, but nobody else seemed to be on the story. It was enough to go to air as it was, but then just before eleven, she got a major break. The white production trucks she'd seen pulling out of the park had to mean a movie or a television shoot. She checked the schedules of all the productions around town, and then a couple of Web chat rooms. The TV series *Urban Battle* was shooting there that night.

Next call went to the police station main switchboard. She punched numbers until she finally got a human, non-recorded voice, and explained to a Corporal Nesbit that she had gone through the channels to the official media spokesperson and got nowhere. She questioned him about half a dozen scenarios—a stunt-related accident, a domestic altercation, a labor dispute—with Corporal Nesbit denying each. When she mentioned the TV show, there was a long pause. Finally, perhaps to get her off the phone and perhaps because he'd received authorization to release the news, he told her the victim was actor Jason Wheeler.

This would be big.

Vivian Brooke, the late-night anchor, balked at using Chelan's copy at first, demanding to know who had approved the insertion of this new item in the late news. But when Chelan got the police to email the news release directly, Vivian agreed to lead with it.

When Chelan got back to the park, the police blockades were gone. She drove the perimeter, along the seawall, without seeing another moving vehicle. There were a few romantic types parked at the water's edge, looking at the North Shore lights, but otherwise she seemed to have the place to herself.

Of course, that was just the edge of the park, the threshold. Walk even a few yards inland on the west side and you would be surrounded by ancient trees huddled as close together as men in a rugby scrum. And you would not be alone. People lived deep in the park, unseen and unapproachable.

Stanley Park was a wilderness in the middle of a city. Small parts of it had been developed and visitors could amuse themselves at an aquarium, a restaurant or an open-air theater. Or they could traverse the circumference of the park, along the seawall on foot or on Park Drive, passing the majestic Lions Gate Bridge. But the vast majority of the park was old-growth forest, dark and thick with moss. Just a few steps away from the path that hugged the water's edge would take you along an ancient trail into caverns of vegetation where sun and suburban people rarely penetrated.

Chelan drove at the slug's pace required by the posted speed limit. The rain wiped out her view of the Lions Gate Bridge, just ahead. She turned on her windshield wipers and cleared the water off the glass just in time to see a dark shape streak across the road in front of the car. She slammed on her brakes and peered into the dark. A squirrel, maybe? No, bigger. A raccoon? Chelan didn't think they moved that quickly.

She turned on the radio. She was so jittery at this point that she didn't care what station she listened to, just as long as it obliterated the silence of the park and smoothed out her goose bumps. But of course, it didn't. No matter how loud she played it. She was alone, driving through a dark, isolated place where someone had recently died a violent death. Very recently.

Chelan circled the park twice but saw nothing new. Yellow caution tape blocked off a section of the seawall and she thought she caught a glimpse of a police patrol, but otherwise nothing appeared to be any different than on any other night. The rain was coming down hard now and there were puddles covering the road. She had to slow down to make sure she didn't drench the engine and end up stranded in this dark place. Somehow old-growth forests and nature are a lot more appealing in the daylight hours.

She wondered whether Keith was giving any thought to their conversation from earlier that evening. She hoped she had been tactful enough—but was there really any diplomatic way to tell someone you didn't want him? She had been on the receiving end in these situations herself, once or twice, and found that time and a generous supply of vodka helped move you on to the next phase. But it was never easy.

Ξ

The next morning at 6:45 Keith Papineau stepped out onto his apartment balcony. The previous night's downpour had washed the air clean and the sun was already raising the curtain on what would be a record-breaker of a spring day. Down at street level, a garbage truck inched along the narrow street, its gears grinding and brakes squealing. High above the ground, outside Apartment 909, the air was still, as if all sound had been erased.

Keith slid the glass door partly closed behind him. He walked to the railing and scanned the Vancouver street below. He carried a coffee mug in his left hand and the scent of a full-bodied mocha java spilled out into the warm, sunny morning, mingling with the salt smell of the ocean, only six blocks away. Keith inhaled and raised his cup in a silent toast to the glory of the day.

A set of wind chimes, hanging high in the southern corner of the next balcony over, jangled in a random breeze, spoiling the silence. Keith watched the cars pull in and out of the no-parking zone in front of the apartment building. The

West End was the highest-density living space in the city, and while the sense of action, the restaurants, and the buzz were outstanding, the traffic could make you insane.

It wasn't usually so busy on the street this early. Keith still had two hours until he was expected at work, and the morning newspaper had only been delivered half an hour ago. The sweetness of the dawn had probably enticed a few more fair-weather strollers than usual. It didn't really matter. He watched as a seagull dove toward the ground, desperate to win the race to scoop up some prize piece of garbage on the sidewalk below. Through a slender view corridor to the right of the building opposite, the water of the bay sparkled and glistened in the sun. A perfect day.

Time to go.

2

When Chelan awoke at seven, it was already clear that it was going to be one of those legendary Vancouver days, when you could head out with a snowboard and a racquet. Play tennis in the morning, ride in the afternoon, and go sailing at sunset. And throw the golf clubs in the trunk, just in case the spirit moved you. The sky was a gleaming blue and the warmth of the sun had already absorbed last night's puddles.

From the window of her two-bedroom rented condo on Fairview Slopes, she could see the North Shore mountains and the Lions. That was about the only feature that justified what she considered an outrageous rent. It probably wouldn't seem so high to many people, but she had a long way to go before her income met her aspirations. She bridged the gap by pairing up with roommates—the current one, Layla, was a stockbroker between jobs. Someday, she vowed, she'd be in a nice place that she could pay for alone.

Waking up this early was a major accomplishment. She hadn't turned her lights out and her television off until the east coast morning shows on cable were signing on for the day.

She was unsettled after the conversation with Keith and terrified after the conversation with Matthew. Sleep hadn't been an easy catch. But she felt better when she thought about the way she'd taken the initiative on the Jason Wheeler crime story. That had to give her enough brownie points to wipe out the eavesdropping mistake.

She took an extended shower and shoveled in a high-protein breakfast, but nothing helped cut through her grogginess.

The newsroom was full of people when she arrived.

"Chelan you're late," Elliot did not like any entrance or departure to go unreported.

Chelan didn't look his way. Why was that any of his business? She searched the clutter on her desk for a memo or a note, commenting on her work last night, or giving her a follow-up assignment. Nothing. Oh, well. You live in hope or you don't bother getting out of bed in the morning.

Nevada sat at the next desk, hidden behind the *New York Times*. "She's not late, she's early for the night shift." She put down her paper. Nevada, the master of spin. No matter what the facts, she could pick and choose and polish until she had you looking at the story the way she wanted you to.

Chelan managed to twist her face into something that might pass for a smile. "Thank you. Is there any coffee?"

Chelan had addressed her question to Nevada, but Elliot felt that any question or comment, voiced in his vicinity, was fair game.

"Why don't you bring in a cup of the good stuff, like everybody else?" As assignment editor, Elliot was entitled to an office of his own, and Chelan spent at least half an hour every day wondering why he wouldn't get one and spend some time in it. One of these days, when her own position was a little more secure, she just might suggest it.

When or if.

"Because—" Chelan sat down and opened her copy of the local newspaper, "coffee prices are ridiculous. And I don't have time to turn an ordinary coffee break into a major expedition. And sometimes I enjoy drinking vending machine coffee."

"That's repulsive. You'll ruin your stomach." Elliot's brown hair and pale skin came into focus far above Chelan's desk.

THE LION'S SHARE OF THE AIR TIME

"It's my stomach."

Nevada folded her paper and brushed off her navy blazer. She was in her work uniform—blue jacket, blue pants. "Where's Keith?" He's usually here by now. He has to tell us when he's going to pay out on the hockey pool."

Chelan picked up the local papers. The story of the Jason Wheeler stabbing screamed from the front page. There had not been much time to gather details before going to press, but all four papers dug up a publicity or candid photo, which they blew up to fill half the space above the fold.

A celebrity stabbed, on the seawall. It was the subject everyone was talking about in the newsroom, and everywhere else, that morning. The media went to work, gathering information and risking, as always, the accusation that their interest was prurient, intrusive and ghoulish, and insisting, as always, that the public had a right to know.

Chelan waited for some kind of pat on the back for her initiative in calling the photographer and writing the copy for Vivian's late-night newscast. None of the other stations had coverage last night. But no one said a word.

She went over to look at the Assignment Board. Lead item: Wheeler stabbing, there it was, top of the list. With Amanda Crystal's name beside it.

Chelan found her own name on the board. At least it wasn't in the stand-by column today. But what did the "AGC" slug written beside it mean?

Nevada stood at her elbow. "Association of Government Communicators."

Chelan stared at her, without comprehension.

"They usually get the receptionist or somebody from PR to meet with the tour groups," Nevada commented.

The fog cleared and Chelan found her voice. "I worked my butt off last night. I followed up on a police report that came in very late. I went over to the park, I wrote a script for the newscast, I'm back in here before 9:00… okay, before 10:00 a.m. I thought for sure Matthew would give me that story today."

Leonard Chu, the new general assignment reporter from San Francisco, came up on her other side, pen and pad in hand. "Amanda was here before eight and Elliot sent her over to the park and to Wheeler's apartment. Oh, look, I've got a hunger strike over at the Immigration Department. And the network wants a piece for the Cross Country News." He wrote down the assignment in his notebook, looking as smug as a retired guy driving a red sports car with a blonde in the passenger seat. Chelan wanted to punch a wall.

"Too bad, Chelan," Nevada was sympathetic, as usual. That and a five-dollar bill would buy her a cup of coffee.

"I don't know what you have to do to get a break around here," Chelan slammed her newspaper on her desk and rearranged everything on it as noisily as she could.

"You have to know what to do with the cards you're holding," Matthew was standing behind them and he didn't look friendly. "Chelan, you called out a cameraman at ten o'clock last night. Do you know what I have here in my hand? This piece of paper is an overtime claim from Thomas Patranos, for triple time. Triple time pay! And he's entitled to it. He worked the night before last, at double time, and so he's entitled to triple time for last night. Do you know the size of the premium they get if they have to work after midnight? Then, he had less than eight hours between finishing last night and coming back in to work this morning. That adds up to a sixteen-hour day with less than a full break and not enough turnaround time. His overtime check is going to be into four figures!"

Chelan's head hung lower with each additional detail. Matthew was calm, but he was breathing as if he'd just run a hundred-yard dash. "And we ended up running with stock footage anyway! Chelan, you can't just take it on yourself to spend the station's money. You have to check with Elliot or me on things like this."

"Okay, I understand. It won't happen again. I promise, it will not happen again." Chelan looked up and stared

THE LION'S SHARE OF THE AIR TIME

Matthew in the eye. "But I still think you should let me follow up on the story today. I did a lot of work on it yesterday."

Matthew shook his head, rhythmically, five or six times. "It's Amanda's story now. I want you to meet with the government communicators and tell them how TV news works." He turned his back on them and was gone, back to the executive floor.

"Unfairly, that's how," Chelan muttered as she slumped into her chair. "This place is absolutely toxic."

Nevada tilted her head sympathetically. "It's a bummer, I know. And a complete waste of reporting talent."

That cheered Chelan up a bit. "You think I'd do a better job than Amanda?"

"With Amanda, we risk getting ninety seconds on what he was wearing when he died." Nevada's phone rang and she spoke quietly into it for a few seconds. Sounded like she was confirming a time and place for some meeting. "Chelan, I know you're disappointed but really, is this the kind of story you want to get your shorts in a twist over anyway?"

"What do you mean? It's big. He's a movie star—okay, a TV star—he's known around the world, nobody knows how or why he died…"

"But who is really affected? Do people suffer or starve because of anything to do with Jason Wheeler? Does he make decisions that drive people into poverty or insanity?" She saw Chelan's eyes glaze slightly. "Alright, you're right. Too much newsroom philosophy so early in the morning."

"And before I've had even one cup of coffee," Chelan picked up her phone and punched in a number. She let it ring twelve times—no answer at Keith's apartment. He must be on his way in to work.

"What's Keith working on these days?"
Nevada looked up from her computer screen. "Something quite hush-hush. Ever since he finished up on the smuggling story, he hasn't talked about anything new."

"Maybe he's taking a break, looking for the next idea?"

25

"Keith never takes a break," Nevada leaned back in her chair. "And he's never looking for the next idea. He always has a list of about ten that he's trying to get to. So I'm sure there's something. It's just too soon to talk to us about it. He practically works around the clock, that guy. Which is why I'm a bit curious about where he is this morning."

"Maybe he's out, tracking something down."

"It would be here, in the intranet planner. Matthew has us all enter information about whether we'll be in the newsroom or out for an interview, research, or a shoot, every segment of the day."

"Seems a bit intrusive."

"It took me some getting used to," Nevada admitted. "But I can see that it does have some security advantages."

"Would Keith let Matthew know if he changed his plans?"

"He'd just type it into the system from wherever he happened to be." Nevada called up the schedule onscreen. "And this says he's going to be here this morning."

"Maybe a traffic problem or something. I'm sure he'll call." Chelan looked up as one of the public relations staff called her name across the room.

It took two hours to escort the tour group through the station and answer their questions. While she was standing with them by the trophy cases as they read about the various awards LV-TV had won, Chelan saw Amanda bustle through the front doors of the station and head straight for the editing rooms. Still no sign of Keith, though.

She really wished she could talk to him. She doubted that he would be very excited about the death of a Hollywood movie star, but maybe the circumstances would intrigue him at least a little. Usually, though, it took at least thirty million dollars, a few dozen bikers, and a very extensive cover-up to stir his interest.

Very unlike him to be late on the morning of a hockey playoff pool payout, though. He told her once that it was important to have some small hobbies, some ordinary, even

THE LION'S SHARE OF THE AIR TIME

mundane interests to use almost like an anchor, while corruption and evil swirled around you, trying to blow you off course. He'd make a big fuss about some sports event results one morning, and you'd hear later that he spent the rest of the day interviewing a man who had chopped off the hands of eight people. The trick is compartmentalizing your life, he said.

She called him twice more but he didn't pick up the phone at home or the cell. She left messages at both numbers. Elliot didn't know where he was, and she didn't dare ask Matthew anything. No one else seemed too concerned, and certainly he had been out of the office working on a story for extended periods of time in the past. Still, she just wanted to talk to him. to find out what he'd been doing all morning. Maybe she wanted to reassure herself that what had happened last night wasn't going to put a permanent mark on their friendship.

She settled down in front of her computer and connected to the Internet. As expected, online newspapers all over the U.S. were headlining the story of Jason Wheeler's death and combing the details of the last moments of his life.

They reported that his usual after-work routine took him through the exterior doors of Studio 3B, along a short sidewalk to a parking lot, into the driver's seat of his black Porsche, and home before midnight. As the star of Urban Battle, he was expected to put in a long day. It was usually well into the evening before the director released everyone to go home, but it didn't take long for Jason to speed away from the studio and back to the comforts of his penthouse apartment on the West Vancouver waterfront.

This particular night, however, the usual was not to be.

Audience research had shown that viewers wanted to see Tom Tyrone, Jason's character, going farther afield, being more adventurous, and doing more dangerous stunts. That meant more location shooting. Last week, the producers had unveiled an ambitious schedule that included scenes on a mountain, a suspension bridge, a waterfall, and the ocean floor. Last night's sequence was shot near the Stanley Park seawall.

After signing autographs for a dozen fans who waited behind barriers to the set, Jason walked off quickly, not waiting for any kind of escort. No doubt he was anxious to get home and put this day behind him. As he had revealed in several newspaper and magazine interviews recently, he was annoyed with the way the show was developing. It started out as a relatively cerebral puzzle, a brainteaser of a detective show, set mainly in the cop's office and home. Nobody mentioned hang gliding or cliff jumping or rapids shooting or scuba diving when his contract was signed.

But pull a few people in off the midway at a theme park, Jason grumbled in a recent magazine piece, hand them passes to see a TV show, give them a survey and ask for their comments, and suddenly he was trapped in a whole different concept.

It wasn't that his ego or his box office value had grown too large for stunt work, he told the interviewer. It wasn't really stunt work at all, just outdoor work in unpleasant conditions. But he wanted people to stick to their promises, and he had been promised a certain sort of show. Nobody— no producer, no director, no executive, and certainly no writer—should be able, on a whim, to change his show into an action-adventure with three or four new characters. And two of them were truly bimbos, wearing halter-tops to go out and interview suspects.

Even though it was raining hard last night, a few people were walking or jogging on the seawall. Some of them saw Jason, but no one stopped him. In Vancouver, television and movie people usually got around without being hassled. You saw the occasional exception but it was always a fan, seeking an autograph or photo, and approaching the star in a restaurant or a store. The celebrity hounds had yet to discover Vancouver. It was a good place to be left undisturbed, unlike New York or L.A. or London, where the paparazzi made their living from the moments they could steal from a celebrity's private life.

Public recognition was a new experience for Jason Wheeler. After a dozen years of miniscule parts, innumerable acting classes, and dozens of different day jobs, Jason became a 'face'. An overnight success. One lucky break after another, like hitting twenty-one at the blackjack table, hand after improbable hand.

Being famous was not his goal in life, he mentioned in another interview, but like a lot of people who get even a small taste of it, he enjoyed it. The best tables in restaurants, the best seats in airplanes, concert halls and theatres, the best suites in hotels, the best-looking women. Summoned out of any crowd to the front of the line—no, past the line, and into the exclusive domain. Deference, respect, courtesy—all disappearing from the lives of everyday people, but available to anyone who could achieve celebrity and fame, and was willing to pay the price.

They were even calling Jason these days for political comments and endorsements of political candidates and issues. It was not Jason personally they wanted, of course. It was his celebrity and his success. His name had become a brand.

And the money! Twelve million dollars a year to memorize some lines and do a dream job. Neither a famous face nor an ability to make people believe some character was real should justify paying someone twelve million dollars a year.

None of the passersby took any notice of him that night. That Vancouver cool—or maybe the hat and the slouch did give him some extra personal space or a bigger zone of protection. Jason's pace brought him up behind a middle-aged woman in a tracksuit. She told police that he sped up and moved out to the left to pass her. Three strides and he put enough distance between them to be comfortable. He was a man who made major efforts to stay in shape and keep the athlete's physique.

Jason slowed down and peered out into the blackness

of the night, scanning for the lights near Lost Lagoon. His car was a few hundred feet away. He stood beside it, then crumpled to the ground.

Moments later, the jogger reached the car and saw Jason, lying on the pavement, face down on the spidery network of cracks in the concrete. A knife lay on the pavement beside him. She saw the blood spreading from beneath his body, rapidly diluted by the heavy rain, and she started to scream.

And now the whole city—and people in cities all over the globe—knew about his last moments. Chelan wondered how much ink and airtime would be used up before they had a name and a face for the killer with the knife.

Ξ

Lillian Howe always walked Coaster before breakfast. It was amazing, how big a puddle such a small dog could make, and so she always tried to get him outside before he had a chance to relieve himself inside. He was a Shih Tzu, a name at which her grandsons delighted in laughing. She didn't find it amusing, but then it had been a long time since she was nine years old.

The dog picked his way along the grass beside the sidewalk. He required at least ten minutes to find the perfect spot, but she didn't mind the wait. That was the point of having him, wasn't it? To have a reason to get out, go for a walk, see people, and pass the time. Give some shape to the endless, amorphous hours of retirement.

Lillian sought out the noise and bustle of Vancouver's West End because she didn't want to be entombed in one of the suburbs before her time. She enjoyed the many years of relative serenity during her days as a librarian. Now that she was sixty-five she found that what she craved was noise and action. And independence.

Even if she weren't actually one of the active people, she liked watching them and imagining things about them.

So, to the horror of her son and daughter, she sold the family home in Coquitlam in a down market, and moved to Vancouver's West End, a neighborhood of high-rise towers and heritage buildings on tree-lined streets just blocks away from Stanley Park. She was looking for privacy, and a view of the bay and the Lions.

She loved those two mountain peaks that rose into the sky above the North Shore. In winter, they carried a coat of silvery snow. Now, in late spring, when the sun was setting, they turned the most amazing colors of purple and blue. Native legend had it that the peaks were made when two young women tried to stop a war. They were the daughters of the chief and at a festival in honor of their reaching womanhood, they asked their father to make peace with the tribe to the north. They invited their enemies to put down their weapons and come to the festival. Through some trick of imagination and geology, the chief's two daughters became immortal and were turned into twin mountain peaks, put in place high above the Capilano Canyon for all time, lions guarding the Lower Mainland.

Lillian loved the view and the smaller buildings in her neighborhood. She had no use for buildings that climbed fifteen, twenty, even twenty-five floors into the sky. They shut out the light, blocked the ocean vista, and housed far too many people in one stack.

Of course, Lillian did like to have a lot of people around. But she wanted them all in small-scale, aesthetically pleasing apartment buildings that didn't interfere with her view. Those weren't her only opinions; she had a long list of likes and dislikes, but until she came upon a neighborhood that answered them all, the West End would do.

Many people, her own children included, thought the West End was not really a neighborhood, just a jumble of high-rise buildings filled with transient young people. In truth, it had people of all ages, backgrounds, interests and personalities, just like any community. Lillian smiled at a little boy walking with his own small dog on a leash.

Running footsteps came up behind her and a man in jogging clothes went by. Coaster finally chose the best patch of grass and started to do his business. Lillian stood by, looking the other way, her plastic bag ready in her hand, for any of her passing neighbors to see. People tended to become quite annoyed if you left dog droppings behind. She watched the traffic inch by. It seemed that things got busy earlier every day. People tried to get a jump on the traffic and only succeeded in extending the rush hour further. It used to be that 7:30 a.m. marked the beginning; now there was a steady stream of cars pulling out of underground parking garages or heading for the West End shops and restaurants at seven every day.

Even with the traffic, she preferred the morning hours. She didn't like being out at night, after dark, when it seemed anything was possible. The West End had the high crime statistics that any city had, and Lillian was smart about avoiding trouble. She tried to get Coaster out for his final walk of the day before nightfall, and once the darkness arrived, she was snug, behind a locked door.

But in the magnificent morning hours, when the sun wiped everything clean with a new cloth, there was nothing to fear. Lillian tipped her face to the sky, enjoying the feeling of warmth on her face and feeding her eyes with the sweep of blue. In a couple of hours, she would walk to the market to take advantage of the Friday seniors' discount day.

Then she saw a sudden movement on one of the upper balconies of the high-rise tower across the street. No doubt someone was outside, relishing the fresh air of a new day. She squinted, trying to focus. Her eyes opened wide as she tried to make sense of what she was seeing.

A dark object fell from the balcony. It seemed to pick up speed as it rushed toward the street. Maybe a book, a cup? A piece of clothing accidentally dropped? But would she be able to see something that small coming from such a height? She strained to look and her posture drew Coaster's attention. He stared upward, then started to bark.

THE LION'S SHARE OF THE AIR TIME

The object was not an object, but a person. A man, falling from the sky. Lillian picked up Coaster and hugged him to her.

3

Elliot put down the phone and called across the newsroom. "Chelan, Matthew wants to see you in his office in ten minutes. Finish that voice-over script for David before you go.""

Chelan took a deep breath. This could be it. Maybe this was her last day at LV-TV. Maybe Matthew had decided that listening in on a board meeting plus booking your own cameraman added up to a firing offence.

"I'm supposed to come along with you," Elliott added

Chelan and Nevada exchanged glances. "Maybe it's a story assignment, Chelan," Nevada said.

Maybe. Stranger things have happened. "Maybe he wants to hear more about that documentary idea I outlined last week." She hunted for the right file folder on her cluttered desk. This could be the chance she had been waiting for, to show she could do more than fact checking or research. That the news director could trust her to talk to people, get the story, find the pictures, and write the script.

Nevada picked up the sports section. "Did you know that at other stations they actually let the reporters come to daily story meetings? They pass on what they've been hearing, suggest stories. Even offer opinions on the line-up."

Tim Phelan, the business reporter, spoke without looking up from his computer screen. "No, really? You mean actually let the people who have sources and contacts

THE LION'S SHARE OF THE AIR TIME

make some decisions? I don't believe it."

Nevada nodded sagely. "You're right. It's too dangerous. Must be just a malicious rumor."

"Yeah, couldn't possibly work. Too logical."

Never one to let a conversation go by without his input, Elliot was eager to jump in.

"No, Tim, that's true. I've heard that, too. At the public TV station. Everybody goes to meetings, puts forward ideas. I hear it takes forever for them to get anything done."

Nevada stifled a smirk. "And they probably have way too many ideas and way too much information."

Tim nodded, pounding away on his computer keys like a pianist playing Bach. "Bunch of left-wing kids."

Nevada crossed her legs and turned a page of her paper. "I'd much rather be here, waiting to find out what Matthew decides the newscast will be about today. After all…"

Tim chimed in. "He knows news."

Elliot looked suspiciously between them. Irony was a foreign land to him. Chelan had waited out this little play, but now she was getting impatient. She headed for the stairs leading to the executive floor, Elliot on her heels.

"Do you know what this is about?" Chelan took the steps two at a time.

"No idea." Elliot concentrated on conserving his oxygen supply, wheezing with the exertion. For a tall, thin man, he didn't seem to be in very good shape. "Nothing big, I don't think. No Cinderella stuff."

"No, Elliot, I know that's your department."

The instant Chelan said it, she regretted it. Partly because she had been taught the Thumper doctrine years ago by her grandmother—if you can't say something nice, don't say anything at all. She always had an attack of conscience after she took a shot at someone.

And partly because Elliot had clout. The last thing she needed at this TV station was an enemy.

She hoped this meeting was about her documentary proposal for a short series on computer hackers—or maybe

Matthew was ready to grant her request to work with Keith or Nevada on one of the big stories. She knew he thought she hadn't shown signs yet of being pushy enough but it was the old Catch 22—how was she going to learn the tricks and methods that worked if he wouldn't give her an investigative assignment or put her on the A-team?

Each morning Elliot and Matthew talked about the assignments and made their decisions in Matthew's office on the executive floor. Then Matthew's assistant e-mailed them to the newsroom. Elliot often told Chelan to copy them to the large whiteboard on the wall, a task that she thought fell into his job description, not hers. It would be very unusual for Matthew to call Chelan to his office to give her an assignment, but she'd rather speculate that a leap to hyperspace, rather than a crash-and-burn, was on her flight plan this morning.

If she were fired today, it wouldn't be fair. Not today. She'd had other bad days, when maybe somebody could have justified cutting her loose, but she really thought she'd shown her stuff last night. She wished she'd been able to get in touch with Keith and get his take on it. She wanted to be the best journalist she could be, and eventually run a television station. If they gave her a pink slip here, she wasn't sure what her next step should be.

One of the more frustrating aspects of working in the media was that no one laid out a simple, direct career path. There was no farm-team system, no evidence that taking a journalism degree was necessary to finding a good spot or staying in one. Chelan knew high school dropouts who were at the top of the ladder, and PhDs who sent out tapes and résumés to a resoundingly silent response.

Unlike law or medicine or even pipefitting, no person or committee laid out a specified length of time and set of skills you needed to qualify, no body of knowledge you had to prove you had mastered, no exams to pass.

And unlike sports, you had no clear opponents, no rules of competition, no referees. All's fair in love, war, and

THE LION'S SHARE OF THE AIR TIME

media career planning. It was enough to drive you nuts with frustration, if you were inclined that way.

Chelan was too impatient for journalism school. After four years on a swimming scholarship at the University of Washington, doing a Bachelor of Arts degree in history, she was sick of classrooms, dead people, and of the water. No money was available for any more education anyway—her father had made that very clear. Chelan wanted to live in Vancouver and so went calling at LV-TV, asking the news director for some career advice. And Matthew had pointed her north and east, to the coast and then to the Canadian prairies, to servitude at small-town stations.

She was a big believer in following the advice of mentors. Since her father felt that he had very few useful suggestions to offer her, and her mother hadn't been in the picture since she was five years old, she had started to seek out older, wiser, successful people when she was in high school.

She had done a stint of one year at each small station. That was considered a suitable apprenticeship at most places. Chelan knew of some hot shots who had done a much shorter time in the boonies and moved right into choice assignments in the big city. There were others who had stayed on longer, sometimes meeting and falling in love with a local, settling down to a life of covering business club luncheon speeches and the annual Summer Fair.

She paid her dues, at the tiny TV stations. She fumbled her way through her first few stories and gradually developed confidence and skills. She winced, now, when she thought of some of the howlers she perpetrated. There was the time she went on the air to report a scientist's discovery of "microscopic orgasms". And the time she described a port city that was a popular sailors' recreation destination, as "awash with seamen, looking for a night out on the town".

Still, she continued to learn. Her ignorance and joy in the job shielded her from the embarrassment that might have accompanied mistakes of this sort. She paid her dues

37

and she was ready for more responsibility.

After two years, she called Matthew again. The conversation was forever branded on some neuron in Chelan's brain. "I've learned a lot and I'd like to come to work at LV-TV," she said.

"We have no openings right now," Matthew's voice was remote.

"But I heard last week that Evan Kendall has given notice."

"Your information is sound, but outdated. We've already filled that spot."

"Matthew, you told me that it would be a good idea for me to pay my dues at a small town station. I've done that for two years."

"Yes, and now you're two years farther ahead than you were before. But you still don't have the qualifications we're looking for. We don't hire people directly out of a small town."

"That's not what you told me two years ago, you jerk," the words formed in Chelan's brain, but she bit them back, resisting the urge to build a pyre of her career ambitions just for the pleasure of seeing the Matthew bridge go up in a glorious blaze. Instead, she decided to aim lower.

"Could I come aboard as a researcher or an assistant?"

Those were the magic words that got her in the door, three months ago.

But Chelan wouldn't let Matthew and Elliot forget, even for a day, that she wanted better assignments. She peppered both of them with proposals for documentaries, series, mini-series and features. She followed the police blotter the way day traders follow stock market fluctuations. Every time she heard of a big story, she called and asked for the assignment. Invariably, she was told she was too late; it had already been assigned.

From time to time, she got angry and frustrated, but Keith was there to talk her out of the blues. One of these days, Keith said. One of these days, there would be a story it

THE LION'S SHARE OF THE AIR TIME

would be impossible for them to deny her.

So far, there were few signs of any road leading to a position as a full reporter. At the beginning, she was enthusiastic and willing to do all the jobs no one else wanted. Running tapes back and forth. Calling to check dates, places, facts. Hunting for obscure pictures in the stock library.

The novelty wore off after about six days. She still felt she was in the right place—a newsroom where people were paid to dig up facts, find the truth, comfort the afflicted and afflict the comfortable, as the saying went. But she was tired of watching others do the job. True, she hadn't trained at a journalism school for four years, and she hadn't grown up in a family connected to broadcasting, nor to any other business.

She faced Matthew. "Please don't fire me, please don't fire me," she silently pleaded.

"Elliot, I changed my mind. I'd like to speak with Chelan alone," Matthew barely looked up from the memo he was reading. Elliot gave a thumbs-up and backed out of the room, closing the door as he went.

"Chelan, I have a meeting with Mrs. Cunningham and Mr. Stratton-Porter in five minutes and I don't have a lot of time for this," Matthew shuffled files, gathered his day book, PDA and cell phone, and rose from his chair. "I had a complaint about you from one of the guests you escorted this morning."

Chelan was speechless.

"A Ms. Tremelo from the Supply and Services Ministry says you were less than gracious, even brusque with their group. She said some of them felt that the tour was a waste of their time, because you wouldn't answer their questions."

"She asked me for the name of the person to contact when she wanted to get one of her press releases read verbatim on the air! If I'm thinking of the right woman, she was an arrogant..." Chelan read Matthew's facial expression and struggled to get herself into professional mode. "She seemed to think that the purpose of the tour was to get tips on manipulating the media, Matthew. She asked for the anchorman's direct phone number and was very cranky when I wouldn't give it to her."

Matthew stuffed his papers into a briefcase and snapped it shut. "Chelan, how can you possibly expect to function as an investigative journalist—follow leads, cultivate sources, extract secrets from hostile people—when you can't even manage communication with an "arrogant" whatever it was you called her? Look, I'd like to upgrade you and put you on reporting full-time. We need the extra pair of hands—we're going into a big push on ratings. We have to bring them up, and more people will watch our newscast if they think it's better than the competition. Our newscast could get better if we had more resources and more reporters."

Why did she feel as though he was lecturing an eight-year-old?

"Please show me that I can trust you, that you aren't so self-absorbed that you can't exercise some tact and diplomacy occasionally. Show me that, and I'll be able to put you in the game. Otherwise… I'll have to get another reporter from somewhere else."

Chelan could feel the blood pounding beneath her skin and she knew her cheeks were fire-engine red. "Matthew, I understand. Really. You don't know me that well, but I'm all about getting the story. And I really do want to take on more responsibility."

Matthew nodded. "That was strike two. Let's see if you can't hit one out of the park, sometime soon."

Ξ

The ambulance arrived with flashing red lights and silent siren, inching its way down the narrow West End streets. The paramedics did their jobs swiftly and professionally, lifting the body from the pavement to a stretcher and loading it in. Half an hour after the fall, there

THE LION'S SHARE OF THE AIR TIME

was no dramatic evidence of tragedy.

But Lillian could see many other, sublte signs. Yellow crime-scene tape still blocked the entrance to the apartment, white chalk outlined the body's position on the ground, and dark brown bloodstains showed up against the grainy texture of the concrete. A small drop of blood was deposited in each microscopic pit and groove of the pavement over a wide radius, leaving a pattern that looked like a waving fan.

The crowd drifted away, each person disturbed by this early morning evidence of the precariousness of life.

The police were inside the building, systematically knocking on every door and interviewing the residents. They had already taken statements from the three people who had been on the street when the body came down. Lillian and the other witnesses were still there when the reporters started arriving.

Outside the art deco apartment building, Liam St. Clair of Eyewitness News was the first one out of his car. He directed his cameraman to pan the scene, slowly up to the seventeenth floor balcony, down toward the street, zooming in on the bloodstained pavement.

Tight shot of the building's address, #683, in large gold digits on the glass front door, and its name, Point After Apartments. Pan over to Liam, who had the microphone in his hand, ready to record his stand-up, before he asked a single question.

He spoke earnestly, forcefully, and even gave a solemn shake of his head at one point, his mouth a grim line of reportorial sympathy. He paused for dramatic effect, and then said a few more words—probably his name and station ID. Motioning to his cameraman to follow, Liam strode toward the three people standing about half a block away, near the yellow tape. He made a small movement to signal the cameraman to continue shooting and stepped forward confidently, his microphone extended.

"Excuse me, could I ask a few questions? Did any of you see what happened?"

41

Lillian shuffled behind the taller of the men and tried to make herself inconspicuous. Maybe other people liked the idea of being seen on the television news, but she could not think of anything more dreadful. She tried to make herself invisible and edged backward, inch-by-inch, until she and Coaster could slide away down the street without being missed.

Ξ

Chelan walked into the newsroom, bracing herself for a wave of questions about her meeting with Matthew. But no one paid her any attention. The place was under a pall, like the smoky haze over a forest after a fire has killed every living thing in it.

Chelan finally made eye contact with Nevada. "What's going on?"

"It's Keith, Chelan."

"What's Keith? What's going on?"

Nevada's eyes were red. "They found his body this morning."

Chelan sat down on the edge of her desk and stared at her. Keith's body? What was she talking about?

"They found him outside his apartment." Nevada covered her hand with one of hers. "He's dead."

Chelan's hands clenched into fists. There was a roaring in her head that she hadn't heard since the frustrating days of her teenage years. She had to move, had to do something. She paced across the newsroom, ending up back at Nevada's desk.

"What happened to him?"

"We don't know much."

Chelan turned to see that Matthew had walked through the newsroom door.

"He was found on the pavement outside his apartment building." Matthew moved around Nevada's desk to face Chelan. He put out a hand, as if to touch Chelan's shoulder,

THE LION'S SHARE OF THE AIR TIME

then dropped it. "I know you two were close. Why don't you take the rest of the day off? You're free to go on home."

She didn't want to go home. Home to the four cluttered rooms she shared with a succession of roommates? She spent more time in the newsroom than she did anywhere else; did that qualify it as 'home'? She shook her head.

"Right," Matthew said soothingly. "I understand. When something like this happens, people usually want to be together. We can all stay here and talk about Keith."

This was a bit of a surprise. Chelan hadn't known Matthew to be much of a source of comfort in times of stress. Had he been reading some new management style book?

"He was brilliant," boomed Elliot, who had been hovering nearby, looking for an opening. Nevada raised her coffee cup in a toast.

Daniel Merritt, the anchorman, had emerged from his office to join them. "How did we hear about it, Matthew?"

"His brother-in-law called me. Apparently the family was contacted by the police and they're all together at his sister and brother-in-law's home." Matthew leaned against the edge of Nevada's desk.

"Not at his house? His and Heather's house?" Elliot seemed to think he was sniffing out a story.

"Heather and Keith split up a couple of months ago, Elliot," Matthew supplied. "He was living on his own in a small apartment in the West End."

Chelan dropped into a chair, as the talk floated around her.

"Keith was one of the best," Tess Cunningham's low, slow voice turned everyone's head. She rarely dropped in on the newsroom unannounced, although it wasn't completely unprecedented. Legend had it that the one time they had won a ratings book, she showed up with a case of beer. Didn't stay to have any of it, though. Today she looked pale and tired.

" We need to do something, to focus," Matthew decided.

"Nevada, I want you to get on the telephone to the police and the hospitals. See what you can find out. Felix, the weather segment will have to go short tonight. And the sports… we won't have a sports report. Elliot, you just check the scores and mention anything that's really important."

"It's a Tuesday, there won't be much."

Elliot liked to look at the trees, not the forest.

Daniel, Nevada and Elliot sat down at computer terminals and booted them up. Matthew held the glass door open for Tess as she left the newsroom, then followed her out.

Chelan sat, frozen, for hours. She stared at the metal desks, the wall of monitor screens, and the baffles surrounding the three workstations of the investigative team. From time to time, when anyone looked her way, she pretended to be reading. In truth, she was concentrating on each breath, in and out, so that she could prevent herself from screaming.

The Vancouver Police Department called a news conference for five o'clock. After an argument with Elliot over who would cover it, and about half an hour of solitary time in a dark corner of Studio 1, Chelan was eager to get out of the building. When Nevada stopped by her desk on her way out to cover the newser, she let herself be walked toward the door.

"Did Matthew really assign both of us to go?"

"I need somebody to carry the tripod," Nevada said. "The cameraman's been complaining, lately." She saw from Chelan's expression that she was in no mood for banter. "Alright, Chelan. Sorry. I just think we all need to be in motion right now. It's no good to sit around."

"Fair enough. Let's go." She'd found no answers and no comfort at the TV station; maybe the cop shop would surprise her. And if she had to be with anyone right now, Nevada was the one she minded the least. Nevada was a 'dame', as Grandma would call her. Early forties, well-read, well-traveled, well-heeled, well-built. Every time she sat down and crossed her legs, men sneaked a look and had to smile. She had covered stories from murders to political scandals. She was comfortable around everyone, and did not change the atmosphere every time she joined a group of men, the way many women did, deliberately or unconsciously. She didn't mind salty language and in fact, her own was usually raunchier than anyone else's.

Every seat was taken in the Media Conference room at the police station. Chelan did a quick count and came up with forty. A side door opened and Chief Rupella walked in, followed by the media liaison officer, Barbara Sewell, and two detectives, one round and rumpled, the other looking like an athletic Burnaby boy, in a Canucks jersey and ball cap. The chief put on a pair of glasses and read from a prepared statement.

"At about 0700 this morning, a man died in a fall from the ninth floor of an apartment building in the West End."

Nevada took notes, her hand moving while her eyes did not leave the police chief's face.

"The man was dead at the scene. Next of kin have been informed."

Nevada waited, pen poised. Chelan straightened up, trying to ride with the idea that there might be a surprise, that a mistake had been made, that it was not Keith at all, but some other resident of the Point After Apartments, and that Keith was just AWOL, maybe on one of his famous spontaneous and unannounced trips to Vegas.

The other reporters all waited, like runners on the starting blocks.

"The man was Keith Papineau."

There was no need to specify age, occupation, address. Everybody knew Keith Papineau. The journalist was a regular presence in their living rooms, via their television screens. He was on everyone's career radar, too; he was the standard they all used to judge their own success as reporters. He was the master.

Several faces turned toward Nevada and Chelan. Neither gave away anything that any of the other reporters could use for a sentence or two about the reaction of Keith's colleagues.

Reporters pulled out cell phones. This would be front page.

The buzz lasted two or three minutes, then refocused on the front of the room, as the questions started to flow.

"What was the cause of death?"

"What was he wearing, Chief?"

"Where did he land?"

"Any witnesses?"

Nevada slowly raised her hand. "Did he fall or did he jump?"

Chelan wasn't sure she heard right. Chief Rupella began to gather up his papers, and for a moment it looked as though he wouldn't answer. "Our preliminary investigation indicates a deliberate action. I presume all of your outlets' editorial policies, and your own sensitivity to the feelings of the family, will dictate your handling of that information. That's all, ladies and gentlemen."

The reporter sitting next to Nevada turned to her, a puzzled look on his face. "What does that mean? Our preliminary investigation indicates…"

Nevada was still scribbling her notes. "It means he wants us to sit on the information."

Cass Murphy, a longtime radio reporter who had known Nevada since their salad days in the early seventies, leaned over to join the conversation. "What are you going to do?"

Nevada didn't answer for a moment. Two or three other reporters tilted their heads toward the conversation, and two cameramen hovered nearby, gathering up electrical cords and information they could pass on to their reporters.

Nevada finally shut her notebook. "Say it, without spelling it out." She stood up and walked out.

The young reporter sitting next to Chelan was still

THE LION'S SHARE OF THE AIR TIME

unsure. "How the freak do you do that? I've got to report it or not report it. I don't want to leave it out and have my boss turn on LV-TV and find out about it."

Cass nodded. "On the other hand, you don't want to report it and be the only one in town showing something that everyone else had the class to leave out." She went up to the table, thinking things over while she reclaimed her microphone. When she came back, she had an answer. "I think you're going to hear it tonight on the LV-TV supper hour news. Nevada won't be too lurid or graphic about it, but she's going to report it. So we better all get on board."

Chelan was outraged. What 'preliminary investigation'? What business did Rupella have, giving all of these bozos this information, and then suggesting their 'sensitivity' should dictate what they did with it? It was like giving a loaded gun to a chimp. Keith hadn't committed suicide. Were they insane? A guy like Keith would never commit suicide.

4

Zack Esher shoved around the stack of files on his desk, trying to open up a little space. He was overloaded as it was with the Jason Wheeler stabbing, and now the chief had asked him to see the Keith Papineau case through. Not that there should be much to do there—seemed pretty obvious that with a balcony rail that high, something intentional was going on.

Still there was a procedure to follow. Zack tossed his ball cap onto the chair on the other side of the scuffed chrome desk and sat down to hunt for anything new from forensics or the medical examiner. Nothing. A bit early yet.

A lot of the reporters at the news conference he'd just left looked pretty stunned by the notion of suicide. Not that that was a sign of anything. It just meant that Keith Papineau was better than a lot of others in keeping the media out of his personal business.

He booted up his computer and pulled up the Wheeler file. So far, he and Kenny had talked to TV production people, an agent, a lawyer, a manager, a publicist and a personal trainer, and they had yet to get a bead on why anyone would want to kill this actor. So far, everyone had nothing but good things to say: Wheeler was a generous guy, a friendly guy, wrote notes to people's mothers, threw parties on the set. A stickler for contracts and a little temperamental, sometimes, about things he was asked to do, but who

THE LION'S SHARE OF THE AIR TIME

wouldn't be, they all said, when it came to matters of safety?

Zack sighed and patted his empty shirt pocket, groping for the cigarettes that he'd given up in 1999 when the blanket of anti-smoking regulations in Vancouver finally smothered his will to search for places and times he could light up. Funny how the unconscious memories of the habit hung on, long after he'd taken his last drag. He pulled a bottle of water out of the bottom desk drawer.

He'd been working long hours forever and Marla was ready to explode, but she'd just have to understand. It looked as though they'd have to go back for a second go-round with all of these people. After the initial shock of the death wore off and everyone had said their polite phrases, more of the truth about Wheeler's life might come out. Three years ago, Zack had cut corners on the time required to investigate the Hyack Docks case because of pressure from Marla, and he'd lost his promotion as a result. He'd worked his way back to the front of the line and he wasn't going to make the same mistake twice.

Just as he was about to close the computer file, one of Kenny's notes on his interview with Wheeler's manager caught Zack's eye—"recently settled a law suit with former partner in a restaurant." Now that had some possibilities. People often got desperate about business deals gone wrong or money lost, and the feelings were just as searing as jealousy or passion. Was it a big law suit? Who was the plaintiff? Was the restaurant a success or a failure? Had the former partner gone on to success in something else, or was he down and out in an alley somewhere? Was it a male or a female? Who won in court?

This definitely looked like a good place to start.

Ξ

Chelan stumbled out of the media conference room, barely noticing where she was going. The only thing she knew for sure was that she wasn't going back to the

49

newsroom for a while. She walked toward Pacific Boulevard, looking for a friendly door.

The sky hung low over Vancouver, creating one of those weird days when the light was so dim at three o'clock in the afternoon that the streetlights came on. The clouds seemed to hover about six feet from the ground, leaving Chelan with the urge to duck. Something was pressing down on her from above; her shoulders slumped, her neck protruded forward, and she had to make a conscious effort to stand up straight. The bar down the block looked intimidating, not the right place for a woman alone. She couldn't face the Scribbler, and all of the questions from the other reporters. A lounge at one of the downtown luxury hotels—that would be a better place. Chelan speed-dialed the taxi company's number on her cell phone and within fifteen minutes sat at a quiet corner table, contemplating a Scotch and water.

She gulped down her drink and ordered another one. She figured she needed at least one more before she would be ready to walk the few miles home and hole up in her apartment. She needed to be alone to think about Keith. Keith, who mentored her, showed her the ropes, gave her a shoulder to cry on when she was going through yet another day of feeling invisible. And how did she pay him back?

With friendship, certainly. But he had wanted more. Needed more, if he was that close to taking his own life. If she had said the right thing that night, instead of the wrong thing, could she have saved him from such a horrible, irrevocable decision?

Chelan opened her throat and poured down the amber liquid. He was a talented, successful journalist and no one had seen this coming. Sure, he had a few problems but what man in his early forties didn't? His marriage hadn't worked out, he missed having daily contact with his son, and he was looking for a chance to climb higher in his profession. An ambitious man would have migrated to Toronto, or even to New York or L.A., but Keith, like so many before him,

THE LION'S SHARE OF THE AIR TIME

decided he loved Vancouver too much to leave. Over drinks once or twice, when he and Chelan were trading life stories and observations about people and the world, he confessed to some regrets about that decision—but in the next breath, he noted that he was not exactly kicking retirement and could decide to go to take a shot at the majors next year—next month, even—if he chose.

There's always next year, he sometimes said. Chelan took a swipe at the tears stinging her eyes and a swallow from the crystal glass in front of her.

Hours later, she was still warming the same lounge chair, but her posture was quite a bit more relaxed. She had settled into a rhythm: a Scotch, a beer, a Scotch, a beer, and except for one quick question ("you planning to take a taxi home?") the waiter had brought on the brew and held back on the chitchat. Good understanding of his job, that waiter.

Chelan wondered briefly whether Nevada or Elliot or anyone else had noticed her absence, and whether she would get a slap on the wrist for taking a bit of unauthorized personal leave. She didn't care, particularly. It wasn't as if she had some responsibility for some important report on that evening's newscast. She had spent the whole freakin' day out doing very little of freakin' consequence. She was completely irrelevant and extraneous to that newsroom and she knew it; her absence or presence made no difference to anybody. It was the story of her life. When she wanted to be in the middle of the action, circumstances sent her off to the sidelines. When she felt it all crowding in on her—too many people, too much fuss—and she wanted to get away and be alone, fate would dump her into a situation that had no exit. The story of her life—no luck, no future, no talent, no truth, no friends. She signaled for another beer.

A new waiter came over, took her order, then went behind the bar and turned on the television set. Chelan heard the familiar chords of the Channel Two Evening News and turned to watch, heavy head propped on one hand.

"I work there, you know," she told the waiter who

51

arrived with her drink..

The man was intent on putting down the tumbler and a new bill. "Is that right."

No comfort there. But then, Chelan thought, he probably doesn't believe me. He probably hears sixteen people a day brag about what they do, who they know, how much money they have, what they're going to do to score. The only thing the world has more of, than liars, is skeptics—and that's the liars' fault. Everybody is so intent on making sure they don't buy a line of bull, they're suspicious of everything.

Daniel's face came up on the TV screen and Chelan braced herself for the report. It came soon into the broadcast, short and to the point, no more than half a minute. Keith Papineau died that day, cause of death unknown, station's condolences to the family.

She asked the bartender to change to Channel Four's Eyewitness News. There was Liam St. Clair, covering the story of Keith's death. He had a group of people gathered around him.

"Can you tell me what you saw?"

The two witnesses looked at one another. Liam held out the microphone, as if offering a dog a bone, pointing it at the man dressed in a business suit.

The man stepped back, but mumbled a reply to the question. "A man fell from his balcony up there, I guess."

"Did you see him fall?"

The man nodded. His face was a mask, but his eyes were wide with the terrified look of a child who has just witnessed a beating.

"Can you tell us more, sir?"

The man shook his head, then turned away. Liam then pointed his microphone at a man dressed in jogging clothes.

"Did you see him fall?"

The man ignored the microphone and spoke with the confident air of a person used to the podium. "I wasn't looking up, you know, I was looking toward the park. But I

THE LION'S SHARE OF THE AIR TIME

saw a lady looking up at the building. I didn't slow down at first, but then I saw the look on her face. I stopped beside her, but I kept on jogging in place. You can't let the muscles seize up, you know. About two seconds later—no, maybe less than that, this body landed on the pavement. Right there," he said, staring at the white chalk mark outline. They all stared at it in silence for a moment, picturing the face, the hair, the eyes, and the person that the white mark represented.

Chelan turned her back on the television and fished in her wallet for her credit card. Time to go home.

Ξ

The turnout for Keith's funeral three days later was huge. Chelan stood with hundreds, maybe even thousands of people, most of them either weeping or wearing the stricken look of the deeply bereaved. They stood in the driving rain, gathered around Keith's final resting place in the cemetery. The coffin was a gunmetal gray, polished to a high gloss that reflected the blurred outlines and shapes of the scene surrounding it. Droplets of water clung to the shiny surface. The rain began before dawn and continued, without a break, throughout the day. Heavy, glowering clouds seemed to hang only inches above Chelan's head, and if her mood had not compelled her shoulders to slump, the cloud cover certainly would have.

The cemetery was high in the North Shore mountains, which throbbed with six different shades of green, thanks to the Vancouver rainforest climate. Somehow, Chelan thought, it was easier to ignore all the rain, or laugh about it, when you were driving around in it, or even sloshing through puddles of it. But when you were standing out in it, to bury a friend, it became much more than background.

Several hundred people made the trek from the church to graveside, some moved by grief and some by curiosity. Many of them stood under somber black umbrellas, but quite a few stood unsheltered, with heads uncovered, letting the rivers of rain pour down their faces.

Chelan thought the saddest moment of the miserable day came when Keith's teenaged son insisted on riding with the funeral director in the car carrying his father's body. And the worst moment came when Chelan looked into her rearview mirror, as she drove away from the gravesite, one of the last to leave.

Where only a short time ago a community of people had stood, there was now only a solitary coffin, still on its wooden platform, the only object higher than the headstones. In an hour, the workers would finish lowering the coffin and covering it over with its shroud of earth. Chelan had a searing sense that they were all leaving Keith alone, in the cold, the dark, and the rain.

She turned her mind to following the directions to Jayne Granville's house. Keith's sister was hosting the traditional post-funeral gathering. Chelan found her way to Campbell Road and pulled into a driveway that curved in a semi-circle in front of a house too large to be believed — not a house, a mansion. She didn't know Keith was from a wealthy family. Maybe it was his sister's money—or perhaps, her husband's?

Chelan parked beside a gleaming Jaguar and got out of her car at the same time as the driver of the Jag. She recognized the tall, self-assured man from newspaper photos: Bob Venice, former golden boy, high school hero, Olympic gold medalist, law firm star, politician, and now, owner of half a dozen of the most popular night spots in the Lower Mainland.

He looked right through Chelan. Squaring his shoulders, he strode off toward the house. Chelan was about to follow when she heard a familiar voice.

"Should be quite an interesting group." Matthew wore a black suit that probably cost as much as Chelan's car.

"Did you know Keith was connected with the Granville family?"

THE LION'S SHARE OF THE AIR TIME

"Of course, Chelan. Didn't you?"

That was a bit of a slip. Of course, she should have known, or at least she shouldn't have admitted she didn't know. If she was going to get anywhere in Matthew's newsroom, she had to earn a reputation as knowledgeable and astute. At least, that's what Nevada kept telling her. She tried to recover ground. "Well, yes, but I didn't know they were still doing this well. I thought the real estate slump hit them hard last year."

"They diversified." Matthew seemed to be in no hurry to go inside. He folded his arms and surveyed the field of parked cars—luxury vehicles almost every one. Chelan had heard that Matthew liked expensive cars. His other hobby, besides cooking, was playing blackjack—also an interest that required a certain amount of coin. "How are you doing today, Chelan? I know you and Keith were close."

"Yes, we were. He was a good friend."

Matthew ran a hand over his blond hair, watching the cars and speaking past Chelan. "I suppose he was like many people. You think you know what's going on in their lives and in their thoughts, and then they do something like this, and you realize just how little you really knew about them."

Chelan folded her arms and watched the arriving cars, too. "There were a lot of days when he pulled me out of a slump."

Matthew stared at an arriving sports car as if it were part of a journalism award entry and he the chief judge. "And all the while, he was in a major slump himself. A terminal slump."

Chelan's face throbbed with heat. "It's so hard to believe."

"Yes, of course it is," Matthew said, in the soothing tones of a father comforting a sobbing six-year-old. "The truth is hard to take." He gave Chelan a sad, enigmatic smile.

"What do you mean?"

Matthew moved toward the twin columns guarding the front door. "Chelan, you didn't know Keith very well. He

GAIL HULNICK

was a man with a very stressful job who obviously didn't have the strength to deal with it. He screwed up sometimes—he'd disappear when the pressure was too much. In a lot of ways, I think he was in the wrong occupation, given his personality type. But it was what he'd trained for, he was well-known for it, and he just couldn't switch into something else that easily."

Matthew handed his raincoat to the butler who opened the door and turned right to plunge into the lake-sized living room, disappearing into one of a dozen eddies of people in conversation. Chelan handed over her umbrella, then turned left into the dining room, where she stood, shifting uncertainly from one foot to another. What were you supposed to do in this situation? They hadn't covered it in any class she had ever been in. She had been to a dozen weddings in the past few years, and knew all of the etiquette there, but the only funeral she had ever attended was that of an elderly aunt, fifteen years ago, when she was at an age when people expected very little understanding of the events, and she had experienced even less.

She saw Keith's sister, Jayne, across the room, seated in a leather armchair, staring off into space, her carefully streaked blonde hair needing a wash and her black suit flecked with dog hair. Someone bent down to hand her a cup of coffee and she briefly sparked, with the flash of a lovely smile. Chelan wasn't sure of the protocol, but speaking to her seemed like the right thing to do. The room was large enough to hold a football game, and it looked as though a few of the members of the pro team were here to play it. As Chelan made her way toward Jayne, she spotted half a dozen celebrity athletes and quite a few other familiar faces. Although Bob Venice was probably the highest profile person in the room, many of the others would ring a bell on the recognition door—the pro quarterback, half a dozen hockey players, the mayor. She saw many of these people's names mentioned at the sports events and gala fund-raising functions she read about in the paper. Sort of like a small

THE LION'S SHARE OF THE AIR TIME

town within a small town. She had no idea they were part of Keith's life. Tess Cunningham stood near the fireplace, teacup in hand. She had the tense look that people get when they're working with too much pressure and too little sleep. Chelan felt a sort of kinship with her, since it seemed that both of their positions would be very shaky if things didn't improve at the station.

Chelan picked her way through the maze of dark suits and black dresses, toward the leather chair beside the grand piano. She waited while Keith's sister finished her conversation with the anchorman from one of the other stations.

"Hello, Mrs. Granville. I'm Chelan Montgomery. I worked with Keith."

"Chelan, thanks for coming," Jayne looked into her eyes for a nanosecond.

Chelan felt as though she should pat her shoulder or squeeze her hand, but again, she just wasn't sure about the right thing to do. "I wanted to tell you how very sorry I am."

"Thank you. We'll all miss him." She seemed to have reached the end of her store of remarks, but Chelan did not feel ready to move on. She hunted for something else to say, something to keep the exchange alive.

"He had a lot of friends."

Jayne focused on the crowd. "He did, didn't he? Well, he certainly spent a lot of time with them. Even those who go way back are here."

Chelan followed her gaze across the room and recognized Keith's wife, Heather, standing alone near the fireplace. She had met her once at a station party a while ago. With her shaggy gray hair and Birkenstock sandals, Heather stood out in this crowd of spa-soothed skin and facelifts like a tattoo in a convent.

Jayne glanced past Chelan, toward the French doors leading to the back of the house. A dark-haired teenager wearing the hip hop uniform of hoody, baggy pants and reversed baseball cap came in, walked across the room, acknowledging no one, and stood at Jayne's side.

"Chelan, have you met Kevin?"

Chelan put forward a hand, which Kevin shook for a fraction of a second. "Aunt Jayne, can I talk to you?"

"Kevin, I have to stay here and meet people. We can talk later."

Kevin looked as though he was about to argue, then shrugged. "Would it be alright if I play some video games in another room?"

Jayne nodded and Kevin slouched out of the room, his shoulders held stiffly as if he felt that everyone were watching him walk. Jayne directed a shrug of her own and a smile toward Chelan, which she took as her cue to move on, and make way for the two tall, prosperous men in Bond Street suits, waiting for their turns to offer condolences.

She wandered down a short hallway and spotted a small group of media types in the kitchen. Nevada was holding court.

"So a bunch of us get on the hotel elevator and there's this guy in a suit who turns out to be one of the cabinet minister's flacks. He assumes we all know who he is and he starts telling us about their itinerary for the next day. As if we care. Then he says to me, 'You know the boss really likes to meet young reporters like you. I'm going up to his suite now. Would you like to come along?' So what to do? Is it a set-up, or will I get an interview? And of course I'm a TV reporter, and I need my cameraman, but I can't figure out whether he's invited."

Nevada stopped for a long gulp of her drink and Amanda prompted her. "So, what happened?"

"Keith stepped forward to rescue me. Offered to come along, too. The government creep just laughed and got off the elevator at the next floor. 'Maybe another time', he says." Nevada raised her highball glass in a toast. "To Keith."

Chelan reached past Nevada to the wine bottle on the counter and poured herself a glass, ignoring the disapproving stare of the waiter. The catering staff were also in the

THE LION'S SHARE OF THE AIR TIME

kitchen, doing their jobs, and trying to avoid the journalists. They held off on commenting, though, saving their observations for wash-up time, after all the guests had gone home.

"Have you talked to Heather?" Nevada asked as Chelan refilled her glass from the vodka bottle.

"Keith's ex? No, have you?"

Nevada nodded. "Briefly. She's very upset. So is Kevin."

Amanda interjected. "Well, what do you expect? Bad enough to lose your dad, but to have him go that way…"

Chelan drained her wine glass. "Are the police firm on that?"

Amanda sipped her wine, and then declared, "They found a suicide note."

Nevada perked up like a golden retriever spotting a squirrel. "How do you know?"

"Sources." Amanda winked.

"Where did they find the note?"

Amanda sipped her wine, taking her time, no doubt enjoying the attention.

"On his kitchen table, under a coffee mug."

Nevada's intensity was growing. "What did it say? Did your contact tell you that, too?"

Amanda picked up a wine bottle and poured herself a refill. "Just made it clear it was suicide."

Elliot held out his half-empty glass toward Amanda and she topped it up. "The coward's way out."

Chelan tried to tune him out, but this was too much. She turned on him. "You've got no way of knowing what was going on in his life. Absolutely none. Suicide isn't cowardly." Nevada covered her hand and squeezed it warningly. "But I can't imagine what reason he would have."

"Sometimes people don't have reasons," Nevada said. "Sometimes it's just… an illness."

Elliot ignored her and gulped his wine. "You didn't know him that well, Chelan. He had a very complicated life."

59

Amanda was intrigued. "Like what?"

"He was very popular with the ladies and he had a weakness for the high maintenance types, the party girls and the high-profile career types. I guess he had a weakness for almost all women. He had three or four relationships while he was married, who knows how many since he and Heather separated."

"Where are you getting this stuff?" Chelan felt as though all of the air in the room had been sucked up by all of these people, breathing in the oxygen and breathing out poison. What party girls?

Amanda was puzzled. "Why would that make a man kill himself? You'd think it would be the opposite."

"Maybe he caught something." Elliot made a face as he downed his glass of wine. "Or maybe he was depressed all along and the new girlfriends were part of the symptoms."

Nevada set down her wineglass and took over the conversation. "Do you remember the *Lift Your Spirits* charity auction, when Keith put up his share of a racehorse up for sale? I thought Bob Venice would blow a fuse."

"Keith was such a clown. One time a bunch of us went to ..."

Chelan drifted away from the revisionist history being done on Keith's life. Party girls and a complicated life? Maybe he caught something? She had an ache in the back of her throat and she needed some air. She looked around the living room, crowded despite its large size, filled with people who probably all had some skewed opinion of who Keith was and why he died. Even Matthew—saying Keith was in the wrong job and screwed up all the time. That was completely inappropriate. Were they all jealous of Keith's ability? Or was there some truth in all of this? Threading her way past the conversational knots, she went out into a long hallway.

"Chelan, are you okay?" Nevada had followed her out of the kitchen.

"Yeah, I'm fine. Just needed some air."

THE LION'S SHARE OF THE AIR TIME

"You look a bit rough." Nevada stared into Chelan's eyes, her head cocked to the right. "Keith's death hit you pretty hard, didn't it? Are you here by yourself?"

Chelan nodded.

"Well, what's the matter with that boyfriend of yours? You just tell him, being eye candy is not enough. When stuff happens, he has to be there for you." Nevada reached around Chelan's shoulders to give her a hug.

"He did call last night actually. He was concerned, but I didn't want him to come over. I just wanted to be alone." Chelan heard a distant beeping, then ringing sound.

" What about coming along with you to this? Funerals aren't easy, even when you don't know the dead and departed."

Chelan winced. "Uh, no. I wouldn't want Twain to come along to this. It wouldn't help."

"Why?"

"Because he wouldn't fit in. He's a bit—"

"I've met him. He's charming. And he's the most gorgeous thing on two legs I've ever seen—except for Owen, of course. Why wouldn't he fit in?"

"Because he's — " Chelan waved vaguely toward the grand living room and the crowd of professionals and millionaires gathered there.

"Because he's a tradesman? Because he drives a pickup truck? Chelan, I'm shocked at you. Shocked and appalled." Nevada said it with a grin on her face, but there was an undertone of criticism, no question.

This day was difficult enough. Analyzing her boyfriend was just too much.

"Nevada, I'm going to go outside for a while." Chelan walked away down the corridor toward the back patio.

The beeping, ringing sound grew louder as she walked. Through a door, not quite closed, she could see Kevin sitting on the floor, back hunched over, hands methodically working the controller of an electronic video game, with only the glare from the screen for light.

Poor kid. To be fourteen and lose your father. Maybe better to grow up with none at all? Chelan didn't know which was worse. She was about to move on when Kevin spoke. "Want to play?"

Chelan walked in, sat down and picked up the green controller. Kevin switched to a two-person game and for several minutes they both concentrated on racing the little characters through an obstacle course.

Kevin concentrated on the screen. "Why did the station give so many details about the way my dad died?"

Chelan wished she were on another planet. For several minutes she focused on playing, and thought about whether she could get away with ignoring the question, or evading it.

"Why?"

Apparently not.

"Well, Kevin, I guess that's the way news is. Telling the truth."

Kevin shoved the joystick impatiently, trying to make the on-screen characters move faster. "Why is it anybody's business? Anybody outside the family, I mean?"

Chelan was at a loss for words. Conversation with teenagers wasn't in her usual daily routine anyway, nor was this topic.

Kevin shook the game controller and pushed the controls. "You didn't have to say where he was found."

"It was in the police report." Chelan stared at the screen.

"You didn't have to say it." Kevin's voice was a monotone.

Chelan sent her character through a jungle landscape, dodging pythons and exploding dynamite. "Kevin, I'm sorry. But the police say that your dad... "

Kevin's interruption was explosive. "Why, Chelan? Why did he kill himself?"

Oh, God, she just wasn't equipped for this. "Kevin, I'm so sorry. I don't know why... there must have been a lot going on in his life that I didn't know about. Stuff in his

THE LION'S SHARE OF THE AIR TIME

heart that even you, even the people that he loved, didn't know about…"

Kevin didn't reply. It was as though he'd withdrawn behind a blank, acrylic wall. She could see him but he was ignoring her.

At least he'd stopped shouting. Calm was better than upset. She barely knew him and she had no way of predicting what he might do if he got really agitated. The last thing she needed was to be found in a private room with Keith's son roaring at her.

The game ended with Kevin winning. He started up another round, and they played for another ten minutes in silence. Chelan had been an ardent gamer in her youth, but she had a much shorter attention span for it these days. She wanted to get out of this darkened room; the sympathy she felt for Kevin was strong, but not enough to smother her desire to be alone. To her relief, when they finished the round, Kevin set down his controller and stood up.

"Gotta go."

He towered over her, and that elevator between childhood and adulthood that went back and forth for fourteen-year-olds was definitely stopped on the top floor.

"Okay, Kevin." She stood up and laid a tentative hand on the boy's shoulder. "I'm really sorry about your dad."

"Are you? Are you really?" He said the words with such anger—was he going to hit her? She wanted to look away from the boy's eyes, two bullet holes ripped in an anguished face, but she was pinned by his pain. "If there's anything I can do for you…"

Kevin's gaze burned into Chelan's eyes. She took a step backward, ready to make a run for it, if he came any closer.

"Find out why. You know how to ask questions, find out things, you're a reporter. You know who to call, how to do it. Find out why my dad killed himself."

He was so intense that she was speechless for a long ten seconds. The video game repeated its theme music over and over, while Kevin waited for an answer. Certainly, Chelan

63

wanted to know the truth about Keith's death. But she was also afraid to know it. What if she investigated and found out that his suicide did have something to do with her, with their conversation the night before he died? There were a lot of things Chelan could rationalize or repress but she doubted that this would be one of them. She had been barely functional for the three days after his death as it was—how could she cope with knowing that she was responsible for it?

"Kevin, I can't. I don't know. I..." She reached out to touch his arm but he backed away.

"Never mind. I knew nobody would help."

This was no good.

"I'll try," she promised.

5

Robson Street was a magnet for anyone in the Lower Mainland with money and a memory for brand names. Chelan plodded past the chic boutiques, every window filled with mannequins sporting up-to-the-minute styles on the trendiest body shapes. While her own clothing preferences swung with her moods and would probably have leaned to jeans and T-shirts most days, she worked on building up a work-appropriate wardrobe over time. She believed that jackets and low-rise shoes were crucial in eking out that little bit of extra respect that her chronological age denied her.

Today she headed for a small store tucked away on an interior courtyard near three coffee shops. Floor to ceiling, the walls displayed hundreds of items of electronic equipment, each silver piece smaller and more multifunctional than its neighbor.

She had given up on waiting for the newsroom to equip her with top-of-the-line tools. "No budget for that" was one of the most popular phrases in the place, and top-of-the-line equipment for a researcher was not likely ever to get approval. Maybe one day, if she got a promotion, or if the ratings went up and there was more money, she would get her share of the toys. In the meantime, she was on her own.

Chelan asked the clerk for a tape recorder and was overwhelmed when he put nine boxes on the counter in front of her. She was still feeling so low that she had very little energy left for anything. She just wanted someone to sit her down, tell her exactly what supplies she needed and what steps to follow to lay Keith to rest properly.

She forced herself to look over all the gear and make a choice. A tape recorder, obviously. A battery charger that she could plug into the Mini. A pile of blank tapes. She let the salesman show her the latest in cell phones, the ones that took pictures, did your email, held your calendar and address book, and would one day do your laundry. One look at the price tag almost put her into a state of shock. One day, when she'd reached her first-stage goal of being a political reporter, she'd be able to justify spending that much on a tool to stay in touch. In fact, one day she'd be able to justify getting the station to pay for it.

She opted for a sleek, compact, dark gray number with a voice-activation feature and dropped it into the depths of her bag.

Ξ

Everyone was back to action in the newsroom, with the needle bouncing back up to the normal level of buzz, but Chelan couldn't go five minutes without thinking about Keith killing himself. She felt as though she had passed through the center of a hurricane, that zone of absolute calm and stillness, and now she was back on the other side, with wind whirling around her, debris flying, dust cutting into her skin. And the floodwaters rising. She had to get out for a while, and decided that lunch break was the perfect time to start her Keith research by talking to his wife of twenty years.

Heather and Kevin lived on one of the busiest streets in Kitsilano. Since its days as a hippie haven, way before Chelan's time, through to its present life as home to hundreds of university students, the district held onto its charm and unique character. Many of the buildings were old,

THE LION'S SHARE OF THE AIR TIME

but all were in good repair. The houses were painted in vivid colors that made an entire block look like a school of brightly colored fish. Chelan recognized the Craftsman style in most of the designs, with a few French Provincials and faux Southern Colonials scattered among the gabled structures with their wide front porches. The lawns in front were the size of a hand towel and the parking was non-existent, but the beach was less than a mile away, so all of those minor flaws didn't matter.

Chelan parked on West 4th near a shop selling crystals and offering tarot readings by Madame Giselle. The walk to Heather's place was only four blocks and she made it last as long as possible. The spring breeze was sweet and the sun was warm on her face and hands. Heather's house was one of the newer ones on the block. At some point, someone must have brought in bulldozers to knock down the original structure, probably a pre World War II old-timer with sagging front porch, gabled windows and patchwork renovations, then put up this chic West Coast post-and-beam. The landscaping was lush. The front yard was framed by a wrought-iron fence with two short river-rock columns on either side of the sidewalk to the door. The metal bars of the gate were crafted into diamond shapes. It was locked.

Chelan had about half an hour before her absence from work would be noticed. She had to remember that she was on probation, and that until she figured out how to get back on Matthew's good side, she needed to leave no room for criticism. She'd done her shopping during yesterday's lunch hour and she'd already used up half of today's, going to see the detective who was investigating Keith's death. It turned out he was not the round, rumpled one from the news conference—he was the muscular one in the baseball cap. But today he was wearing a dark suit, with a white shirt and striped tie. Said he was going to court and could only give her five minutes. It only took him half that to refuse to show her Keith's suicide note. Said as she was not a member of the family, it was none of her business.

Chelan shook the gate in frustration a couple of times before she noticed a bell and a speaker on the left column. She buzzed and after an uncomfortable pause, an answering buzz and a click told her she was in.

Heather led Chelan through the open-plan living room to the kitchen at the back of the house. The room was a comfortable clutter of table, chairs, and an ironing board in the corner. One wall was dominated by a huge bulletin board covered in family pictures: on the beach, at Whistler, on the ferry. The kitchen table was scattered with a pair of water shoes, a stack of copies of the alternative newspaper, a couple of Motown CDs, a sewing kit, a tennis racquet and a purple cat collar. What did Heather and Kevin do when they wanted to sit down to eat?

Heather's face looked weary and pale. She had exchanged the long blouse and baggy skirt she'd worn the day of the funeral for a pair of faded blue jeans and an over-sized T-shirt with *Kelowna* printed on the front.

Chelan looked past her to the bulletin board on the wall, snapshots pinned to every inch of it. A dozen photographic Keiths were looking at her—Keith proudly displaying a salmon the size of a suitcase; Keith on skis; Keith at the wheel of a sailboat; Keith holding toddler Kevin; Keith with an arm around Heather's shoulders, at the eighteenth tee at Hazelmere. Chelan felt the tears coming and decided she had to cut to the chase. Preferably without Heather getting any clue about the guilt Chelan felt over Keith's death.

"Would you like some coffee?" Heather asked.

"Thanks, anyway, Heather, but I can't stay long. I'm supposed to be at work."

Heather dropped into a chair and Chelan followed her lead. "It was nice of you to stop by."

"How are you doing, Heather?"

"It hit me harder than I expected. I mean, he did move out months ago—" Heather had a puzzled look. "But I feel like I'm moving under about forty feet of water. I took a

THE LION'S SHARE OF THE AIR TIME

leave of absence from the college…" She stared off into space.

"Heather, I spoke with Kevin at the funeral."

Heather's face was tense. "What did he say?"

"I'm sure you know, he's very upset." Chelan was groping for a way into this topic. "He asked me to find out why Keith killed himself."

She didn't know exactly what she expected from Heather, but the flat, expressionless nod was probably her last guess.

"Nobody knows. I'm not surprised."

"I heard there was a note."

"The police haven't given it to us yet, ' Heather said. "But apparently it only says Good-bye, and that he's sorry." Heather was on the verge of shattering, and as crass as it felt, Chelan knew she had to push, to something in the few minutes she figured she had left before Heather crumbled.

"Why would he take his life, Heather? Was he sick? A terminal illness? Was he depressed? Had he ever consulted a psychiatrist, that you know of?"

Each question brought an exhausted shake of Heather's head. "He used to get blue sometimes, when he talked about stories and sources where he hadn't been able to get justice, hadn't been able to stir up enough of a fuss to get the powers-that-be to listen. There was one, I remember, whose name he promised to conceal, and he wasn't able to. That seemed to bug him for a long time."

Chelan ran through the rest of the list of possibilities she had come up with so far. "Could it have been blackmail? It sounds farfetched, I know, but he does meet some tough characters in some of the stories he's covering."

"No." Heather paused for so long that Chelan thought the conversation was over. "There are only two reasons I can think of. Either he was in love with somebody new and it was going really, really badly— "

Chelan held her breath: Oh, don't tell me that. Please, let it be something I can work with…"

"—or it had something to do with the money."

"What about money, Heather?"

"I don't know how well you knew Keith—"Heather stared at Chelan as if she were trying to read her mind. "He was a brilliant reporter and a great writer, but he wasn't very good with money. And…he liked to gamble. He won a few big pots in Las Vegas and then he started to place a few bets around here. The casino, the racetrack. I never really knew how much he spent, or whether he was winning or losing. We kept things separate. He grew up with money and he was just not used to having to think about it.

"A couple of years ago he asked me to cash a bond, said he needed to bridge a small cash flow problem. He replaced the money almost right away, and when I asked him about it, he laughed it off. But obviously, it had turned out okay, because he had the funds to pay me back.

"Then a few months ago I started to hear that he was borrowing money from our friends. And Revenue Canada was calling here, leaving messages. I guess he was behind on paying his taxes. He moved out shortly after that. Money wasn't the reason, though; we had a few other problems." Heather's blue eyes were filling up and she seemed to have come to the end of her story.

"You think he might have killed himself over the embarrassment of owing money to his friends and not being able to pay it back?" Chelan prompted.

Heather pressed her palms into her eye sockets. "Maybe. Or maybe he felt overwhelmed by the pressure. Maybe he couldn't see any other way out." She held her head in her hands. "But I don't know why he wouldn't have just come to me again. Or talked to his sister—there's family money."

"Maybe it was a really huge amount," Chelan suggested.

"He could have gone to Bob, then."

"Bob?"

"Bob Venice. He's an old friend of Keith's, from college days." Heather rummaged through some of the items

THE LION'S SHARE OF THE AIR TIME

on the table and pulled out a battered, black address book. "His number's in here."

Chelan leafed through the pages. "Heather, could I borrow this? Just for a couple of days? I'd like to talk to a few of Keith's other friends."

Heather nodded, her eyes glazed as if she had barely heard the question. The seconds ticked by on the wall clock and after about ninety of them, it became clear that she had nothing more to say. Chelan tried a few more questions but Heather just sat there, her shoulders shaking slightly as she cried. Chelan stood up and reached across the table to pat her on the shoulder.

"I'm so sorry," she said. "If there's anything I can do, please call."

Heather nodded through her tears. "You know, I always thought he would come back, eventually. That it was just a matter of time, that all I had to do was wait. And be there."

6

Zack Escher and Kenny Burnett rode the elevator to the penthouse in an Italian marble high-rise building set on the West Vancouver waterfront. Quick work with the building manager's pass key and they stood on the threshold of Jason Wheeler's apartment. It easily covered three thousand square feet. A luxuriant golden broadloom complemented the honey and amber shades used for the furniture; the ceiling and upper part of the walls were painted a turquoise tint and the paintings were framed in white. It reminded Zack of standing on a prairie field, in Alberta or Saskatchewan somewhere, with a wide sky so blue above and a feeling of endless space and distance.

He walked across to the balcony door and took in the view: Kitsilano and the university to the south across the water, and a line of apartment buildings, including a pink one, to the east. Stanley Park and the Lions Gate Bridge to the southeast. To the west, Vancouver Island, and beyond that, Japan, probably.

He and Kenny set to work, investigating the contents of Jason's apartment. The actor had travelled light—the closet was barely half full, the kitchen drawers and cupboards equipped with just the basics for one, maybe two people. No books, no videos, no stuff—obviously, he must keep most of his life's accumulation at his home in L.A.

They had more luck in the second bedroom, which

THE LION'S SHARE OF THE AIR TIME

Jason used as a den. The desk was covered in scripts, file folders, and mailing envelopes. A laptop computer sat open on the black, Chinese lacquered desk. Zack closed it and put it by the door, so that he'd remember to take it along. When he got back to the office, he would go through every web site Jason had surfed in the weeks before his death, every email he'd received. There might be something they could trace through an IP address.

Kenny was flipping through the stacks of paper. "Lot of stuff related to the TV show. Fan mail. Hey, now, what's this?"

He paused to read a document festooned with the massive letterhead of a multi-name law firm. Zack came to read over his shoulder.

"Something about being in court next month. A law suit of some kind." Zack stared at the piece of paper. "That may have to do with the restaurant deal we heard about."

"Will you call the lawyer or should I?"

"How about you do that and I'll follow up with the manager or agent, or whoever he is."

"I think they have both," Kenny said as he sorted through more of the papers.

Zack made a face. "Too damn complicated, being famous."

Ξ

When Chelan looked out of Bob Venice's office, across False Creek toward the green-glass wall of downtown buildings, the sky was still a granite gray, but with a bit of yellow light sneaking in at the edges. It was as if the city were in a bubble or under a misty, opaque dome, separating it from the world beyond. It was weird weather for spring, but Vancouver was used to the clouds and fog rolling in at any time.

Chelan was surprised at how easy it was to get an appointment with the man. Some reporters, once they were on air for a little while and their names and faces became somewhat familiar, liked to think that they were important people, rather than just a means of communication for the people who really had significant clout. Chelan understood, however, that any entrée she had to the corridors of power came only because of her association with LV-TV and her access to the airwaves. Chelan Montgomery, the person, was nobody, and fraternization with the city's famous, rich or powerful was possible for her only because they recognized the TV station's name, not hers.

But there was a limit to her newly acquired access and it stopped long before you reached Bob Venice's circle. So Chelan was puzzled by the enthusiasm of Venice's secretary for setting an appointment. Maybe something was going on with this new developers' disclosure debate that was worth tipping Nevada about—or worth trying to investigate by herself.

The offices of Infinite Enterprises Inc. reminded Chelan of a big-name casino in Las Vegas. Everything was very up-to-date, yet tinged with colors and shapes that recalled ancient times. The photographs on the wall were windows on the company's assets: sky-clawing towers, monumental ships, and breathtaking aircraft. The man who owned a place like this ate steak, not fish, drove a gas-guzzler, not an electric car, and drank old Scotch, not new wine. Living large, as they say. And loud.

Of course, you never could tell, by appearances. It all looked expensive, but that didn't mean the bailiffs weren't hovering near the back door, ready to cart off stuff that had been repossessed for non-payment of bills.

Bob kept her waiting an hour. Maybe it was tactics, maybe just time management. When the receptionist finally rose and opened the door to the inner office, Chelan was ready to explode like a rodeo bull coming out of the chute.

Bob was out of his chair, extending a hand. "Ms. Montgomery. Nice to see you. What docs Channel Two want with us today?"

THE LION'S SHARE OF THE AIR TIME

He was the kind of man who would attract notice wherever he went, whether or not he was driving his Jaguar or wearing his designer suit. Obviously in very good shape, strong jaw, green eyes. The only real clue to his age was the salt-and-pepper hair.

Chelan sat down in the leather chair in front of the desk. "It's not the station, Mr. Venice. It's me personally this time."

"Please call me Bob." The words seemed automatic. The smile didn't falter and the eyes didn't move. But somehow, the mood in the room wasn't friendly.

"It's a pleasure to meet you. Bob." Chelan leaned forward from the waist to reach across the teak desk to shake hands. "My friend, Keith Papineau, always spoke highly of you."

Bob's eyes narrowed. "Keith and I played some golf together."

"So he told me. Apparently, you have quite the drive." Chelan reached down for her briefcase. "He mentioned that you used to play cards together, too."

Bob leaned back in his chair. "No, Ms. Montgomery, you must have me confused with someone else. I never play cards."

Chelan smiled as warmly as she could. "An investment, perhaps."

Bob pretended to search his memory. "No, we weren't together on any investment. That I know of. Sometimes the press reports my stock purchases and people follow what I do, but…"

"Yes, maybe that was it." Chelan pulled a file from her briefcase, opened it, and pretended to read from a page of notes. She wasn't sure how she was going to get around to discussing Keith's financial affairs, nor what it was that she was looking for. She had to make this last long enough to give her time to nose around a little.

"No, here it is, somebody said something about a racehorse you two owned together—"

Bob grinned and the temperature in the room went up a notch. "Oh, yeah, Denman's Dream. Hah, took a kicking on that one. Beautiful horse, though. Worth the price just to look at her."

"I heard you sold her."

Bob coughed. "Not exactly. We donated her. We were at some charity do and Keith got into a generous mood. Decided to contribute his share of the horse to the auction. I didn't want to be left owning a racehorse with some stranger—or worse, somebody I knew and didn't want to be in business with—so I sucked it up and tossed in my share, too."

Chelan laughed. "Weren't you just a bit annoyed with Keith about that?"

"Annoyed? I guess I was, at the time. But hey, it was a good cause." Bob grinned at her once more, then did a quick, but obvious glance at the smart phone lying on his desk pad. "What can I do for you today, Ms. Montgomery?"

Chelan put on the most serious, earnest look she had. "Bob, do you have any idea why Keith might have killed himself?"

"Is the station investigating this?"

"No, it's just for me. And for Kevin, his son. There was a note, apparently, but it was only two lines long. There are a lot of questions—"

Bob nodded sympathetically. "Of course there are. But I can't really help, Ms. Montgomery. I wondered whether he was sick, with something terminal. I'm pretty sure that might make some people decide to cash it in. Although," he said, picking up his phone, "...I think maybe Keith was more the type to fight it. He might search around for some doctor in some obscure hospital with an experimental treatment that might lead to a cure."

Chelan nodded. "That's my take on him, too, although I didn't know him very long." She pretended to be looking over her notes. "I thought there might be money problems, but if he had enough money to be buying and selling

THE LION'S SHARE OF THE AIR TIME

racehorses…"

"Well, Keith's finances were up and down." Bob caught himself as he realized he had rushed in to fill in the blank that Chelan had set up. "I heard that somewhere once. I really don't know much about it. We were social friends, you know? Attended some of the same functions, saw each other at the golf club once in a while. That's all. I think you need to talk to some of the people he was really close to." He stood up and began to gather folders into a briefcase. "You'll have to excuse me now, Ms. Montgomery. I have a meeting out of the office in half an hour."

Chelan rose. "Of course. Thank you very much for your time."

"One other suggestion I could make. You're a journalist, go the research route. Find a suicide expert. Ask him why Keith might have killed himself."

As soon as Chelan said good-bye to the Infinite Property Development receptionist, she wandered down the hall looking for the ladies' room. Ducking into a stall, she pulled out her notepad to write down the main points of the interview before she forgot anything. It wasn't much—she hadn't had the nerve to come right out and ask if he had given Keith a big loan. All she had was a sort of confirmation of Keith's shaky financial picture, a suggestion to call a psychiatrist, and an overall impression of someone unpleasant. No doubt he had to have a lot going for him to end up a player, but whatever it was, he wasn't showing it to Chelan. Grandma used to say the key to happiness was to want what you have. No doubt Bob Venice would put that kind of happiness way down on his 'to do' list.

Ξ

Irritating as the suggestion of consulting a suicide expert was, because it came from Bob Venice, when Chelan examined it during her drive back to the station, it started to look like one of the better ideas of the day. She still thought the financial question was a good one, but she'd have to find some other way of checking into it. Finding an authority on suicide was a much easier matter—the Web and the universities were loaded with information

Dr. Margaret Dodge called her back within the hour. She sounded polite, but rushed. "Do you want just a general outline or do you have some specific questions?"

"Both." Chelan had a list that covered three notebook pages.

"Let's see, then." The psychiatrist's voice became brisk. "The signs that a person might be thinking of suicide can be very obvious or very subtle. Sometimes they come right out and tell a friend or a relative that they're planning it. They may give away all of their possessions, or certain prized objects. Sometimes they spend a lot of money—all of their savings, perhaps. Certainly, anyone who is suffering from depression or substance abuse problems should be watched carefully. But then, sometimes it's something as indirect and elusive as a change in their topics of conversation. Maybe they resist discussing anything about the future. Or they suddenly take an interest in the properties of various kinds of pills and medications. They may just make vague references to a conclusive solution to their problems. I don't mean to say that a person showing those indicators will commit suicide, just that people who commit suicide often display those behaviors.

And there are some people who talk and talk about it who have no intention of ever following through. It's just manipulation and emotional blackmail."

"Are there people who do kill themselves who never talk about it ahead of time?"

"Yes. Some are so private—and decisive—that one day they make their preparations and they're gone." Dr. Dodge seemed to sense Chelan's grief. "It's tragic, for their friends and families."

"I wonder, if they knew that, if they'd go through with it."

THE LION'S SHARE OF THE AIR TIME

"I wonder, too. We do have anecdotal data, from people who've attempted suicide, that they often aren't aware of the impact their passing will have. And sometimes they're just so caught up in their personal turmoil that they give no thought to the reactions of others."

"What are the most common reasons people take their own lives?"

"Almost any sort of pressure and any sort of human emotion can lead to suicide. Financial pressure, relationship pressure, work pressure. Despair, hopelessness, the desire to avoid or end pain."

Chelan wanted to ask her next question, but was worried that it would sound silly. Still, she had to take the plunge; it had been tormenting her for days. "Would someone commit suicide because someone else wasn't interested in him—for a relationship, I mean?"

"It's possible. It's possible that the disappointment would be so intense that a person might decide to take that drastic action. Some people turn their disappointment outward, onto the person who rejected them, but some do turn it onto themselves. It would depend on the individual, on his or her particular personality."

"Dr. Dodge, thanks very much for your time." Chelan hung up, feeling just a bit farther ahead than she had been at the start of the conversation. It was clear, though, that she had a lot more questions to ask about Keith's life before she could offer any conclusions to Kevin or resolve any of the guilt she felt.

Ξ

That afternoon the whiteboard showed a new assignment beside Chelan's name. "Keith farewell." She was staring at the words on the board, mesmerized, when Elliot appeared behind her.

"Chelan, we need a two or three-minute feature on Keith's life," His voice was brisk and bossy. "Retrospective on his career, his highlights here at the station, that sort of thing."

When she didn't respond, Elliot pressed her. "Do you know what I mean, Chelan?"

"Of course she does, Elliot," Nevada's voice carried across the newsroom.

"I do, Elliot. But I'm just curious—why today?"

"Mrs. Cunningham, by way of Matthew, says it's the right time to air something substantial about him and his career. Viewers have been calling and asking."

"I'll start right in on it." Chelan walked back to her desk and sat, motionless, for half an hour. She knew she should make a move, but she felt as though her body and brain were submerged in tar. Farewell, Keith. Nevada came over to lay a hand on her arm and give her a gentle push.

"Go on," she mouthed, and gave another, firmer push.

Okay, it was time to do something. Maybe if she followed the trail into Keith's past, the reason for his suicide would emerge from hiding. Cecil Hall, the editor, roamed through a couple of times. He was at least sixty, a small man with sparse gray hair and an inexhaustible supply of plaid shirts. He was also a millionaire several times over, so the stories went, through speculation in the stock market. Chelan had often seen him during the slow morning hours, hunched over the financial pages of a newspaper. Most people nowadays edited their own material but that had no impact on Cecil; he was union-protected and would be at the station until he was ready to retire.

Cecil had never passed on a stock tip or responded to anybody's efforts to discuss investments in general. Chelan figured that if a million dollars came her way, she'd resign in a flash and travel the world. But obviously, LV-TV gave Cecil something his bank account couldn't, and so there he was. He was the best editor in the place and had been around since the days of film, razor blades, and splicing tape.

There was a newsroom legend that he had once— but only once—exercised his editorial opinion while cutting

THE LION'S SHARE OF THE AIR TIME

a story about some politician or personage. One version of the tale had it as a British princess. Cecil spliced in the pictures of the VIP upside down, and, for good measure, added a few feet of film shot in the barns during the Royal Ontario Agricultural Fair. When the item went to air, some viewers enjoyed the amusing sight of the dignitary appearing to stand on her head, looking at cattle backsides, while others were outraged by the lack of respect.

Cecil wasn't fired. Matthew said management had decided that after thirty years of service, Cecil would be allowed one lapse in judgment.

Chelan timed her work on the piece about Keith so that she could have Cecil edit it. She had the feeling he wanted to be the one to do it, too. About four o'clock they sat down together, in a booth, and watched the footage.

Chelan's throat was thick and raw. The images of Keith at the anchor desk, reporting from the field, in Europe on assignment—it was impossible to believe they wouldn't be seeing him again. Cecil had gone into the archives and found film from twenty-five years back, worked his software magic and edited the material, past and almost present, into a dazzling five minutes.

Chelan knew Keith had started in Toronto, had won awards, even that he once covered a frog-jumping contest, but she hadn't known that he was once a sports reporter, travelling the globe to cover world championships, and was an elite athlete himself. A diver.

Keith had never referred to it. Of course, he never had been one of those bores who constantly refer back to their glory days—nor was he one of those who led you to believe they were going to let you off the hook, by saying "back when dinosaurs roamed the earth" or "of course, it's ancient history". Next they almost always go on to tell you how much better it had all been done in their day. Keith was a man who lived for the present. Chelan scribbled a note on her pad. Maybe that was the first line for the script.

They labored over the piece for more than three hours,

81

fitting the pictures to Chelan's words and changing the copy to reflect the visuals they had. Five minutes of heartfelt, dignified tribute to a good friend. As she sifted through the stories he'd covered over the years, the probes he'd initiated and the scandals he'd uncovered, Chelan was amazed at how little she actually knew about the scope of his career. The script almost seemed to write itself. Her only hesitation came over a shot of Keith shaking hands with a hockey star, while Kevin, age about six, looked on adoringly. It was too personal. Cecil raised an eyebrow, which was enough to solidify Chelan's opinion. She left it out.

She walked down to the bank of vending machines and bought a chocolate bar. She returned to the newsroom and turned on the television that was perched high on a shelf at the south end. Five minutes to airtime.

Half an hour ago, the place had been in chaos. Daniel blazed through the newsroom three or four times, asking for his copy. Nevada was typing like a mad fiend, having left her story to the last minute, as usual. Earlier in the day, she went to a news conference called by a local agricultural association, something about the positive health impact of milk, apparently. She started writing her story at 5:00 p.m.. Said the tighter the deadline, the sharper she was.

Two minutes to air time. Many nights Chelan went over to the set and watched from a chair a few yards away from Daniel's anchor desk. But tonight she felt detached, a bit numb. She wanted to look at a screen, not a human face. She sat down at Tim's desk and looked up at one of the monitors.

The commercial string was just finishing. The news theme began, with a globe and various throbbing graphics, demanding attention. An authoritative voice-over introduced Daniel and the newscast was underway.

"In the news tonight—the city's traffic engineers have come up with a new blueprint for the downtown core..."

There was more of the same, Daniel on camera for about forty-five seconds before the end of the opener. Then,

THE LION'S SHARE OF THE AIR TIME

cut to commercial. That was it. No mention of Keith at all.

Chelan chewed on her chocolate bar. After the commercials, Daniel came back with a script about a looming garbage strike. Then, she heard stories about a shooting, severance packages for government employees, and a new treatment for cancer, but nothing about Keith. What happened to her piece? Tape broke? Hah. Computer froze? File accidentally erased?

"Tonight we say farewell to a prominent local journalist," Daniel announced. "Forty-eight year old Keith Papineau of Lions View Television died on the sidewalk outside his West End home after falling from his apartment balcony last week."

Chelan checked the clock. Twenty-six minutes after the hour — for a story like this! Eighth on the line-up, after items about bureaucratic red tape, minor medical discoveries, and a flood in India?

She listened to her own voice and watched the bleak scenes in front of Keith's apartment building, then the dynamic scenes of a young Keith, dominating the room at a press conference, then wielding his microphone in a political scrum like a sword. Suddenly, it was over, and Daniel was doing the hand-off to Felix for the weather forecast.

Chelan checked the clock again. Thirty-five seconds? The piece had been re-edited and cut short. The broadcast rolled on, but Chelan didn't hear a word. The telephones in the newsroom were ringing, but she let the machines pick them up. Thirty-five seconds! When the program was over, and Daniel walked by, bidding Chelan good night, she didn't respond. But moments later, she headed up the stairs to the executive floor, taking the steps two at a time.

She caught Matthew just leaving, turning out the lights, his Burberry raincoat over one arm. "Why did you cut my story?"

"There was a lot of material today, Chelan. We ran out of time."

Chelan exploded. "Every other station in town has

done better coverage on Keith than we did."

"We don't put out the tabloid stuff they do."

"There was nothing yellow-rag about this. He was our guy. We should be giving him just as much prominence as they did. More."

"Chelan. I know you worked hard on that piece, and I know you wanted to see it go to air. And it was done very well…"

"This has nothing to do with it being my piece. I don't care about that. I'd feel the same way if Nevada had done it, or Tim, or anybody. We should have given Keith more than thirty-five seconds." She was choking up. How embarrassing.

Matthew turned out the lights. "I have things to do, Chelan. Good night."

Things to do?

So had she.

Ξ

Chelan spent the evening on the telephone, calling some of the names in the address book Heather had allowed her to borrow. All of the people were kindly and willing to talk, once she explained that she was a friend of the family, making some calls to help out Kevin. Not one had any idea why Keith might have decided to kill himself.

By the next morning, most of Chelan's anger about the careless way the station had treated Keith's tribute had ebbed, but her drive to find out the truth about his reason for dying was in full flow. She needed to soothe the awful thought that it was all her fault. Even more, she had to find an answer for that tragic fourteen year-old-boy, left reeling and perhaps irrevocably hurt by his father's suicide. She couldn't imagine what it would be like to lose a father at that age. She had her own cross to bear, trying to get her father's attention in the shadow of a talented younger brother, but it would be worse to lose him outright, she was sure.

THE LION'S SHARE OF THE AIR TIME

She was about to get on the phone, to call the next person on her list, when a thought struck her. Had Keith's desk been checked yet? It was one of three grouped in a special area of the newsroom dedicated to the investigative journalists—Keith, Wayne Austen, Sam Nakano. Some cardboard boxes were stacked beside Keith's desk, and nothing looked as it used to. The piles of paper, cardboard files, sticky notes, and newspapers that usually surrounded the desktop computer were gone.

The old-fashioned, solid mahogany pedestal desk was one of a kind in the newsroom. Keith had brought it in from home, over Matthew's objections. Matthew thought that everyone would want to buy their own desk and bring it in, if he let one person do so. Keith insisted that they wouldn't.

Keith's personal effects had been claimed by his family right after his death, but no one had made arrangements yet for the desk to be moved out. Chelan hunted through the three left side drawers—just a few notepads and copies of scripts. The middle right drawer had stacks of story drafts, edited in heavy blue pencil. Keith was quite a pack rat, too. Chelan found dozens of pencil ends, pens, sticky notes, buttons, coins, and paper clips.

In the middle of the debris, a leather-bound appointment book stood out from its surroundings like the last autumn leaf on a dormant tree. It was red and embossed with some sort of graphic design image, done in a classical style. Nicer than the typical day timer you buy in an office supply store. Obviously, Keith had also used it as a doodling pad—there were inky squiggles, mostly triangles within triangles, running down the left front. She hesitated—clearly, this was a very personal item and should be given to his family. On the other hand, if she read it before passing it along, who would know?

"So, he liked to keep some of his notes by hand and off the computer," Chelan muttered, as she tucked the agenda book into her purse. She would return it in half an hour or so, after she'd had a chance to flip through it.

The top right hand drawer held files of research and correspondence. Chelan sifted through pages of interview requests, notes on conversations, and lists of contacts. Keith wasn't much for daily filing, obviously.

The letter lay at the very bottom of the drawer. It was handwritten in a kind of blue-green ink on a thick sheet of paper. Some feminine color. Pink. Or peach, maybe.

Dear Keith,
You are the best reporter on LV-TV — the best in the whole city, actually! I've been watching you for years and I never miss your reports. The most recent one — on the smugglers at the airport — was very good.
I have a story idea for you and I think we should get together sometime. I'll call you...

Your biggest fan,
T

The letter was dated about three weeks ago. Chelan had never heard Keith talk about any particular viewer, or having any fans at all.

Chelan picked up the telephone receiver and punched in Nevada's cell number. "It's Chelan. Do you know whether Keith had any weird fans?"

"Do rabbits make babies? Of course he did, we all do."

"I don't."

"Well, you're too green. Wait till your mug's been on the tube a few years. People think they know you. You get some nice folks contacting you and you get a few nut bars."

This was intriguing. "Like what? What have you had?"

"My two favorites were the dental fillings guy and the graphic designer. The dental guy thought he was getting messages from me by way of the fillings in his teeth, and he phoned to ask me would I please use the mail, like normal people. The graphics guy sent these elaborate pages with letters and words cut out of magazines and pasted into boxes and shapes of airplanes and rocket ships. No sentences or

THE LION'S SHARE OF THE AIR TIME

ideas—just words. None of it made any sense—except to him, I guess."

"Anything come of it?"

"No, they were both harmless. But I did report it to management and they had the police check them both out. You can't be too careful. Why do you ask?"

Chelan was not ready to give Nevada any details just yet.

"Have you ever had something that turned out not to be harmless?"

"No, not really. Once I had a guy calling me each night, right after my story on the late news, but I changed my number and made sure it was unlisted."

"Ever get fan letters?"

"Oh, yeah, at least a hundred a day." Chelan thought she heard Nevada inhale deeply at the other end of the phone. Was she sneaking a cigarette? "No, really, I think one did come pouring in last month. What's going on?"

Chelan saw Elliot heading her way across the newsroom. "Gotta go. Let's have drinks at the Scribbler after work." She tucked the letter out of sight in her purse.

"Chelan! Hold off there!" Elliot crossed the room in five strides.

Chelan stood up, clutching her purse. "What's up?"

"What are you doing?" Elliot leaned against Keith's desk and crossed his arms.

"Just—just looking at this desk." Chelan smiled and tucked her bag over her shoulder.

"It was Keith's. His sister is sending someone for it this afternoon."

He stood guard near it until she returned to her own desk. The hours crawled by. She had expected that handling Keith's things would give her an unbearable and overwhelming sense of loss, and of missing Keith, but that had not happened. If anything, she felt as if she did not even know him. She had spent hours with him in restaurants, in bars, and in the newsroom, hashing over the day's news and questions of journalism ethics. She had played some tennis, some golf, and done some snowboarding with him. They hung out and they became friends.

Just friends, she thought. But for him, there was some sort of attraction. He wanted her. But how much? Enough to speak up, certainly, and to try to find out whether there was any chance the attraction was mutual.

But enough to kill himself over it?

She had never seen him lose his cool. Never heard him speak in anger to anyone, never seen him afraid or hurt. She doubted that he was immune to those feelings; it was just that she had never seen them. What kind of man was he, really? Was he the kind who would commit suicide? Over a rejection?

Was it her fault?

Elliot glanced her way frequently as the hours passed, and she had no chance to read through Keith's planner. The whiteboard showed no other assignments for her, so even though it was only five o'clock, Chelan put on her coat and got ready to leave. She took the steps of the three flights of stairs to the door leading to the parking lot one by one, slowly, like a toddler not sure of the distance needed for each step. She couldn't get past the feeling that she should have noticed some sign in the weeks before Keith's suicide, some clue of some kind. Was he signaling for help from his friends and his colleagues? Had they all been so self-centered that they missed it?

Chelan remembered Brian Bain, from her high school days. The class clown, the best party guy—and then one day, they heard he was in the hospital, after taking a razor blade to his own wrists.

Chelan had seen a lot of blood at crime and accident scenes over the years, but the thought of cutting into herself, deliberately, made her stomach heave. But somehow Brian had not been deterred by any abhorrence of blood. Somehow he had felt that the clouds of fear and depression gathering overhead were too thick to ignore, and he had

THE LION'S SHARE OF THE AIR TIME

tried to get out from under. Permanently. It was incomprehensible. No one saw it coming, with Brian. Maybe it was the same with Keith.

Chelan walked out into the spring sunshine. When she got to her car, she sat behind the wheel for a few moments, and then pulled Keith's appointment book from her bag. She stroked the leather cover, wishing she could get some hint of the truth through her fingertips. Looking left and right, she slouched down low in the seat.

She thought she would feel that she was invading Keith's privacy by flipping through his appointment book, but she didn't get so much as a pang of regret. She needed to know why Keith killed himself—why he left a teenaged son who loved him and a career that had some meaning. She doubted very much that his act had anything to do with their conversation at the Scribbler that evening. What kind of person commits suicide over being turned down for a date? Maybe somebody in a movie, or maybe somebody who had had a mega-rash of rejections and failures, and just couldn't take one more.

But that wasn't Keith. Was it?

She opened the dark red cover and flipped to last Thursday's date. May 8. Her finger traced down the lined page, past about half a dozen entries, appointments on Keith's last day. Bob V.   JW. Garage.   T.

Her head ached and she leaned it against the car window. She was just nicely settled into a semi-trance when a loud noise right beside her left ear sent a surge of adrenaline through her. She turned and saw a hand in a fist, knocking on the glass.

7

Lillian awoke in a cold sweat, just moments after smashing her fists against the bakery glass, trying unsuccessfully to break it and get to the loaves of bread on the other side. This dream, or variations of it, had plagued her nighttime hours for months now. It wasn't difficult to figure out. If one believed that dreams reflect fears, then obviously she was anxious about going without, even starving.

She wearily crawled out from under the covers and checked the time on the clock. Ten p.m. She hated these nights when she awoke after being asleep only a short time. It was as if a short nap recharged her just enough and something in her brain turned her battery back on. It would probably be hours now before she could get back to sleep for the night. Coaster snuggled in closer beside her. She stretched her legs and arms, then sat up slowly. The dream, as usual, was so vivid she could almost feel the shatter-resistant glass against her hands.

But there was something different, this night. She had dreamed of something else. A vestige of a memory of something else happening, before the attack on the grocery store window, teased at the edges of her thoughts. Lillian shook her head to try to clear the sleepy fog and squinted at her reflection, as if the dream were a vision or a scene through a window that she might be able to see, if she got

THE LION'S SHARE OF THE AIR TIME

her mind into the right frame.

She remembered that in the dream something was happening outside. She was looking up, the sun was shining; then a sensation of surprise, of shock—so strong she felt as if she might vomit.

Lillian stared into the glass, trying to bring back more detail. But the more wakeful she became, the further the recollection retreated, until all she was aware of was a silver-haired woman staring back at her. A woman with eyes the color of the Atlantic during a November storm, eyes surrounded by a network of fine lines. It took only a second for the last trace of slumber to recede; once fully alert, she recognized herself.

There would be no returning to sleep now. She pulled the covers closer and opened her folder of coupons and fliers. She picked it up and began sorting through the week's offering of bargains and discounts.

Ξ

Chelan jumped six inches, then looked through the driver's window to see Nevada grinning at her. Chelan pushed Keith's appointment book underneath her purse on the passenger seat. Nevada waited while she fumbled with the window control. By the time she got the window open, she was totally flustered.

"Nevada. Hi. What's up?" Chelan wondered whether she would ever be smooth enough to function as an investigative journalist.

"Chelan, we have to talk. Let me in." Nevada walked around to the passenger side and opened the door. She picked up Chelan's purse and the appointment book, putting them on her knee as she sat down. "I'm going out to a TV production shoot to talk to the director who worked on Jason Wheeler's show the week before he died."

"I thought you weren't interested in lightweight stories about entertainment people."

"Normally, I'm not, but Matthew was so determined to hand this to Amanda at the beginning, I thought I'd just nose around and find out whether there's anything we're missing." She pulled out a cigarette, then caught the look on Chelan's face, and put it away. "Plus he's assigned me to do a daily update on this one story now. Supposedly, we're after a much bigger share of the ratings in the next book. I guess Matthew thinks this is what will make more of them tune in."

Chelan worked on keeping thoughts of Keith's book off her face.

Nevada smiled at her. "I thought maybe the agent or the manager could help us answer some questions, too."

"Us?"

"I'm overloaded with this municipal taxes in Whistler story that Matthew assigned me last week. But I thought that maybe working together..."

"I don't know if I have time either. They've got me doing a lot of research, and I'm doing some things on my own, finding out about Keith. I talked with a suicide expert. And with Bob Venice. They were old friends, apparently. "

"That was probably a blind alley, Chelan. Venice is so slick—he wouldn't tell you anything."

"I don't know, I think I got a few things out of him." Chelan grinned, trying to put this conversation into a lighter tone.

"Chelan, pardon me for saying, but you're not the world's best judge of character."

Was she born thinking she knew everything, or was this an attitude that grew on you after you reached a certain age? Or maybe it was a lack of respect for Chelan, in particular.

"Still, I've got some things going on, Nevada, and I can't take on anything more. I promised Keith's son, Kevin, that I would try to find out why his dad killed himself. There's so much to do I hardly know where to start. I have to talk to his friends, to Sam and Wayne, maybe to Matthew, maybe any women friends he's had in the past few

THE LION'S SHARE OF THE AIR TIME

months… "

"You don't want to work with me?" Nevada watched Chelan's profile.

"I think I have to go my own way for a while, Nevada, that's all I'm saying. I'm not assigned to the Jason Wheeler story and I just don't want to do anything to get Matthew mad at me."

"Chelan, Matthew isn't God."

Chelan stared through the windshield — how do you break off a conversation when somebody is sitting in your car?

"Nevada, my job is on the line. I have to figure out how to get the people upstairs back on my side, how to show them I'm somebody with potential, somebody they should pay attention to."

"They?"

"Matthew. Mrs. Cunningham, Mr. Stratton-Porter."

Nevada screwed her face up as if Chelan had just taken out a blue-cheese sandwich. "Chelan, you're wasting your time. Those people don't know you exist. I thought you were smarter than that —"

"Smarter than that?" Who the hell did she think she was?

"You know, you could go far, but you have to pick carefully when you're deciding who to trust, who to copy. And so far, you're making quite a few mistakes."

"Who the hell do you think you are?"

Nevada sighed. "Just somebody who's trying to help you walk through the minefield here."

"Nevada, you're way out of line here, telling me I'm not smart, that I'm making mistakes. We have a lot we could talk about, you and me, but you have to treat me like an equal, not like some kid."

"I'm honest, Chelan, what can I say? I just call 'em as I see 'em." Nevada opened the passenger door, finally realizing that she'd overstayed her welcome. "Call me if you change your mind."

93

GAIL HULNICK

Ξ

Chelan drove around for half an hour, thinking over Nevada's demands. Maybe it was a bad move, but her first priority right now was investigating Keith's suicide. Maybe there was something to be found out in the details of his final morning. She got nothing but voice mail when she tried phoning Detective Esher at the police station but Liam St. Clair picked up his phone on the second ring and invited her to drop in.

The Eyewitness newsroom was pretty elaborate, compared to LV-TV. Every reporter had a semi-private workspace, and the computers on the desks looked brand new. The furniture and carpets appeared to be crisp and fresh, and there were even art prints on the walls. Liam's desk was covered in yellow sticky notes, with a pile of about fifty spiral notebooks making a pillar on one corner.

Chelan stuck out a hand. "Liam, thanks for agreeing to see me on short notice."

"Hey, no problem." Liam half rose from his chair and shook her hand. His eyes made contact somewhere south of her shoulders, but maybe that was because he was only about five foot six. His hand squeezed hers tightly.

"Damn shame about Keith. He was a good reporter."

The highest praise.

"Do you want to see it?" Liam pulled the video up on his screen without waiting for her reply.

Scenes from the street in front of Keith's apartment building filled the monitor. Chelan kept her face frozen as the camera panned across the body outline on the sidewalk and then up to the balconies of the upper floors.

"Do you want the sound?" Liam asked.

She nodded, concentrating on the screen like a laser beam.

"…neighborhood residents say they were shocked when they saw the man falling…"

THE LION'S SHARE OF THE AIR TIME

Well, who wouldn't be? Chelan knew it was often difficult to come up with enough script to cover the length of the visuals that a producer or news director wanted to use, but she still thought Liam could have filled the time with a few more facts.

Chelan grabbed the remote control and froze the frame. "Look at this group of people." She touched a fingertip to the cold, slippery surface of the monitor. "Here, two men and a woman. Then a cutaway to a Q and A with this guy, this jogger. Next shot, only two men."

Liam studied the second group shot, then ran it back to the first one. "You're right. There was a woman there at first, an elderly woman with a little dog. Then a few minutes later, she's gone. So?"

Chelan ran the tape in reverse and then forward, five times. "She probably didn't want to be interviewed."

"Nah, everybody wants to be on TV. She probably got left behind when we ran over to talk to the police." Liam leaned near to take the remote controller from Chelan. She leaned away—there was a budget cigar in his not-too-distant past.

She thanked him and went out to her car. Her next stop would be the West End.

Just two blocks away from the Point After Apartments, customers lined up outside the restaurants on Denman Street to sit at a patio table and watch the neighborhood stroll by. Chelan parked as close to Keith's building as possible. She planned to wait until the woman with the dog came out for its evening walk.

Coaster emerged around a corner of the building first. He marched past, looking like he owned the world, a fitting match for the silver-haired woman who followed him. She was slender, with a great sweep of hair over her left eye and ear, like a flag waving in a gentle breeze. She was dressed in a lumpy pair of brown pants and a black sweater.

Chelan raised her voice, but kept her distance. "Hello, could I speak with you for a moment?"

Lillian greeted her with the wariness that is wise in those who live near downtown. "Yes? What is it?"

"I am a friend of the man who died here last week." Chelan took a step or two closer. "I wanted to ask you about it."

Lillian waited for her to approach. She looked Chelan over, and then nodded.

"I worked with him. His name was Keith Papineau." she said. "I—we are trying to find out more about what happened, and I just wondered if maybe you saw anything…"

"We? Do you mean you and the rest of his friends?" Lillian asked.

"He has—had a fourteen-year-old son who is very confused by all of this." Chelan bent down to pet the dog and hide her eyes.

Lillian seemed to be wrestling with something in her mind. Then, the self-censor lost and Lillian opened up.

"I was just standing in the park across the way while Coaster did his business. I was looking around, then for some reason I looked up.

"An object was falling. A dark object, irregular shape." Chelan straightened up. Lillian wrinkled her brow and her gaze turned inward. "A jogger went by me, and then stopped—I think because he noticed I was looking up. Then in front of the building, a man in a business suit looked up, too. Coaster was yapping and pulling at his leash. The rest of us were all frozen.

"The thing is—he came down like a platform diver. His head was down, arms stretched out like this, chin tucked in, knees together, as if he were diving into a pool."

Lillian's voice was compassionate and dignified. Chelan was in tears.

"But he hit concrete, not water, and he died," Lillian said quietly. "I wondered afterward why I didn't scream. But I was just frozen. The police came, then the other people. And the reporters." Her smile was strained. "So Coaster and

I left."

Chelan's gulped back a sob and tried to smile. "We all miss him so much."

Lillian nodded. "I'm sure you do, my dear." She stooped to pick up Coaster. "My name is Lillian Howe. Would you like to go for a cup of tea?"

She led Chelan up the block to a small café with green plastic resin seats arranged outside tables at the edge of the sidewalk. She settled herself in at a table, coaxing Coaster to lie down underneath, while Chelan went inside to get the tea.

"I brought milk and sugar just in case." Chelan laid out everything on the plastic table.

"Thanks, anyway, but I like it clear. And strong." Lillian inhaled the steam and smiled. "Delicious. You know, I'm feeling better than I have in days."

"Because of the tea?"

Lillian grinned. "Because of telling you about Mr. Papineau, I think. I've been having bad dreams about that morning, and I think perhaps I've had a need to recount it to someone."

Chelan nodded. "I can understand that. The image of him coming down in a dive is pretty disturbing."

"Yes, I've wondered why he would do that."

"I guess it was a bit typical of his personality. Once he made up his mind to jump, I guess he decided to do it as deliberately as he could."

"Perhaps." Lillian pulled a small biscuit out of her purse and reached it down to Coaster. "But the other thing I keep dreaming about, and can't get out of my mind, is the sense that he wasn't alone up there."

What?

Chelan stared into Lillian's eyes as intently as she could. "Are you sure?"

Lillian stared back. "No, I'm not, which is why I haven't spoken with the police since that first morning. But every time I dream about it, or even think about it, the image gets clearer. That's funny, isn't it? Memories usually become more vague with time. Anyway, each time it's a little longer, goes back a little further. At first, all I thought about was him. Hitting the ground. Then it was the sight of him, diving through the air. But lately, I've been remembering seeing him up on the balcony. Just a second before he fell." Lillian stopped speaking. Chelan waited. "I think there was another person up on the balcony with him."

Another person? This was the first anyone had heard about another person. Was it even possible for Lillian to have seen that, from street level?

"Man or woman?" Chelan asked.

Lillian shook her head. "I couldn't tell. I'm sorry I can't help you more."

Chelan patted her hand. "But you have helped. If there was another person there, someone may be able to answer our questions about why Keith killed himself."

"Or whether he killed himself at all," Lillian gently corrected her.

8

No question, those people at LV-TV News were an aggressive bunch. Zack had just finished a telephone conversation with a Matthew Dixon about Jason Wheeler's death, and he felt as though he'd gone ten rounds with a champion kick boxer. Yesterday, it was Nevada Leacock, quizzing him about police procedure that night in Stanley Park. She'd even gone toe-to-toe with the chief at the news conference about Keith Papineau's suicide.

Now he had another phone message—that a Chelan Montgomery from Channel Two wanted him to call back. How was he supposed to get any work done if he all did was talk on the phone to reporters all day? They all knew Barbara Sewell in Media Liaison was the person they were supposed to call, but they seemed to think that they weren't required to go through channels. The chief aided and abetted them, as far as Zack was concerned, by insisting that public relations and media sucking up was part of every police officer's job description.

The message from Chelan Montgomery said that she wanted to ask him some questions about Keith's death. So far, LV-TV had done no follow-up on Keith's story. Seemed as far as they were concerned, they had laid him to rest with dignity and the story was done. The other media chased down interviews with his family and friends, who seemed convinced there was no motive for suicide. There was no terminal illness, no history of battling the black dogs of depression, no looming personal crisis, no financial problems, and no previous instances of impulsive escape. The reporters probed every corner of Keith's life and found nothing, except copious detail on a well-rounded, relatively happy existence, filled with family, health, money, success and what for many would be a 'fantasy' job. Yeah, there was a marriage breakdown and a few girlfriends, but that was hardly unusual. The reporters visited Keith's apartment building again and again, talking to neighbors and local merchants. They traveled up the highway to Whistler and tried to meet Keith's neighbors at his cabin. They hung around Kevin's school and tried to speak with him and his classmates, until an outraged principal phoned Zack, who came over to help him throw them off the property and ban them from the sidewalks outside the fence, as well.

Every day, year after year, the Vancouver reporters watched the American press cover the twists and turns in their celebrities' lives. Now, with a chance to show their stuff on a homegrown story, they were throwing a lot of resources into trying to "find the color" on Keith's story. The trouble was, there wasn't much to go on. There was a brief foray into the neon end of the palette when Liam St. Clair found an old university classmate of Keith's who said he sometimes got morose when his diving wasn't going well, and went for long walks in the forest beside campus. Bit of a stretch, especially when it turned out there was a house full of sorority sisters that Keith often visited on the street at the end of the forest trail on those pensive nights.

It was even a bit of a stretch for them to cast him in the celebrity role. He wasn't an anchorman or a sportscaster. His name wasn't in the society columns or regularly in the arts and entertainment pages. Still, he did show up on TV regularly and that was enough.

Zack checked his look in the mirror; today it was

"business casual", with a bit of golf pro tossed in. He cranked the wheel and pulled the aging sedan over to the curb. It wasn't a glamorous ride but he had no complaints. Not a shiny red SUV or a black truck up on big wheels like the boys chasing highway speeders had, but it still took him where he wanted to go.

Which today was only about three miles through downtown to LV-TV. Despite what those media people might think, the wheels were turning in the Jason Wheeler case. The autopsy was done, and the report would be ready any day. There could be something there that could shed more light on the attack. The search of the stretch of seawall and park where he died had turned up nothing they could use. They had dozens of footprints, no physical clues, and no murder weapon.

The interview with Jason's manager and a search of the court records in Los Angeles had put the restaurant partnership gone sour to the top of the list as his best lead. The individuals started out with a strong plan, a theme that hadn't been done before, and a wad of cash behind them. Five years later, they were stalled over who owned what, who put what in, and who got to take what out. A year ago, the courts finally decided in Jason's favor. The manager told Zack that Jason's partner was still holding a grudge. The newspapers had spilled a lot of ink on the Jason Wheeler killing, but nobody had come up with this information so far. They would continue to focus on this case, though, because there were unanswered questions. Violence, celebrity and a mystery. But that would soon subside, once they got a new sensational story to pursue. Then it would only come up again, Zack figured, on each anniversary of Jason's murder.

Unless, of course, he caught the killer.

Ξ

"Chelan!" Layla rarely spoke to her in the morning, let

alone shouted, so there must be something she needed. Chelan rolled over and tried to go back to sleep.

"Can I borrow the car?"

Chelan surfaced. "It's not 'the' car, it's my car. And, no."

"But I need it."

"I need it, too. And I paid for it." Chelan rolled through the twisted sheets to check the time on the alarm clock. It was late. "Get a job."

"I'm on my way to a job interview. I need the car."

"It's not 'the' car, it's my car. Go away."

With a huge effort, Chelan stumbled out of bed, walked across the chipped and peeling linoleum, and groped toward the shower. A torrent of scalding water opened her eyes. A few minutes to clean up, and wake up, and she was in front of the closet, looking over her wardrobe. Definitely black.

When she came out into the living room, Layla was pawing under the couch cushions for loose change. "Don't suppose you could give me a ride downtown?" Layla paused in her quest.

"Not going that way."

"The bus, it is then," Layla went back to searching for the fare.

Chelan stared out the window at the killer view. No question, this location was top of the line. Too bad the rent was, too. She should be happy, she supposed, that she had Layla to help pay the bills. Recently graduated from the University of British Columbia, she was a smart girl, just a little disorganized. Smart, disorganized, and ambitious. Chelan suspected they might have been quite good friends, if they weren't sharing space. Maybe she should be a little more generous with her.

Not this morning, though. Chelan felt like dirt and she couldn't blame it entirely on the bottle of Scotch last night. How would anybody feel if they lost a friend? The practicalities of getting up and getting mobile had consumed what small bit of brainpower she had this morning. But once

THE LION'S SHARE OF THE AIR TIME

she got to work, sitting in silence in front of her computer, thoughts and memories of Keith came crashing in as relentlessly as surf on a shore.

She knew she had to do something with the information Lillian Howe had given her yesterday. It was possible that the older woman's eyewitness account was all baloney, but she seemed credible to Chelan. Something about her intensity and her certainty. But how was she going to find out who that second person was? She could try asking around at the apartment—

"Daydreaming, Chelan?" Matthew's voice was a bit kinder than usual, but no less startling.

Chelan whipped around to face him. He was carrying a briefcase, as was Tess, who stood just a few feet back of him. "Just thinking over some new information I came across yesterday."

Maybe this was something she should share with Matthew. He was Keith's boss, after all. And she should probably let him know that she was making some inquiries about Keith's suicide. Wouldn't hurt to let Tess hear about some of her activities, either. "I met a woman who lives in Keith's neighborhood and was out on the street that morning when Keith died."

"There were quite a few bystanders, I heard. Several witnesses."

"Yes, but she says she actually looked up and saw him jump." Chelan watched Matthew's face closely for a reaction. "She says he looked like he was actually diving to the ground. And that there was another person with him up on the balcony."

Matthew made a thoughtful face. "Do the police know?"

"I encouraged her to talk to Detective Esher. She was quite upset about it, she thinks it was proof that someone pushed him." troubled. "That would be quite a development, w

Matthew's face

Chelan nodded. "But you know so far we don't really have any clear reason why Keith killed himself. So maybe…"

"Weren't there some money problems?" Matthew said. "I thought I heard that he was under a lot of financial stress."

Tess stepped forward. "Nothing's been solidly established about that. All that's known absolutely is that he wasn't under treatment for depression and he has no history of suicide attempts."

"And no one in his family or at work had noticed any signs of mental disturbance or despair." Chelan was eager to add her findings.

"Matthew, we really have to get this meeting underway," Tess gave Chelan a friendly smile. "Chelan, we want to speak with all the news people briefly about our new initiative."

"New logo? Theme music?" Chelan was anxious to keep the conversation rolling.

"No, it's more about the types of stories we do, the pace of the newscast, that sort of thing. The winter ratings were abysmal and even though they don't matter as much as the spring book, they still matter. We have to pull ourselves higher and we're going to turn up the heat in every way." Matthew scanned the newsroom, looking for Elliot. "The reporters will be filing more often… and we want more big scoops."

"Our objective is to have all Vancouver thinking that they must watch LV-TV News, every night, or they'll miss something important," Tess said.

Matthew waved at Elliot, who responded by hurrying over to them. "We're all set for the meeting. The camera people will be here in just a few seconds. Oh, Chelan, this package has to go over to Gregory Keene's office."

Chelan gave him a tight smile and took the envelope. She was going to have to find a way to have a serious talk with Matthew about her job situation. With a sigh, she pushed open the newsroom door and headed for the

THE LION'S SHARE OF THE AIR TIME

elevator to take her to the programming floor.

Lions View TV was more than a newsroom. In fact, the newsroom was probably the least important, least profitable place in the building—even less financially viable than the cafeteria. The real center of creativity was the programming wing, where the writers, directors, producers and stars dreamed up the images and stories that kept the viewers coming back to Channel Two on the dial.

No office in that wing was more important than Gregory Keene's. Gregory's show was the top-rated game show in the country. He had been a daily fixture in Canadian living rooms for eight years, if you ignored a brief, six-month period when someone's nephew had been put in charge of programming and had managed to annihilate five years of ratings gains.

Gregory had all the attitude of a star — a minor one. The really major ones tended to be friendly, polite, and normal. He liked to say he did not suffer fools gladly, if at all. Those who wanted to come to the party had to do things his way, and make sure they were properly grateful for the invitation. The game show business is not for the faint-of-heart—or brain.

His office was as familiar as his face. It was used in the opening shots for the show, as Gregory put on his jacket, charged down the hall to the studio and walked on stage with a huge smile, to greet his audience. The suite was decorated in the latest trend — a retro style with a lot of Danish teak in evidence and an expensive espresso machine with Italian ceramic mugs on the credenza. Last year, it was heavy oak, dark green leather, brandy snifters, and barrister bookcases. No doubt he had something in mind for its next incarnation. When they first hired him to host Gregory Keene Presents, he was assigned a small cubicle with powder-blue baffles for dividers, a metal desk and a swivel chair, like everyone else. One call to the national network president and the next day Gregory was in his own office, with a closed door and an open decorating budget. Managers

105

GAIL HULNICK

and staff at LV-TV were told that Gregory Keene was a national network employee, the host of a major primetime network show, and therefore entitled to a private office, as he would be if he lived and worked in Toronto.

But accommodation at LV-TV was cramped, and many of the station staff begrudged Gregory his office, his designated parking space, and his star treatment. They got very grumpy when they saw a new desk and credenza, and various lamps, paintings and pieces of art carried through the building every few months. Gregory liked to say that his profile and the star treatment reflected on them all, but they didn't buy it. He liked to brag about having an open-door policy, inviting anyone to drop in to visit him, any time, but they knew that despite the unguarded entrance to his sanctum, they weren't really welcome.

Even though the style of his office changed frequently, several elements were constant: his wall of photographs with famous people and his big-screen TV. And a framed picture that he kept front and center, next to his telephone. In it, he was wearing seventies-style pants and jacket, hair cut in a shag with long bangs brushed off to the sides, and he was holding a pointer. He was half-turned toward a map of North America, aiming at some spot just north of Minnesota.

Nevada had told Chelan that ever since his beginner days on a small station in Oklahoma, followed by a brief detour into sports reporting in the early eighties, he made time for the people who were on his side, and shut out those who were not. You had to prove yourself to Gregory. He did not have great looks, brains, or powers of concentration, and he knew it. He probably had not read a book, cover to cover, since high school. But he had two things going for him: an instinct for office politics and a high comfort level with the camera. He could chat with anybody about anything when a camera was turned on him. His career had faltered whenever he tried an area of the media that required research, selecting facts and organizing them, writing anything down on paper,

THE LION'S SHARE OF THE AIR TIME

or any effort to impose order on chaos. His one attempt at producing a documentary, on inner city teenagers, had left hurt feelings on all sides. It just wasn't his talent. But when he simply stood there and let his flair for presentation take over, he was riveting. He was interested in people, as long as they had something to say and could say it quickly; he had a charming, warm manner that relaxed everyone and made them want to open up to him.

His second talent built directly on the first. Television station executives and network owners responded to him the same way his on-air guests did. He made an effort to find out who the players were and devoted considerable time to making sure that they knew they were important to him. Over the years, they had responded with decisions that moved his career from the local to the national stage. He met a lot of people along the way and he tried to stay in touch with all of the useful ones. He had had offers to move to a major market in the U.S. and the rumor mill was grinding out the news that he was just about to jump to New York.

His publicist was hard at work, building the buzz. He had his own publicist, business manager, accountant, agent, assistant, office, dressing room, and rented limousine, for special occasions. All of the props that can go with having your own daily hour on the tube.

Some people might find all of this human paraphernalia stultifying, but not Gregory. He seemed to revel in his pressured life, in the number of people buzzing around him, and in the demands of celebrity life. He had a stack of fan mail a foot high on the side of his desk— postcards, business envelopes, personal stationery in every color from purple to peach.

Two hours until airtime. A black suit jacket was draped across the back of his chair. Gregory picked up an envelope from the top of the fan mail pile and took out the letter.

Chelan walked past the empty assistant's desk in

out of Gregory's open door and knocked. "Excuse me, Gregory, I'm just bringing that package you requested from the newsroom."

He had the desk situated so that he could look out at the spectacular view, even though it meant he had almost all of his back to the door. He looked up and turned slightly, not really focusing on her. "Oh, sure. Just toss it on the pile somewhere."

Chelan walked into the office and reached to the right of the desk to deposit the envelope in a small area that wasn't covered in paper.

"Mr. Keene?"

At the sound of the man's voice, she and Gregory both turned to the doorway. Looking very Saturday in a green golf shirt, tan cargo pants and a leather bomber jacket, Detective Zack Esher stood there, notebook in hand.

9

Nevada dug into the bag of potato chips. That flippin' Grouse Grind. Whoever invented such a thing, and who would guess that it would become the biggest problem in her marriage? She knew when she'd fallen for a guy fifteen years younger that there might be a few more hurdles than on the usual track. The age difference would mean that some of their cultural references would be lost on each other. Some of their tastes might be out of sync. But they'd managed to control any friction in their daily life, happy in their apartment diplomatically decorated half in English pub style, with hunter greens and burgundy, and half in "college student in a hurry".

But she hadn't bargained on Owen becoming obsessed with a hiking trail that was inappropriate for anyone over thirty.

She was exaggerating, she knew, and age really had nothing to do with it. Fit women in their sixties could, and did, hike the Grouse Grind. Never mind that it climbed up the side of a mountain that had a perfectly functional gondola to take you up in comfort and with speed. Never mind that in essence it was a steep staircase that took nearly an hour to climb, was covered with roots and slick leaves, and meandered through a forest where bears and cougars made their homes. They still came by the thousands to hike the Grind, the thoughtful ones for the fitness challenge and the reckless ones for the cachet of being able to say they'd done it.

Nevada didn't care about being able to say she'd done it, and it wasn't her preferred choice when it came to workouts. She liked to move her body through the water of a swimming pool or between bed sheets. She and Owen had that in common, and along with their mutual love of books, movies, music, and a good joke, it had carried them through three years of marriage. To please him, she'd once gone along with a plan to hike the Grind—exactly nine minutes into the climb, she'd sworn silently that she would never set foot—or muscle-cramping thigh—on this bloody trail again.

Now that all of the winter snow had melted and the Grind was open to the public, Owen wanted to hike it whenever he had a break in his schedule as a resident at the hospital. Each time he called to suggest she meet him there, she pretended to be considering it, knowing that each time she would call back after half an hour to announce regretfully that she had an assignment she couldn't duck. Then he'd go off on his own, and she would buy a bottle of nice dry red wine to keep her company.

With almost anyone else, she would say exactly what she thought and insist that they go do something civilized. But she had a trail of broken relationships behind her and she was convinced the only way to keep her marriage in one piece was to soften the truth a little, with Owen.

But only to a certain point, and only over irrelevant items like hiking. When it came to work, Nevada was determined to hold the line. Ambiguity was the quicksand that lay between hell and the higher ground. People like Matthew Dixon or Elliot Dahl could handle the truth and needed to hear it. People like Chelan Montgomery—Nevada sighed. She felt sort of sad about the way their last conversation had gone. Chelan was a good kid, and might be a good journalist, if she managed to avoid being sucked into the mire of office politics. She needed to know that truth was the only reason to be a reporter—not fame, not creativity, not ambition. Ambition didn't get anybody anywhere worth going; most of the people at the top of the

THE LION'S SHARE OF THE AIR TIME

heap, with the most money, the most power, and the most toys got there because of luck. Some were ambitious, some were not—it was an extraneous variable, but one that could curdle the soul if you weren't careful, or if you hitched your wagon to a dark star.

She had watched Chelan's eager face when she came into the newsroom during the latter part of the meeting today. Just drinking it in, all the talk about more stories, better journalism, issues that mattered to people. When you're new, of course, that all sounds like the music of the angels. After you've heard it a few hundred times, it's one of those annoying tunes that dig into your brain and won't let go.

Nevada doubted there would be much real change. One of the problems, and one of the reasons they had trouble getting to the number one spot, was that they burned up way too much energy redesigning things, taking "new initiatives", when they should just be concentrating on old-fashioned, solid journalism. And they needed to stop constantly trying to find ways to make the reporter the center of the story. In this Jason Wheeler story, for example, Amanda had actually filed an update where she talked about the first time she'd seen one of his shows and how she felt about it. Gag.

Nevada poured another glass of wine and flopped into the armchair in front of a bookcase filled with medical texts and biographies. On the end table, a pile of four hardcover books drew her attention. She picked up the top one, a brand new novel nominated for the Giller Prize, but it held her interest for only a moment. The second book on the pile, with its glossy black and white photograph of a handsome man with dark hair and a killer smile, pulled her in. Tom Leacock. She opened it and began to read.

Ξ

The silence was thick when Chelan approached Wayne and Sam. Both were hunched over their computer terminals, intent on reading through the thousands of lines of text in some dense, official document. Keith's antique wooden desk had been replaced by a standard issue metal number.

That was an odd thing, seeing Detective Esher outside Gregory's office. Was it possible that Gregory knew something about Keith's death? Unlikely, though, because the police department wasn't looking into Keith's death anymore. Still, might be worth Chelan's while to stop by for a chat with the game show host. Or to make an appointment — she'd heard he wasn't terribly friendly. Maybe Esher was there about some complaint of Gregory's. A theft or something?

Chelan watched Wayne's fingers sweep across the keyboard. When she cleared her throat, he looked up with the startled, aggrieved air of a cat interrupted, mid-nap. Sam ignored her completely.

"Do you have a minute? I wanted to talk about Keith."

That got Sam's attention. "Sure, have a seat."

Sam was once a sports writer on a major metropolitan daily newspaper in the States, and he always dressed as if he were a kid, on his way out to a game: jeans, T-shirt, windbreaker. Sitting beside him, in his brown tweed jacket, shirt and tie, Wayne could have been his university professor. Or maybe his probation officer. While their clothing styles had nothing in common, they both had about the same gray-hair count and the same slightly distracted manner. Despite the fact that their jobs required them to sit a lot of the time, they both obviously used their off hours to run, bike or swim—neither the T-shirt on Sam nor the jacket on Wayne showed any extra flab.

"What are you after?" Wayne asked.

"Why Keith did it." She waited for the information to come pouring out, but there was silence. "I promised Keith's son I'd ask a few questions."

"Nobody in the family knows? Maybe Heather?" Sam said.

"Heather his wife?" Chelan paused. "Wife he was

separated from? Heather says maybe he had money problems and felt he couldn't get out from under."

"Who else? Father, mother, sister, best friend?" Wayne's voice had the efficient tone used by supermarket clerks. "How about family doctor? Psychiatrist? Counselor? Golf buddies, ski buddies, hockey buddies? Barber?" His eyes continually flicked back and forth from his computer screen to the general region of Chelan's face.

Chelan was rattled. "Well, I was kind of starting with you guys. His closest co-workers."

Wayne raised both eyebrows, and Chelan wasn't quite sure how to interpret that—maybe skepticism and maybe derision.

Sam laughed. "Come on, give her a break. Anybody she talked to could suggest a dozen other possible sources. And it's only because you're the asshole that you are that you're telling her she should have gone everywhere else first, before coming to us. And the reason you want her to do that is so she has a big pot of information that you can take off her."

Wayne muttered something incomprehensible as he took a drink of his coffee. Chelan looked from one to the other—this was like stumbling into a party where everyone had been friends forever and had some secret language they all spoke.

"Did he ever mention to either of you anything that was bothering him, that might have made him do this?" Chelan asked.

Wayne shook his head. "Have you tried talking to the cops?"

"I avoid the police as much as possible." Chelan sensed disapproval in the way they were looking at her and tried to explain. "I did go to the initial news conference about him. But they haven't been very helpful and they don't seem to want to talk to me."

Sam moved his chair closer to his desk and started to type on his keyboard. Chelan was about to leave when he spoke. "There was one very pissed-off source, after that drug smuggling story. Keith seemed to think the guy may have had a point, that maybe he wasn't treated completely ethically. I don't know, I wouldn't kill myself over that, but Keith prided himself on never making mistakes in his work. I don't know the details."

"Who should I ask?"

"Ask Matthew."

Ξ

Zack piloted his car through the traffic jam on Highway 1 East. Too bad Kenny hadn't come along, so he could use the HOV lane with a clear conscience. He made the turnoff and rolled along, watching for the sign to Butterfield Hospital. He was on his way to interview some of Jason Wheeler's colleagues in the television business, and they were shooting scenes there. The mental institution had been long out of use as a home for patients, and was now rented out as a film location. Ironic.

As he waited for the production assistant to direct him to a parking spot, Zack reflected on the morning's interview with Gregory Keene. Keene had something on his mind, no doubt about it. He'd been quite polite and anxious to cooperate, and he hadn't said anything self-incriminating. But something about his way of talking, smiling just a bit too much—Zack's antennae were up.

He was operating at a bit of a disadvantage today, because Kenny had had to take another sick day. Sure wasn't easy for a guy whose wife couldn't function. Usually, he and Kenny did the good cop, bad cop routine; on his own, he found that the authoritarian style was his most productive.

Keene had confirmed that he was in the restaurant business with Jason Wheeler and sued him when the business went under. There was another participant, a silent partner. Gregory said he'd only seen the guy's money, not his name, that Jason had been the one to bring him in. Wheeler's lawyers had drawn up the initial paperwork with

THE LION'S SHARE OF THE AIR TIME

clauses that left Keene with sole responsibility for paying back the secured creditors. Wheeler didn't make any money on the restaurant, but when it closed, he walked. Keene would be paying for about four more years. Understandably, he was furious with the way things turned out and had dragged Wheeler into court. The judge didn't see it his way, and now he had lost his investment. Plus, he had to pay court costs.

The night Jason Wheeler took a knife in the back, Gregory Keene said he was at home on his acreage near Abbotsford, listening to Handel while the aroma of a superb fettuccine alfredo filled the air.

Throw in all the details you want—it's still not an alibi. For people who live alone, alibis are like five-foot NBA players.

The producer was waiting for Zack at the front door. But for the short beard, Zack would have guessed he was about twelve years old. "Rob King, Officer. What can I do for you?"

"I'll only take a few minutes. Mr. King. I imagine you've got your plate full, trying to work around Mr. Wheeler's death." Zack showed his identification.

"The whole thing is just sad. Nobody feels much like working, now that Jason's gone. But we have to keep on shooting scenes while the execs figure out what to do about the show."

"I only have a few questions. Did he ever mention to you anyone who was an enemy?"

Rob considered. "No. I mean, he was the same as all of us, he had people he liked and people he didn't like, but nobody I'd say he thought of as an enemy."

"Any fights on set?"

Rob shook his head. "None that I know of."

" Anybody trying to come in to see him that he wouldn't put on a visitors' list?"

"Nope. We keep everything pretty tight, as you can imagine. Have to keep the actors safe. Some of them have some nutty fans, obsessive, and we have to provide security."

"Obsessive. What do you mean, what did they do?" Zack had a pretty good idea, but you never knew when you'd hear something fresh.

"Send letters, photographs, gifts. Wait around outside, trying to get an autograph or just meet him. He told me once that one particularly persistent woman turned up at his house in L.A. All she wanted was to see him in person, but you gotta admit, that seems a bit over-the-top, going all the way to some actor's house. She was from Germany, of all places. And he had another one who sent him a letter a day for a year, he said. Three hundred sixty five frickin' letters, do you believe it? "

"Did he ever seem concerned when he talked about it?"

Rob reflected before answering. "I'd have to say no. He didn't joke around about it, but he didn't seem worried about it either."

"Did you know Mr. Wheeler socially at all, Mr. King?"

"No. He kept to himself, pretty much. Came to the wrap parties each season but that's about it. Can't help you there."

"Could I get a list of his visitors in the past three weeks?"

"Sure thing."

"Thanks." Zack put out a hand. "You've been very helpful."

On the drive back downtown, Zack went over the possibilities. Too bad Kenny wasn't here. It was always useful to hear his thoughts out loud—usually gave him a few new ones. Zack supposed he could just start talking as if Kenny were there, but that might cause some commotion on the freeway—if anyone he knew happened to see him.

So, Jason Wheeler has a business deal with Gregory Keene that had gone so sour it had ended up in court. Keene insisted there were no hard feelings, that it was all in the past. Jason's will hadn't yet been read but that was one event Zack would definitely keep tabs on. Another possibility—it

THE LION'S SHARE OF THE AIR TIME

was a random attack in a dark park by a psycho. And another possibility—a carefully planned killing by an obsessed fan.

Ξ

Chelan walked into the Scribbler, looking for a familiar, if not an actually friendly face. She saw Liam St. Clair and a group of Eyewitness News reporters at a table and was on her way over to them when Nevada stepped into her path. She extended a white paper napkin.

"Truce, Montgomery."

Chelan had to laugh. "Yeah, okay, truce."

"Want a beer?"

Lunchtime suds had gone out at the end of the eighties, the old-timers said, particularly in a hotbed for the healthy lifestyle like Vancouver, but once in a while there was an occasion for an exception. Like maybe a cease-fire. Chelan allowed herself to be led over to Nevada's table, where a pitcher of draft awaited.

"You know, you gotta stop being so thin-skinned," Nevada remarked as she poured the beer.

"You're too rough," Chelan protested. "Too direct, too tactless, too rough."

"Too honest, you mean," Nevada dove into the foam. "No such thing, you know."

Chelan shook her head—what was the point of getting into this? "What have you been up to?"

"Matthew's got me on the Jason Wheeler story. What did you do?"

"No kidding." Chelan shook her head at Nevada's offer of a cigarette. "Quit trying to corrupt me. You're not allowed to light up in here anyway." She waited a moment, to give Nevada time to do her usual muttered rant about fascists. "I talked to Wayne and Sam about Keith. Have you ever heard about some source he allegedly burned? And that he might have been feeling so guilty about it that he was getting depressed?"

117

Nevada frowned. "News to me."

"Sam suggested I ask Matthew."

"Well, yeah, any confidential source crap has to go through Matthew or Elliot. At least one senior person has to see your notes and know your source's identity. But, Chelan, I'd walk softly on this, if I were you." Nevada's blue eyes lost their familiar ironic flash. "Seriously. If you want Matthew in your corner, you shouldn't let him know that you're investigating something personal on company time."

"But it's Keith!"

Nevada shrugged. "Won't matter. To Matthew, you're either professional or you're not. Doing anything unrelated to your clearly stated assignment is unprofessional. And that can get you canned." She drained her mug. "Let's shoot some pool."

Nevada led the way through the dim, cluttered room. Chelan had leaned over a billiards table a grand total of three times previously in her life, but sometimes 'no, thanks' was clearly the wrong answer. She wanted to be cool again with Nevada, and if she had to wave around a long stick to do it, she would. Nevada broke the balls with a sharp, crisp shot. Two reds dove into the side pockets. She knew what she was doing.

Nevada strolled around the table, sizing up her next shot. "Have you dug any deeper on Keith?"

"Talked to Wayne and Sam, and to Liam St. Clair. I also met an old lady who was there the night Keith died."

Chelan looked past Nevada's face to the tip of the cue as it tapped a red ball and dropped it neatly in the end pocket. She watched as one by one, Nevada put away all the red balls.

"Yellow ball, side pocket," Nevada announced. As she bent to make the shot, she said, "That's interesting." The sharp smacking sound of the cue ball hitting its designated target was followed by the inevitable thump of the ball falling into the side pocket. Sunrise, sunset. Up, down.

"It gets better. She's had her memory coming back

more and more. She remembers seeing him fall. Except that it wasn't a fall. It was a dive." Chelan kept her eyes on the pool table.

Nevada stopped, leaned against her cue stick, and looked Chelan full in the face. "You believe that? Just like that? Chelan, she might be making it up to get attention."

Chelan twisted the pool cue in her hands. Nevada tapped the cue ball smartly; it looked like it was intended to bank off the right side and come over to knock the green ball into the end pocket. But she didn't have enough power on it, and it came to rest against the brown ball. "It's all yours."

Chelan took a sip from her glass of beer, surveying her options. A light tap to the left on the cue ball should send it far enough to sink the green in the end pocket. She leaned over to take her shot, but her elbow touched the black ball and knocked it several inches out of position.

"You knocked the black ball. My shot." Nevada bent down to take another turn.

Chelan shrugged and stepped back from the table. Nevada sank the green ball, then put the brown into the end pocket and the blue into the side.

"You're a pro," Chelan commented.

"Yeah, missed my calling," Nevada muttered as she focused on her next shot.

"This lady also says that she saw two people up on Keith's balcony."

"How does she know it was Keith's balcony?" Nevada sank the pink ball. "And wouldn't that be a hell of a long way away?"

"She says she's extremely far-sighted."

Nevada snorted. Just the black ball left on the table. She calculated the angles and turned her attention to the most likely shot.

"Go slow on this, Chelan. You got a lot of people's feelings hanging on it, and you don't want to go around putting stuff out there that isn't absolutely solid." Nevada put the black ball in the side pocket.

Chelan raised her beer glass in a toast. "You win. What a surprise."

Nevada laughed. "My misspent youth."

They returned to their small table and Nevada ordered another round.

"Now let's talk long-term plans, Chelan. What's next for you in the newsroom?"

Chelan felt a bit wary, but decided to answer the question. "I'm hoping Matthew will give me better assignments and then maybe put me on City Hall."

"City Hall? No, no, that's just a dead end. And the office is so far away from the station—you're out of the loop."

"How do you know so much about it?"

Nevada made a face and gulped her beer. "Been there, done that. Fifteen years ago. Nothing's changed."

Chelan should have realized that. Nevada had covered City Hall, years ago, when she was in her twenties. She had covered the Legislature, Parliament Hill, and even a couple of wars, somewhere. She could have had any beat at the station, but preferred to go for variety. These days, she viewed a beat assignment as a sentence to sameness: the same contacts, the same sources, the same stories, the same cycles, nothing changing. As long as she continued to turn in the occasional scoop, win the occasional award, and be available to fill in any gaps in a given news day, Matthew let her choose her own burrow and dig it however she liked.

"Still, it has to be better than filing and writing background all day."

Nevada conceded. "Of course, it is. I'm sorry. You're ready to celebrate, and I'm dumping on your parade. It's just that I think Matthew has treated you badly so far and I'm not ready to give him a round of applause now, for this."

"He hasn't treated me that badly. He's had me pay my dues, like everybody has to. And he has the bigger picture in mind, I guess. He has to think of the best interests of the whole newsroom."

Nevada made a gagging sound and Chelan got up to go to the bar to order another beer. The room had filled with chattering, bantering media types, relaxing over their meals and trading gossip, stories and information, snug in a place of their own, while the rainstorm howled outside.

Chelan came back to the table with both hands full.

"A peace offering. Thank you." Nevada downed the last bit from her previous bottle and poured the new one into her glass.

"You're welcome, Trip." Chelan filled her own glass. "Where did that nickname come from? Trip. Some foreign assignment?"

"In a way. It's short for 'triple threat'. Somebody from the Washington Post called me that on a Royal Tour one year and it stuck. Or maybe we were on an election campaign..."

"So it's because you can do three things at once?"

"Either that or it had something to do with the Secret Service..." Nevada made her wide-eyed bimbo face, then pushed the bowl of peanuts toward Chelan.

"What about Nevada?" Chelan asked. "Is that a nickname, too?"

"No, that's my name. My mother picked it, for some song that was on the radio the year I was born. How about you, any family?"

Chelan sipped at her beer and looked around the room. "My father. My mother died years ago."

"Any brothers? Sisters?"

"One brother. How about you?"

Nevada snorted. "Hah. More people in the picture than at a Smith family reunion. Mom, dad, two brothers, two sisters, nieces, nephews, cousins. And Owen, of course. And the hospital. The hospital is like another family. Or another wife, or something."

"Must be nice to have so much social life."

"A nice twenty-two year old like you—"

"Twenty-four year old."

"Twenty-four year old … should be happy with her social life."

"I am, I am," Chelan laughed. "It's my work life that's the pits."

"Well, what is it that you want, exactly?"

Chelan's face set. "I want a big piece of the pie. I want the whole pie. Ever since I was a little kid, my brother was given the bigger piece of everything—first, because he was the boy, then because he was the favorite, then later on, after he left home and did drugs for about eight years and then came back, because he was the prodigal son. I would have thought it was unfair, even if there was nothing that I wanted for myself. But I've got my own dreams, too, you know? I don't think I'm just here to help somebody else fulfill his. I've been taking the scraps for years, and it's my turn for the lion's share."

"But it's early days yet, in your career. We all had to take the scraps for a long time at the beginning."

"I know, and I can cope with that. But I don't want to get complacent, or forget why I'm there." Chelan downed her beer. "Let's go."

10

The telephone line to L.A. was as clear as the water in the Caribbean, and so was Jason's agent. "I know nothing. I'm sorry I can't be more helpful, but really, I have nothing to add."

They had been on the phone for less than ninety seconds, but Zack could tell the guy was champing at the bit to move on. "No other suggestions of people in Jason's circle that we should talk to, Mr. Maxell?"

"Can't think of anybody."

"We had someone suggest yesterday that we should consider the possibility that a member of the public stalked Jason and killed him."

"Jason never mentioned to me anything about a stalker."

"Had he ever taken anything to the LAPD Threat Management Unit, that you know of?"

"The…? No, nothing that I ever heard about. Certainly there was nothing formal, no restraining orders, no arrests, or I would know about it. Any successful actor has thousands of fans, maybe millions, Detective. Knows millions of people. Some have problems with the odd one or two. It's rare. You want to find the one person who might be emotional enough about Jason Wheeler to try to kill him — it's like looking for a needle in a haystack. Sorry—what a cliché. Good thing I'm not a writer."

123

Zack laughed, trying to build a connection. "Yeah, really. That's why we're trying to narrow it down, looking at possible motivations—"

"Why don't you try looking at evidence? Look, I'll have to go soon, Detective, but I just want to say my best guess is that Jason happened to be in the wrong place at the wrong time, when some tragic jerk who didn't take his medication came wandering through your park up there. Okay? Are we through here?"

"What about his personal life?"

"Ex-wife, no kids. Look, all this is information that's available on the Internet."

"When's the will going to be read?"

"No idea. Call his lawyer."

Zack resisted the urge to shout at the guy. "Thanks for your time, Mr. Maxell. We'll be in touch."

He hung up and walked out to the coffee machine. The desk sergeant was waving at him, and when he arrived at the counter, he saw a tall, silver-haired woman waiting.

"Detective, this lady would like to speak with whoever is investigating Keith Papineau's death."

Zack looked around for someone to delegate this to, but there was no one. "Ma'am, there isn't an investigation going on right now, but I was one of the people involved when he was found. Would you like to come in to speak with me?"

Lillian followed him into his office. Her baggy clothing and well-used running shoes suggested that she was not living in one of the high-income postal codes, but the way she carried herself implied some experience with the better things in life.

"What can I do for you?" he asked once she was settled in a metal chair across from his desk and offered coffee.

"I was present the day Keith Papineau died."

"Present? Do you mean—"

"I saw him die."

"You saw him die?"

THE LION'S SHARE OF THE AIR TIME

"He came down like a diver."

"Do you mean you were an eyewitness, Ms. — "

"Mrs. Howe. Lillian Howe. Yes, I was on the sidewalk in front of his building, and I saw him come down."

"We didn't see you there, Mrs. Howe."

"I left right away. I didn't want to talk to the police, and I particularly didn't want to talk to any journalists. But recently I've been reconsidering, and I think the right thing to do is to come forward."

Witness? Or victim of too many TV shows?

"Believe me or not, Detective. Of course, it's up to you. At least, I will have done my duty. I was walking my dog, he started barking, I looked up, and I saw Mr. Papineau dive from the balcony." She bowed her head for a moment, and then stared Zack in the eye. "There is one other matter. When I looked up, I saw two people on his balcony."

She was credible, there was no question about that. Over the years, Zack, like any policeman, had developed some intuition. The courses in spotting a liar had helped, too. So, what were the possibilities? Someone was up there, when he fell, and was now somewhere in the city in a state of shock over being unable to prevent such a horrendous accident. Or was somewhere in the city in a state of shock over being so close to someone committing suicide.

Or was up there with him, and gave him a push.

Ξ

Several hours later, Lillian and Coaster hovered in the doorway of the building across the street from the Point After apartments. She saw the unmarked police car pull up and the man she had met earlier at the police station get out from behind the wheel. Another man, shorter, slower, and also dressed in a suit, got out from the passenger side. She watched them enter the building and stop to talk to the manager through the intercom system. A young man in sloppy jeans and a kangaroo sweatshirt passed in front of

125

her, blocking her view for a moment.

The police officers were still by the front door. Was there a problem in getting inside? Now that she had finally made up her mind to tell her story, Lillian was anxious for progress to be made. She wanted them to search the man's home, find something conclusive, and establish definitively why this television reporter had fallen nine floors to his death. And why he was doing a beautiful dive as he fell.

Someone was watching her. She turned as Coaster tugged at his leash and pulled her toward the young man who had passed her a moment ago.

He bent to pat the dog. "He's cute, what's his name?"

Lillian smiled. "Coaster."

"I was going to get a dog, but I moved back and forth so much, it would have been confusing. For the dog." The teenager had dark circles under his eyes and his hair hadn't been washed in a while. But when those two items were cleared up, he was probably quite a handsome boy. Chestnut hair, dark eyes, tall. Nothing to make you cringe.

"I wanted a golden retriever. But they're pretty big and my dad was living in a small apartment." It was if he were telling Coaster all this. "And I do a lot of stuff, go a lot of places where a dog wouldn't be welcome. If I had a dog, it would have to be my dog. I would be the one to feed it, and walk it, and pick up the…"

"That sounds like your mother talking." Lillian smiled.

The boy rose and smiled back at her. "I'm Kevin," he said.

"Mrs. Howe." A rain shower began and Lillian stepped back under the shelter of the building entrance. Coaster followed her, and Kevin followed him. "Do you live near here?"

"No, I live in Kits. I bused over to—to take a walk."

There was an odd tone in his voice; he seemed to be thinking about something disturbing. Perhaps it wasn't a brilliant idea to be so friendly with him. Lillian scanned the area around them, planning an adroit way to step around him

THE LION'S SHARE OF THE AIR TIME

and move away, along the sidewalk. She studied his face again, just in case she needed to identify him for some reason later. A tear rolled down his cheek.

"Are you alright?" Lillian picked up Coaster and got ready, just in case she had to make a move.

He reached out to pat Coaster's head. "My dad died. Just the other day."

So it was suffering she saw, not mental illness or criminal intent.

"He lived over there, and I like to come by and just walk up and down his street, you know?"

Over there? Over where? Across the street?

Lillian tipped her head back to look at him directly. "Kevin, is your father Keith Papineau?"

The boy nodded.

In the faces of the almost grown, you can still see the two-year-olds and five-year-olds and eight-year-olds they once were. She wanted to put her arms around him, give him a hug, even pick him up—but, of course, that was ludicrous. A pat on the arm would have to do.

"I'm so sorry for your loss, Kevin. Of course, you want to walk by his home and think about him."

Kevin seemed to be leaning toward her and it was a natural movement to pass Coaster into his empty arms. He lowered his head to the dog's and rubbed against it. Coaster licked his chin. That brought on a bit of a smile.

"I miss him an awful lot. Even though we didn't live together all the time for the last while, he picked me up at school all the time, to drive me home. And I saw him every second weekend." Kevin rubbed his eyes against Coaster's head and held out the dog to Lillian.

"Thanks for listening, Mrs. Howe. I gotta go."

"Of course. You take care of yourself now."

The boy nodded and loped off down the street. His life would be so changed now.

Ξ

127

GAIL HULNICK

Keith's apartment had been thoroughly searched the day of his death. The forensics people had been in, and had literally combed every surface. The coroner's report had come back with a finding of suicide. Nonetheless, after Lillian Howe's appearance, Zack couldn't shake the thought that they needed to take another look. A hunch, as the old-timers would say. He got her to give a statement and assured her again that her decision to come in was a case of "better late than never". Now he and Kenny waited for the building manager to let them into Suite 909.

Kenny was having a rough time this month. His wife was very high-maintenance. It had started out with just a few problems with reliability. He got calls from the school about permission forms not handed in, calls from doctors and dentists about missed appointments, calls from the kids about needing a ride. Her home phone and cell phone seemed to be permanently forwarded to voice mail and no one could reach her. Lately, she needed hours and hours of his time, to talk about her problems, and Kenny often came to work on only three hours' sleep, after a long night of being that shoulder to cry on. This morning, she'd been unable to get out of bed and function at all. Zack pushed him to call a doctor and get her into therapy, but Kenny just kept hoping it was something that would blow over.

Made him glad that Marla's only fault was ragging on him about the long hours he worked. Yeah, but things could change at any time.

The manager probed them with questions as she opened Keith's door with the passkey. Keith's lease didn't run out until the end of June and everything was paid up, so no major cleaning or advertising for new tenants would happen for a while. The family was due to come over and pack up his effects next week.

The apartment had been closed up for more than a week and the air was stale. The door opened on a standard one-bedroom layout. Bathroom to the right, kitchen to the

THE LION'S SHARE OF THE AIR TIME

left. Living room opening onto the balcony, bedroom in the northwest corner. Zack walked in and stood in the middle of the living room to get his bearings. Nice-looking leather coach, big screen TV, couple of extra chairs. Beige walls, a real guy's color. A few prints—one with a lot of odd-looking people and strange buildings where the lines led in and out, fooling you into thinking you were looking at a front when you were really looking at a back. Another one with an amazingly accurate drawing of a black bear.

The bedroom had a king-size bed, covered with a dark blue quilt. Just a box spring, no fancy furniture. Couple of night tables, a dresser. He'd get to the closet later. In the bathroom, the basics. And in the kitchen, barely anything. Clearly, a guy who ate out a lot. Zack roamed through the apartment, not looking for anything in particular, just anything unusual.

He walked out to the balcony, where Kenny stood, looking things over.

"Trying to get a feel for it," Kenny said.

Zack studied the balcony railing, again. "Could go either way, couldn't it? Not so high that somebody would never fall over it, accidentally. But high enough that it's unlikely."

"But there was the note, don't forget."

"Yeah, the note." The note was typed on Keith's computer and left under a coffee mug on the kitchen table. It would be that much closer to a slam-dunk, if the note were handwritten. But you work with what you got.

"We got any signs at all of this second person the old lady talked about?"

Zack shook his head. "The building manager says nobody rang the buzzer that she heard. She says she's got the closed circuit channel that shows video of the front lobby on most of the day, on her kitchen TV, but, you know, it was before seven in the morning." Rain was falling and the air outside on the balcony had a crisp, clean smell. "I think we gotta go over every inch of the place again, and look for

129

anything that might not belong to a forty something guy living on his own."

Kenny nodded. "And we do the door-knocking thing again."

"I'll take the kitchen."

Meticulously, they searched the apartment, stopping only to compare empty notebooks after about two hours. Zack had pretty much given up on any expectation of finding something worthwhile. Then he noticed the flashing green light on Keith's computer printer. Bingo.

Ξ

Chelan sat perched on a plastic chair, watching people line up for their French fries, or sushi, or whatever. The smell of grilling hamburgers, mingled with the unmistakable aroma of pizza, was overwhelming. She wasn't much for the Food Court, ordinarily. Given her choice, she'd rather walk up to a small café with its own door to the street. But she wasn't given her choice today. When Twain called, he didn't ask her where she wanted to eat or even ask if she wanted to go to the shopping mall. He just told her to meet him there at five.

Much as his bossy style annoyed her sometimes, she was glad to see him today. She needed a change of scene from the newsroom, after having yet another run-in with Matthew. Ignoring Sam's advice, she approached Matthew to ask for the name of the source that he had insisted Keith reveal on the whistle-blower story. Matthew snapped at her, told her to pay attention to the assignment she'd been given, and she felt like crawling under a rock. She needed to talk to Twain and spend a few hours forgetting that she worked at LV-TV.

She spotted him walking over, maneuvering among the tables. Very hot. He was about six foot three or four, with the build of a football player. Not one of the gargantuan men who tackle everybody, but one of the muscular, fast

THE LION'S SHARE OF THE AIR TIME

ones who threw and caught the passes. His blond hair was a bit longer than the fashion, but his three-day stubble of beard was right in style. She liked the longer hair, anyway. Kind eyes and an inclination to make jokes whenever the going got tough made him almost perfect.

He said that his mother gave him the name Twain because he was born a Gemini, and she wanted something unique. He liked to snowboard, golf, play tennis, swim, and see movies. The only flaw—okay, the only one other than his bossiness—was that he had no ambition. Whatsoever. He liked his job, building kitchen cabinets, and he had no quarrel with the pay scale. One night, when she questioned him about his choice of occupation, he admitted that he could imagine himself quite happily doing the same thing when he was forty. Or fifty.

That was not the only night that Chelan had brought up the subject of Twain's line of work, and she could tell that her persistence was bugging him. But, really. What was life about, if not about having experiences, many different experiences, and jobs building toward more knowledge, more responsibility, more power?

He turned around several times to talk to a homeless man who seemed to be following him through the Food Court. The man wore an old combat jacket, jeans and running shoes with no laces. He swayed and almost lost his balance a couple of times—drunk or stoned, no doubt. As they moved closer, Chelan's shoulders slumped. She recognized the face beneath the heavy beard. Twain had no business bringing him here, trying to put the two of them together. She stood up and walked toward the exit.

Ξ

Zack inserted the computer paper that Kenny had had to go down the street to the drugstore to get, when they couldn't find any in Keith's apartment. He pressed the start button and the machine swung into action. A single page came out.

If anyone reads this, and I am gone, you should know that someone came after

"What? Someone came after all? Someone came after eight? Or maybe someone came after me?" Kenny asked.

"That's my guess." Zack pulled out a plastic bag and slipped the piece of paper into it, handling it by its edges. "Let's go interview some of the other residents."

Ξ

Chelan expected to hear from Twain after she had ditched him at the Food Court, but he didn't call. She didn't wait around—she had work to do. She needed to find out more about Keith's state of mind after he had to burn his source. She made a list of people to call. Heather Alcott was at the top.

"Heather, I want to pursue the possibility that Keith was depressed over having to burn an informant. Sam at work says it was really bothering him. Matthew wasn't any help, and I was wondering if you could tell me the man's name."

A pause while Heather thought. "It was a story about a shipping company. The source was some guy on the fringes of a gang—unusual last name. Ted... Ted... Bougie, I think."

"Bougie?" Chelan made her note.

"But Chelan, that doesn't matter now. I've got some new information about Keith's death." Heather sounded shaken. "I got a phone call from Detective Esher. He's had a visit from a woman who lives near Keith's building."

Lillian Howe? Did she get over her fear of the cops and actually go in to tell them what she saw? "This woman says she saw Keith jump, and that there were two people on his balcony just before he did it." Heather exhaled. "And he found some sort of note in Keith's apartment—another note, something they think he wrote that last morning."

THE LION'S SHARE OF THE AIR TIME

"What did it say?"

"He didn't tell me, but he said that when they add up the woman eyewitness's information and this new note, it gives them reason enough to treat it as suspicious." Heather's breathing was so loud that Chelan became concerned.

"Heather, are you okay? Is anyone there with you?"

"Kevin's here. And I'm okay. It'll just take me a while to absorb the idea that Keith might have been killed. Killed on purpose, I mean."

"Is that what they're saying? Foul play is suspected?"

"Not in so many words. Just that it was a suspicious death."

Words enough.

11

Nevada's list of new story ideas lay before her like a shelf filled with bottles of expensive French wine. She studied each one, trying to decide what to chase next, now that Matthew had backed away from his intention that they run an item on the Jason Wheeler killing every single day. She toyed with the thought that the new residential/ retail high-rise project going up on Fairview Slopes could use some attention. Maybe she should take a walk downtown, visit a few sources, and find out what was new on the street. Maybe drive up to Whistler, have lunch in the village, and talk to some of the merchants about business prospects, now that ski season was over.

She scanned the list again. The important thing was to have something on the go—a defense against Matthew's next irritating assignment.

Chelan sat down in Sam's chair and rolled it over so that she was sitting beside Nevada. "You'll never guess what I heard last night."

"Is this high school? Or twenty questions? Come on, Chelan, spill." Chelan hesitated for a second and Nevada was all over it. "Or let me get back to work."

"Whoa, you're intense. Alright. Heather Alcott, you know, Keith's ex-wife?"

"Estranged wife."

"Estranged wife."

"Accuracy comes first."

"Yeah, accuracy comes first. Okay, Keith's estranged

wife called me last night, to say the cops called her, to say they're now treating Keith's death as suspicious."

"Is that exactly what they said?"

"More or less. I mean, it has gone through two people, so maybe it's not the precise words, and maybe we don't know exactly what the procedure will be, but they are going to investigate further." Chelan smiled with satisfaction. "Those are exact words."

"Wow." Nevada would need some time to think over the ramifications of this.

"Excuse me." Nevada and Chelan looked up as they heard Tess's friendly voice. "Good morning."

"Hello, Tess," Nevada greeted her as a fellow traveler on the road of life. Chelan groveled, but at the edges of her submissive posture Nevada could see a few flashes of expression that signaled she just might be only a few meetings away from actually making eye contact. Was it really necessary to be so deferential? Nevada realized it was the beginning of Chelan's career, and times had changed in twenty years, but still, she questioned whether it was necessary to be so respectful. Didn't people higher up the ladder appreciate a little personality, a little sass? She knew she would.

"Chelan, could I speak with you for a moment?"

Chelan nodded, but she didn't seem to get it, that Tess wanted to draw her away for a private conversation. Apparently it wasn't that private, because Tess plunged in, ignoring Nevada's attentive face.

"I just wanted to comment on the retrospective you did on Keith's life. I know you felt it was cut a bit short, but as a viewer, I thought you conveyed a lot of emotion and information in a very short time." Tess smiled warmly and Chelan lapped it up like a kitten given real cream. "Good job."

"Thank you." Chelan put on her modest face. "He was an impressive man."

"A good reporter." Tess seemed somber and

approving.

"A good reporter." Chelan dutifully repeated, as if it were some sort of insight. "I heard last night that the police are investigating his death again. They think the circumstances are suspicious, and that maybe suicide isn't the story."

Tess's face was unreadable. "If that's the case, maybe we should be re-examining things, digging a little more."

"Re-examining what?" a cheerful male voice asked. Oh, good, Matthew's here now. This was quite the morning for mingling with the peons.

"Keith Papineau's suicide," Tess said. "Oh, yes, that's just the place we want the police devoting their scarce resources, don't you think?" She was becoming quite agitated. "We've got strangers walking up behind people on the Stanley Park seawall and stabbing them, but by all means, we should have the police spending time poking around into the sad story of a man with some problems, who decided to take matters into his own hands and end it all."

Nevada tried to come up with the best response to that remark. Chelan was speechless, but Matthew seemed to think he had to try to calm Tess down. "The motivations for suicide are often difficult to determine. But if there is a possibility that the police believe it was not a suicide, and not an accident, isn't that appropriate information for us to have, here at the station?"

Tess took control of herself. "Yes, of course. Thank you for the information, Chelan." She smiled tightly at all of them, then swept out through the newsroom door.

Nevada and Matthew exchanged a look. Chelan had to question the vibe.

"What? What's going on?"

"Nothing's going on, Chelan. Per sé," Nevada answered. "But it's no wonder she's bit touchy. Her husband committed suicide ten years ago."

Ξ

THE LION'S SHARE OF THE AIR TIME

The little boys rushed up and down the soccer field, some of them pouring their whole heart and soul into pursuing that black and white ball. Most of them ran as though they still enjoyed the pleasure of running, arms and legs pumping. A few others had already reached their limits; they were slowing down and had incessant complaints about sore ankles, sensitive calves, or painful hamstrings.

Zack loved being on the sidelines of his son's soccer games. Marla almost spoiled it for him, back in January, when she told him in the middle of a fight that if it weren't for the soccer games, he wouldn't spend any time at all with his kids. But he just shook it off. He expected her to be cranky from time to time, and to jerk his chain about the hours he worked and the way work distracted him from paying attention to the family, even when he was at home. It was part of the stress she lived with, as a police officer's wife. Each time he went out to work she had to wonder what he would encounter that day, or night, and whether he'd be back. If she needed to rattle the chain she was on, once in a while, it was understandable.

One of the best things about the soccer was that Kenny had no objections to meeting him at a game and talking over cases, while they watched Zack's son Lucas play goalie. Kenny's kids had ditched soccer many years before, along with music lessons, gymnastics, and dance. They were majoring in the mall. Kenny liked to come out to the games, holler when somebody scored a goal, and pretend to be a young dad again.

They stood off by themselves, away from the other clusters of parents. No shame in that; lots of them were in small groups, self-selecting according to their interests. There was the parents group, mostly mothers who wanted to compare notes on homework loads and video game rules; the competitors group, guys who watched every play as if it were World Cup and who had to bite their tongues repeatedly to avoid screaming at the young referee and getting thrown off the field; and the citizens of the world group, who talked about politics and current events, and acted as though they just happened to be at the sidelines of a soccer game on a Saturday by accident. Marla would say that Kenny and Zack were the workaholics group, but Zack would say that they were just taking advantage of an opportunity.

"Go, Steve! Good work!" Zack applauded a particularly smart move. "So the asshole of an agent was about as much use as balls on a pimp. What I think I'll do now is see if I can subpoena all his files on Wheeler. Take a look at the correspondence, the deals, and whatever he's got on these fans."

"Particularly the one from Germany. Come on, Lucas! Go, go, go—good save!" Kenny pumped the air and let go a few whoops. "Did you get anything when you talked to Keene about the restaurant deal that went sideways?"

Zack made a face. "He's a performer, man. He explained it all away, and said the whole thing had been resolved, satisfactorily, as far as he was concerned."

"What did he have to say about Wheeler's death?"

That was one of the great things about working with Kenny. He asked the questions that allowed Zack to work over the case in his mind. "Totally suitable. Shocked, sad, tragic... you know the drill. Thinks it has to be some kind of rabid fan."

"That's interesting, coming from somebody else in the business. This must be something they worry about."

"Come on, Ben, big kick! Yeah, way to go! Come on, carry it, move it—" Zack concentrated on the field action. "Run, run, yeah, center it... yeah!" Zack and Kenny leaped around and clapped their hands for the young shooter.

This was another of the great things about Kenny. You could stop talking to him while you were distracted by something athletic and his feelings weren't wounded.

"I don't know if they talk much about it, but no doubt it goes with the territory. The really famous, successful ones

THE LION'S SHARE OF THE AIR TIME

spend a mint on personal bodyguards. The ones who are famous but don't have much money are the ones who must lie awake nights."

"Hey, maybe there's a future job opportunity for us, once we retire from the P.D." Kenny spoke through the right side of his mouth, while he watched the kick off.

"As if."

"What's our next move, boss?"

Zack had a list in his mind, a list that he had gone over at least thirty times since he awoke this morning. "Follow up with the L.A. agent. Follow up with the lawyer, about the will. And I think I'll go out to LV-TV and talk with Gregory Keene once more."

"He's a suspect?"

Zack watched the play. "Yeah. Shit. I don't know. Motivation's there, opportunity's there. We should go over his credit card purchases in the past few months, see if he bought any knives. Maybe look over his video store rentals, see if he had an unusual interest in Jason Wheeler. Maybe talk to all the TV show crew and cast again, see if anybody can put the two of them together, either on the set or somewhere else."

"Talking to him again is a good idea, though. Use your buddy-buddy thing. Who knows? Maybe he's just looking for a chance to confess to somebody."

Zack nodded, and watched as four boys on the opposing team charged up the field toward Lucas. His boy ran out into the open and scooped up the ball. One more reprieve, one more moment of staving off a loss. Still a lot of time left in the game.

Ξ

Zack wasn't sure Gregory would still be in his office on a Saturday, but he hoped so. If not, then he'd have to call Marla and let her know that he had an hour's drive out to Abbotsford to do an interview. An hour there, an hour back—she would have to do bedtime with the kids on her own.

Zack just had a feeling about the game show host. The pieces seemed to fit and the motive was certainly there. He and Jason Wheeler had known each other well enough to become partners in a business venture. When things went bad, Wheeler wouldn't return Keene's phone calls, stopped payment on items for the business, let his lawyers do all the talking. Suppliers started pressing Keene for payment; as the less high profile guy, it was easier to get to him. The whole sorry mess ended up in court, and then Keene lost. He was on the hook for millions, had put up his house as collateral for the restaurant loan, and had no other assets to liquidate.

Gregory Keene had tried to contact Jason Wheeler dozens of times since the court judgment. When they checked Wheeler's computer hard drive, they found emails from Keene; in Wheeler's apartment, there were letters. The tone in some of them was pretty emotional—well, who wouldn't be, if they lost millions of dollars after trusting some guy and then he wouldn't even take their phone calls?

But emotional enough to kill? That was the core question. There were as many variations on the motives to kill as there were sands on a beach. But he believed that murder usually required an extreme of human emotional temperature—either very hot or cold, as cold as the blood in a snake. Anybody whose frame of mind was calm and moderate was unlikely to be a killer, no matter how great the provocation.

When Zack visited Keene in his LV-TV office the first time, he had hoped to determine the TV show host's feelings about his financial straits and Jason Wheeler's courtroom victory. But the man had given away no clue. He acknowledged the facts, denied having any residual resentment, pointed out that he had had business dealings with a number of people over the years, and that Wheeler had known and been involved with many people other than himself. He had no alibi. He seemed a bit restless, but that

THE LION'S SHARE OF THE AIR TIME

may have been his normal state just prior to going on the air. He'd shown none of the usual indications of lying and he hadn't burst out with any expressions of burning hatred against Wheeler.

So—frame of mind, unknown. Motive, yes. Opportunity, yes.

Zack had called the number he had for Gregory's assistant and was told that Mr. Keene was working in his station office that weekend. The security guard at the reception desk informed him that Mr. Keene was still in the building. Zack waited ten minutes while the guard tried Keene's local without a reply. He got the voice mail a couple of times and left messages, then went on the public address system and asked Keene to come to the reception area.

After ten minutes, the security guard was quite concerned and Zack was exasperated.

"Look, couldn't I just go and look around for him? I know the way," Zack said.

"I can't let you leave the lobby area alone, even if you are a police officer," the guard repeated.

"Could you escort me?"

The guard was troubled. "I guess so. I'd have to get Jerome in here, to sit in for me."

Only one light was burning in the programming wing—under the door of Keene's office, at the end of the corridor. Zack moved cautiously, scanning the shadows around them. He paused outside Keene's door, but heard nothing but the whir of computer equipment left on. When he leaned an ear against the door, he could hear classical music, playing softly.

"Mr. Keene? This is Detective Zack Esher. Could I see you for a moment?"

When there was no reply, Zack gently unholstered his weapon and held it ready. He signaled to the security guard to move away from the door. He put a hand on the knob and slowly turned it.

Zack pushed the door open and let his gun lead the way.

Gregory Keene lay slumped over his desk, a gaping wound in his back. Blood soaked the papers, files, computer, and coffee cups on the desk.

12

Chelan's fingers were on the keyboard, and her eyes stared at the words "Story Proposal" on the computer screen, but her mind had no thoughts except Keith. She couldn't help picturing him, hands together, chin tucked to his chest, diving toward the pavement and his death. Such an image of intention, of somebody wanting to die. Her eyes filled and her heart ached every time she thought of it.

But if it was not intentional and if he was pushed from that balcony, then what was the message in that dive? That he had to take one final bit of control over his life, the last seconds of it? That he was thumbing his nose at whoever had killed him? Embracing death, at the moment when it seemed inevitable, with one last, independent gesture?

She was hunting for a box of tissue when the news popped up on the headline scroll running across the bottom of her computer screen. *TV Game Show Host Found Dead in Dressing Room.* How bizarre. She called across the newsroom to Nevada. "Did you see the bulletin on the Web?"

Nevada looked up from her newspaper. "Have I ever told you how much I miss the old days when we had wire machines churning out copy and three bells going off when there was big news?"

"Many times. At least a million. And have I ever told you all you have to do is leave your computer connected to the Net and customize your news page?"

"Yeah, yeah, yeah. What's up?"

"Some game show host was killed in his dressing room." She stopped to read more of the details on the screen. "Unbelievable. It's Gregory Keene."

Nevada across the newsroom to lean over Chelan's desk. "Now there's a big loss. What happened?"

"They found him slumped over his desk in his office. No sign of forced entry."

"Ooh, the locked room."

Chelan turned around in her chair to look into Nevada's face. "You're very hard-hearted about this."

Nevada reached into her jeans pocket and pulled out a single cigarette. "Met him once. Couldn't stand him. He was screaming at a young associate producer who came with him to this book launch or charity auction or something. Treated her like dirt. Gregory Keene seemed like an egotistical, arrogant jerk to me. But I don't feel strongly about it." She grinned. "Want to keep me company outside for ten minutes?"

"Chelan, I want to speak with you. "Matthew's voice was neutral, but there was no smile to take the edge off his voice. Nevada rolled her eyes and reluctantly put her cigarette back. Experienced and union-protected as she was, she would not zip outside for a smoke break just when the news director showed up.

"Chelan, I want you to do the obit on Gregory Keene. Some footage from his show, shots of his office, his car, go over and get anything you can from the cops. Do about a minute ten."

"Right away, Matthew." Bonus. It wasn't a lead story, but at least he was giving her air time.

"Everybody else is busy on something, and Nevada isn't dressed to go out," Matthew glared at her jeans and T-shirt "I spoke with the programming vice-president just now. They are all extremely paranoid, worried they have some kind of psychotic killer in their midst."

THE LION'S SHARE OF THE AIR TIME

Nevada perched on the edge of the desk, folding her arms across her chest. "Does it look as though it's someone inside?"

"Hard to tell, from the facts they have so far. He often kept his door closed. There was no sign of someone having to break in. He had some good electronic stuff in there, but nothing was stolen."

"Did he see the killer, do they think?" Nevada asked. "Scratch an incriminating initial or two into the top of his desk with his diamond pinkie ring, just before he died?"

"They think he was stabbed from behind. Probably didn't see anybody." Matthew scowled at Nevada and she had the grace to wince.

Matthew seemed to be in a rather unfriendly mood. What would be the best way for Chelan to let him know that she already had an appointment for this afternoon? It wasn't, strictly speaking, a work-related assignment, but it was important.

"Matthew..." he turned on her and stared at her so fiercely that she instantly revised her plans. She stood up and started to put on her suit jacket. "I'll have that piece ready for four o'clock."

"Two famous people killed in Vancouver in less than a month," Nevada was already writing the draft of a script in her head.

"Not just two famous people. Two famous TV people." Matthew corrected her.

Ξ

The first news briefing on Gregory Keene's death had already been held and if LV-TV couldn't get its act together to show up, too bad. Of course, they didn't come right out and say that to Chelan. The media liaison officer did some smooth stuff about making a special arrangement for her, but she wasn't holding her breath. She was able to get the name of the lead detective from her, though, and through dedicated lurking around the police station lobby, she caught up with Zack Esher just after lunch.

"I'm Chelan Montgomery, Channel Two News. We've spoken on the phone a few times and I've seen you at the station and at police briefings. Could I ask a few questions about Gregory Keene's death?"

Zack's face tensed for a split second before being disciplined back to a neutral mask.

"Don't have much information so far, but go ahead."

"Where was he found?"

"Already out there. It's on the wire."

"Cause of death?"

"Don't know." Chelan could picture this prickly cop guarding the Mint, hoarding facts like gold nuggets.

"Time?"

"Don't know. Coroner's got it right now."

"When will you know?"

Silence. Zack didn't actually shrug, but he might as well have.

"We heard that he was stabbed."

"From whom?"

"Jungle telegraph. Come on, a lot of people work at the station. Stuff gets out."

Again, a long, intimidating silence. Then "Not confirming that, at this time."

"Any sign of forced entry, a struggle?"

"Nope." It was like picking slivers out of a child's finger. He stared at her while she groped for another question.

"What was he doing when he died?"

"What do you mean? He was sitting at his desk in his office."

"Yeah, but doing what? Talking on the phone? Reading the paper?"

"He had fan mail open in front of him. Just a minute." Zack pulled out his ringing cell phone and muttered briefly into the receiver.

THE LION'S SHARE OF THE AIR TIME

"Anything else?" Zack covered the mouthpiece with his hand.

This guy was really helpful. Chelan fished. "Anything you want to add?"

Zack wouldn't bite. "No."

Chelan cast one more time. "Are you linking it to the Jason Wheeler killing?"

"What for?"

Chelan was flustered. "Well, both TV stars, both stabbed, both killed in Vancouver."

Zack stopped and pinned her with a stare. "Look, we're conducting a police investigation here, not writing four or five short sentences for a TV news report." He seemed to be on the edge of turning his back on her and just walking off. Something restrained him. "You can say we're not ruling anything out. Anything else?"

Chelan looked around the lobby desperately, trying to find a reason to prolong the meeting. "I have a few other questions—"

"I apologize, Ms. Montgomery. I have a meeting." Zack walked toward the door.

Chelan surrendered. "Thanks for your time, Detective Esher. If anything else comes up, I would appreciate a call."

When Chelan got back to the station and looked at the video and her notes, it was even worse than going through it the first time. She'd have to rely on archival footage, then. No point in trying to include an interview with an officer who had nothing to say.

Matthew asked to see the item before it went to air. He had a few comments—that it was too short, had no flair, not enough facts, no interviews, boring visuals. Totally not okay. She had to agree with him, but he didn't have to go on and on about it. It was totally embarrassing when he told the line-up desk that she didn't have anything ready. He was on the verge of reassigning it to Amanda, and only Chelan's solemn promise to put up something solid right away changed his mind.

She needed something to pull herself out of the doghouse and back to the best chair in front of the fire. She had footage of Gregory's show and Gregory's office, but she needed something personal. There was no family, but maybe she could use something like footage of Gregory's home. Helicopter shots, that would do it.

Hah! Matthew would go for that about as quickly as he would approve an all-expenses paid trip to London. But she could try for just a few long shots of the exterior, a tight shot of Gregory's front door. She was pretty sure his address wasn't public, but she could get it from the station database.

Matthew wouldn't authorize Chelan to take a cameraman out to the valley to shoot footage of Gregory's house, but Chelan was able to persuade Thomas to take her along on his afternoon assignment. When he finished, she asked him to head east on Highway 1 toward Abbotsford. He had no immediate deadline and he was willing to go exploring with her. Maybe he figured he owed her, after that immense overtime check he'd been able to claim, thanks to her decision to cover the Wheeler story. Thomas drove like a pro, cutting in and out of the downtown traffic, around illegally parked cars and slow-moving delivery trucks but it still took them nearly an hour to move two miles. They tried a detour through the West End and got stuck on a one-way street.

Thomas put on his emergency flashers and flung an arm over the back of the seat as he put the truck in reverse to get out of the dead-end. A few minutes later, they were back on Burrard Street and on their way. It would be a treat to get out of the city core.

Four hours later, Chelan was not so sure. She wished she had thought to stuff something to eat in her pocket. She and Thomas were roaming the flatlands around the river, hunting for anything that looked like a game show host's mansion. Nothing. Not a sign, not a clue, not a huge front gate.

She had an address but it didn't exist. Not only could

THE LION'S SHARE OF THE AIR TIME

they not find the street number, they couldn't find the street. The GPS was no use whatsoever. Chelan called back to the station to check, and the station receptionist insisted that the address she had was the one the station had on record as Gregory's. Maybe it was fabricated, to throw inquisitive fans off the trail.

Chelan trudged up to a farmhouse, climbed the porch steps and knocked on the door. Instantly, two large black dogs came bounding across the yard, looking like something set loose to catch escaped convicts. She considered trying to make a break for it, back to the truck, but the dogs stopped short of attacking and took up a post behind her, at the foot of the steps. The barking continued, as a woman opened the door about three inches.

"Duke! Shut up," she ordered.

Chelan handed her business card through the door.

"We're looking for Gregory Keene's house," she explained, not taking her gaze away from the silent, vibrating guard dogs.

The woman shook her head, handed back the card, and shut the door in her face.

Chelan and the dogs stared at one another. She didn't want to make a move, but she was losing time. Again, she wished she had brought something to eat. Gingerly, she took one step down from the porch. So far, so good.

She edged her way down and slowly backed toward safety. She felt like throwing up. The dogs didn't move. Thomas leaned over to open the passenger door and Chelan jumped in.

"She was a gold mine of information, I bet." Thomas backed the truck down the driveway.

Chelan made faces at the dogs as they chased the departing vehicle, barking furiously. She shook her head.

"Maybe we should try the back roads around the fields to the south," Thomas suggested. He looked closely at Chelan. "You okay?"

She forced herself to breathe normally. "Yeah, yeah,

I'm fine. No problem. Sounds good. We've stopped at twelve of these farmhouses now, and it's not working. Let's do something else. I'm not going back empty-handed." She took a look at her watch. "We're running out of time."

Thomas gave her another doubtful glance, then wheeled around and concentrated on heading south.

The sun was high in a sky like Hawaiian water, and in the distance, they could see the Coast Mountains. After eight months of the wettest year on record, the fields and forests were a brilliant emerald shade of green. It would have been a terrific day to be out for a long distance cycling trip, a hike, or even just a drive, but Chelan couldn't savor anything until she had the film in the bag.

Thomas pulled off the highway onto a side road and turned south. They drove in silence for half an hour, scanning the horizon for any sign of a large home.

But there was nothing. Mile after mile of crops, fields, pasture.

Thomas sighed. "What a way to make a buck. You hungry? I got a stack of junk food under the seat there."

Chelan pulled out a bag of chips and a chocolate bar. "Thanks. I'm starving."

"Somebody told me a long time ago. Keep the reporters fed or they get ugly."

"Must have been some PR guy."

"Yeah, I think. With one of the sports teams." Thomas pulled over to the side of the road. "What's that?"

Across the yellow fields, a thick stream of gray smoke lifted over the horizon. Chelan wished she had a pair of binoculars. "Let's go check it out. Even if we don't find Gregory's house, we might get a story out of this."

The cameraman put the truck in gear. He drove as far as he could on the dusty country road, then headed cross-country. The station 4x4 took the ruts in the road easily.

As they drew nearer to the column of smoke, Chelan scanned the horizon for movement. Then she saw two figures in the distance.

THE LION'S SHARE OF THE AIR TIME

"That way, Thomas."

The cameraman pulled the steering wheel over and they bumped along in a new direction for about fifteen minutes. Then Thomas stopped in front of a ditch. All they could see on the other side was an old shack. They climbed out of the vehicle and Thomas went to the back to get his camera.

Slipping and sliding down the bank of the trench, they saw two young boys watching them from the other side.

"Hi, there," she called. "I'm Chelan Montgomery, from Channel Two News."

"I'm Tom and he's Paul," the taller one offered.

"Where's the smoke coming from?"

"We're playing cowboys on the range." The boys led Chelan and Thomas behind the shack and showed them a small fire with a makeshift spit built over it. Why weren't these kids at home playing violent video games? A piece of some sort of meat, skewered by a stick, dripped grease on the fire.

"It's squirrel," Paul said. "Not sure if we'll eat it."

Chelan nodded—she could understand why the novice chefs were still debating that point. Thomas turned his back on the cowboy campfire and squinted off into the distance.

"Have you boys ever heard of Gregory Keene?"

"Yup."

Chelan waited for more help. None came. "Do you know him from TV?"

"Yup." Tom stirred up the ashes with a stick.

Moments passed while Chelan tried to think of a question that would get her more than a "yup" or a "nope". Paul saved her the trouble.

"He's a neighbor of ours."

Ξ

The house was only a few hundred yards down the country road, hidden from view by a stand of arbutus trees. The black wrought-iron gate was standing open and Chelan had no trouble making up her mind to leave the truck behind. Thomas was right behind her, camera up on his shoulder.

Wow, she had no idea the game show business was this profitable. The house was an amazing construction of golden Cotswold stone, stained glass windows, and cedar shingles. Its one floor was laid out to take total advantage of the mountain and valley views—the sunrises must be awesome. A five-car garage stood to the north of the mansion, with a guesthouse, tennis court and swimming pool to the south behind it. Lots of space for a man who lived alone.

Chelan was about to go up and ring the front door bell when a voice challenged her.

"Something I can help you with?" A dark-haired young man, built like a bulldozer, stood near the corner of the house.

"Who are you?" Chelan smiled as she rummaged in her purse for her business card.

"Who are you?" Turning on the charm hadn't worked.

"Chelan Montgomery, Channel Two News. We're doing a report on Mr. Keene and we just wanted to get a few pictures of his home." She handed over the card and he read it about twenty times. "And you are… ?"

"The caretaker. Nobody told me you were coming."

"It was a spontaneous decision. Look, we'll just take a few shots and we'll be out of your way."

"I dunno…" He raised his head to listen to a distant sound. "Hey, that's my phone. I'll be right back."

Chelan urged Thomas to take advantage of their stroke of luck, and bag a few shots while he could. Just long shots, nothing too intrusive, not through the windows or anything. While he was rolling, she walked around the corner of the house to take a look at the pool. Beautiful. It was one of those infinity pools where it looks as though the water is dropping off a cliff. A gorgeous scent of roses came from an elaborate, well-tended garden that rivaled the one in Stanley Park. Floor-to-ceiling French doors backed the patio that

THE LION'S SHARE OF THE AIR TIME

surrounded the pool.

Chelan couldn't resist a peek. Just inside the glass, a black baby grand piano was the showpiece in a room that included two walls of books, a colossal fireplace, and leather furniture to die for. Just beyond the living room, she could see a corridor leading to a kitchen with a stainless steel refrigerator.

"You almost done here?"

She nearly had an accident. The caretaker stood, arms crossed over his chest, just inches behind her. "Yes, yes, I'm done. The photographer is still at the front of the house. We'll be on our way." She sidestepped past him and then walked to meet Thomas as quickly as she could.

Just after they edged out of the gate, it swung shut behind them. As Thomas checked for oncoming traffic, Chelan noticed a green plastic can by the side of the main road.

Paydirt!

Garbage day in Gregory's neighborhood. Chelan grabbed the two plastic green bags from Gregory's trash can and loaded them into the back of the TV station truck.

Ξ

Orange peels, coffee grounds, and sodden plastic lay strewn across an old sheet on top of Chelan's kitchen table. She'd never gone through anyone's garbage before, and she was sure she wouldn't be in a hurry to do it again. The stench of rotting ham and old cottage cheese was overpowering.

She pulled on a pair of rubber gloves and pawed through the pile. Nothing but old food and odds and ends like the rubber sole of an old running shoe. Chelan didn't know what she was looking for, precisely, but you could tell a lot about a person by their garbage. Until the police came forward with anything solid to report, her best chance of turning up some clue about Gregory's death and getting some respect from Matthew and the other newsmen lay in thinking outside the box. Or outside the can.

The entire first bag revealed nothing but a man who liked to cook, used expensive ingredients, and didn't hang onto or recycle elastic bands. Chelan poured the garbage into a super-size bag and tied it back up. She dumped the second bag onto the table—this one was full of stuff from the laundry room and from Gregory's home office. Dryer lint, bent paper clips, a couple of damp paperback books—and paper. Pages of notes, letters, envelopes, junk mail. Chelan picked up the page on the top and started to read.

She worked her way through nearly every scrap, most of it completely ordinary—it was just the heap of superfluous trash every householder sheds every week. She shook out of the last third of the material in the second bag, and in between two socks with holes in them, she found one more piece of paper. A letter.

Dear Gregory,

I played the game along with you last night and I almost won. When do I get a chance to come on your show? You know, I am your biggest fan. If you don't invite me soon, I'm going to have to turn up and insist that you give me a seat!

Please send me tickets, #6 Red Street, Delta, B.C.

Love ya forever,

Tara

13

"So we're back to square one." Zack slammed the files down on his desk, and saw Kenny looking at him with raised eyebrows. Yeah, well, maybe he was showing a bit too much reaction, but Gregory Keene's death had come as a very unwelcome surprise.

"Okay, let's go over it. What have we got?" He prepared to add three sugars to his coffee while he gave Kenny the floor.

Kenny was brief. "Two victims stabbed. No witnesses, although both died in a place with people all around."

Zack looked through the papers in the file on his desk. "We won't have the formal autopsy report for a while but so far we know that Keene was stabbed three times, from the back. Just like Wheeler."

"No issue about time or cause of death in either case." Kenny continued. "No weapons found."

"Are we still searching the surrounding areas in both cases?"

"We are."

"Any info on knife size or make?"

Kenny shook his head. "Not yet."

"Stabbed with the same hand?"

"Don't know."

Zack started to pace. "It could be completely coincidental that two TV performers were murdered by stabbing in less than two weeks. Could be one has a relative looking forward to the reading of the will, and the other one was messing around with somebody with an irrational husband."

"On the other hand," Kenny said, "let's suppose both were killed by the same person. What are the connections?"

Zack sat down and started to make notes. "Who else was in the restaurant deal with them? Did they ever work in the same place, on the same job? Any family or friends in common?"

Kenny leaned back in his chair, closed his eyes, and put his hands behind his head. "Attend any of the same events? Join the same clubs? Take a vacation in the same place?"
"Physical evidence." Zack set the topic while he stirred his coffee slowly, staring off into space.

"Not much. Heavy rain the night of the Wheeler killing. No prints. No fibers. Small gold earring found nearby. Could have come from the killer, could have been lying there for three years or whatever."

Zack winced. "It's not much. Anything from analyzing the blood spatter patterns?"

Kenny shook his head. "Not in either case. One funny thing—they found lipstick on one of the coffee cups on Keene's desk. Enough for a print. But it could have been any one of hundreds of women working in that building. Or visitors that he had."

"Yeah, well, let's try a few other things before we start asking every woman at LV-TV for lip print samples."

Kenny nodded. "If nothing turns up, we could always try publishing a picture of the earring at the Wheeler scene in the newspaper. See if anyone recognizes it."

"As a last resort."

"Yeah, okay. And in both cases, no murder weapon."

"Nope. And no witnesses." Zack consulted a sheet of notes from the file. "I got the log from the security people and called every visitor to the station that day. Every one of them checks out and we can establish their whereabouts at the estimated time of death."

THE LION'S SHARE OF THE AIR TIME

"So does that mean somebody inside, do you think?"

"Either that or the killer slipped in, without going past security. Might not be that hard to do. They've got a couple of doors to the side and back where somebody might have walked in while somebody else was coming out."

A voice interrupted them. "Excuse me."

Both men looked up. A uniformed delivery man stood at Zack's desk, holding a large box. "This has been cleared. Could Detective Esher sign for it?"

Zack took the clipboard and scribbled his initials on the page. The box had come from Los Angeles. He tore open the top.

"These are Wheeler's files from the L.A. agent's office. I got him to overnight them."

"You take half, I'll take half." Kenny grabbed an armful of folders and retreated to his own desk.

Over the course of the next hour, Zack expanded his knowledge of Jason Wheeler's life and business dealings and got a glimpse of the inner workings of the entertainment world. Most of the material was dense and complicated; Zack started a stack of contracts and correspondence that he wanted to read at least twice.

The fan letter files were the thickest of the bunch. They only covered the previous two weeks, and had a note attached, indicating that any older ones were in storage, but could be retrieved if the Vancouver police department wanted them. Zack sifted through and found a few names that repeated—Tara. Cindy. Darlene. He made three piles for those. The flow of Cindy and Darlene letters each ran out after two. The Tara count rose to fifteen.

Kenny looked over and noticed Zack staring off into space. "What have you got?"

"Letters from a fan. Fifteen in two weeks."

"Fifteen?"

"Yeah. Maybe it's nothing, you know, maybe just an enthusiastic supporter." Zack rifled through the pile. "But maybe not."

"Do they come from Germany?"
"Nope. Postmarked Vancouver."

Ξ

Zack couldn't keep his mind on the spaghetti and meatballs during dinner, nor on his son's long, sad story about some teacher who had done him wrong in math class and some girl in science who told on him for teasing her about her new haircut. Could it be some sort of obsessed fan, stalking Jason and Gregory, overcome by a yearning to possess, in some way? Or maybe not a fan at all, maybe someone enraged by something Gregory had said on air, or that Jason had said in an interview. Could be someone hunting for instant fame, he thought. Someone with no sense of the real human beings these two men were, when their images weren't being packaged and distributed through the one-way screen.

"Dad, you didn't say." Lucas's ten-year-old voice rose above the sound of the two-year-old happily bashing away at her plate with a spoon.

"Didn't say what, pal?"

"Didn't say if you're coming to my game next Saturday."

"Do my best, like always." He felt Marla's eyes on him and looked over to see her glaring. "What?"

She didn't answer him, just stood and began clearing away the dirty plates. She whisked his half-eaten meal away to the kitchen, before he had time to decide whether he was done with it.

He followed her to the sink. "What are we debating tonight?"

"It's not a debate, Zack. It's just a question." Her whisper came out as a hiss. "The same one as always. Why do you have to spend so much time away from us?"

"Because of the job I have. I don't punch a clock, I don't start and finish in a specific place, like a bus driver or

THE LION'S SHARE OF THE AIR TIME

something. You knew I was a police officer when you married me."

She plunged the stainless steel pots into the soapy water.

"Why can't you move into another position? Something that doesn't require so much night work, so much weekend work." She scrubbed at those pots as if they'd been covered in grime for six weeks. "And maybe something that pays better."

Yeah, both barrels. "And how do you suggest I arrange all that?"

"I don't know, apply for things. Upgrade your credentials, maybe. Get a degree. Or put your name in for something higher up the ladder in another city."

"I don't want to move." Their window of free time was closing. The kids would find them any second. "And if I was studying for a degree or angling for a promotion I'd be away from home even more, Marla."

He tried to turn her to face him but she was like a tree stump. A small body wrapped itself around his left shoe and he reached down to pick up Emily. He waited for Marla's reply, but when none came he beat a retreat to the living room.

Ξ

Chelan waited through sixteen rings before the phone was picked up. This was the only T. Bougie in the telephone book.

"Mr. Bougie?"

"Who wants to know?"

"I'm Chelan Montgomery, from Channel Two News. I was a friend of Keith Papineau's."

"That lying son of a bitch." The man's voice was flat. At first it reminded Chelan of a listless, enervated snake, but she revised her impression to a cougar, crouching to attack.

Chelan hoped he would say more, but after the silence

159

went on for ten seconds, she knew she was going to have to work for this one. "What was your connection with him?"

"My connection with him? My connection with him? Let's see, I went to him in confidence, gave him private information about corruption in my workplace, got his promise that he'd protect my identity, and he friggin' blew me out of the water."

"Did he report your name?"

"He gave so much detail about me in the report that everybody figured out it was me. Then the assholes went to the station, and the news director confirmed it for them."

By this point, Chelan was on his side. This was pretty terrible. "What happened then, Mr. Bougie?"

"I got fired. No pension, no reference letter, no severance pay. It's been six months and I haven't been able to find another job. Credit cards are red-lined. Bank account's dry. Got a mortgage payment coming up in three weeks."

"Oh, Mr. Bougie, that's horrible. I wish there was something I could say or do."

"You gotta be kidding me. You reporters are the scum of the earth. Phony as hell. So don't you be calling here, telling me you wish there was something you could do." He was breathing hard and Chelan doubted that she had much time left before he hung up.

"I'm trying to find out more about Keith's work and I was hoping you could tell me something about—"

"I'm not telling you anything! Keith Papineau is dead, and it's no loss."

Ξ

The phone call with Ted Bougie left Chelan with a desire to stay in her apartment, hidden under a quilt, watching some mindless music videos on TV. But the remaining time in her weekend was shrinking and she faced a Monday morning with a plateful of research demands from

THE LION'S SHARE OF THE AIR TIME

Elliot and no room for any of her own projects. The Gregory Keene obit had gone to air without any more criticism from Matthew, but she didn't know whether that meant that it was good or that Matthew had given up on her. She was sitting on the fan letter she'd found in Gregory's garbage until she had time to check out the address.

At first, as she worked her way through the list of Keith's contacts and friends, she avoided approaching Kevin for information. A bit weird, she knew—a reporter feeling timid about asking questions. But her confidence was building and she recognized that she couldn't ignore Kevin's possible usefulness. So she dialed Heather Alcott's number, hoping to speak to him. Fifteen minutes later, she was on her way over the Burrard Bridge. She made a quick right turn, then another onto Beach Avenue, and hunted for a parking space under a dignified tree that was just getting its summer foliage.

The Aquatic Center was packed with competitors and volunteers. Chelan spotted Kevin on the deck with a group of other mid-teenage boys, toweling off and digging into bags of potato chips. Kevin looked up frequently, scanning the bleachers. Looking for his mother, maybe? When Chelan called Heather to ask for another meeting, Heather had asked her to come by the swim meet where Kevin was competing

Chelan waved, but it took a while before Kevin noticed the waving hand and realized he recognized the face that went with it. Clutching his snack and a can of pop, he walked up to sit with her.

"Hey, how's it going, Kevin?"

"Hey."

For a long while, it seemed that that would be the end of the conversation.

Talking to a young guy usually wasn't that difficult for Chelan, but then usually she didn't have an agenda, some huge and intimidating topic she wanted to scale. Keith's death loomed in front of her, just like the ladder to the high

GAIL HULNICK

diving board. Chelan watched as six boys lined up at the starting blocks. They dove in and began grinding through the water at a respectable pace for a fifty-meter backstroke heat. She didn't speak again until the winner pulled himself out of the water.

"Kevin, I'm so sorry about your dad. You know that." She looked into his eyes for confirmation. "I've been talking to a few people, asking some questions."

Kevin watched the swimmers in the next heat get ready. "Did you find out why he did it?"

"Not yet," Chelan said. "So far, I'm just finding out more about him, the work he was doing, the people he knew. I'll tell you if I find out anything for sure. But I did want to ask you for any information you might have about his life outside the station that I might not know. What did he do on the weekends, for example?"

"Played golf, went running sometimes." Kevin seemed to be replaying some private memory in his mind, and several more silent moments went by. "Oh—and he belonged to a gym. He usually worked out every weekend."

"What was the name of the place?"

"Pump it Up. It's on Marine, going out toward the airport."

"Kevin, did your dad ever mention any fans to you?"

Kevin made a face. "What do you mean, like women chasing him? Some did, I guess. He used to joke about it."

This was more information than anyone else had given her so far. Kevin didn't seem uncomfortable with the subject, so Chelan pursued it. "Did he ever mention any fan letters?"

"What do you mean?"

"I found a fan letter to your dad and it was kind of a weird one. It got me wondering whether he knew this person very well."

Kevin shook his head. "The only one he ever mentioned by name called herself Sherry. She comes up to him when we were at a basketball game once and she goes

'Keith, how come you don't return my calls anymore?" And he's like 'I'm sorry, I think my voice mail isn't working right. Have you been leaving me messages?' " Kevin laughed. "She knew he was ducking her. He told me later she left him forty messages once—in one day! Anyway, after that night he said she never called him again."

"Did he have a lot of girlfriends?" Chelan saw Kevin's eyes go dark and she knew she had crossed the line.

"He and my mom were just separated. Not divorced."

Chelan pulled the letter out of her bag. "Have you ever seen a letter like this?"

Kevin shook his head again then they watched the next heat without speaking. When Kevin said he had to leave to get ready to swim, Chelan knew her opening was shrinking quickly.

"I wonder where your dad might have met this fan. Maybe at the gym, do you think?"

Chelan thought Kevin had shut down completely, when suddenly he spoke. "I met somebody who saw Dad, near the end. She's a little old lady, walks her dog near Dad's apartment building."

Chelan smiled. "Mrs. Howe! I've met her, too."

"I've been to see her three times. She's cool, talks about all kinds of stuff."

"About your dad?"

"No, other stuff. The war and the Depression and what it was like when she was a girl."

"It's nice of you to ask her questions and listen to her."

"I like it. She's kind of peaceful to be with, you know? And I like to walk in that neighborhood."

Chelan looked up as Heather approached and sat down. "Hi, Chelan, nice to see you. Kev, your next heat is coming up."

Kevin nodded at Chelan as he gathered his swim bag and turned to go back to the blocks. Heather smiled as she watched him go. She was looking a little better, as if she were getting some sleep, but still not her usual self.

"How's it going, Heather?"

She shrugged. "You know." She watched as Kevin dove into the pool at the crack of the starter's pistol. "They read the will yesterday."

"And?"

"Almost nothing there. He changed it, since we split up, wrote a new one. Left everything to Kevin, in trust. The executor says they'll be paying off the credit cards, his credit line. I've been hearing from some of his other creditors, too. Bob Venice gave him a loan, but I've told him there's not enough in the estate to pay it off. Seemed to be a surprise to him."

"So what will he do, will he just let it go?"

"Says he's going to approach Keith's sister and the rest of his family about it. Debt of honor, he called it." Heather shook her head. "Good luck with that, I told him. They're tough people. I'm just glad none of this will stick to Kevin."

"He won't have to make good on Keith's debts, from his part of the estate?"

"The lawyer says no. But what if all this comes up again, in the future, and Kevin is the one to get caught up in it?"

They turned to watch the final seconds of the heat, which Kevin won by two strokes.

"Have the police made any progress?"

Heather shook her head.

"Heather, I'm still trying, too," Chelan risked putting an arm around her shoulder, briefly. "Kevin's given me a couple of ideas of places to meet some of Keith's associates, try to find out more about what went on in his life during those last six months. I just don't have nearly enough time, to do as much as I'd like."

Heather smiled. "We appreciate anything you can do, Chelan. Thank you."

When Chelan walked into Pump It Up, half a dozen people looked up from their bench presses and squat thrusts. It was a place to see and be seen; many celebrities used this

THE LION'S SHARE OF THE AIR TIME

gym. A lot of regulars were there because they could count on seeing a pro athlete or a television actor once or twice a month, and use the story to amuse and impress their friends. The celebrities came because they could count on seeing quite a few people they knew from the charity banquet or club scene. They could also count on the other members to be cool and leave them alone to do their workouts. And the owner gave them full and preferred use of the facilities at no charge. Fame is currency.

Chelan approached the buff blonde behind the reception counter. "Hi."

A megawatt smile. "Hello. Are you interested in joining the club?"

"Just a drop-in today." While she filled out the form, Chelan turned around and leaned back against the counter, surveying the room. Five guys were power lifting in front of the mirrored wall. Six others were on the treadmills and exercise bikes. "A friend of mine used to work out here. Recommended it."

She pushed the form toward her. "We have a lot of satisfied clients. Who's your friend?"

"Keith Papineau."

The receptionist nodded. "We all miss him here, too." She watched Chelan fill out her name. " Chelan Montgomery. Do you work at the TV station, too?"

Chelan fished in her wallet for the money. "Yeah."

Tracy put the cash in the till. "He was a really nice guy, you know? He'd stop and talk to me all the time. Some guys, you know, they just rush right by the desk, don't say anything. But not Keith. He talked to everybody. And he was nice to everybody."

The crash of a weight on one of the biceps machines falling too quickly caught their attention and they looked across the room, toward the windows. A huge man in top shape stood over the machine, cursing it.

Tracy frowned in disapproval, for an instant resembling a Sunday school teacher more than a girl who had barely

165

reached drinking age. "Unlike some people."

The face was familiar and as Chelan watched the man move on to the rowing machine, she realized the muscles and the movements were, too. Conrad Davis was the star of the Vancouver Cougars hockey team. Every home game, he skated out onto the rink accompanied by the roars, cheers and whistles of fifty or sixty thousand fans. Before Conrad arrived, interest in the team was at an all-time low and the owners were seriously thinking of selling. It was discouraging to go to a game—discouraging for the fans, who had to sit among rows and rows of empty seats, and discouraging for the players, who lost week after week. Who knew which came first, the losing record or the fan apathy? Either way, it was more like going to see a train wreck than a pro sports event, and the fans were starting to get hostile. Many of those who did still attend the games, season-ticket holders mostly, booed and jeered their own team. The sports writers made fun of the players' efforts (or lack of them). It was just getting ugly.

Then Conrad showed up. In two months, he turned everything around, showing fans, sports writers and the team owners how a hard-working, motivated pro athlete did his job. He put the puck in the net and set an example that the other Cougars began to follow.

Unfortunately, the best of Conrad was saved for the rink and the game. There wasn't anything left over for his personality. He soon became notorious around town for his prodigious drinking capacity, his bad manners and his rude mouth. He lipped off to almost every maitre d', restaurant hostess, bartender, and waiter in the city. He stomped past the line-ups of fans outside the dressing room wanting his autograph, ignoring even the kids. He got into arguments over parking spots and he confronted his neighbors over minor issues in his condo building.

And every time, it made the papers. The papers, the radio sports casts, and the TV evening news. Keith had done a profile of Conrad for the city magazine and won an award

THE LION'S SHARE OF THE AIR TIME

for it, two years ago. Conrad was the biggest star athlete in the city and the most colorful. Too bad he was such a jerk, but the truth had to be told.

Chelan could see that Conrad was having a bad day. After the biceps machine, he took issue with the rowing machine and a treadmill. A set of free weights drew a stream of abuse as wide as the Fraser River. Chelan tried to ignore the tirades while she worked out, but the atmosphere in the gym was definitely 'center ring', rather than 'day at the beach'.

"You gonna take all day there, sweetheart?"

Chelan's chin was tucked down as she strained to push the metal plate controlling the weights on the quadriceps machine. Droplets of sweat rolled from her cheeks and soaked into the damp front of her gray T-shirt.

"Hey. I'm talking to you."

Chelan looked up. "Pardon me?"

"Pardon me. I love it." Conrad Davis loomed above her. "You just about done here?"

Chelan mopped her face with the towel around her shoulders, while she thought about her next move. Conrad Davis was a very large man. And a loud one. She hated being pushed as much as the next person, but you had to be smart.

"Why, certainly, sir. Absolutely. I was finished ten minutes ago, I was just hoping someone would come along and give me an excuse to stop," Chelan rubbed her face once more. She took her time, getting up from the machine— wouldn't want the guy to think she was sucking up. On the other hand, Chelan really didn't relish the thought of a confrontation with somebody as powerful as this, either. Maybe on occasion, over something important, but not over a quadriceps machine.

She stepped aside and Conrad dropped his muscular butt onto the leather seat without so much as a sideways glance. He gave a push at the plate, snorted in derision and got up to change the pin on the weights, moving it to the slot that would give him the most weight possible to lift. As

Chelan walked away, she could see Conrad's knees pumping back and forth, almost effortlessly.

As the hour wore on, Chelan overheard Conrad do his "you gonna take all day?" number on half a dozen other people in the room. It actually provided a bit of entertainment value in an otherwise mundane afternoon. Somebody flipped on the TV set in front of the front row of stationary bicycles and rock music floated out over the noise of the exercise machines.

Chelan was just about to wrap up her workout and go back to ask the receptionist a few more questions, when angry voices rose above the buzz of exertion in the room.

"You don't shush me." Conrad loomed over Tracy like a Douglas fir over a mushroom.

Tracy stood her ground, her head cranked back to look up at him. Her blonde hair almost reached her knees. "Mr. Davis. Some of the other clients have been complaining that you are forcing them off the machines. Interfering with their workouts."

Conrad became aware that his public was watching. He waved his arms wide, to include everybody, or maybe to collect a round of applause.

"Yeah? Anybody here get kicked off a machine? Anybody feelin' intimidated?" No one spoke a word or moved a muscle.

"It's your imagination. Now why don't you go back behind your reception desk there and do your job and let me get on with mine." Conrad turned his back on her and she shrugged. Minimum wage wasn't enough to justify pursuing this any further.

Chelan tried to concentrate on peddling the exercise bike. Anybody who needed to make so much noise and throw his weight around like that had to be compensating for some fairly major problems. She wondered whether Keith's path had ever crossed Conrad's here at the gym, and whether they'd spoken, particularly after the magazine piece Keith had written. She peddled harder—she had only a

THE LION'S SHARE OF THE AIR TIME

couple of hours before she had to be ready to go out to the News Congress banquet. Wouldn't be appropriate to pull a no-show there, since Matthew had given her a free ticket.

When Chelan walked by the desk an hour later, Tracy was absorbed in a copy of *War and Peace*. She put it aside to sign Chelan out. "Hope we see you again. This is a great place for reducing stress. Things are a bit tense at the TV station, I'll bet."

"No kidding." Chelan handed over her locker key.

"Interesting that they all worked at that station and they all belonged to this gym."

"All of them?"

"Yeah. Jason Wheeler was here the most often, but we saw Keith and Gregory Keene about once every two weeks or so."

At that moment, Conrad emerged from the change room. Looking for towels or for another confrontation? Chelan didn't wait to find out.

14

The exterior lights of the luxury hotel reflected on the black water—the whole place looked like a fairyland. Chelan had never attended the annual News Congress Awards dinner before, and with the prices as high as they were, it might be never again, unless the station continued to spring for the tickets.

Clearly, it was a five-star night. She wished she'd had the time, or the finances, to drop by a spa for a massage and a facial after the workout at Pump It Up, but even without the luxury treatment, she was feeling pretty special. She was wearing a black, clingy thing that Layla insisted on lending her the minute she got wind that Chelan was thinking of showing up in just a shirt and top, with a pair of boots. Not Chelan's fault—black-tie affairs just weren't on her list of activities, growing up. Layla had also insisted that jewelry was called for, and loaded her up with a little bling.

She was flying solo. Since the evening that Twain had tried to engineer a meeting with her brother, she had been dodging his phone calls and emails. She wasn't sure he was Mr. Right anyway, and then to have him act as if he thought he was Mr. Best Friend—well, it was a bit much. She preferred to go to work-related events alone anyway. Somehow you looked like less of a loser if you were wandering through the crowd, than if you were one half of a desperate-looking pair, frantically talking to one another to

THE LION'S SHARE OF THE AIR TIME

avoid appearing to be unwanted and out of place. Also, she wanted to talk to as many people as possible about Keith. Somebody might be able to give her another lead on his activities and state of mind before he died. If an opportunity came up, also she wanted to ask Nevada what she thought about Ted Bougie and about the Gregory Keene fan letter.

She rode the elevator up the mezzanine floor and stepped out into a field of black, white and gold. Tuxedos and gorgeous dresses—reporters could clean up pretty good, when they wanted to. She located Nevada and Owen across the foyer near the ballroom doors and headed their way.

"Hi, you two!" Hugs and cheek kisses all around. "Doesn't this look awesome?"

Nevada made a face. "I can only put up with this if we get to throw buns after dinner."

"You start." Owen grinned at her, and Chelan smiled at him. Owen Heintzman was one of those people who just makes you smile. He always seemed to be upbeat, his good-looking face beaming about eighty per cent of the time. Not in a dopey way, though. Signs of his genius-level IQ were obvious in his eyes, and when you talked with him, you knew you were with someone wise and brilliant. His look was so cool, he could be a movie star or a model—certainly, the type of appearance to divert your attention quite readily. A handy thing to have in an oncology doctor.

"Hey, Chelan, how are you?" Owen reached for two glasses of wine from the tray of a passing waiter and handed them over.

"I'm good, Owen, thanks."

"Things okay at work?"

"Yeah. Still trying to get a chance to play, but you know."

"It'll come, don't worry."

"What will come?"

The three of them turned to see Matthew, totally at home in a tuxedo. "Hi, Matthew." Nevada waved a wine glass in his direction. "Owen was just giving Chelan some career advice."

Matthew was too polite to actually roll his eyes, but Chelan thought she saw the vestige of a twitch in that direction.

"Has anyone seen a program for this party yet?" Nevada was scanning the north end of the room. "Who do we have to listen to, before they hand out the prizes?"

"Nevada, I love handing out free tickets to these events to you, because you're always so appreciative." Matthew was also vigorously scanning the room, glancing over Chelan and Nevada's shoulders. "The keynote speaker is Des Johnson, from Toronto. Mrs. Cunningham is introducing him."

"Tess Cunningham?" Chelan was surprised that Tess would have a prominent role at this event.

"Yes. She has a background in news." Matthew seemed somewhat testy about Chelan's question. "And sports. Business. The arts." He plastered a networking smile on his face, and took off. "Murray, how've you been?"

Nevada was replacing her empty wine glass on a tray and commandeering another. Chelan declined a second.

"Why was he cranky at me for not knowing Tess Cunningham's résumé?

"Matthew is always quite protective about Tess. It's just executive-level sucking up." Nevada signaled to a waiter passing with an hors d'oeuvres tray, then bent her head over the selection of angel wings, spring rolls, and sushi.

"Or maybe he's just providing information that Chelan didn't have," Owen picked up a Swedish meatball and fed it to her.

"No, there was an edge there," Chelan took a napkin and loaded up.

"They go back a long way," Nevada juggled her drink and a pastry. "In the eighties they worked together at a TV station in Victoria before Matthew went to the States."

"What did he do there?"

"News in Atlanta. Sports in L.A. Then back to the east—Boston, I think. That's where he met Gregory Keene."

THE LION'S SHARE OF THE AIR TIME

"He knew Gregory before Vancouver?"

"Oh yeah. He got Keene his first job in Canada, in Montreal. They had a bit of a falling out, though, when Tess got Keene the game show and a national profile, but Keene wouldn't give Matthew a job as his executive producer."

"Tess got Keene the game show?"

Nevada tugged at some part of her dress that wasn't sitting quite right. "Yeah, they've known each other forever. He was in the States for a while, then she hired him back and got him his big break."

"Nevada, is that true, or is it just gossip?" The affection in Owen's eyes took the sting out of his words.

"That's both, dear heart," Nevada waved at someone across the room who was trying to catch her eye. "Come on, let's mingle a bit before we get trapped in our seats."

Owen and Nevada headed south and Chelan north toward the ladies' room—by way of Matthew's track. She hovered about ten feet behind him, watching as he moved from group to group, spending less than five minutes with each cluster. Everybody seemed to know him—although everybody probably knew almost everybody here, except for the relative newcomers, like herself.

"Hey, Chelan, " Liam St. Clair called to her from a post near the grand piano.

"Liam, how ya doin." She shook her head as he tried to hand her one of the two glasses of wine he was holding.

"Good, how are you? Listen, did you ever catch up with that woman who was on the scene when Keith died? Did she have anything to say?"

Chelan looked for an escape. "Well, you know—oh, there's Elliot over there, I have to go say hello."

Matthew was at the other side of the room, hugging a petite, blonde woman in a spectacular red dress. When he moved to the left, Chelan could see that it was Tess Cunningham, owning the room, as usual. Glamour to burn. She was wearing ruby chandelier earrings and a phenomenal ruby pendant. But the most startling thing about her this evening wasn't her jewelry—it was her escort. Conrad Davis stood to her right, and it looked as though she had her hand tucked under his arm. He leaned forward to murmur something in her ear.

She wished she knew what they were talking about.

Ξ

Table 23, Chelan's table, was located within bun-throwing distance of the back wall of the ballroom. She was seated with Amanda, Wayne, Sam, Nevada and Owen, enjoyable dinner mates to be sure (except for Amanda, to be honest) but definitely not A-lister types, not the ones who had seats at a table right beneath the podium. A table where George Stratton-Porter shared a bottle of wine with Daniel, the anchorman, and Tess Cunningham held court, shaking hands with each arrival. Conrad Davis sat to her right, not speaking to anyone. Bob Venice, occupying the seat to her left, scanned the room almost as attentively as Chelan did.

The meal was as good as it could be when eight hundred plates had to arrive simultaneously, hot and aromatic. Chelan really wasn't interested in the caviar, endive salad, salmon or rack of lamb. Even the northern Italian dishes contributed by two famous Vancouver chefs didn't seduce her taste buds. Although she was able to nod and ask a question or two, she wasn't really listening to the conversation at the table, the announcements of the award winners or their interminable speeches. Most of them were far better writers and reporters than speakers, with the exception of Christina from the Vancouver Times, whose speech was as witty as her columns. But most of the time Chelan's mind shuttled from Gregory's and Keith's fan letters to Gregory's, Keith's and Jason's membership at the same gym. Was there a connection? Or was Ted, the burned source, the most likely lead?

"Chelan, pass the buns. For the third time."

"Oops, Nevada, sorry." Chelan handed over the basket

THE LION'S SHARE OF THE AIR TIME

and tried to force herself to focus. "Where are we in the program?"

"Near the end, I hope." Nevada pretended to get ready to throw a bun.

Owen took it away from her. "Don't you start a war in here, like you did that time Warner spoke."

"How did you know about that? You weren't there," Nevada's words and tone were rebellious, but she put the piece of pumpernickel on her plate.

"Someone told me the story. You're famous." He was trying to appear critical and failing completely.

"We have had some good times. It's such a shame Keith isn't here." It might have been the wine and it might have been that her guard had dropped just a little, but Nevada's edges were a bit softer than usual.

The mention of Keith sent everyone at the table into silence and most were probably more than ready to go home once the speeches finally ended. As the women were gathering purses and the men were putting jackets back on, Tess and Matthew approached their table.

"Nice to see so many women here," Tess commented, nodding at Chelan. "Especially you younger ones."

Chelan glowed at being noticed. "It was wonderful for the station to invite us. Thank you, Mrs. Cunningham."

"Events like this are so important in making contacts, finding out what an industry is all about," Tess scanned the room. "It's difficult enough for women to be taken seriously, and to make the decision to put forward the kind of effort and time that any success requires. We bump up against that glass ceiling, and so often it has to do with a lack of reputation. No one knows who you are, no one knows what you can do. But if you come out to these events, meet people, it can make all the difference."

Amanda leaned toward Tess and tried to draw her away from the group. "Mrs. Cunningham, I've been wanting to ask you something about that…"

Nevada saw her opening and lunged for it. "Thanks

175

GAIL HULNICK

again for the tickets. We have to be going." Taking Owen by one elbow and Chelan by another, she started to steer their trio out of the crowded ballroom, Matthew, Wayne and Sam tagging along behind them.

They had moved two steps when Bob Venice loomed in front of them, like an iceberg in the north Atlantic.

"Good evening, everybody. So, Tess, this is your crew from the newsroom, is it?" He was only one man but to Chelan it seemed as though the front four of the New England Patriots had suddenly sprouted, shoulder-to-shoulder, between Table 23 and the door.

Tess seemed no more inclined to hang around, talking to him, than Chelan did. "Yes, Bob, it is. Lovely dinner, wasn't it?" She blazed a megawatt smile at Bob, leaned to the left, then moved to the right, forward, and past him. Deked him out completely. She beckoned to Amanda and swept off toward the ballroom door.

Bob stared after them, then nodded politely at the rest of the group and made his own exit. The atmosphere lightened and Nevada pasted a big smile on her face. She tucked her arm through Owen's and turned to Chelan.

"Want to go for a drink with us somewhere?" she asked.

"No, I'm on my way," Chelan rooted around in her purse for keys.

"Say, Matthew, have we heard anything new about Keith's death?" Nevada asked, as Amanda and Tess emerged into the hotel lobby.

"Not lately, but I'm sure the police have the investigation well underway—for all three killings," Matthew commented. "They've done another search on Keith's apartment and they've scoured Gregory's house from top to bottom, I heard. They've been going through Keith's files and the desk we sent back to his sister. I hear they're close to finding a prime suspect already."

"And who is that, Matthew?" Nevada asked.

"I can't say, of course, but we should all hear something

THE LION'S SHARE OF THE AIR TIME

official soon." Matthew looked over her head at Tess, approaching in full confident sail. "Mrs. Cunningham, I have to be going. May I offer you a lift somewhere?"

"No, thank you, Matthew. Dmitri, my driver, is waiting downstairs." She distributed smiles and eye contact all around, then swept off toward the elevators. A short nod to the group, and Matthew was crossing the lobby toward the door.

Nevada watched Tess go. "Funny kind of date. I wonder why Conrad Davis isn't driving her home."

"You noticed them, too?" Chelan searched the bottom of her purse for her keys.

Owen put an arm around Nevada. "She notices everything. That's her job, she thinks." He smiled at Chelan. "Are you okay for a ride, Chelan?"

"Yeah, I'm good. See you guys another time."

Chelan was tired and would have liked nothing better than to go home, take off her stiletto heels and put her feet up. But she was still carrying Keith's planner around in her trunk, after borrowing it from his desk that day, and she knew she had to do something with it. She didn't want to return the planner to Keith's sister, or to Heather, and to have to explain why she had it in the first place. The police would soon talk to somebody who would mention that he'd seen Keith with a day-book—if they hadn't already—and they'd be looking for it.

All she had to do was take it back to the station and put it into a filing cabinet somewhere in the newsroom. Somewhere that it would be logical that it might have been overlooked.

As Chelan picked her way across the dark and silent studio, she had second thoughts. This could have been done the next day, when the surroundings weren't quite so creepy. But, on third thought, there would be too many people around, too many people who asked questions for a living.

The studio had the atmosphere of a mummy's tomb, or at least as she imagined one might be, having seen dozens on

GAIL HULNICK

TV and in the movies. All of the cameras had been wheeled off the sets to the edges of the enormous room. A few lights were scattered around, like scarecrows in a cornfield.

She'd sat in her car for a few moments in the station parking lot and made notes on the last two weeks of entries in the planner. Lots of initials, appointments for interviews. Nothing in the pages for names and addresses in the back. Keith must have had an address book or a business card file somewhere, but Chelan hadn't come across it yet.

She tripped over a stepladder left lying on the concrete floor. Maybe it was a mistake to come in this way, but it was the shortest route to the newsroom. Nevada had loaned her a key to the side door, which led to the main studio and past the sets for *Captain Fogblast, Smart Kids Compete* and *Cooking with Syd*.

They kept the studio very cold, perhaps due to concern for the props and equipment, or to make sure Captain Fogblast stayed awake during the drowsy afternoon hours. Chelan shivered as what seemed like a faint breeze blew through and she picked up her pace. She heard footsteps echoing through the immense cavern, but she assumed those were her own.

A door slammed somewhere in the distance. Was it in the studio or on another floor, in some faraway corridor? The station was never completely empty. There were people there twenty-four hours a day, seven days a week, either working late because of sports broadcasts and late movies, or getting there early because of the breakfast TV shows. Make-up people, camera operators, Master Control technicians, reporters, writers, producers—there were hundreds of people, coming and going all the time. There was absolutely no reason, at any hour of the day, to take notice of the sound of footsteps or a door closing.

Nevertheless, Chelan looked over her shoulder a few times and quickened her pace. She had only a few dozen feet to go to the north door, the one that led to the main corridor. The metallic sound of the double doors to the east

THE LION'S SHARE OF THE AIR TIME

scraping against the concrete floor stopped her in her tracks. Instinctively, she searched for a place to hide. But why hide? She had every right to be here. She was simply on her way in to pick up something from the newsroom. There was nothing wrong with that.

Still, she wasn't in a hurry to meet anyone or to have to explain herself. The cooking show set was just to her left, and she backed up slowly towards it, all the while gazing around, trying to pierce the darkness and identify whoever had entered the studio. The heels of her dress shoes made a clicking sound every time she took a step. She tried to step as carefully and quietly as possible, without slowing down to a crawl, as she edged onto the black and white checkered linoleum floor and shrank back into the space between the refrigerator and the pantry.

Her follower had some problems with noisy footwear, too. Clearly he or she was in a considerable hurry. At first the pace sounded like a determined stride; then it picked up to a rhythmic jog.

Chelan had seen camera operators and reporters hustle to ensnare a departing dignitary and she'd even seen them jog to catch up with another crew from a competing station, but she'd never seen anyone actually run out of the newsroom or through a studio. But maybe she hadn't been around long enough to see a big enough story.

Maybe something huge had broken—a hostage-taking in Victoria or an earthquake in Richmond—and maybe she heard a photographer, taking the shortest way through the station to the parking lot. Maybe there was an extra seat in the car.

Chelan stepped out from her spot next to the refrigerator and called out. "Hey. Who's there? It's me, Chelan Montgomery. Are you on a story? Hey, wait up!" The tempo of the footsteps behind Chelan reached allegro and then, a figure brushed past her. Peering through the gloom, Chelan thought she could see a child's back, hunched forward, a few yards away, moving toward the south door.

179

This was definitely weird. Chelan started to run after him. She had no real plan in mind, it just seemed like the logical thing to do.

As she pursued the runner through the dark studio to the far door, it seemed as though she was gaining on him. The door opened and the parking lot lights illuminated the entrance just moments before Chelan got there. But there wasn't enough light to identify the runner, and by the time Chelan arrived at the door, whoever had been in such a hurry to leave the building was gone. Nothing moved in the parking lot, and the only vehicle was her Mini.

Chelan stood in the doorway, catching her breath and hugging Keith's planner to her chest. She turned to go back into the studio. The heavy door to the cavernous studio swung shut behind her. She had only taken two steps when the impact of something heavy—a stick? a chair? forced her to her knees and then out of consciousness.

15

When she came to, Chelan was lying on the concrete floor, her feet halfway underneath Syd's refrigerator. Her instinct was to leap up and run, but when she tensed her muscles and tried to sit up, nothing happened. She was numb, no feeling or movement at all for a few seconds, then her eyes widened as a tide of pain swelled through her head. She took a deep breath, then sent a direct order to her left arm. Bending her elbow, then rolling to support her weight on one side, she managed to push herself to a half-sitting position. Good Lord. Her brain throbbed like a drum skin and she almost rolled back. Another deep breath and she was ready to drive herself to a crouch, on hands and knees.

She got that far and had to stop. She was shivering with the cold and her headache was horrendous. If there were any justice in the world, at this point a gorgeous hot guy would appear, bend down and put strong arms around her and lift her to her feet.

Chelan edged toward the refrigerator and gripped the door. She managed to get her right foot planted, then pulled herself upright. With eyes closed, she waited for the nausea to pass. Breathe deeply, she coached herself. You'll be alright. She had no idea how much time passed before she thought she could open her eyes.

The studio was still dark, and steeped in silence. The cooking show set, with its maple cabinets and checkerboard floor, gave no clue that anything had just happened here.

Keith's planner was gone.

Ξ

The next morning, Chelan took a long shower, trying to wash away the memory and the fear. Then she made copies of Gregory's and Keith's letters—maybe she was being paranoid, but she wanted to have something solid, her own proof that the letters existed. Her next step was a call to make an appointment to see Detective Zack Esher. He didn't sound happy to come out on a Sunday, but he didn't say no.

"Ms. Montgomery, what's this all about?" He waited until they settled in at a small table on the outside deck at Granville Island. On a Sunday he wore baggy jeans and a skateboarder's black T-shirt with some sort of Asian logo in red. Small children chased seagulls and the seagulls came flapping back, trying to dive for bits of muffin and bagel that had fallen to the pavement.

"Detective Esher, there were letters sent to Keith and to Gregory Keene that I think may have something to do with their deaths. I found Gregory's in a bag of garbage left outside his home and I found Keith's in his desk at work." She unfolded the letters and laid them out on the table.

Escher's face showed no reaction. "Thank you, Ms. Montgomery. This is very helpful."

"That's it? I'm not in any trouble for … poking around a little?"

Still a face of stone. "I appreciate that you brought these to me. I hope you'll stay in touch about anything more you may turn up."

This had turned out to be not quite as painful as she expected. Her experience with cops was miserable; she remembered the first time they brought Ronnie home.

Her father had been incredulous as he stood at the door, talking to a weary man in blue at four o'clock in the morning. Chelan got out of bed when she heard the doorbell and looked through her bedroom curtains. Through the driving rain, she could see the police car parked in the driveway, with a shadowy shape in the back seat that must be her brother.

Her father's voice, pitched half an octave higher than usual, carried up the stairs. "My son? Are you sure? Maybe it's one of his goofy friends, giving his name as a joke."

A low murmuring, followed by a long silence. Then her father "all right, bring him in, then."

"Ms. Montgomery?" Esher's voice snapped her back to the present. "You did the right thing, bringing this to my attention."

Maybe, maybe not, she thought.

I was going to look into it on my own, you know?' she said. "I thought I'd just drive out to Delta, take a look at this woman, this Tara. I didn't really think it was a big enough deal to call the police about. But I haven't had a lot of free time lately, and I've had a lot of stuff on my plate, from work, and—"

"What made you decide to call me today?"

"Well, something happened last night and — "

"What happened last night?"

"Someone attacked me at the station."

"Did you report it?"

Chelan inhaled her Arabian Mocha Java. "I'm reporting it now."

She grinned at him but he didn't respond. Guess he wasn't too pleased with that reply.

"I was at the station late, and as I was walking through the studio, someone hit me from behind. I just fell down, the person ran away, then I got up and went home."

Esher took out a small, spiral-coiled notebook and flipped to a page halfway through. He produced a pen from his jeans pocket and made a few notes.

"After I woke up this morning and thought it over, I realized I should talk to someone about it."

"Did you go to a hospital or to a doctor?"

"No, I'm not hurt."

"Did you see anyone, hear anything, that might help you identify who it was who hit you?"

Chelan shook her head. "No idea. I heard some footsteps, running. I was trying to follow them, find out who it was, you know? Then, boom! I was on the ground."

Esher looked up from his notebook. Even though he was probably less than ten years older than she was, she felt as though it was her father or her elementary school principal, gazing into her eyes. "What's your best guess, Ms. Montgomery? Why would somebody want to hit you from behind?"

She gulped her coffee.

"And why were you at the station late, anyway?"

"Working." Two seagulls scrapped over a discarded muffin wrapper and Chelan pretended to be interested in their squabble. She hadn't intended to tell him anymore, but there was something about the way he was questioning her that made her want to tell him about Keith's planner. Good trick, that. She wondered whether the police had a special school for it. Reporters could use one of those.

"Working on what?"

"Detective Esher, I went in to return a planner of Keith Papineau's that I found some days ago."

"A planner."

"You know, an appointment book." He was staring at her as though he could see right through her. "After he died, I read through a lot of his things at the office. I held onto his planner, but then I thought I should put it back. That's what I was doing last night, when someone hit me."

"Do you have the planner now?"

She shook her head. "I think whoever it was took it. I do have notes that I took on some of the pages that I can give you." She fumbled in her bag and handed them over. He looked at them then tucked them away with the letters she'd given him earlier.

THE LION'S SHARE OF THE AIR TIME

Zack's grim face was quite a bit intimidating, but she had stared down worse. Her father, for one. Matthew for another.

"Ms. Montgomery, we'd appreciate it if you kept this information to yourself for a while, let us get on with our investigation."

She said nothing. Did silence mean yes or no?

Ξ

Red Street in Delta was a quiet road, barely big enough for two late-model SUVs to pass one another without scraping. Zack and Kenny turned in at the double-digit end of the street and cruised along slowly, looking for #6. The family who lived there wasn't big on lawn mowing or weeding, but the place looked fresh enough. A blue front door added some color to the gray siding and roof, as did the blue shutters next to the bedroom windows. It was a single-story house, maybe about 1,800 square feet, with a bay window and a dilapidated fence. Kenny looked around carefully for signs of a dog; at one of their stops last winter a Doberman came lunging around the corner at him and almost gave him extra laundry.

A chunky woman, middle-aged, partly blonde hair, old clothes, opened the door, and stood, wiping her hands on a tea towel. A yellow mutt stood behind her. Both men showed her their identification.

"Mrs. Carle, we'd like to speak with you. Could we come in?"

Before she could reply, a man roughly the size of an adult black bear loomed behind her in the hallway. That would be Norman Carle. Gray hair, blue eyes, regular daily exercise just a distant memory.

"What do you guys want?"

"Mr. Carle? We have a few questions to ask your wife."

"Regarding what?"

"A police matter." Zack looked the man over. He could

185

GAIL HULNICK

picture this man spending a lot of time in the bush. "Could we come inside please?"

Mr. Carle led them to the kitchen that was shabby but well cared-for. Bright yellow curtains framed a window that looked out onto a barren back yard. The cupboards were small and old; the blue paint that covered them was probably just the latest in about thirty coats that had covered them over the years. Short stretches of countertop were cluttered with coffee pot, toaster, blender, and a knife block. Various utensils and oven mitts separated elderly appliances. A Vancouver Cougars calendar hung on one wall. The table was a utility-grade, dark brown metal job that might have been made back in the seventies. Mr. Carle took a seat, then motioned to Mrs. Carle and the detectives to sit down.

Zack cleared his throat. "Mrs. Carle, have you ever visited LV-TV?"

"Yes, a few months ago. I went to a taping of the Gregory Keene show."

"You are a fan of the Gregory Keene show?"

"Yes, I watch it almost every day. If I'm not out driving the kids around somewhere."

"What did you think when you heard about his death?"

She shook her head. "Just a tragedy. Why would anyone want to kill such a talented man?"

Norman's patience had run out. "What's this all about?"

"Just a few questions for Mrs. Carle. About Gregory Keene and about Jason Wheeler."

Tara Carle squinted at Zack. "Jason Wheeler? The TV actor?"

Norman's mouth was a tight line, as he looked back and forth between Zack and Kenny. "The TV actor who was killed on the seawall a few months ago. What's this all about?"

Zack ignored him. "Mrs. Carle, were you a fan of his?"

Tara didn't know yet where all of these questions were leading, but she seemed to get the gravity of the situation.

186

THE LION'S SHARE OF THE AIR TIME

"No, I'm not a fan of Jason Wheeler. I've never seen him, I don't watch his show, I don't read about him. Officer, what is this all about?"

Kenny spoke up. "Mrs. Carle, we're investigating the deaths of these two men. We also think there might be a link to the recent death of Keith Papineau, from LV-TV. We're talking to dozens of people who knew them and following quite a few leads. We have information that you were interested in all of their careers and that you were in contact with all three ."

Tara's face flamed red and tears moistened the corners of her eyes. Guilt? Or intimidation? Her next words would be significant.

She never got them out. Norman was on his feet, swaying like some wild creature about to attack. "That's it, you're outa here. I don't know what this is about, exactly, but you're not asking her any more questions unless we get a lawyer."

Zack sighed. "Fine, Mr. Carle. Why don't you make that arrangement, and we'll be in touch about continuing this later." He stood up and gazed around the room, lingering on the dirty dishes in the sink. Would be nice if he could score something for the DNA lab. No judge would like it, though. "You wouldn't mind if we look around your home a bit, would you?"

"You bet I would. Out." Norman herded them to the front door.

Zack stopped just before they walked out onto the front step. "Mr. Carle, it's important that you and your wife remain available.

No reply from Norman as he ushered them out of his house and closed the door. Zack and Kenny got back in the car for the drive back to town. Zack hadn't really expected a major breakthrough on this interview. There would be a lot of work yet to do.

16

The young man burst from the door of a decaying flophouse, his face the incarnation of terror. In less time than it took Nevada to chew her gum twice, he burst into flames. Stumbling down a slick street, he screamed for help as the yellow and orange fire consumed his body.

"Cut."

The director's voice was bored. Or maybe it was a neutral tone, designed to imply authority, control, and calm. Either way, Nevada recognized the sound of somebody who'd been doing his job for a couple of decades. She watched him consult with his sound engineer, assistant director, camera people, lighting people. They stood on the make-believe street, pointing, pacing, talking the shot over. And over. She would go mad if she had to work at this pace, with this much attention to detail. Get in, get it done, go home—that was more her style.

Nevada much preferred real life to the artificial, tight-focus existence of a film location. In a former lifetime, she'd done her time on set, and her memories were of a place where the colors weren't quite genuine, sound could only be heard properly if you were wearing a headset, and time stretched on, endlessly, like the "song that doesn't end" that she'd learned as a child.

The smell of rotting garbage added a bit of authenticity

THE LION'S SHARE OF THE AIR TIME

to this scene, though. They were in an alley in one of the poorest parts of town in the lonely hours of the morning.

She had had to beg and plead with the *Escape!* showrunner for permission to visit the set to do this interview with Josh Dickens, the director who had been employed at *Urban Battle* the week that Jason Wheeler was killed. She had tried going through the director's agency but they were less than helpful, suggesting that they could put her name on a list and fit her in for an interview when a shooting break came up next November. So she had tracked him down through production schedules and had managed to get a message to him by making friends with one of the production company assistants. It wasn't easy to make contact with these film and TV people, but she understood why. They worked longer hours than almost anyone except medical people; the pressure was high and the meter was always running. If you wanted ten minutes of a director or an actor's time, you had to wait. She'd been taught that when she was five years old.

Finally, she'd received a reply, saying that if she were willing to show up at 3 a.m., he would speak to her. If Matthew knew that she was taking this approach to the Jason Wheeler story, he'd probably hand her her butt on a sword. He said he wanted this TV star stabbing covered, but he didn't want a lot of time or effort spent on it. Nevada didn't think it deserved any coverage at all, at this point, now that the initial flurry of interest had passed. She thought they should just bide their time, until the police came up with somebody to charge. But Matthew was insisting that she file something each and every day on this story, to "sex up the newscast a bit". So, she was going to take as much time as she wanted—get the interviews nobody else was getting, find a story that hadn't been done to death. Wait until he saw her overtime charge.

It was Chelan's idea to look up Josh Dickens and pick his brain. Good angle—something different. Man, that garbage was putrid. You'd think they could get somebody to move it away someplace. She watched while they peeled the fire-resistant shirt off the stunt man and got ready to set up for the next shot. So much effort to create three on-screen seconds of phony terror. Hurry up and wait, as Tom used to say. Once she had found this whole scene exciting, but after her tenth birthday, when she pulled back the curtain and showed him up for what he really was, she never again had any illusions about it. It was full of treachery, not glamor.

Her memories were interrupted when Josh hurried over to her, pulling off his headset. He was a burly man, with more hair on his chin than the top of his head. He wore jeans and a sweatshirt that read *Banff Springs Hotel.* "Hi, Josh Dickens, nice to meet you." He extended a hand to shake.

Nevada took it, smiling, trying to summon up some energy. She was almost asleep on her feet. "Hi, Nevada Leacock from Channel Two." She handed him her contact card.

"I hear you want to ask some questions about Jason."

"I'm doing some follow-up coverage on his death, and it occurred to me that no one had talked to you about it."

Josh shook his head. "Not sure I have that much to say. I was only on *Urban Battle* for that one week—oh, and one other episode last season."

"How did he seem?"

"Normal. Same as always. He was very professional, you know. Came out, did his job. You can't ask for more."

Nevada could see that the crew had everything ready for the next shot. "Do you have any theories on why he was killed?"

Josh stared her down. "Anybody with an imagination could come up with half a dozen scenarios. You shouldn't be asking somebody who makes up stories for a living. Just stick to what the police are absolutely sure of. Don't be discussing "theories". Jason was a good guy."

The producer was heading their way. Nevada hurried to fit in one last question. "Did he go anywhere unusual that week?"

THE LION'S SHARE OF THE AIR TIME

Josh shook his head.

"Have any visitors?"

"Yeah, a few. Not as many as usual, actually, because we did a lot of night shoots that week. But he did have a guy from L.A. drop by."

"Do you know his name?"

"No, sorry. I was introduced but it went in one ear and out the other. I heard later he was a producer, talking to Jason about a movie role." Josh heard some crackling in his headset and pulled it back into place. "A couple of TV types later in the week."

Nevada was trying to engrave all of this in her mind, so that she could write it all down later. She didn't want to pull out her notebook at this point, in case it dried up the flow. "Do you remember any names?"

Josh concentrated. "Naw, sorry. One was a woman, forties, red dress, heels. Looked more like an actress than a businesswoman." Josh started to move toward the camera. "The other one was introduced as a journalist, I think. Or maybe an investor. I forget, exactly. Although, who knows, that might have been just smoke."

Nevada fell into step beside Josh as he picked up speed.

"Do you think the killer might have been somebody Jason worked with?"

"I told you, I don't think it helps anything to speculate. Maybe it was somebody he knew, but maybe it was completely random. Just being in the wrong place, at the wrong time, you know?" Josh stopped suddenly, putting out a hand. "It was nice meeting you. I have to get back to work."

Nevada shook hands. "Would you go on camera, if I come by tomorrow at a quieter time?"

Josh shook his head and snorted. "No, thanks."

Nevada had to accept the inevitable. The interview was over. The production assistant materialized at her side, Josh walked off, and she was escorted her toward her car, parked a block away.

She huddled in her front seat, typing notes into her computer. Not a complete waste of time. She had a couple of quotes she could use, and she could run the script over some big-action visuals from the *Urban Battle* TV show. Who the hell would want to kill a famous guy like that, somebody who was making money for a lot of people? A stalker fan? Some starlet that he dumped? Maybe somebody named in his will?

She yawned and put her pen aside. It had been a lot of years since she pulled all-nighters with no consequences the next day. She hoped she had a slack day at the station tomorrow. Owen was working the night shift at the hospital so she would have the bed to herself—make it easier to bag some serious zee's before she had to head back to work.

Ξ

Chelan pushed open the door of the newsroom and had the unique experience, for her, of being the only person there. Not surprising, given that it wasn't yet 6 a.m. Things were precarious for her there, she could feel it, and she had decided it wouldn't hurt to put in some exceptional face time. First one in, last one to leave—her father used to preach that that was one of the keys to success, no matter what you did.

The voice to her left made her almost jump out of her skin. "Chelan, what are you doing here so early?"

Tess's face was stern but her voice was kind. Amazing that at 5:45 in the morning, she looked as perfect as if she'd just stepped out of a salon. Her blonde hair was shaped into a new style—it seemed to be slightly different every time Chelan saw her. Her suit was some kind of elegant gray fabric that shimmered slightly and clung to her body just the right amount. Chelan knew that her own shirt and pants outfit was totally lame.

"Are you in early to work on a story?" Tess seemed to be in less of a hurry than usual.

THE LION'S SHARE OF THE AIR TIME

"I have a couple of big research projects in the works for Elliot, and the first draft of a script that Matthew wants to see." Chelan dropped her hand and let the door close behind them.

"How is it going, Chelan?" Tess walked over to Tim Phelan's desk and leaned against it. Somehow she managed to give the impression that she owned the desk, the paper on it, and every last pen and paper clip in the room. She motioned to the chair and Chelan took the invitation to sit down. Invitation or command, perhaps.

"It's going well, I think." How to play this? Like a job interview? A performance review? Tell the truth or cover up the real situation? The total, stinking misery of being stuck in a research job. Would Tess appreciate getting the real 411 or would she rather hear from a happy camper?

Tess tilted her head and looked at Chelan as if appraising her for auction. "Are you on deadline for anything this morning?"

Chelan shook her head.

"I have to go over to the university to do some interviews for next year's intern positions. Would you like to come along?"

The drive to the campus took them over the Burrard Street Bridge, which had done frequent duty as a movie location over the years, then west on Second Avenue. Chelan leaned back and relaxed in the passenger seat of Tess's silver Lexus convertible. No conversation seemed to be necessary, which made the ride even more enjoyable. Much as she appreciated every opportunity to be with Tess Cunningham, she really had no idea what to say to her. 'Speaking when spoken to' seemed like a good strategy.

Vancouver in late spring is a feast for the eyes and nose. The trees and shrubs they passed displayed the benefits of all those winter months of moisture, almost vibrating with shades of green from hunter to emerald. Flowerbeds and baskets spilled over with huge blossoms of red, yellow, pink, orange, and blue. Tess drove a little quickly for Chelan's

193

comfort level, but perhaps it just felt that way because she wasn't used to the wind in her hair and on her face while in traffic.

She heard only one word from Tess on the whole drive. As they passed Kits Beach, packed with young people playing volleyball, Tess turned to look at the scene, made a face and muttered "slackers".

Outside the J-school boardroom, four smartly groomed people in suits, three men and a woman, sat waiting. Chelan had wondered whether there would be any grads still looking for jobs or internships, now that it was June, but she should have known better. Always strong demand for journalism jobs.

Tess's interviewing style was brisk and intimidating. Chelan almost felt sorry for a couple of the candidates, particularly the one who had the nerve to maneuver Tess into playing straight man for his joke about investigating drug abuse. When she asked him how he would go about researching a report on heroin addiction, he replied, "I'd call my brother, Joe." When she asked why he would call his brother, and he triumphantly announced, "Because he's a heroin addict!", Chelan thought Tess's face looked so tight with suppressed animosity that she was just seconds away from standing up to leave. But she just nodded, made a note, and ended the interview with a couple of other questions. Chelan liked that guy the best, but she doubted he'd get the job.

On the way back, Tess seemed much more relaxed. "Well, Chelan, which one would you hire?"

"I thought the tall guy from Calgary — was his name Jordan? — I thought he was very sharp."

"Mmm," Tess commented. "I thought the young woman seemed very bright, too." She pulled out to pass a driver who was taking a mellow pace through the forest at the edge of campus, then cut back in front of him with just a few feet to spare. Chelan didn't turn around, but she could imagine the look on his face. "I thought the man from

THE LION'S SHARE OF THE AIR TIME

Calgary looked a lot like a younger Jason Wheeler."

"The TV actor?" Chelan ordered herself not to put a hand on the passenger door or the dashboard to brace herself, as Tess had a rather carefree interpretation of the speed limits.

"I knew him for years, you know," Tess's right foot seemed to have grown a magnet, drawing it closer and closer to the floor. "I was very upset when he died. And then when we lost Gregory, too ... We'll be making some changes around the station. We've had a new security company in and we'll be putting surveillance cameras in all the private office and the studios."

She suddenly realized that she was driving way too fast and eased off on the gas. "You know, I saw Jason just the week before he died. Visited him on the set. And Gregory—we had dinner a few months ago, and I dropped by his studio for the show whenever I had time."

Chelan searched for the right thing to say. "It's very sad. You never think that some moment might be the last one you have with a person—"

"That's exactly it," Tess turned to glance at Chelan. "We all go on, of course, but in some way, it just seems wrong that everything should continue as normal when someone important is gone."

Chelan didn't say another word, not wanting to disturb the comfortable silence that seemed to rest between them. Tess Cunningham had shared her thoughts with her, and had revealed some of her feelings. It was like playing a brilliant piece of jazz, improvising a new series of chords and changes that filled your ears with sounds that seemed so perfect, so right, that you didn't want to touch another key. If you launched into another piece, it might take away a part of the memory of the howling success you'd just delivered. On the other hand, it might get even better.

Chelan decided to stay silent, and save the next step with Tess for another day.

195

GAIL HULNICK

Ξ

The news naming Tara Carle moved at about eight a.m. Within four hours, the scene at the airport was pandemonium. Matthew sent Chelan out to do chauffeur duty for a camera crew, reporter and producer from one of the major American networks. LV-TV had a reciprocal arrangement with them, sharing footage and resources, production services and personnel. Until now, all that meant was sending tape of the occasional item of interest to the bigger audiences down south, and taking a daily feed of items from the American network's foreign news bureaus.

But apparently this crime story was big enough that they wanted their own people on it. And they were not the only ones. While waiting for the luggage, tripods, briefcases and other gear at the baggage carousel, Chelan met four reporters coming in from New York, Los Angeles, Chicago and Toronto, and two from the British tabloid newspapers. Obsessed Housewife/Fan Suspected in Three TV Killings. The local newscasts had been full of the story through the night and the newspapers ran 72-point headlines in the morning.

Mostly because of Jason Wheeler. Gregory was not international news, but the star of *Urban Battle* was. One of the visiting reporters explained that the story had all of the ingredients he needed: lovesick housewife with a killer's streak, celebrity victim, exotic location, violent death. All it needed was a little sex, and they would find that, or cook it up.

The Vancouver Media Murders.

Chelan drove the visitors to a downtown waterfront hotel, then headed back to the station. All of the monitors were tuned to the all-news station, which was carrying a report on Tara and her neighborhood. Amanda was bragging that she had convinced Elliot to have LV-TV News break into kiddie programming at 8:15 with a bulletin.

The police had refused to confirm or deny that Tara

196

THE LION'S SHARE OF THE AIR TIME

Carle was a prime suspect, but the information had leaked out somewhere. The newspaper had it as "The Vancouver Times has learned" and while a few of the out-of-town media had attributed the story to the Times, many had moved beyond that and were just trumpeting it as truth.

The footage showed a shot of the suspected killer rushing from her car to her front door. Chelan could not have imagined a more unlikely looking murderer. She was round and short, with dull blonde hair, and wearing a lime-green tracksuit with a pair of ancient running shoes. She held her chin up, turning her head in jerky motions to look left, then right, then over her shoulder.

"Have charges been laid?" Chelan heard a note of disapproval in Nevada's voice.

"Probably soon," Amanda answered without taking her eyes off the screen.

Suddenly, Chelan heard muffled shouting from the corridor outside the newsroom. A man burst through the opaque glass doors, almost shattering them.

"You people got a lot to answer for. Tara didn't kill anybody. This is just a load of bull!"

Chelan pressed the security alarm button under her desk, knowing that half a dozen other fingers were doing the same.

Max, the security guard from the front lobby, came through the door just a few moments behind the intruder. "He tricked me. He tricked me into letting him though the door. I'm sorry. It won't happen again."

"You people have no conscience. You'll say anything, the more outrageous the better," the man raged. "No matter how big a lie it is. You don't care who you hurt. Anybody knows Tara knows she's no killer."

Matthew appeared at the newsroom door and smoothly took charge. "It's alright, Nicholas, these things happen. We're okay here, you go back to the front desk and let the police in. They should be arriving at any moment."

He faced the stranger, who towered over him by about

GAIL HULNICK

six inches. "And who are you?"

Chelan had already guessed, and she was quite sure Matthew was on the same track.

"Norman Carle. Tara Carle is my wife."

"Why are you here?"

"I want you to stop all this. You started it, you stop it. Tara didn't kill anybody, and I want you to tell everybody that. Whatever happened to innocent until proven guilty? Everywhere but on the TV!"

Norman Carle clenched his fists. Chelan and the others glared at the newsroom door. Where was the cavalry?

"All we do is report the news, Mr. Carle," Matthew was calm. "The police arrested your wife. We reported it. That's all."

"That's not all and you know it. If that was all, you'd report her name and then get on with the real news. But you put on pictures of our house, you talk to our neighbors…"

Chelan saw Amanda duck her head and become very busy working with some papers on her desk.

"And what's it going to be tonight? Video of my kids going to school? Tara's pictures from high school?" Norman began to pace across the newsroom, stopping to brace his massive hands on either side of Chelan's desk and lean forward, yelling into her face, "You drop the word 'alleged' in there, and you think that makes it all right? Back off, I'm telling you!"

Matthew pulled out a chair and sat down, pulling another one out and motioning to Norman to join him. Chelan saw him raise an eyebrow to Daniel who pulled up another chair. Norman looked back and forth between them.

"Mr. Carle, let's talk." Daniel had the actor's ability to project authority and serenity simultaneously. It was impressive, especially combined with the power that Daniel's recognition factor gave. This was a face and voice that spoke to Norman every night, an important face and voice. If he asked you, or told you, to do something, you were inclined to comply.

THE LION'S SHARE OF THE AIR TIME

Chelan watched Norman waver, and then succumb. He sat down and glared suspiciously from Matthew to Daniel and back again.

"Mr. Carle, we're just doing our job. Your wife is of interest to the public, if the police have arrested her. The public has a right to know what the police are doing." Daniel's two-tone blue eyes gazed earnestly into Norman's.

"But you're not just talking about what the police are doing. You're talking about her as if she actually killed somebody. My wife couldn't kill anybody."

"The police think they have evidence that points to Tara."

"What, those fan letters? Shoot, if you arrested everyone who's ever sent a fan letter, you'd arrest pretty much everybody!" Carle made an effort to bring himself under control and then matched Chelan's earnest expression with one of his own. "Bought a new knife? Lots of people buy knives. Look, she's just a nice, ordinary woman. A wife, a mother. She works at the grocery store part-time. She watches TV, she goes to movies, she cheers at the hockey games. Once in a while she gets to liking one of the stars and she sends a few letters. She spends a little time in chat rooms on the computer, talking to other women who like to watch the same guy. Where's the harm?"

Matthew tried to keep eye contact with the man. "She also visited the station to watch Keene's game show numerous times. And she hung around Jason Wheeler's shooting locations."

"So she was a fan, so what? She didn't kill anybody. She's not some hidden psycho, and the police will find that out, as long as they keep looking. But if they decide the job is done and if you guys in the media convict her, the truth will never come out."

"Mr. Carle, all we do is report what happens. The police arrest somebody, release a name, we report it. That's all."

"Aww, that's bullshit and you know it. If you want to make a big noise about somebody, you do. And if you want to hush something up, maybe about somebody rich enough, you do."

"You're very cynical, Mr. Carle."

"Naw, I just see things the way they are. Just think about it! She's a forty-five-year-old housewife. Do you really believe she stabbed somebody? Pushed a grown man off a balcony?"

The door opened and two officers in uniform came in. They quickly assessed the situation and hung back, waiting to see what Carle would do. Chelan noticed that one man put himself in front of the door and one next to the windows.

"Mr. Carle, go home," Matthew leaned closer to Norman but didn't touch him. "Call Tara's lawyer, find out what you can do. Don't come to the TV station again."

Carle glowered at them all and muttered a bit but his fury had dissipated.

Matthew stood up and looked at Carle with a sympathetic air. "This kind of stunt doesn't help Tara. You have to stay in control, for her, and for your kids." He waved an arm around the newsroom. "And look at how you've alarmed all these people." There were a lot of white faces around the room, now that Chelan took a look, her own probably one of them. "I don't think you're a bully by nature, Mr. Carle. We all understand how concerned you are for your wife."

Chelan had to admire Matthew's ability to make a connection with this man who had been a complete stranger just half an hour ago, and a berserk one, at that. Matthew escorted Carle over to the police officer by the door and held it open for them to leave. Through the newsroom window, Chelan saw the police walk him over to a battered white van. Were they just going to let him go off on his own? Apparently so, Chelan realized as Norman heaved his considerable bulk into the driver's seat, slammed the door, and drove out of the station parking lot.

Chelan wasn't scared of him, exactly, but the encounter had been pretty intense.

THE LION'S SHARE OF THE AIR TIME

That was why, later in the day, she called Detective Esher at the Vancouver Police Department and asked for a meeting.

She drove down to headquarters on Main Street and parked at a meter. His office was just down the corridor from the media conference room. Today, Esher was dressed in a blazer and gray pants. He pointed to a narrow, folding chair for Chelan and took its twin, facing the reporter across a small round table. He took a sip from a cardboard cup, and then waved it at Chelan.

"Tara Carle's husband was in the newsroom today."

"I heard."

"He wants the media to back off on the coverage. Wants to give the police a chance to figure out that Tara couldn't possibly be a killer. She was a fan of all three, yes, but she couldn't possibly..."

"He said that? She was a fan of all three?"

Chelan backtracked. "Not specifically that, no, but..."

Esher shook his head and stood up. "Look, if you want me to give you the time of day, you gotta get your quotes absolutely, perfectly right. Don't come in here telling me about a conversation that you're making up. I don't have time for this."

"Alright, alright." Chelan put her hands palms up in what she hoped was a humorous gesture of surrender. "Word for word, he said she's just an ordinary woman who develops a liking for a star once in a while, sends a few letters, looks him up on the Internet chat rooms. She's not some psycho stalker fan and if the media would just back off, the police wouldn't be in such a hurry to wrap up this investigation."

Esher spoke as if talking to himself. "He's got something of a point there. There is a certain—momentum at play here." He downed the last of his coffee and pitched the cup at the wastebasket in the corner. "What do you think, Ms. Montgomery?"

Chelan considered her words and tried not to make a

201

fool of herself. "I think all three were murdered. I think it's significant that they were all on TV. I think we need to know whether they knew each other, and how well. Whether they went to any of the same places—like Jason Wheeler and Keith belonging to the same gym."

Esher raised an eyebrow. "Ms. Montgomery, we would certainly like you to stay in touch, let us in on whatever you're finding out." He made a note. "Which gym is that?"

"Pump it Up, it's called."

He nodded. "I appreciate this. Make sure you keep me in the loop."

"I don't think I can find out anything you wouldn't already have access to."

Esher shook his head. "That's not true. You news people have leverage nobody else has."

"What do you mean?"

"You can threaten to put people on TV who don't want to be on TV. And you can threaten to keep people off TV, when they want to be on. Either way, you have something to promise somebody when you're asking for information."

Chelan wasn't about to let that go by without a challenge. "It's nowhere near the crowbar that cops have. You guys have the force of the law behind you."

Esher smiled with no warmth. "That impresses some people, but not many. Not the really bad guys."

A telephone rang. "Anything else, Ms. Montgomery?"

Chelan stood up. "Nothing I can think of."

"I will add Mr. Carle's input to the mix, although I should tell you we had the same visit from him today that you had. I don't think you should worry about him. Just take your usual precautions. I should also tell you there is one other point we'll look at very closely, in addition to the very fine suggestions you've made."

The telephone buzzed again but both ignored it.

Esher's look was determined. "Whether they had the same enemies."

THE LION'S SHARE OF THE AIR TIME

Ξ

"I don't know, Chelan, I don't know if you'd call them enemies, but certainly he had non-fans. Just like every well-known person has." Nevada parked her jeep. Cypress Bowl Road was deserted, despite the amazing June evening. Maybe it was too early. The white and gold twinkling of the city lights was just beginning to show up against a dark blue land mass that would turn to deep purple and then to black, as night fell.

Chelan leaned back against the headrest and sighed. "What a gorgeous view."

"Yeah, yeah." Nevada smiled and lit a cigarette. "When I first moved to Vancouver I rushed around looking at all that stuff all the time. Now I'm used to it. After all, what is it, really? It's just scenery."

"I guess."

Nevada slid down in the seat, rested her head against it, and closed her eyes. Chelan watched the sun sending shouts of gold, orange, pink, and finally purple, as it slid below the western horizon. "So that was a bit scary, Norman Carle in the newsroom."

Nevada's face was so serene Chelan thought she had fallen asleep. She tried another topic. "Elliot told me this morning that Tess is concerned about the impact that the killings are having on everyone. She is going to get the newsroom working on something major, something we can all get behind, help get our minds off —"

Nevada snorted. "How altruistic of her. 'I'll let you work harder for me so that you feel better.' Hah." She opened her eyes and stretched. "What I wonder is how the police found their way to Tara Carle."

Chelan considered, then decided to bring Nevada up to speed. "They have letters. Fan letters she wrote. To Jason and to Gregory."

"Like that one you found of Keith's?"

Chelan nodded.

"Are you convinced?"

"I don't know. It seems plausible. It's certainly not a new story, that an obsessed fan got to a star. That's why they're all so well-protected most of the time. But I can't stop thinking about the source who thinks Keith burned him. He could have quite a grudge." Chelan leaned her head out the window. It was such a glorious night. She wondered whether Nevada would be up for a walk along the mountain road. "I've tried calling him a dozen times, but all I get is voice mail."

"A word of advice. If you do get in touch with him? Don't make any plans to meet him alone."

"Yeah. Maybe. I also wonder whether Keith's death might have had something to do with that story he was working on. About the marijuana grow-ops."

"Keith wasn't working on a grow-op story last month," Nevada sat up. "Well, maybe he was, on the side, in a minor way, but I know he wasn't too interested in doing anything more on drugs because he'd just finished that long project on smuggling."

"How do you know?"

"He told me. He was onto something about corruption in sports. That's all he would tell me, not which sport, not who, nothing more. Said he picked up a tip when he was doing the airport smuggling story and was following it all over town."

Chelan tried to fit that into the mental files she'd created so far about Keith's death.

"I also keep thinking about that gym they all belonged to, and that noisy athlete."

"Which noisy athlete?"

"Conrad Davis. I met him at the gym that Keith used to go to. And Jason."

"He's a piece of work, isn't he?"

"Needs an attitude adjustment." Chelan peered through the darkness at two runners who went pounding by on the trail.

THE LION'S SHARE OF THE AIR TIME

"You can't blame it all on him, though. He had a hard time, growing up. His older brother was killed when Conrad was only about ten. Killed in a hit and run accident, and they never found out who was responsible. One of the profiles I read about him—maybe it was the one Keith did, actually — said that Conrad idolized his older brother, wanted to follow in his footsteps. There was no dad, as I recall. The older brother—Cal, his name was, Cal Davis—was a talented athlete, too."

"Hockey player?"

"Diver."

Chelan stared at the grid of white city lights that blazed on the other side of the darkness that smothered the inlet and the park. The line of lights that outlined the Lions Gate Bridge rose and fell in a wave pattern that mimicked the incoming tide of the water below. It was a view that always made her feel large and powerful, and yet very small, at the same time.

"Conrad might just be the type of person who'd have an obnoxious personality, even if he had a great childhood and grew up to be a circus clown, or a tax consultant," Nevada snickered, amused at the image. "But maybe not."

"I just don't get it." Chelan shook her head. "Are we trying to link too many things together? Jason, Keith, and Gregory were all high-profile on TV, and got fan letters from Tara Carle. They all went to this same gym and Keith, at least, had an enemy—excuse me, a "non-fan" in Conrad Davis, because of the magazine article he wrote. Maybe Conrad had reason to hate Jason or Gregory."

"Let's not forget that Conrad Davis is high-profile on TV, too, and Mr. Carle mentioned that his wife is a hockey fan."

"Did he?"

"Yeah, when he stormed the newsroom today."

"So maybe rather than possible suspect, Conrad is possible victim?"

"Or maybe complete blind alley."

"I think this whole situation needs a lot more investigation."

"Right on." Nevada sat up and put the jeep in gear. "Another day. Let's leave that for another day."

Ξ

The music in the Eagle gym was set at 'break the sound barrier' level; the better to keep your mind off your problems and your aching muscles, Chelan thought, as she zigzagged through the room, looking for Conrad. She spotted a group of about ten people gathered around a triceps machine. Sure enough, there was Conrad in the middle of the crowd, answering questions about the upcoming season. The Eagle was known as a singles gym, a place to see and be seen. Did he ever get much of a workout here? But of course that wasn't the reason Conrad showed up. Chelan knew from Tracy, the receptionist at Pump It Up, that Conrad's membership there had been cancelled. At his new fitness venue, it seemed, more value was put on celebrity than good manners.

Chelan joined the cluster of admirers and listened.

"So it's tied at 2-2, with less than a minute to go and the Leafs got nobody injured. We got three guys on our bench, moanin', and the coach is looking kinda green around the gills." Conrad spotted Chelan through the crowd and his smile faded. "I know you, you're an LV-TV reporter, aren't you? What are you doing here?"

Chelan stood up straight and tried to make herself look as tall as possible. "Could I speak with you for a moment, Mr. Davis?"

Conrad scowled and made a move toward Chelan. The crowd parted and in seconds, the two of them were face to face.

"Privately?" Conrad nodded and his fans drifted away. "I'm trying to find out who killed Keith Papineau, and I think there might be a connection with the Pump it Up gym.

THE LION'S SHARE OF THE AIR TIME

And maybe with Gregory Keene and Jason Wheeler."

"Yeah?" Conrad was so tense he almost started shaking, like a primordial volcano heating up to explode.

"I think you might be in danger, Mr. Davis."

Conrad snorted and flexed his fists once or twice, sending ripples through his biceps.

"Can you tell me anything you might have noticed about any of them when they were at the gym?"

"Not a thing." He practically spat the words at her. "Are you done?"

"One more thing, Mr. Davis. I heard about your brother's death in 1983—"

Conrad stared at her, then stomped toward the exit. He was within five feet of leaving when he stopped and returned to face Chelan. "Wait a minute. This is my gym."

Chelan didn't move quite quickly enough for Conrad's taste. Waving at the staff working behind the desk and near the machines, Conrad bellowed, "Get this reporter out of here. She's not a member and she shouldn't be here."

Chelan moved toward the door, signaling her surrender to the staff. Pretty touchy there, big guy, she thought, as she walked out into the sunlight.

Ξ

The phone call came while she was pounding away on the cheap keyboard she'd bought to calm her craving for a piano.

"Your brother wants to see you.," Twain said.

Chelan had called her boyfriend when she first got home and left a message on his voice mail. She was just looking for some distraction from the fear she felt after Norman Carle's threats and the bump on the head she'd taken at the TV station Saturday night. She didn't want more drama right now, she wanted soothing and pampering. Boyfriends were supposed to give you glimpses of another, better life—not force you to look at the ugliest corners of your own. She wanted to feel like a girl for a while and put the curiosity that was driving her these days into low gear. She didn't want any family drama.

Chelan hadn't heard from her brother in a year. He'd come out of prison, visited her and asked for money, then dropped out of sight.

"I gathered that, when I saw you with him at the mall. How did he find you, Twain? Has he tried to borrow money from you?"

"A little. Nothing I couldn't spare. Relax. He didn't find me, I found him. Got chatting to this guy sitting on a grate outside a club in Gastown, he bragged about having this terrific sister who works at a TV station. We put two and two together."

His voice was like melting chocolate, and it really was kind of sweet that he'd cared enough to try to build a bridge between her and Ron. It was not his fault that he had no idea how wide the chasm was. She'd never told him.

"Twain, I appreciate what you're trying to do, but really, there's a lot going on here that can't be solved with a cup of coffee and an apology."

"What did he do that was so bad?"

"It was what he did and who he was. He was given everything, Twain. He was the golden boy, my father's favorite and my mother's, so I'm told. And he trashed it all. He took the expensive education, the vacations, the car when he turned sixteen, and basically, he kind of spat in my father's face. When he got older and it was clear what a loser he'd grown up to be, my father still kept on trying—financed him in two business that went under, hired lawyers for him."

"He had a lot of bad luck."

"It wasn't bad luck, it was his own doing," Chelan exploded. "He had opportunities and support, but he rejected it all. Then he started doing drugs. He disappeared for months at a time and every time he came back, my father welcomed him. He was stealing money, stealing cars, robbing houses, and finally he got caught. My father hasn't been the

THE LION'S SHARE OF THE AIR TIME

same since."

"It might be different this time, Chelan. Won't you see him?"

"No."

They sat in silence for a few minutes, then Twain said good-bye. Chelan couldn't move for a long time. Her insides were churning, the way they always did when she saw Ronnie, or even thought of him. She hadn't told Twain that she'd welcomed her brother back almost as often as her father had, and been disappointed every time. She hated him for letting them down and hated him for causing her father such pain. She hated him for getting the unreserved attention from her father that she yearned for. She hated him for throwing his life away.

She loved him, too.

Ξ

The Downtown Eastside was not an easy place to walk through and Chelan was hoping she could find Ronnie without having to leave her car. The traffic light turned red and she waited, watching a man on the corner who was drinking from a bottle in a paper bag. He swayed against the lamppost and she thought he might fall. These streets and gritty sidewalks had filled numerous hours of air time, as a backdrop for dramas and news reports. But none of the on-screen footage revealed the true nature of the neighborhood, in Chelan's opinion. You had to actually go there, smell the smells, see the erosion of lives and faces, and feel the fear, theirs and your own, to get anywhere near the real tragedy of the place.

She drove as slowly as she could, trying to glance at the forms lying in sleeping bags on the sidewalks, while keeping her eye on the traffic and the people who frequently staggered out onto the street. She didn't want to park and get out, but it looked as though that would be inevitable. She knew she could have asked Twain if he knew where to find

Ron, but she didn't want to let him any further into this area of her life.

A parking spot opened up in front of a window advertising cheap rooms and she tucked the Mini into it. Usually, the way to avoid trouble in a rough neighborhood is to avoid eye contact, but Chelan had to stare into every face she passed. She didn't know what Ron looked like now—long hair or shaved head, bearded or clean-shaven, healthy or sick. What if she walked right by and didn't recognize him?

She needn't have worried. He was sitting against a building, wearing an old green jacket and baggy jeans. He looked a lot like a hundred other lost souls in this swamp of narcotic quicksand and she might have missed him entirely, if she hadn't instantly recognized the man standing over him. Her father. This she couldn't handle. She turned away before anyone saw her.

17

This had to be one of the longest days that Zack could remember. He leaned back from the computer screen, rubbed his eyes, and groped for his mug. It was half full of lukewarm coffee; refilling it with strong caffeine to carry him through the next hour was a good excuse to get up from the desk and walk around for a while.

Man, he was drowsy. He'd been up since daybreak, letting Marla sleep in because she'd been up all night with Sara. Lucas had slept through all the commotion, with the coughing and the crying, and was up at six, looking for his breakfast. Then the phone rang at eight, waking up Marla and the sick baby. Kenny was on the line, telling Zack that the chief was looking for him and he'd better get his butt in there. Zack could tell that Marla thought he should stay home long enough to take Lucas to school for her, so that she wouldn't have to take the baby out, but he couldn't ignore Kenny's call. He hurried out of the house, calling over his shoulder that he might have to work late.

Once he got in the car and turned on the news, he understood the urgency in Kenny's voice. Tara Carle's name was all over the radio. The chief was furious about the leak, but seemed to accept Zack and Kenny's assurances that they would find out how it had happened. They really had no idea where the press got her name, but there were at least a dozen possibilities Zack could think of. It seemed to originate with the Vancouver Times, and their reporters had connections that twisted through the station, the courthouse, and the law firms like the root system of an old-growth forest. Zack knew that every time he made an inquiry, someone might be watching or listening. If that someone was a journalist, the "public's right to know" might trump his investigation.

The day had gone from bad to worse. Tara's husband was going around, stirring up trouble. Kenny had to leave mid-afternoon, to take care of some emergency at home. And the chief was on the phone three times, unheard of in a single day. He wanted to know details on how the investigation was proceeding, whether Zack thought they had enough to take to the crown prosecutor, whether charges could be laid. Said there was a lot of interest "upstairs", whatever or whoever that might mean.

The cookies in the tin beside the coffee pot were giving Zack an unmistakable come-on, he could swear it. He scooped up half a dozen and carried them back to his desk. He would need to do something about his lack of exercise, if he planned to go on scarfing down cookies like this. It was just so damn hard to find any time in a day. He knew he should be running four or five miles, four or five times a week, but usually by the time the work day was done, he was already unforgivably late in getting home, from Marla's point of view. Maybe he should suggest she could express her aggravation by chasing him around the track a few times, waving a baseball bat or a frying pan or something. Would be good for both of them.

Somehow, he doubted she'd see the humor.

He picked up the photocopies from Keith Papineau's agenda book and flipped through them. He hadn't decided yet whether this TV reporter, Chelan Montgomery, was an asset or a nuisance; time would tell, probably. In the meantime, at least there was a pipeline there, or the beginning of one. He couldn't really see much in these photocopied pages that added to the investigation, but then, you never knew. Same thing with the information about the

THE LION'S SHARE OF THE AIR TIME

workout club they all belonged to. Maybe coincidence, maybe not. Worth checking out.

Tomorrow, maybe. His final task today he would put under the label 'possible enemies'. He was combing financial records, looking for the name of the third partner in Jason Wheeler and Gregory Keene's restaurant deal. The 'silent' partner. It turned out to be a numbered company, rather than a human being with a name and an address, but that was a minor delay. These guys might have their ways of hiding in the weeds, but Zack had his methods of smoking them out too.

Methods that didn't let him down today. Zack watched, a smile forming on his weary face, as a name appeared on his computer screen. So the real estate tycoon was also a player in restaurants.

Ξ

When Owen walked through the door, Nevada had every intention of pampering him within an inch of his life. She hadn't seen him in three days, partly because of his schedule at the hospital and partly because of her late-night interview with the TV director. He dropped his medical bag and she slipped into his arms, rubbing his cheek with hers and seeking out his lips for a long kiss.

"Mmmm. Nice to see you, too." Owen hugged her tighter. "Let's have a glass of wine, okay?"

She got out a bottle of red, polished a couple of glasses and set them out with some cheese and walnuts, while she listened for the shower. Usually when he came home exhausted he wanted to stand under a steaming hot blast of water for about twenty minutes. But tonight he wandered back into the living room and collapsed into his favorite chair, long legs stretched out almost to the TV. She put on his favorite Ella Fitzgerald CD.

"Rough day?"

"Brutal. How about you?"

213

"Totally crappy." She poured the wine and handed him his glass. "Loser Elliot wouldn't assign anybody to cover the Drummond inquiry. Matthew is still demanding an item a day on that actor's murder. And Tess Cunningham is pushing everybody to shoot for the number one spot in the ratings. As if we have a hope in hell."

"But at least it wasn't a boring news day." Owen closed his eyes and rested his wine glass on his chest. He had slipped further down in his chair and was almost horizontal. "I heard all about Tara Carle, was that her name? It was all over the radio and the TV news in the doctor's lounge. Kind of sad, in a way. She looked terrified."

"Yeah. But... that's the way it works. If she's innocent, she has nothing to worry about."

"I think you're a bit naïve," Owen gulped some of his wine. "It's not usually that simple."

He was calling her naïve? That was rich, given that she'd been on the planet quite a bit longer than he had.

"Try to put yourself in her shoes." His words were coming out so slowly, she wondered if he were about to fall asleep. "Or suppose it was someone in your family. Your father, let's say. Suppose he was accused of something and his picture was all over the papers and TV, as if he were convicted already. You'd be on the warpath."

"My father? Not quite. I'd be the first in line."

Owen sat up. "You're kidding, right? Before he was charged with anything, before he had a chance to defend himself?"

"He's always loved the limelight, Owen. This would just be more of it. He'd be as happy as a pig in poop."

"Oh, come on, you're being silly. Nobody wants public attention for something like that."

"One thing I never am, Owen, is silly." She grabbed one of the couch cushions and folded her arms over it in front of her chest. She was ready for her apology now, and maybe for a little cuddling. A conversation about her father was the last thing on her list of fun things to do with your

THE LION'S SHARE OF THE AIR TIME

husband when you haven't seen him in three days. No, not the last thing on the list. Not even on the list.

"Why are you so hostile about your dad, Nevada?"

Oh, man. Beam me up, Scotty. Was there any way to avoid this discussion?

"Come over here and sit by me on the couch," she invited. "We need some more wine." She went to the kitchen and returned, carrying the bottle of cabernet sauvignon. He hadn't moved.

"We never hear from your father, Nevada. And I know he comes to town from time to time. Doesn't he approve of us?"

She filled the glasses to the rim, then sat down with a sigh. "He barely registers that you exist, Owen. He barely registers that I exist. He's been Tom Leacock, the movie star, since he was twenty-two years old. Everything is all about him. When I was a kid growing up, everything we did, everything we wanted, every thought or plan we had came second to his career. There was a lot of money, once in a while there was some glamor, but there was never any love."

"Never? Nevada, that seems a bit exaggerated."

"Never."

Owen ignored the wine and leaned forward, his forearms on his knees, his gaze fixed on hers, as if he were a businessman trying to sell an investor on a new idea. Maybe this was a subject he had wanted to raise for some time.

"Even if that is true," he reached for her hands, "maybe it's time to forgive and forget."

"It goes beyond an unpleasant childhood, Owen. It was more than that. I can't tell you ... but just trust me, there's no possibility that I can ever forgive him."

"What was it?"

"I can't tell you."

"You can't tell me?"

"No."

They sat in silence for a few minutes, and then Owen tried again. "Nevada, you can talk to me."

"Look, sweetie, I know you're terribly sensitive and all that, you talk to people every day about terrible things happening in their families. But I'm the kind of person who has to have a little privacy. You have things in your life you don't want to discuss with me, I'm sure. Let me have the same... the same... " What was the bloody word? "The same space."

He stared at her as if he didn't recognize her, then stood up, walked to the door and left.

Ξ

Nevada finished the last third of her beer in one swallow and ordered another. After Owen left, she decided she couldn't face the empty rooms—or her own thoughts. She needed the Scribbler and a little noise. She knew she would have to come to grips with what had just happened with Owen. Damn. She had scared off so many men in her life, for one reason or another, and she didn't want to lose this one. But his game was pretty intense. She wasn't sure she could step up to the plate the way he wanted, but she was sure she didn't want to think about it right now. Tomorrow would be good.

For tonight, she just wanted to talk shop and hang out. She spotted Chelan across the room and challenged her to a game of darts. But minutes after they started, Chelan had diverted the topic of conversation to the media murders and Nevada realized there was no escape from heavy subjects tonight.

"Chelan, it's really not that hard to believe that this Tara Carle is a crazy fan who murdered Keith." Nevada let fly with a dart that hit the board right in the bull's eye. The Scribbler was crowded, even for a Thursday night, but the area near the dartboard had plenty of empty seats, and they were able to talk in comparative privacy. "Some movie fans and TV fans do get obsessed. And even TV journalists have fans that follow them around. Keith even had a web site."

THE LION'S SHARE OF THE AIR TIME

She put a second one in, right beside her first.

"So what? Lots of people have web sites. It's the new version of the black and white glossy. Or your résumé. " Chelan was itching to get her hands on those darts and fling a few.

Nevada threw her third and sat down to her beer. "No, I'm not talking about the kind you put up yourself. His fan club put this one up. They keep track of his public appearances, post photos. They run a chat room. All these ladies get together and type messages to each other about what he's wearing, where he's going, what he should do next with this career next."

"You're kidding."

"No. It's wild. Keith showed it to me one night when we were both at the station late."

"What's that all about? Do these people have so little going on their lives that they have to fall in love with a total stranger?"

"Chelan, don't you get it? With a perfect stranger. One who never picks his nose or belches in public. One who is fantastic in bed — he must be, because he's special enough to be famous. That's part of it, I think. The other thing is they just fall in love. Just like in real life, you know? Something attracts them, they start thinking about the movie star or TV personality or whoever it is, all the time. It puts some sparkle in their life, makes them look forward to getting up each morning—come on, you know what it's like to fall in love."

"With a real person, yeah. Not with a celebrity."

Nevada's face had a faraway look. "Of course, you're in love with a fantasy, with who you think the person is. But that doesn't make it any less intense."

"But it's a long way from a crush like that to a freaky obsession that turns a person into a killer."

"I know, right?. It's unlikely. But not impossible. Maybe she got angry with them. Maybe they didn't respond to their letters the way she thought they should, or maybe something made her mad when she went to see them in person."

Chelan went over to the board and pulled the darts from the speckled surface. She stood at the masking tape mark on the floor, and started to throw.

"Did you know Keith was only twenty years old in '84 when he almost went to the Los Angeles Olympics?" Nevada asked. "He could have been on the Canadian diving team. Ten-meter platform was his event."

"What happened?"

"Last minute injury."

Chelan threw her last dart and sat back down at the table. "Were you there, Nevada?"

"No, I missed the '84 Olympics. I got to the ones in '88, in Seoul, but not the '84."

"Do you think that's why he didn't just fall from his balcony, but actually dived? That in his final moments, he wanted to go out doing one of the things he loved best to do in the world, one of the things that made him who he was?"

"Maybe. Or maybe it was his way of taking back control, of thumbing his nose at whoever pushed him off."

"You're sure someone pushed him?"

"Positive." Nevada drained her mug of draft. "Or threw him."

A powerful female voice wailed from the speaker. "Who are we listening to?" Chelan asked.

"Janis Joplin. *Piece of My Heart*. We've finally got someone playing the tunes who understands that music in a bar has to have its roots in the blues somewhere. The only thing missing is the sweet smell of cigarette smoke," Nevada said.

For a few moments, they listened to Janis's pain, then Chelan had an idea. She had to give herself a few seconds to settle down.

"What is it?" Nevada stared at her.

Her face must be as informative as a fire bell, Chelan thought. She really should practice doing some kind of poker face.

THE LION'S SHARE OF THE AIR TIME

"Nevada, what if he deliberately put himself into that dive to give some kind of clue about who pushed him off?"

"Seems a bit far-fetched."

"Isn't it far-fetched to think an obsessed serial-killer fan stalked him, and Jason and Gregory, and murdered them?"

"Is it?" Nevada drummed her fingertips on the tabletop. She seemed distracted. "Come on, we've been over that. Famous people do sometimes have crazy fans who come after them. Why do you think they all travel with bodyguards?"

"Maybe for the totally famous, the movie stars who get millions a picture. I know Jason Wheeler was right up there, but Gregory wasn't really in that league. And Keith was a TV reporter. Do you think TV reporters should be going around with bodyguards?"

"Yeah, make mine tall, dark and Latin."

It was a typical Nevada joke, but Chelan felt dismissed. She stood up. "You know, it's so obvious. We should have thought of this ages ago. We've got her address. Let's go talk to her."

Ξ

The front windows of Tara Carle's house were dark and no porch light shone on the front door. Chelan's courage had disappeared during the drive south to Delta, and she would have preferred just to drive up, take a look at the house and the neighborhood, and then double back to downtown. But Nevada had jumped on the idea and she wouldn't settle for anything less than ringing the doorbell and meeting Tara Carle, face to face.

Norman Carle opened the door. His wary expression morphed into something resembling what you might find on a rabid dog. He turned beet red and his eyes bulged. "Get away from my house!"

Chelan would have been more than happy to comply, but Nevada had a hand in the small of her back. "Mr. Carle, we're from LV-T —"

"I know who you are."

That was all that Chelan could manage to say. Nevada stepped around her. "Mr. Carle, we were wondering whether Mrs. Carle would agree to an interview. Tell her side of the story."

"Get off my property. I'm calling my lawyer." Norman slammed the door.

Chelan was just as intimidated as he intended her to be, but Nevada appeared unfazed. She stepped off the front porch, but rather than taking the path back to the car, she veered off onto the lawn.

"What are you doing?" Chelan hissed. Let's get out of here."

"We drove all this way. I just want to get a sense of the place before we head back." Nevada looked up into the windows, but heavy drapes, drawn tight, blocked her view.

"What if he comes back out?"

"What if he does? Just let me do the talking. Or run," Nevada suggested as she stepped carefully over an abandoned badminton racquet and three plastic action figures.

Her right foot landed in the flowerbed, among some tattered geraniums and a drooping Dusty Miller, and on top of something not quite level. She was thrown off-balance and had to plant her left foot on a solitary begonia, stomping the last bit of life out of it. She reached down, probably to check out what it was that had tripped her, and came up holding a knife. An eight-inch, serrated kitchen knife with a white plastic handle. With something brown clinging to the edges.

Chelan felt her temperature rise and her breathing quicken. She stared at Nevada's hand, gingerly holding the blade between thumb and forefinger. "Drop it," she urged. "I'm calling Detective Esher."

THE LION'S SHARE OF THE AIR TIME

Ξ

Esher got the call just as he was shutting down his computer for the night. He was so tired that when the telephone rang he swore he wouldn't lift another finger even if there were a gun battle going on in the police parking lot. But training trumps fatigue, every time.

"Esher."

"Detective Esher, this is Chelan Montgomery from LV-TV."

Terrific.

"I'm out at Tara Carle's home in Delta."

"What are you doing there?"

"I'm with Nevada Leacock, also from LV-TV News. We were asking for an interview."

"Have any luck with that?"

She was too upset to notice his tone. "No, they were uncooperative. But when we were leaving, we stumbled over something in their yard. I think it might be the murder weapon."

Esher grabbed the cell phone and punched in Kenny's pager number. "Stay put. We'll be right there."

18

The next morning, Chelan arrived at the station front door just as a black luxury SUV pulled up into the no-parking zone. Nevada had called to wake her up, long before she was ready to surface, with a heads-up that there was a special meeting and all hands were expected on deck. It was very late when she'd arrived home last night, after showing the police where they'd found the knife, and she'd had trouble getting to sleep. Esher said it would take less than twenty-four hours to determine the nature of the substance on the knife, do a DNA test and establish whether or not it was the knife used on Jason Wheeler and Gregory Keene. If they arrested Tara Carle, with this knife as the evidence, the next few days would be even busier than the last.

Chelan watched an enormous man in an immaculate suit get out of the driver's seat and walk around to open the passenger door. Tess Cunningham glided out, both hands clutching leather briefcases.

She turned to the man holding the door. "Dmitri, I have a lunch meeting at the Bayshore. Bring the car up at 11:30, would you? I won't need anything done until then." She smiled briefly and took off for the door, moving faster than the rest of the pedestrian traffic, despite the five-inch heels on her shoes.

Just moments later, all eyes in the newsroom were

THE LION'S SHARE OF THE AIR TIME

focused on her as she stood, in her red suit and expensive jewelry, in front of the anchor desk.

"Thank you all for being here," Tess began. The vibe wasn't good, Chelan thought. Surely it wouldn't be layoffs, when they were talking about more resources and a big push at first place in the ratings. At most downsizing stations, the protocol was last in, first out, with a few exceptions where management used the economic squeeze as an excuse to replace people who were no longer needed or popular. If layoffs were on the agenda, Chelan was sure she would be one of the first to go, unless her help at the intern interviews had raised her a peg or two on Tess's chart.

"We have some changes in personnel to announce." Tess consulted a clipboard. Terrific. Station president as coach, changing a line-up.

"As some of you may know, Rick O'Neill, our vice-president of programming, has left us for personal reasons. Matthew Collis is to become the next LV-TV vice-president of programming." Tess paused as a buzz built in the room. Chelan looked at Nevada, whose face was as blank as a supermodel's. Matthew was clearly very pleased. Elliot seemed puzzled and Leonard was focused on his shoes.

Tess tucked her clipboard into a leather briefcase and gave them all a corporate smile. "I'm making the time to tell you this personally rather than sending a memo because it will have an impact on the newsroom, obviously. Your new news director is Leonard Chu. I'm sure I don't have to tell you of his extensive experience in San Francisco, and I'm sure you'll give him all the support you can."

The buzz was building, but Tess wasn't finished. "As you know we're planning to mount an exposé on the marijuana industry in B.C. Leonard will decide on the staffing for that. I'm confident we'll soon see the results of these changes reflected in our ratings share." Smiling and shaking a few hands, Tess made her exit to the elevator. Chelan expected that Matthew would go with her but he remained behind to share a few final thoughts with his team.

223

GAIL HULNICK

"I want to thank you all for all your hard work on the news since I've been here," Matthew's tone was humble. "I appreciate it very much and I hope I'll find as high a caliber of work ethic and professionalism in the other departments. Of course, I'll still be involved in the news, just one step removed."

"Still taking credit, you mean," Nevada muttered near Chelan's ear.

Leonard's speech, after Matthew's, was short enough to make everyone happy. He knew he was an unknown quantity to most of them and nothing he could say would have any impact on their evaluation of him; that would only come through watching his daily decisions and his style.

"Got time for coffee before you go back to the salt mine?" Nevada seemed as antsy as a boxer seconds before the bell.

They went to Django's, a little coffee shop a block from the station where the coffee was excellent and the music was jazz. Nevada barely sat down before she erupted.

"Leonard Chu as the news director! What are they thinking? He's been a reporter a grand total of six years and he's never worked in Canada before—yes, thanks!" Her fervent acceptance of the menu startled both Chelan and the waiter.

" Well, six years is ... it's not like he's completely green, right out of journalism school or something. A latté, please."

"Espresso. Double shot. And a slice of the chocolate cake." Nevada intercepted the glance between Chelan and the waiter, lifted her chin and squared her shoulders. "What? I need something, and they won't let you smoke anywhere in this prissy city any more."

Chelan leaned back in her chair and let the slide guitar notes waft through her brain. Best to let Nevada just blow till the storm was over. She'd learned that from trying to deal with her brother.

"You watch, for a while it will be business as usual, then he'll start to try to put his stamp on things. I don't think

THE LION'S SHARE OF THE AIR TIME

he's the type to make big changes overnight. It'll be little, niggling things, annoying things. 'Make your stories shorter, make your voice-overs stronger, walk slowly down the Courthouse steps for your stand-ups'. Then he'll start to change the newscast into something tabloid. More car chases, more live-action from the scene of a home invasion, more fires."

The waiter arrived with two steaming mugs. They smelled like Italy on the happiest day of your life. Chelan smiled at the waiter and he seemed inclined to linger, but after a couple of seconds, he fled back to the kitchen, discouraged by the barrage of Nevada's commentary.

"You think I'm exaggerating, but I worked in Detroit. This is their idea of local news," she stirred her coffee furiously, then speared the gooey icing on her chocolate cake.

"Detroit is a long way from San Francisco. And Leonard is an individual. He may have his own ideas about local news coverage and they may be right in line with yours." Chelan intended to say nothing, but she couldn't resist being drawn into the debate. "Besides, who else could they choose? Unless they brought in somebody from another newsroom or completely new. And you wouldn't like that, probably."

Nevada stabbed the cake and captured a forkful. "What about me?" She stuffed the cake in her mouth.

Oops. Red light. Danger ahead. Chelan leaned forward, wrapping both hands around her mug. "Nevada, I doubt that Tess or Matthew knew you were at all interested in being a news director. I didn't know you were interested in being a news director."

"Well, I certainly think I could do a better job and bring more news experience to it than Leonard bleeping Chu!"

"Of course, you could," Chelan tried to make her voice soothing. "So what you have to do is let them know you're interested. Now, before the next personnel change comes up. Go see Tess or Matthew."

225

"I don't think I could ask either one of them for anything."

"But if they ask you, that's different?"

"That's different." Nevada tossed the fork on the empty plate, then went to work twisting the rings on her pointer and middle fingers.

Chelan shook her head like a Saint Bernard trying to remove a hat that some joker had put on its head. "Too deep for me. You want more cake?"

"No, I want a cigarette. Let's pay and get out of here."

She yanked her wallet out of her purse and pulled out a ten-dollar bill. Her chair made a hideous scraping noise as she stood up.

Chelan put down her share of the bill and a generous tip. "One good thing to come out of it all. It will help the newsroom to have Matthew as VP programming."

Nevada whirled on her heel to face her. "How do you figure that?"

"Because of his news background. Rick, the guy who was in there before, came from children's TV."

Nevada made a face. "Matthew Collis will be no friend of news, now that he's made it to the VP job. He'll just figure out which way the parade is heading and find his way to the front."

Chelan followed Nevada out into the June sunshine. "Geez, you're cynical. And wrong. Matthew is a good guy and the newsroom is going to miss him."

Nevada probed the depths of her purse for her package of cigarettes and her lighter. She inhaled like a drowning man just pulled out of the lake. "Maybe Matthew was a good guy to you, Chelan, but he didn't have the time of day for most of us."

"He hasn't hung out with me the way you have, and hasn't told me nearly as many spectacular stories, but I did get the feeling that he wanted to teach me something, that he was looking out for me."

"Chelan, you're too easy to please." Nevada had her

THE LION'S SHARE OF THE AIR TIME

balance back, now that she was free to flood her system with tar and nicotine once again.

"You underestimate me. Or overestimate me. Or something," Chelan said, just as her cell phone rang. "Chelan Montgomery, LV-TV News." But it was too late. The caller had already been sent on to voice mail. Chelan leaned against the building and scrolling through the numbers. "I have to pick up some of these calls."

Nevada waved at her as she took off down the street.

Ξ

Tony Prinelli reached for a socket wrench. Tools were a mechanic's second set of hands and he took as much care with them as he did with his body. Ever since the age of eleven, Tony had taken the time and made the effort to keep his body functioning like a well-oiled machine. He turned his back on the burgers, fries and pizza so popular among his friends. He looked for excuses to take a long walk or climb the stairs. If the choice were to stand up or to sit, he would stand; to walk or run, he would run, and count his blessings. Any time he got an opportunity to swim, he was in heaven.

When he was that young, he hadn't really thought much about it, he just did it. Later, when he was in training, he found out a lot more about fitness and the body's potential. Then when he got his independence, in his late teens, and discovered the North Shore mountains, he poured as much energy as he could into cycling and running the forest trails.

The main pleasure was in being outdoors, in the clean air, in the shadow of ancient trees, catching sight of wildlife. But the by-product was the satisfying feeling that he lived inside a perfect machine. He probably remembered that joyful feeling of running as a child, picking his feet up high with each step, trying to get his feet and legs moving so fast he could kick the back of his butt with his heels.

Tony took a step back to look over the old Ford 289 that was his current project. His small sideline business,

227

repairing cars and trucks, gave him more money than his regular job at the fire station these days, and he'd been lucky to get the capital he needed to buy his tools and get started. But it wasn't quite enough to take the leap and quit, even with the money that had come from his latest silent partner. He knew a lot of guys who gave up firefighting once they could make a reasonable living doing something else, but he wasn't ready to make that leap yet. For a long time, he thought he never would be, and that he would be on the job until the official day he could start collecting full pension.

Then last year an unexpected bonanza had appeared. Not a bonanza, exactly, because the money came with a ten percent interest rate, but since he'd been turned down at every bank he'd tried for a business loan, it was a windfall, in way.

Being a firefighter left him with a lot of free time. Time to ride his mountain bike, pedaling furiously for marathon distances, at dawn, as often as he could arrange it. Starting at the Capilano River, east to Lynn Valley, and right across to Deep Cove, he raced against himself, pushing his body into high gear, into that zone where the dripping sweat, the pounding heart and the aching knees took him to a timeless, crystallized moment. A moment of forgetting.

It probably would have been better, for his business profits and his loan repayment schedule, if he'd spent more of that time actually working. But what was life, if not a balancing act? You made your choices, about time and about people, and you tried to keep any one thing from dragging you down.

Tony glared at the Holley 750 carburetor in his hand. The damn thing seemed to have a loose needle rattling around in it. He reached for a pair of pliers and poked around. A couple of times he had it, then it dropped back. The sucker just didn't want to come out.

Frustrating as hell. Tony stopped short of kicking the workbench and took a few deep breaths. Calm down. Change your location when you get angry. Good advice

THE LION'S SHARE OF THE AIR TIME

from a smart wife. Too bad he didn't listen to Yvonne more often—as she was constantly reminding him.

Had it stopped raining? Maybe some fresh air would do the trick. Tony jabbed at the automatic door button and the garage door slowly opened, revealing the car whose engine he was working on, parked in his back driveway. He hadn't planned to start a home-based car mechanic business, fourteen years ago, when he and Yvonne had bought this old house on the east side, but he couldn't have chosen a better layout if he had. Back alley, big driveway. His customers could come and go without the neighbors getting irritated about the extra traffic or jealous of his extra income. Roomy, detached garage at the back where he could go to work out of the rain. Far enough away from the house that Yvonne and the kids left him alone out there.

No rain. Tony gathered up the parts and a few tools and carried them out to the weathered picnic table in the back yard. He straddled the bench, his back to the garage and went back to work.

Ξ

When Yvonne arrived home at 11 a.m., she looked out the kitchen window and thought she saw her husband hunched over the picnic table, tinkering with one of his car parts, as he'd done on any one of a thousand previous days. Vic, the neighbor who talked to Chelan when she went door-knocking after hearing the police report, said he looked over the fence just after lunch and saw Tony taking a nap, head cradled on his arms, out in the beautiful sunshine of a June afternoon.

Clouds moved in and the rain began to fall just as Yvonne was starting to make lunch. She grabbed a large cookbook to hold over her head for shelter and went out into the yard to shake her sleepy husband awake.

The raindrops seemed to be the size of double shots and in just a few minutes there were puddles on every low-lying area and around all four of the picnic table legs. The neighbor told Chelan that he saw Yvonne shake Tony, then stop and stare at the puddle for a long minute. Then she started to scream, a horrible, gasping, heaving, almost psycho sound, and Vic had gone running from his back kitchen, down the path, out his gate, down the alley, and across the Prinelli's yard to the picnic table. The puddles were turning from a muddy brown to a throbbing, vital red, and blood gushed from Tony's wound. Tools lay scattered on the ground around him. Footprints in the mud led to the gate.

Chelan stood in the back alley the next day and imagined the scene. The rain was still coming down, and all previous traces of Tony's life and death had been washed away. The police report would say death by stabbing. The theory was that Tony Prinelli, sitting at his picnic table tinkering with a drive shaft, did not hear the stealthy approach of a robber, did not see the hand that reached for one of his tools. The upward thrust, the twist, falling forward on his table.

How long was he conscious? What pain did he feel? Chelan stared at the yard and the table, now looking like any one of a dozen or a thousand yards and tables anywhere.

But not the same as any other. This one was the home of a murder victim, a man who had called Chelan just hours earlier.

The call was one of almost a dozen on the tape, most of them callbacks from sources she had contacted. The next-to-last was from Twain, the first time Chelan had heard from him since their argument two days ago. She was pondering her next move, to call him or not to call him, and almost missed hearing the recording of Tony's message.

"Chelan, my name is Tony Prinelli," the voice was nasal and confident, with just a trace of an accent. "I have some thoughts about those media killings and I was wondering if we could get together to talk."

Yeah, yeah. Chelan's finger hovered over the '7' button, ready to delete the message. As if she had time to get together to talk with every viewer who had thoughts about something in the news. She'd never get any work done.

Tony's next words stopped her. "I'm an old friend of Keith's... or I was, I guess. I saw the report you did on his life. And on Gregory Keene. I knew him, too... and Jason Wheeler."

Where? When? Chelan wanted to shout at the tape.

"There was quite a group of us, quite a few still in Vancouver."

Us? Why us? Who was he talking about?

But there was nothing more, no more information. Just a phone number. Chelan played and replayed the message half a dozen times, trying to find something more, something revealing in his tone of voice or his phrasing. Nothing. Finally, she decided to make the call. She listened to twenty or thirty rings before hanging up. That was about ten o'clock.

By then he was already gone.

19

Lillian was about to step down from the curb into the crosswalk when a small brown car raced in front of her, sloshing through the puddles and splashing some of the rainwater up onto her shoes. She made eye contact with the young woman in the passenger seat, but instead of the lips mouthing "sorry" or the sheepish smile she expected, she got a middle finger raised toward her and shaken. No, it was not really shaken, but stabbed, into the air, as the woman's face twisted into a threatening glare.

When had people become so rude, so angry? She saw it every day: everyone so combative, so unwilling to grant a moment's charity to their fellow humans. We are all on the planet just for a short while, just trying to get along and get through the day; would it be so difficult to take the chip off your shoulder?

The impatient honking of a car horn interrupted her reverie and she willed her feet to move more quickly. God forbid anybody should lose forty-five seconds out of his day while she crossed the street. She was heading for the library on Denman Street, to return her book and borrow another, and to make her weekly call to her daughter in Maple Ridge.

Lillian was meticulous in making that call every Friday afternoon at 4 p.m. She was fairly sure that if she missed it, Gloria would be on her way to Vancouver, to check up on her. This way, a call came, like clockwork, from the elderly

232

mother, and Gloria's mind could be at rest and her guilt in hibernation for another week. And Lillian was left alone, as she wanted to be. She always made certain she sounded vivacious and strong, whenever she called. She hadn't had to receive a visit from any of her children for eight months now, and with any luck they'd stay away for another eight.

"Hey, Mrs. Howe." The voice was deep, like an adult's, but the inflection was youthful.

Lillian turned. "Kevin. Very nice to see you. Are you going to the library?"

"Just out for a walk in the neighborhood. How are you, you doing okay?"

"Yes, and so are you, I can see." His hair was combed and he didn't look as exhausted as he had the last time she'd seen him.

"Better, I guess. It's still hard." His eyes met hers and they said all the things that couldn't be said aloud.

She motioned toward the bus stop. "Sit down with me on this bench for a while. I need to catch my breath."

"Where's Coaster?"

"He was snoozing when I left, so I thought I'd let him be. We took a long walk early this morning." Lillian settled onto the bench. Her knees and hips ached, but that was nothing new. What was new was the cracking she heard from her lower back. Kevin slid onto the long seat, his body bending and twisting effortlessly. Oh, they have no idea, the young. They have no idea what's in store.

Kevin's gaze roved along the line of stores and restaurants on the other side of the street. The smells of grilling hamburgers and frying onions mingled in the warm air.

"Hey, do you want to get something to eat?" he asked.

Lillian smiled, and decided to be direct with him. "Unless you're offering to treat, Kevin, I'm afraid we'll both have to wait until dinner. I don't have enough money with me to pay for a restaurant meal."

He nodded. "You have to be careful with your money,

don't you?"

"You're very perceptive. Yes, I have to be careful. A few years ago, I had a bit of a … a setback, shall we say… and now I'm very careful."

Kevin's face had a compassionate, canny expression. "Did you lose a lot on lottery tickets? Or maybe the casino?"

She laughed. "No, Kevin, I have some problems but gambling's not one of them, thank goodness. No, I just trusted the wrong person and made a bad investment. There's no use crying over spilled milk. The money's gone. So now I'm just very careful. Watch the pennies and the dollars take care of themselves, have you heard that saying?"

He shook his head and she laughed again. "I'm not surprised. I think someone came up with it about a hundred years before you were born. Now, enough about money. How are things at home? Is your mother all right?"

"She's doing okay. She seems better since everybody stopped talking about Dad killing himself. To me, there's no difference, he's still gone …" Kevin wiped the back of his hand across his eyes. "But she's all cranked up about finding out whether somebody killed him. That's almost as bad."

"What do you mean?"

"That somebody would hate him that much."

Lillian wished she could put an arm around him, but she knew however much he needed it, he would resist it. Teenage boys. A hug would be so much easier to deliver than the right words; maybe silence would be the best choice. But that could appear to him as a rejection, or as an inability on her part to deal with the appalling matters under discussion. She believed that all young people need to feel they are surrounded by capable adults — surrounded and supported. If the adult shows fear or confusion, the child shuts down. Lillian didn't want Kevin to think that her silence meant she was overwhelmed by the violent circumstances of his father's death. So, despite her apprehension that she might choose the wrong words, she waded in.

THE LION'S SHARE OF THE AIR TIME

"Kevin, I don't think it's clear that he died because somebody hated him that much. So many of the facts are still missing. Who was it up there with him on that balcony? It might have been a friend or an acquaintance who just happened to be present during an accidental fall. He could have had a medical condition that made him dizzy. He might have eaten or drunk something that made him sick or weak and made him fall."

She saw a group of people approaching and hoped they weren't planning to wait at the bus stop, within earshot of her conversation. "The other thing to consider, Kevin, is this suspect in whom the police are interested. This fan."

Kevin turned to look at her. "Tara Carle."

"Yes, Tara Carle. What do you think of that?"

"I guess it's possible. Makes more sense when you think about the TV star, but maybe she was obsessed with my dad, too."

They watched the people pass by, a mother pushing a stroller, then a young woman dressed in yoga pants and a tight top. So much skin showing. The whole world's gone mad, Lillian thought.

She glanced at her watch. "Kevin, I'm very sorry, but I have to leave for a while to go and make a telephone call. Do you want to wait for me?"

He gave her a smile that would charm an angel. "No thanks, Mrs. Howe. It's been good to talk to you. I have to get going, too."

"I'm sure we'll get some clear answers very soon. The police are working on it and they'll find out what happened to your father."

"Thanks, Mrs. Howe. Say hi to Coaster for me." And he was gone, merging with the crowd passing by, heading in the direction of the beach.

Ξ

The next day, Chelan sat at her favorite spot on

Granville Island, having a coffee, starting the weekend slowly, watching the passing parade. She saw a gaunt-looking man with a soul patch looking her way. Oh yuck, it was that awful guy from Layla's last party. Chelan pulled the newspaper up in front of her face and hid behind it for what she thought was a reasonable length of time. Slowly, she lowered the paper. He was still there, drinking coffee with a friend, only four tables away. Chelan raised the paper again and went through it page by page, making it last. Eventually, she wound up at the classified section and the obituaries. A familiar name caught her eye. Tony Prinelli.

The photograph showed a man in midlife with a full head of dark, thick hair, a strong jaw and a huge smile. What was it he had wanted to tell her before he died? Was it possible that he had known Keith, Jason and Gregory?

Chelan read the details:

Prinelli, Tony.
Survived by his wife, Yvonne, and children, Olivia and Tony. Tony was a member of the Vancouver Fire Department for 16 years and was one of the nation's top swimmers in his youth.

Chelan stopped reading, folded the paper and clutched it tightly, her knuckles white, as she picked up her bag and headed for the parking lot, almost at a run. The Mini was wedged into a slice of a parking space beside a sculptor's studio. She wriggled the little car out into traffic and headed for the library.

It was calm and quiet there. In mid-winter, on a blustery February night, no doubt there would be hundreds of people, roaming the stacks or setting up camp in a study carrel. But on a warm Saturday afternoon in June, Chelan saw only a few busy readers and print-gatherers. Everyone else must be out enjoying the beach or the bay.

The smells of old leather and new ink floated just below the surface, barely detectable, but somehow adding to the

THE LION'S SHARE OF THE AIR TIME

sense of comfort Chelan found in a library. This one, in Vancouver, with its Roman amphitheater architecture and proximity to stores and restaurants, was a beacon for any reader. Many times Chelan had drifted through on her way from the station's downtown offices to the hockey arena, just for the pleasure of looking at it.

Today, however, she was there with a purpose, not just passing through. The librarian at the Social Sciences counter pointed her in the right direction and she settled at a table with a stack of old magazines. She intended to find everything that she could about Tony Prinelli, and everything that was in public view about Keith's life. While she was at it, she would hunt down any references to Jason and Gregory, too.

Several hours later she had a file folder bulging with articles and notes. She had a couple of sports articles written by Gregory Keene for the Vancouver Times and for the university student newspaper, numerous clippings about Jason's television career, and some local pieces about Keith's diving results. Tony's swimming career had also captured a lot of attention in the sports pages of the day.

A search through the Internet gave her reams of information on Jason, Keith, and Gregory from the nineties onward, but nothing about Tony and nothing pre-1989.

Halfway through a page-by-page trawling of a massive, impressively bound collection of all of the issues of *Canadian Scene* Magazine published in 1983, a small photograph that was part of a collage stopped her cold. It was a group of young people, smiling at the camera, and she was sure she recognized Keith. No caption, no photographer credit. She stood in line at the photocopier and made five copies.

She had to get back to Heather and find out more about Keith's life in the eighties. Did he know Tony Prinelli? What was the link? Did it really all have to do with high media profile and an obsessed fan, with Tony Prinelli just a random casualty of a property crime? Or could it be the Pump it Up gym was the common denominator, with

Conrad Davis and others at risk as future victims?

Chelan's phone rang and six people in her immediate vicinity glared at her. How embarrassing, when there were warning signs all over the place about turning off cell phones. She turned her back, lowered her head and tried to look like a doctor on an emergency call or a mother whose children needed her.

"Chelan Montgomery," she hissed.

"Ms. Montgomery, this is Ted Bougie. When can we meet?"

Ξ

Chelan studied the reddening skin on the neck of the man sitting in front of her at Nat Bailey Stadium while she waited for Ted Bougie to arrive, or the game to begin, whichever came first. The magnificent June weather brought the sun worshippers out, but many forgot their sunscreen on the way. It was just after lunch and many business types were skipping their Wednesday afternoon obligations, basking in the warmth of the sun, the sizzling smell of hot dogs with onions, and the mellow pace of a baseball game.

Ted had suggested the stadium as a meeting place and Chelan thought it was perfect. If he did turn out to be a psycho, it would be a lot harder for him to pull off any sort of attack on her, surrounded by hundreds of baseball fans. He'd expected her to pay, and told her to leave a ticket for him at the wicket. That was not quite so perfect. Seat fourteen, on the aisle, row six.

She leaned forward in seat fifteen to look at the people streaming in along the aisles. She didn't really know what she was looking for—would he be one of these guys in business suits or one of the young ones in droopy pants and baggy shirts? All she knew from checking the archive transcript on Keith's report was that an "unnamed source" at the airport had revealed the flaw in the security system that allowed for the drugs to pass through.

THE LION'S SHARE OF THE AIR TIME

The crowd stood for the national anthems and a young singer named Jacqui somebody held them spellbound. The announcer introduced the teams and play was underway. Chelan watched half an inning—still no sign of anyone showing any interest in seat fourteen. She turned to the right, stretching her neck to scan the seats behind her, and then she sensed someone settle beside her. She had only a second to look at him before he muttered under his breath, "Keep your eyes forward. I don't want it to look like we're together."

She could tell that he was shorter than she and very slightly built. She'd had a quick impression of brown hair, worn long, and an unshaven face. The arm on the seat next to hers was tanned and skinny. He wore a gray T-shirt and a red ball cap, which he pulled down low over his eyes as he slouched in the seat.

He watched four pitches before he spoke. "Why do you keep calling me?"

"I want to talk to you about Keith—"

"Pipe down!" He almost spit the words out, still looking straight ahead.

Chelan took a deep breath and tried to focus on what she needed out of this interview. She had a feeling it wouldn't last long. "Okay, sorry."

"Hey, thanks for the ticket. I got no money for anything these days, thanks to your friend, Keith. Lost my job, got nothing coming in at all." He spoke so quietly that she was sure no one behind or in front of them could possible hear.

"He didn't force you to answer his questions. And he didn't use your name in his report."

"Maybe not, but he gave it up to somebody. And pretty damn quick, too. Right after that report, I got fired. They had this fancy paper trail of meetings to discuss my poor performance, breaches of discipline, unsatisfactory work history—and it was all made up, phony dates, phony meetings. Then I turn on the TV and I have to watch stuff about what a great guy he was—makes me want to puke."

"Mr. Bougie, you seem to be very angry about this." Chelan was terrified, but she was unlikely to get another chance like this.

"I didn't kill him, if that's what you're thinking. I got no grudge. I'm the good guy here, you know? I'm the one blew the whistle on those jerks making all that money. I didn't want any thanks for it. I didn't expect to get anything out of it. But I didn't think that reporter would screw me over and make me lose my job, you know?" He risked a quick turn of his head to look at her. "He told me he could guarantee me that he wouldn't broadcast my name, but that he'd have to reveal it to his supervisor or to one of the executives. That he wasn't allowed to operate completely independently. Is that true?"

"Yes, that's the policy for everybody. Even on major stories, confidential sources have to be identified to at least one senior manager."

"So that would be…"

"Matthew Dixon, the news director. Or maybe Tess Cunningham, the VP." Sweat was bursting from the pores on Chelan's forehead. Whether it was from the midday sunshine or the tension of sitting next to this enraged man, she didn't know. She wiped her face with the back of her hand and wished she had thought to buy a cold drink. "But it's very unlikely it was any one of them, Mr. Bougie. Journalists would rather go to jail than give up the names of their sources to the authorities. Look it up, you'll see. There have been many of them, throughout history."

"Yeah, yeah, yeah."

"Really. It's a relationship of trust that has to be maintained, otherwise the whole system would collapse. No one would ever tell us anything, unless they had something to advertise or to sell. You know, there's another possibility, Mr. Bougie. Have you thought about the people you work with?"

He snorted. "Possibly. Plenty of snitches and whiners in

the place."

"Maybe one of them saw you meeting with Keith. Or heard you on the phone with him. Where did you meet him? Were you ever at his apartment?"

Ted ignored the questions. "High-profile TV people got no idea what it's like. Being invisible. Guys like Papineau and Keene, they don't do much, but because they do it in front of a camera, everybody thinks they're somebody special."

He gripped the armrest and rose to his feet. In a second, he was gone. He didn't waste the ticket, though. Throughout the second inning, until she decided to leave and call Nevada, Chelan saw him leaning against a wall, watching the action. She had no idea whether he stayed right to the end.

Ξ

They sat perched on tiny chairs in front of a coffee shop on Commercial Drive, one of the city's best spots for Italian food and interesting people.

"Okay, show me this photo," Nevada commanded as she moved her cappuccino to one side to make room.

Chelan reached into her briefcase and pulled out a manila envelope, taking a quick look over her shoulder to make sure they were still alone. "Do you recognize any of these people?"

Nevada took out the photograph. "Where did you get this?"

"Did some research at the library. Magazine archives."

"Definitely the eighties, look at the clothes." Nevada squinted carefully at the picture. Nine young people stood near a group of empty chairs in front of a CPAir counter at an airport. The clothes and the hair would look weird today, but to Nevada, they were an attractive bunch. Quite a few of the guys had moustaches or beards that covered all of their cheeks—more hair than the goatee style favored by most men who wore beards now. Most of the girls had their hair in a sort of wavy shag. Their clothes were brightly colored and form-fitting. The shoes had thick, platform soles. The four in front beamed at the camera, not a sullen or pensive face in the bunch. Two of the faces of the men in the back row were partially hidden by the people in front of them.

"There's Keith. I'm sure you picked him out. What's the date on this picture?"

"1983."

"Keith... and there's Heather." Nevada studied the youthful faces. "That one looks like Gregory Keene. And there's Bob Venice."

Chelan grabbed the picture. "Bob Venice? Where?"

"There. The guy in the leather jacket. So what?"

"So we know they all knew each other."

"We know they all stood beside each other once for a photo."

"We know they were all together in the same place—probably an airport—in the early eighties, going somewhere together."

"No, we know they were all at an airport, possibly going to six different places." Nevada thought that Chelan was really stretching here, trying to make something out of nothing.

Actually, she was unclear on why Chelan was still chasing off down these other roads. Not long ago, they'd stood together near a flowerbed and found a bloody weapon. The police were all over it, like flies on honey. What they had here was a case of an obsessed fan whose longing for attention from a certain celebrity boiled over into a murderous madness. Nevada had seen, close up, the contortions that big names had to endure to protect themselves from the tiny percentage of their fans that were wacky. Or maybe Tara Carle was not an obsessed fan but a frustrated fame-seeker, someone who had come up with this sick, twisted means of getting her name in the papers.

"You know, Chelan, I don't know why you're bothering with this stuff. I don't always line up with the police, but on this one, I think they're on the right track. Tara Carle had motive, means and opportunity."

"Maybe for the TV people, but what about Tony Prinelli? And Keith?"

"Unrelated. With Tony, it sounds like a property crime that turned messy. And with Keith... well, he knew a lot of people."

"I talked to Ted Bougie today." Chelan sounded as if she were announcing a royal flush with thirty thousand dollars in chips on the table.

"Where did you run into him?"

"I called and he suggested we meet at the baseball game. He only sat a few minutes—wouldn't answer my questions, just wanted to rave on about how Keith had messed up his life."

"See what I mean? So maybe there is a trail to follow there. Did he say anything else?"

"Wanted to know who else at the station might have known his name, besides Keith." Chelan bent to study the picture again. "I don't know why, though, but this picture is just bugging me. You sure you don't know any of these other people?"

Nevada shook her head. "If I get a brainwave, I'll call you. Where will you be?"

"I have to talk to Heather Alcott."

Ξ

Heather brought Chelan in and motioned to her to one of the kitchen chairs. She looked very tired. "What is it you want me to see?"

"I found this in a magazine from 1983." Chelan pushed the photocopy across the table toward her. "Do you recognize anybody?"

"Yes, I knew a lot of these people. I don't remember this photo being taken, though. Maybe it was a day Keith and the others were on their way to some swim meet... "

The sunlight flowed in through the slats of the window blind and left a pattern on the table. Heather leaned over the picture and pointed to the man standing to her left in the photo.

"This guy is awfully familiar. He's—oh, you know who this is? I remember the story now. You know that TV star, the one from *Urban Battle?*"

Chelan was stunned. "Jason Wheeler? But why would he be in this photo?"

"When he was young, he was an Olympic swimmer. Had a different name then, though. Something Polish. I think he was from Manitoba."

A dozen questions crowded Chelan's mind. She tried to focus, to get the chaos into some kind of order. "So this is Gregory Keene on Keith's other side. Why would he be in the picture?"

"Sports reporter with LV-TV at the time."

"Then Bob Venice behind him. Was he an athlete?"

"No, some kind of volunteer team official. Traveled with them to meets, helped with transportation, accommodation, media requests. I think he was associated with the team because of his past Olympic experience—in 1976, in Montreal, I think."

"Okay, Jason Wheeler, then you, then Keith, then Greg in the front. Anything more on these guys in the back?"

Heather shook her head. She stared at the clock and Chelan could see some sort of struggle on her face, as she tried to make a decision. "You know, Chelan, I didn't think much of the idea when Kevin first approached you to ask for help about this. But you seem to be paying more attention to it than the police are."

Chelan shrugged. "I'm trying. I told Kevin I would try, and I am. But it hasn't been easy, finding out about Keith's life. Especially his past."

"There's a function tomorrow night, a reception, that I'd like you to come to. As my guest." Heather ran a hand through her grey hair. "You'll meet Keith's people there.

20

As she drove back along the beach, Chelan stewed over the possibilities and tried to get them in some sort of order in her mind. "Fanatic fan stalks and kills television personalities" was a good story but it just left too many questions. Number 1, did a woman have enough strength to stab a man or push one from an apartment balcony? Number 2, was she anywhere near the scene of each death? Number 3, why would she want to kill these people, when she was a fan and supposedly adored them and their work?

Next, she had "Enraged source murders untrustworthy reporter". But, Number 4, could that tiny man have pushed anybody off over a high-rise railing? Number 5, why did he come out into the open to meet with her? And Number 6, what did he have against any of the others?

And Number 7, what did Tony Prinelli's death have to do with anything?

But perhaps her mistake was in trying to link everything. So far the only firm connection, that she knew of, was that Keith, Greg and Jason all worked in television, and that all had received fan letters from Tara Carle.

She pulled into the parking lot beside Kits Beach and fumbled for her cell phone. She had Zack Esher on speed dial now, although she usually reached his voice mail. She was speechless for a moment when, this time, he picked up.

GAIL HULNICK

Ξ

Nevada pulled a salad bag out of the refrigerator and threw it into a wooden bowl. Bloody marvelous things, never have to wash vegetables or chop them. She was eating alone again tonight; Owen hadn't turned up at home except to sleep and change clothes since their disagreement earlier in the week.

She didn't know why Chelan had so much trouble attaching to the idea that a disturbed fan had stalked and killed Jason, Greg, and Keith. The world was full of oddballs. She didn't know about this fellow Tony, either. Chelan seemed to think his death invalidated the Tara Carle scenario but Nevada didn't really buy it. So he'd called and left a message, saying he knew the three television guys once upon a time. That didn't prove squat. He might be another one who had difficulty separating the private from the public, thinking he knew people when the only contact he'd ever had was with their images beaming in on his television screen.

She paced around the apartment. Every corner seemed dark and the couches looked like hulking rocks. She hated being here alone—which was weird, because it had been her apartment before she even met Owen. She'd spent many happy evenings here alone; she loved her music, her books, and her movies. So why now, all of a sudden, did it have the atmosphere of the most sterile, bland, cookie-cutter room in an anonymous chain of budget motels? Ain't no sunshine... indeed.

She could just friggin' kick herself. Owen was the best thing that had ever happened to her, to use the vernacular of romance. She knew that, and she'd promised herself she would keep a lid on her tendency to broadcast her opinions without screening them for sarcasm and biting honesty. She knew that he expected to be part of her family and that she owed him the opportunity to check them all out and form

THE LION'S SHARE OF THE AIR TIME

his own conclusions. And she was ready to do that, she really was.

Except when it came to the dear old dad.

Ξ

Zack was answering his telephone promptly this afternoon because it seemed to be the one thing he could do well today. Marla had sent out loud and clear signals that she was rating his performance in the husband department as rotten, and the chief was on his case, too. Couldn't understand why he wasn't making an arrest, after they'd found the knife in Tara Carle's front yard.

Zack had taken his share of criticism over the past year about being too cautious. But ever since he'd gone in, both guns blazing, figuratively speaking, on the Simironne case in the early nineties, he had been very careful to make sure the evidence added up to an unshakeable case. He had turned out to be very wrong on that one and he had had to eat his words for years after that fiasco. Thank God no one had died or lost his freedom. But it had come close, and now his method was to work as hard as necessary to make sure that everything was airtight.

Even if it did piss off Marla and Chief Rupella.

"Esher."

"Oh." She sounded surprised to hear his voice. "Detective Esher, it's Chelan from LV-TV."

"Hello, Ms. Montgomery, how are you. What's up, have you found another piece of evidence?"

She chuckled at his humble attempt at humor. "No. No, I just wanted to touch base with you, find out if there's anything new."

"Not too much."

"What about the knife? We were half expecting to hear about an arrest after that."

"You may, still. We're investigating a couple of other leads."

247

"I have one, too. I had a voice mail message from the fellow who was stabbed in East Vancouver last week. Tony Prinelli. He called me just before he died and said he knew Jason Wheeler, Greg Keene, and Keith. I did a little checking on them and it looks like they might have all met each other in the early eighties."

"Where?"

"Lots of places. They were all competitive swimmers or divers."

Esher grabbed his book and scribbled a note. "Interesting. We'll follow up. I'll want that voice mail tape. You didn't delete it, did you?"

"No, I've still got it. What's the lead you've been pursuing, Detective Esher?"

"I can't say much. It's very preliminary. But we're looking into the financial arrangements of some of the victims. That's about all I can say at this time."

He could tell she didn't think it was much. "What about their financial arrangements? Are we talking about investments? Loans?"

"Disputes."

"Disputes with who?"

"Can't say. You'll have to track it down on your own. All I'll say is take a look at the money. That's a good lead any time. Now, listen, Ms. Montgomery, I have to go. Keep in touch."

Ξ

The next evening Chelan discovered that Heather had invited her to one of the glitziest events of the Vancouver social calendar. The embossed invitation described it as a fundraiser for "the new generation of elite athletes in Vancouver". Unlike most of these functions, this one hadn't been booked into a large hotel ballroom, a community hall or a private club. The largest bling store in town had been set up for a reception, auction and formal dinner, with diners to be placed elbow to elbow with the merchandise. What was the psychology? "You have a lot of jewelry at home and around your neck—surely you can spare a few thousand for a struggling triathlete?" Or perhaps "If you can't quite afford fifty-five thousand for a diamond choker, how about helping out a teenage snowboarder who needs five hundred to pay the rent?" Chelan admired the originality of the choice.

The first thing she noticed when she walked into the Sports Champions reception was the crowd of security guards, mingling with the guests.

"Are the guards here for the jewelry or the celebrities?" she whispered to Heather as they made their way down the receiving line.

"Oh, for the guests, I'm sure," she whispered back. "The jewelry cases are all wired. You'll probably be electrocuted if you so much as fog up the glass."

After they picked up auction paddles and programs, Heather released her into the wild and told her to go mingle. This was an intimidating prospect, as most of the people in the room seemed to know each other. If they didn't, many could announce themselves by their sport and year of Olympic participation and have instant conversational fodder. Chelan soon found, however, that all she had to do was approach a group, stick out a hand and say "Chelan Montgomery, LV-TV" and ask a few questions about the individual's event, and she was in. In half an hour, she met a fencer who went to Montreal in '76, a luger from Nagano in '98, a boxer who went to Sydney, and a swimmer who was in Mexico City in '68.

Heather surfaced at her side. "Are you having a good time?"

"Lot of interesting people here," Chelan commented as she took a glass of wine from a passing waiter.

"No question. Most of these people worked for years and made huge sacrifices for one short period. It was the highlight of their lives," Heather downed about half her glass of white wine.

"You sound kind of bitter."

"No, just experienced. I went through it all with Keith. We were in high school together and I went to all his meets, cheered him on, found other things to do while he was practicing for hours every day. The athletes aren't the only ones who make sacrifices for the sport." She polished off the rest of her wine, then looked across the room. "Is that Tess Cunningham?"

As usual, Tess had not a hair out of place. Tonight she wore some kind of red, feathery thing with a high collar and dangling earrings. Real diamonds, maybe. A look that might be too Vegas or Palm Springs on anyone with less class. When she saw Heather smiling at her, she came over and gave her a hug.

"Nice to see you, Tess," Heather said. "Did you know Tess's family is one of the most consistent backers of amateur sport in the city, Chelan?"

Chelan smiled. She wasn't sure what to say. "Congratulations, Tess"? "That's nice to hear." Or how about "excellent" or "well-done"?

Tess nodded agreeably and changed the subject. "Did you see Conrad Davis?"

"No, I didn't know he was here. Where?" Heather scanned the room.

"Over there, by the sapphires."

Did she actually know which cases held which gemstones? Chelan looked around for Conrad. Yes, there he was, his huge frame taking up the space usually used by two or three people. About six blonde dollies crowded around him, hanging on his every word.

Chelan watched Conrad, fascinated by his ability to hold the attention of so many women at once and wary that he might notice her and come storming across the room to shout or throw her out of the party. She noticed Tess giving Conrad the once-over, too. Maybe Tess had a thing for young athletes. She did seem to watch some of the younger guests quite intently.

THE LION'S SHARE OF THE AIR TIME

At times during the evening, Chelan felt as though she were sitting through an Italian movie with no subtitles—she had no idea what was being said but she felt as though she ought to understand it, just by watching the images. She drained a glass of a delicious B.C. chardonnay and tried to spot someone she knew. Donny Shaw, the sports reporter from Pacific Television, was against the wall, talking to two older men with athletic builds. Excusing herself from Heather, she did an end run past the crowd and joined Donny's group. She stuck out a hand to the taller of the two men.

"Chelan Montgomery, LV-TV," she offered.

"Gordon Darby." The man's salt and pepper hair was styled in a mullet. Had he had it like that since the seventies or was that hairdo coming back?

"Paul Soronski." The man beside him did look familiar and as soon as he mentioned his name, Chelan placed him. Paul Soronski had dazzled the world with his display of athletic genius at the Tokyo Games in 1964.

"Hello, Chelan," Donny put out his own hand in greeting. "We were just talking about LV-TV. And Keith. It's not the same without him here."

"Did Keith come to a lot of these parties?" Chelan was curious. She'd never heard Keith mention this event, although he certainly wasn't shy about talking to some of the other parties he'd been to.

"Never missed a year," Paul informed her.

"Funny. Because he rarely talked about them. Or about anything to do with his sports experience."

"Yup, he was like most of the rest of these people. They're doers, not talkers. Rather let other people, the media and so on, call attention to their past achievements. They just want to get on with what they're doing now." Donny accosted a passing waiter and caught a snack of scallops and mussels. "But when athletes get together with other athletes, that's when you hear the stories."

Chelan speared her own hors d'oeuvre and swallowed.

Heaven on a toothpick. "But I bet you've been a fly on the wall more than once, Donny."

Donny beamed. "Yup, no question."

"Have you covered the Olympic Games?"

"Many times."

"Did you go to L.A. in 1984?"

"You bet. Those were the Games the Soviets boycotted, because the West snubbed the Moscow games in 1980. What? Oh, yup, sure, nice seeing you boys," Donny waved hand and glass as Gordon and Paul took an opportunity to melt away into the crowd. "The Americans cleaned up on the gold medals, and Canada got quite a few, too. And those were the first privately-financed games. Made a profit over 200 million bucks."

"Yeah, didn't everything have a sponsor, right down to the towels the athletes used to mop up the flop-sweat?"

Donny laughed. "Pretty much. Still, you can't argue with success and the Americans did a damn good job." He spent a few seconds searching the room for a sign of another approaching server.

"Did Keith go to the L.A. Games?"

"Not as a competitor. Didn't make the team. Came close though, I think." Donny said. "He may have been there as a spectator, I don't know. The diving competition was pretty exciting. Greg cleaned up—he'd been waiting for his turn to win the gold since '76 in Montreal, when Klaus Dibiasi got his third gold and became the first diver in Olympic history to get three golds in succession in the same event." Clearly, Donny kept track of stats other than his own. "There was a young fellow named Cal Davis expected to bring quite a challenge for the silver or the bronze but it just didn't happen."

"Conrad Davis's older brother."

"Yup." Donny squinted at Chelan. "Didn't know too many people knew that. He was one of the top prospects in the early eighties, but he died very young." Donny reached over and grabbed another handful of appetizers from the

THE LION'S SHARE OF THE AIR TIME

nearest server. She extended her other tray, full of glasses of white wine toward him. "Nope, thanks. Do you think you could bring me a real drink when you get a minute?"

Chelan had about a hundred questions. "Did you know Tony Prinelli?"

"Guy who died recently? Not a diver. A swimming champ, I think."

"Did Keith know Cal Davis very well?"

"Don't know." Donny captured the heavy tumbler full of amber liquid the waiter brought him. "You know who might, though. Billy Cuthbert. Best diving coach this town's ever seen. Maybe the country. You should look him up, if you're interested. He used to coach at UBC but I think he's gone to California."

Chelan found a quiet place behind a potted fern and pulled out her notebook. Had to get all these names down before she forgot them. She saw Tess Cunningham looking at her across the room and waved. Not a bad idea, to be seen by one of the execs, out and about, making contacts.

Ξ

Chelan's credit cards could barely take the strain of a plane trip to L.A., but she felt something driving her to follow up the lead Donny had given her. Going online made everything so easy, too. She didn't have to confront the face of a travel agent who might show her disapproval of Chelan's travel plans. She just had to point and click that mouse, type in a few numbers, and she was booked on an early morning flight that put her in L.A. before coffee break time. The day of reckoning on those credit card statements was weeks or months away.

Like airports the world over, LAX was a vast, moving river of humanity, tributaries joining it from airplanes that had come from the four corners of the globe. Thousands of people poured through its corridors, searching for boarding lounges, restaurants, and stores. The flow narrowed at the baggage counters and again at the security checkpoints, then seeped out into small pools of passengers, waiting for their boarding calls, or into streams of arrivals hunting for a taxi.

Chelan always felt anonymous and autonomous in an airport. She went along with the traveling current and enjoyed the sense that nobody knew her and she didn't know any of these people. She was thousands of miles from home and on her own time.

She heard the distant jangling of a cell phone but paid it no attention for the first three blasts. Then two men passing by stared at the jacket over her arm and a woman raised her eyebrows and pointed. She pulled the phone out of the jacket pocket—sure enough, it was ringing.

"Chelan Montgomery."

"Chelan, where are you?" The voice was muffled, but unmistakably Matthew's.

"In the L.A. airport. I left a message on Elliot's voice mail."

"What are you doing there? You have a pile of research to finish back here."

"Matthew, I've just come off working twelve days in a row. This is my own time. I've taken a little trip." And it's my own business, Chelan added silently.

"Chelan, the usual protocol is to ask for a few days off, then wait until you get authorization."

"Look, I'm sorry if I've done something I wasn't supposed to."

"So this is a trip on your own time, correct?"

"That's right."

"And the station is not paying for this, correct?"

Chelan was aware that she'd become a stone in the stream of other travellers and she started to walk toward the doors. "Correct, Matthew. This is my own time, my own nickel." Several million nickels, she thought. The plastic was just smokin' when she finished buying her discount ticket online. She had only a few hundred dollars of credit room left on her card now. She would just have to cross her

THE LION'S SHARE OF THE AIR TIME

fingers that the car didn't break down.

She didn't know why she didn't tell him that she wanted to meet Keith's former coach and this was the place she had to travel to do it. Somehow, although it felt like the right thing to do, the move did seem a bit too impulsive, when she thought about it. So she was trying not to think about it too much, just do it. Success to the swift, not the hesitant.

The sharp California sunshine flashed through the automatic door as Chelan walked through the airport doors. She blinked a few times, her eyes taking some time to adapt to the strong, natural light. A taxi driver approached, hand extended for Chelan's bag.

She leaned back against the taxi cab seat and watched the traffic go by on the freeway. She had visited L.A. twice before and each time she felt as she imagined a tribesman from some isolated southeast Asian island might feel if he landed in Hong Kong—overwhelmed by thousands of cars, miles of concrete, and too many people. She certainly had been in major cities before, but Los Angeles put every inch of her skin on high alert.

Maybe that was why chain hotels were so successful, the world over. Disorienting as the new environment might be, it was the same white bedspread, the same slightly abstract painting, the same sample sizes of soap and shampoo in the bathrooms. It was comforting, a sort of familiar limbo where you could rest until you ventured out into the big city.

Chelan had no plans to do the tourist thing on this trip. She had no plans at all, except to visit the training pool at the university and to locate Billy Cuthbert. An unpremeditated jaunt like this was not exactly out of character, but it was certainly unusual. But she was on a roll now, with each new name and each new piece of information drawing her closer to an answer about Keith's death. If that meant a three and a half hour flight south and a few more numbers in the 'charges outstanding' column of her credit card statement, it was a small price to pay. It wasn't as if L.A. were on the dark

255

side of the moon from Vancouver.

She could hear her father's voice in her head, questioning her common sense in making such a spontaneous journey, but she banished him and tried to focus on her goal in being there.

Olympic athletes were training in the pool, but the front desk clerk let Chelan watch from the seating area. The tank looked like a perfect piece of turquoise. The tower appeared to Chelan to be a hundred stories high and she marveled at the nerve of the people who launched themselves from the safety of the platform, head first to the surface ten meters below. Not just launched themselves, but contorted themselves into twists and somersaults before straightening out into a beautiful, clean, exquisite entry.

She tried to imagine the state of mind of the divers during an international competition with all of the pressure of the Olympic Games. She had watched closely the faces and body language of many athletes as they brought all of their training, concentration and ambition to the 'make or break point' of an event. Striving to bring yourself to your peak at just the right time. Maintaining your focus, often under incredible distraction and provocation. Caring so much about winning but not so much that you disintegrated if things didn't go well.

But even with her brushes with elite competition, Chelan knew she was not even close to comprehending what Olympic athletes experienced, during the event and later, either on the podium with a medal or just inches away from it. She wondered how many of those who didn't win felt they were going home empty-handed and how many felt they'd already won, just by being there, by making that first dive, or first step, or jump.

A girl in a blue bathing suit climbed the ladder and strode confidently out to the platform. Chelan drew in her breath, inhaling the unmistakable smell of chlorine. For several seconds, the diver held a pose as distinct as an etching on glass, rose to her toes, swung her arms up and in an instant, was in the air. Chelan often found that if she let her own concentration falter while watching divers she would miss the split second of the change from readiness to action. Diving was one of the sports for which the slow-motion technique on television had been destined.

This time she didn't miss it, and she saw the transformation from earthbound human into bird. The girl soared toward the water, picking up speed as she went, reaching for the surface rather than shrinking from it, even though she was moving about forty miles an hour. She plunged into the pool and then emerged, five long seconds later, slower, safer, and with the glorious dive successfully behind her.

Chelan watched six girls practice and then it was the men's turn. She observed for a while, then walked around the lobby, along the corridors to the change rooms, the grounds, and the parking lot outside. She wasn't sure what she was looking for—some kind of revelation, perhaps, although nothing was forthcoming. Still, she wouldn't allow herself to be discouraged. It might not come at this precise moment, but she was certain that he was getting ready to recognize it when it did.

In the meantime, she could go and ask some questions of Billy Cuthbert.

Ξ

The man wasn't hard to locate. It took only four calls to unrelated William Cuthberts in Orange County and in Bakersfield, before she found him in the Oxnard directory. Billy's tone was friendly on the phone, but he wouldn't see her right away. He put her off for a day, inviting Chelan to meet him at a chain restaurant not far from his home the following morning.

She took advantage of the extra hours to see a little more of L.A., taking the Hollywood tour and soaking up some sun at Newport. She contemplated trying to find her way to Malibu, until a taxi driver, grumbling that tourists never understood that L.A. was not one city, it was three hundred cities, pointed out that the famous beach wasn't just around the corner, but was hours away. She enjoyed the chance to chat with locals in the stores and restaurants, and with tourists on the tour bus. It was one of the most stress-free days she'd had since the morning Keith died. It was true, there was something about the light, the sun, and the California beaches that seemed magical, even otherworldly. Twice during the day, though, she'd had the sense that someone held her glance a little too long, stood a little too close, but she shook it off as the infrequent traveler's paranoia.

Chelan figured that Billy Cuthbert had scheduled their meeting for the next day to give himself time to check her out. Even though it cost her an additional hotel night, she thought that was fair enough. She was wary about him, too—she was still considering the possibility that Keith's decision to make a dive his final physical gesture had something to do with signaling information about his killer. A public place seemed like a smart place to meet this stranger, but as soon as she saw Billy, she decided that her fear was misplaced. He was at least eighty.

They settled themselves into a booth by the window. The scene outside might include an ocean and a beach, but the décor, the layout, and the laminated menus inside were the same as those anywhere in North America—no doubt, the same anywhere you went in the world. Billy ordered the cheeseburger and fries, and Chelan the chicken Caesar salad.

Billy dug into his food with obvious pleasure. "Don't get to eat too many of these. Doctor's orders."

He had a full head of white hair and the well-preserved look of a former athlete. Here was a man who looked after himself (well, most of the time, not counting the occasional French fry). He had the aura of kinetic energy that runners have. His handshake was firm, his eyes serene, and his smile easy.

THE LION'S SHARE OF THE AIR TIME

"I'm sure once in a while doesn't hurt." Chelan toyed with her salad and wondered how much small talk was appropriate before getting to the point.

"So what do you want to know about Keith?"

Not much small talk needed at all, apparently. "What he was like back then, in the eighties. What he did to train, how he got ready to compete, if he hung out, what his chances of being a champion were."

"Slim to none, as I recall," Billy laughed. "He was better than most, when it came to diving, but he never quite made it into that tiny percentage at the very top of the heap. But you know…" he took a bite of his burger and Chelan waited while he got ready to speak again, "…even though the media focus on the medal winners, going for the gold and all that, the whole thing is a terrific experience for anybody who even trains to get there. Unless they get hung up on the idea that if you don't come first, you're a loser.

"When I was a coach, I always told my kids that if they were swimming at the provincial or college level, they were winners in anybody's book. They're getting ninety, ninety-five percent of the pie. Now the ones who are absolutely on top of their game on that particular day are gonna go home with a medal. And maybe they might get picked for the national team or make it all the way to the Olympics. But that doesn't mean that any of the other ones might not have taken a medal if it was a different day, you know what I mean?"

Chelan began to speak, and then realized she didn't have to.

"Now, of course, there are always a few with a different philosophy, and they take it all very hard. But so long as they get over it eventually, they'll be okay. But some of them don't." Billy seemed to be lost in thought for a moment. "Ambition, you know, Ms. Montgomery? Ambition is like a snake. Or a chameleon, changing all the time. No—it is like a snake. Quiet, just there. But it bites you, if it gets stirred up for the wrong reason.

He sipped at his coffee. "No, that's not really what I'm trying to say. Ambition, we all try to motivate our kids to show some. It's what builds bridges, cures diseases, discovers new worlds. It's the juice. But it's also poison, sometimes. It's like that Japanese fish, you know? The one that's a rare delicacy, an amazing meal, but if the chef doesn't prepare it just right, the diner dies." Billy looked over his cheeseburger, and then dug into it once again.

"Did Keith have a good attitude?"

Billy brightened. "Keith? Oh yeah, he liked to win, did his best—but he was a good loser, too. He was one who was there for the experience, did his best, had a party, lived in the moment. He knew this was a once-in-a-lifetime thing. And boy, did he have a good time. He met girls from all over the country." Billy dug into the fries and Chelan seized the moment.

"But were you okay with all of this, as his coach? Didn't you want them training all day, in bed by nine, eating exactly the right diet?"

"Oh, yeah, of course. We had them paced right up to event time. Pushed every one of 'em to reach their potential. Don't forget they trained for months, trying to reach their peak. For each athlete, you do something a little bit different. In Keith's case, the best thing was to let him treat the experience like an adventure. In another kid's case, it would be to applaud his decision to be a hermit for two weeks. There's no cookie-cutter answer."

"Did you know Cal Davis?"

"I did. Now there's a sad case." Chelan watched Billy's face closely for any sign of wariness or withdrawal but there was none. "Promising kid. Everybody expected him to do really well. We'd seen him at the Worlds and he was fantastic. There was a bit of controversy about him, some people thought he was a shoo-in for the team, others thought there were better divers and that his results that one year were just a fluke. Some stuff was going on behind the scenes... I didn't really know the details. It turned out to be

THE LION'S SHARE OF THE AIR TIME

all irrelevant anyways, when he died."

"He died in a car accident, didn't he?"

"Hit and run. Just tragic."

Chelan reached into her briefcase and pulled out the file folder containing the copy of the photo. "Do you recognize these people?"

Billy wiped his hands off on his napkin, and then reached into his shirt pocket for a pair of reading glasses. Once they were carefully lodged on his nose, he picked up the page and stared at it, pointing at each of the faces. "Gregory Keene. Nose poked into everything. Bob Venice. Much younger. There's Milos from Winnipeg—I should say, Jason. Jason, the actor now. Or was..." Billy's face darkened. "Another tragedy. Now there's Keith's wife... do you know her? Then Keith, Tony, Tony's wife."

Tony's wife. "That's terrific, Mr. Cuthbert. I had quite a few of them identified, but nobody knew who this other woman was."

"Call me Billy, please." He squinted at the picture. "Too bad these fellows' faces in the back are covered up."

"Do you recall Tony's wife's name?"

"It's terrible when your memory starts to go, although they say you can watch all your favorite movies and read your favorite books all over again and enjoy them as if they're brand new. I didn't know her very well, so maybe it's not surprising I don't remember... still, she was quite a character, had Tony on a really tight leash... I should be able to... Angela! Angela Prinelli, that was her." Billy was pleased with himself.

Chelan got out her notebook and took down the name. Something was not right, though. She flipped back through the pages of notes she'd taken in this book since Keith's death. "I thought Tony Prinelli's wife's name is Yvonne."

Billy was confused for a second, but stuck by his answer. "No, Angela. At least it was when I knew her. Maybe she changed it? No, I bet I know what it is. Divorced. He probably divorced the Angela and married an Yvonne."

261

GAIL HULNICK

"Is she still in Vancouver? Angela, I mean."

"No idea."

"Never mind, I'll find her. Mr. Cuthbert, you've been a tremendous help." Chelan tried to take back the photograph, but Billy held on to it."

"Come on now, it's Billy," he said. "Let me just take another look at that." He stretched his arms out to peer at the photo, then took off his reading glasses and held it up close to his face. "In the back row here. These fellows you can hardly see. This one is Tony, beside Bob Venice. Over here, on the far left, that's Cal Davis."

Chelan strained to see the face, beating back the urge to snatch the photocopy from Billy.

"And over here, see, there's another man, in between Tony and Bob, in behind them. I think it might be... yeah, look at the boots... that's Blair Cunningham."

"Blair Cunningham? Related to Tess Cunningham?"

"Husband." Billy put down the photo and applied himself to the last of his French fries. "But that was later, not at the time I was training him. He was extremely talented, Blair Cunningham. The only one who could hold a candle to Cal Davis, in my opinion. Didn't live up to his early promise though. Had the physical skills but not the desire."

An hour later, as they strolled through the parking lot toward Billy's aged Buick and Chelan's rented two-door, they were so busy talking that at first, they didn't notice the low grumble of the shiny black sports car that nosed up behind them. Chelan thought she heard a helicopter and glanced upward, but there was nothing in the sky. Then she turned and saw the black car, creeping along behind her and Billy Cuthbert. She stopped and the car pulled up to within inches of his pant leg.

The man in the driver's seat was wearing sunglasses that covered fifty percent of his face. Big man, dark suit, white shirt, thin tie — could be anyone, from anywhere. Billy backed away to a spot between two parked cars. Chelan

THE LION'S SHARE OF THE AIR TIME

marched over to driver's window and tapped on it. The man turned, pointed his finger at Chelan and pretended to shoot.

Chelan took a step back from the window. The driver burned rubber as he sped away.

"What was that all about?" Billy walked out from his haven.

"You got any enemies, Billy?" Chelan squinted at the disappearing car in a futile effort to read the license plate. "No? Me neither." She thought about chasing after the car, to try to get a better look, but gave it up as useless. Besides, her heart was pounding so hard she doubted she could walk a hundred yards, let alone run. "Must be just a case of mistaken identity."

Ξ

Throughout the entire flight back to Vancouver, Chelan barely sat still in her seat. If she could have willed the giant machine to move faster, she would have. She was eager to share her findings with Nevada and find out more about Blair Cunningham, and eager to try to talk to Conrad Davis about his brother's athletic career and untimely death.

She arrived late, the last flight to land at Vancouver International before the brief interlude that marked the end of one day and the beginning of the next. It was nearly one a.m. when she trudged through the corridors, got her passport checked, then marched past the dozens of weary people waiting at the baggage carousel. She had only her carry on bag—no luggage to delay her and no one waiting on the other side of the opaque sliding glass doors that officially marked the entrance gate to Canada.

It didn't matter, though, because she had something better than a welcoming committee. She had facts.

Ξ

Chelan was back in the newsroom only five minutes

when Elliot sent her to Matthew's office.

"I hope your trip to California was worth it." Matthew put down the document he was reading and motioned her to a chair.

She assumed he meant the price of the ticket and the hotel. "Yes, it was a bit pricey, but… yeah, it was worth it."

"Chelan, this isn't easy for me to say. It never is. I'm sorry, but you don't have a job here anymore."

This had to be a movie, or a dream, or something. "What do you mean?"

"We have to let you go."

"But why? Because I took a few days off?"

"No, of course not. Although you might have handled that a bit differently—given us a bit more notice, for example. Talked to a human being, instead of voice mail." Matthew's eyes didn't look away from hers; there was a bit of kindness in them.

"Why then?"

"We're facing some tough economic decisions here. We're under heavy pressure to bring the ratings up and we have to put more reporters on the air. We're going to be cutting back on the research budget."

"But I'm trained as a reporter. You've been using me as a researcher, but I could do much more on-air work."

"We're going for names that are already known. We'll be making a few changes. Your situation is just one of them."

"Who else is going?"

"I really don't care to discuss that at this time." Small beads of sweat glistened on Matthew's forehead. "On second thought, I guess you'll hear soon enough. Just you for now. Amanda is under discussion."

"What about Leonard? He's new."

"No, he's management. The union seniority rules don't apply to him." Matthew shuffled a few pieces of paper, then stood up, handing her a business card. "You need to go and see Dennis in human resources, to fill out some forms and

THE LION'S SHARE OF THE AIR TIME

get your final check. Good luck, Chelan. I am sorry to have to do this, and I wish you good luck."

21

The light shone through the spaces between the trees and bushes, reflecting off the droplets of moisture still left from the morning dew. A spider web glistened like something made of tiny strands of crystal. Green moss hugged the trees and the branches of the ancient firs interlaced overhead in a sort of canopy. You'd swear that at any moment some sort of magical creature might appear.

Usually, hiking in the Seymour Forest sharpened every sense that Chelan had. But today she trudged along in a sort of stupor. Since the moment that Matthew had told her she was no longer part of LV-TV she was conscious of nothing but her own insides—her gut, which rocked and roiled with nausea and threatened to heave at any moment, and her brain, which persisted in shooting forth arguments and evidence in favor of her continued presence in the newsroom. All the things she should have said to Matthew, all of the dynamic, persuasive facts that would have shown him that he was making a mistake. Instead, she'd sat there like a dummy.

At the very least, if she couldn't come up with a zinger to make him reverse the decision, she should have been able to say something that showed him she already had her eye on her next job, a better job. Something to save face.

Chelan turned her phones off for two days. She came

THE LION'S SHARE OF THE AIR TIME

home, went into her room, and closed the door. Avoiding Layla was easy to do, and nobody from LV-TV had turned up at her place. Maybe there were phone messages, but if you didn't check for them, then they didn't exist and didn't have to be answered.

After two days of hiding under her quilt, she wanted to get out for some air. First the beach and now the mountain. She kept her head down and talked to no one. She probably could have gone on for quite a few more days without human contact any closer than ten feet if it weren't that the memory of her conversation with Billy Cuthbert about the other woman in the photograph repeatedly interrupted her mental replay of the meeting with Matthew. Her curiosity about Tony Prinelli's former wife finally cut in on her self-pity and left it without a partner.

Chelan's first effort to find Angela Prinelli took her to the telephone book, but there were no easy answers there. Prinelli was one of the more common names in Vancouver, and there were dozens. Chelan conscientiously called them all, but none had an Angela.

She was stuck for about half a day—twelve hours that saw her eating a lot of ice cream and halfheartedly trying to write a résumé. She didn't exactly have deep pockets and finding a new job ought to be top of her 'to do' list, but somehow finding Keith's killer seemed to take priority.

As she stood in the gelato store and tried to pick a flavor, she had an idea. Angela Prinelli might not be listed but Yvonne Prinelli was. She decided to go rather than phone. It's harder for people to close a door in your face than to hang up on you.

She needn't have worried about an unfriendly welcome. Yvonne was happy to have someone in who wanted to talk about Tony. She plied Chelan with biscotti and questions about her eating habits and marital status. She had nice nephews for her to meet and lasagna she could cook for her. She told stories about Tony's outstanding qualities as a husband and father, her round, little face beaming at her

267

memories of him. There really was no opportune moment for Chelan to raise the subject of an ex-wife, so she just ploughed in, hoping she wasn't kicking up too much dirt.

"Angela." The word lowered the temperature in the room about forty degrees. Yvonne's smile disappeared.

"I was hoping you could tell me where to find her." Chelan squirmed in the depths of the well-stuffed couch.

"Why?"

"Well, she's… I'm trying to find out some answers about Tony's death…"

"She won't be able to help. She knows nothing. She is a monster." Yvonne struggled to her feet and took the platter of cookies from the coffee table. Chelan followed her into the kitchen.

"Mrs. Prinelli, I think what's at stake here is so huge we have to put aside our personal feelings if they get in the way of finding Tony's killer." Her back was turned to Chelan but she saw her shoulders relax. She shook slightly for a moment—sobbing?—then turned and nodded.

"You are right, of course. We have to find Tony's killer, we owe him that. Even if it means having anything to do with that witch."

"Why do you hate her so much?"

"She treated Tony very badly—when they were married and after he left her. She called here, waited for him after work sometimes. It only stopped when our first baby was born. Then she finally gave up." Mrs. Prinelli started eating cookies, shoving them into her mouth mechanically.

"I couldn't find her in the phone book."

"Her name is different now. She remarried about five years ago. She is Angela Venice Kade now."

Ξ

The small seafood bistro in Yaletown was a huge hit with the artsy crowd and Chelan could see why. Atmosphere, good music, and the intoxicating scent of fresh food prepared by a brilliant chef. For the first half hour, Chelan didn't mind waiting, but after the second, she was becoming a little less forgiving. How much longer would she have to wait for Angela?

Only another few more minutes as it turned out. But she didn't show up, as arranged. The waiter brought a phone over to Chelan.

"Ms. Montgomery?" Chelan imagined she could hear just a touch of a Mediterranean accent. "Would you mind coming up to the house? I have a few things happening this morning and I just can't make it down the hill." She hung up without waiting for an answer.

As she drove the twisting roads of West Vancouver, she wondered why Angela assumed she knew the address and how to find the house. Maybe she had decided that Chelan should figure it out for herself and that if she couldn't, she didn't deserve the meeting that was being granted. Angela's address wasn't that difficult to find, but the lack of assistance offered set off a warning bell.

Certainly Chelan's first impression of her bore out her speculation. Angela was dressed in some sort of satin, tight-fitting jacket over black leather pants, with shiny gold spike heels on her feet. She opened the door, looked Chelan over, then rolled her eyes as if disappointed, did a 180° turn, and disappeared into the house. What, was she supposed to follow her? Wait there? An annoyed voice from the depths of the house answered her question.

"Come in if you're coming. Don't just stand there and let the cold air in."

What cold air? It was June. Chelan shut the heavy mahogany door and looked around the foyer. Nice place. The entranceway alone was bigger than her apartment. The art on the walls was impressive—huge canvases lit museum-style. Somebody liked horses.

Her footsteps echoed on the marble as she walked toward the open French doors at the end of the hall. She had no idea where Angela was but it seemed as good a place as any to look.

"Come in, Ms. Montgomery. I don't have all day." She was sitting on a couch beside the fireplace. A small, yappy white dog sat on her lap and bared its teeth.

"Don't mind Milan, she doesn't bite. Just sit in that chair there and ask your questions." She flipped through pages on a magazine beside her. Chelan obeyed.

"I understand you were once married to Tony Prinelli."

"That's not a question, it's a statement. Why waste our time telling me things I already know. Get to the point, Ms. Montgomery." She didn't look up as she turned the pages of the home décor section.

"I'm looking into the circumstances around Mr. Prinelli's death and a few other... events... that we think may be linked."

"Are you doing a story on Tony's death?"

She could just say she was getting ready to do one. No need for Angela to know that she was working freelance these days. "I'm doing some preliminary research."

A telephone rang somewhere to the west and a maid in a T-shirt and jeans appeared and handed Angela the receiver.

"Hello? ...You need what? Where?" She sighed in annoyance. "Yes, alright. I'll have it sent."

Angela tossed the phone onto the couch cushion and looked up to make eye contact with Chelan for the first time. "Can you believe it? That was my aunt. They were here visiting from Montreal last week. Now they're in Denver and she tells me she left her heart medication in my guest bathroom. I'm supposed to send it right away."

She shook her head in disbelief, then went back to examining the pages of her magazine. Apparently, the aunt wouldn't be receiving her medicine on any kind of urgent basis.

"So you're doing preliminary research on Tony," Angela finished the last page of her magazine and gave her full attention to Chelan.

This had already taken far more time than necessary

and Chelan felt the need to get out of that house. Cut to the chase. "I've found a link between Tony and several other men killed in the past few months. Tony, Gregory Keene, Keith Papineau, Jason Wheeler—they were all associated with elite amateur sports in Vancouver in the early eighties. Swimming and diving—athletes."

Angela smiled, her tanned, lifted face expressing nostalgia. "Except for Greg Keene. He was a junior sports reporter." She focused on Chelan. "I'll bet you were still a baby then."

"I understand from your name that you were once married to Bob Venice."

Angela sighed. "Tony was my first husband, Bob my second, and Mackenzie Kade is my third. I still use the name Venice because it opens doors and Mackenzie doesn't mind. People aren't sure whether I'm an ex-wife or a family member. Either way, it implies money."

"Did you go with Tony to a lot of the swimming meets?"

"Yes, I was always there. It's when I met Bob, too, actually. We had some chemistry, but we were both married to other people at the time, so we just kind of circled each other, you know? Then in '84 sometime, he called me up and we got together a few times. It was nothing serious, but Tony found out and dumped me."

"Yvonne Prinelli told me you didn't let go of Tony easily."

"She's a cow. He could have done much better, but…"Angela stared at Chelan for a few seconds. "Yeah, alright, yeah. I was sad to see him go. But then Bob's marriage ended and he wanted to get together, so… But I always cared about Tony. I even asked Bob to invest some money in Tony's little mechanic business."

"How long were you married to Bob?"

"Five years. Got this house, a car, and an allowance for life."

"Even though you've remarried?"

"Yes, well, that's under discussion."

Angela glanced down at her watch; her attention seemed to be wandering and Chelan knew she probably had only a few more minutes left. Time to sprint.

"When you were with Tony, did these four people spend a lot of time together? Was there anything that might have linked them, some event, or person?"

Angela leaned forward to speak in a hushed tone, although there was no one else in the room to hear them. "Well, they all knew Bob."

"Is that significant?"

Angela dropped her tone again. "People are dying, aren't they?"

"Do you think Bob is capable of murder?"

"Bob is capable of doing anything to protect his financial position and his reputation."

The dog stood up and started to circle on Angela's knee and Chelan held her breath. She didn't want any distractions derailing Angela's train of recollections. "What was he like as a husband?"

"Unfaithful. But generous."

"Unfaithful?"

"He always had girlfriends. I didn't mind that much," Angela fondled the dog's ears. "The fire went out pretty fast. So he had his friends and I had mine. And he always had Tess. But of course, he didn't really have Tess. She was married."

"Tess?"

"Tess Cunningham, you know? Your boss?" Angela picked up a glass of something and sipped at it. "You know, Chelan, your looks might take you somewhere, but you're going to have to pick up the pace in a few other areas. Tess's husband committed suicide ten years ago did you know about that? Bob grabbed her, right afterward. I thought he wanted to marry her, but she wouldn't bite. Too busy building her career to spend any time building up some guy's ego."

THE LION'S SHARE OF THE AIR TIME

"What did her husband... Mr. Cunningham?...What did he do?"

"He climbed to the top of a transportation company. President and CEO. Put a gun to his head in '94, I heard it was because of financial problems. Tess was in a tailspin for a while, then she leveled out and started to build herself a place in the broadcasting scene in this town. Without much help from her very well-connected family members. I heard she's in line for the president's spot at LV-TV, if she can bring the ratings up a bit.

"But we're a long way off-topic, aren't we? None of this has anything to do with Tony. Is the station planning to do a background piece on his life? He was very well-known in his time, you know. I'd be happy to cooperate with LV-TV."

Chelan stood up. "We'll certainly let you know if we need anything further." She started to back out of the room as if she were in the presence of the King of Siam. Or maybe she just instinctively felt that the safest way to go was to keep her eyes on Angela until she was clear of the room.

Ξ

Chelan thought the logical stop to make next was Zack Esher's office. She hadn't talked with him since she'd been fired and Esher had asked her to keep in touch. She found him behind a desk piled a foot high with files.

Esher listened patiently while Chelan detailed all of her movements over the past days.

"You've been busy," he commented.

Chelan sipped at the coffee sludge Esher handed her. "Is any of it useful?"

"Might be. Certainly helps to know about all of the connections among these people. But we're going really carefully with this. We're working on analyzing some of the physical evidence, hoping that gives us some leads."

"What about talking to Bob Venice? If Keith was investigating him for a story, he might have reason to want

273

Keith dead."

"Oh, he's your prime suspect now, is he?" Esher sucked in his cheeks — was he trying not to laugh? "I thought it was Conrad Davis. Or Ted Bougie."

"I still think they're worth keeping an eye on."

"You watch too much TV."

"And this Blair Cunningham is interesting, don't you think? A transportation company president, successful, well-off, then kills himself. And he was an elite swimmer in the eighties, too." Chelan had a thought that slowed her down. She stared at a poster on the wall, not really focusing on it. Esher waited "Maybe he was the first one of this series of killings. Maybe he was the first target."

"Look, Chelan, I appreciate your interest and I'm sure Keith would, too. Just don't get carried away, all right? Stay in touch with me, let me know if you hear anything. And I'll keep you informed, too. But don't take things into your own hands. You're not trained for it."

"Oh, I know, believe me, I know, Detective Esher. I don't really have a clue what I'm doing here. But it's okay if I just meet a few more people, just ask a few questions, isn't it?"

Esher shook his head and sighed. Would it make any difference if he said no?

22

Chelan's little Mini strained to keep up as she tried to follow the dark green Jaguar along the twisting road to Whistler. The highway was virtually free of traffic on a Thursday morning and Bob Venice was making the most of it. His car leaped from curve to curve, and the brake lights didn't flash red even once between Horseshoe Bay and M Creek. He left Chelan in his dust somewhere near Lions Bay and she could only imagine that he hugged the center line, at a steady eighty clicks an hour, all the way to Whistler.

Her original idea was to follow him throughout the day. She waited outside his southwest Marine Drive home at the crack of dawn, and sure enough, shortly after six, the gates opened and he zoomed out into the street, setting a blazing pace at the first turn of the tire. The traffic on Granville Street gave Chelan's small vehicle an advantage, as she deked in and out, finding openings in the lanes that no SUV or even mid-sized car could exploit. She kept Bob in view all the way through downtown, across the bridge and up Taylor Way to Highway One on the North Shore. She managed to keep up through West Vancouver, around the corner past the ferry terminal at Horseshoe Bay, and through the first few turns of the Squamish Highway, but then she lost him.

Good thing she had a full tank of gas, anyway. She would locate him somehow, once she got to Whistler. At least, that's where she assumed he was going. It was possible, she supposed, that he was planning to stop for some backpacking at Alice Lake. Or maybe going to watch the eagles at Brackendale.

As if. In a suit, roaring out of his driveway at six a.m., chewing up the highway? Probably a breakfast business meeting in one of the luxury hotel dining rooms. Or maybe a round of golf. But in a business suit? He must be planning to change. Maybe a breakfast meeting, then changing clothes, then a round of golf.

Angela had told her that he kept a second home at Whistler. Should be a simple matter of finding a phone book. Chelan concentrated on her driving, as the road snaked around the cliffs. The view was glorious, with the waters of Howe Sound the color of cobalt and the hills of the islands covered in evergreen. She glanced over as often as she dared, each time for a micro-second. This road couldn't be taken for granted.

Neither could a wealthy man's interest in privacy. The telephone book had no listing for B. Venice. But, so what? She had a car, a tank of gas, and all the time in the world. No job she was expected to be present for. No boss who cared how she spent her day.

Chelan jerked her attention back to the moment. It was no time to wallow in self-pity or to start plotting her comeback. Most of the articles she'd read and the life story TV shows she'd watched about successful people noted their tremendous ability to stay focused, to set goals, and reach them. She had to stop thinking about herself and try to think about Keith, and about finding Bob Venice.

Of all the places in the world to search for someone, Whistler had to be one of the best. Chelan loved the air in Vancouver, a subtle blend of ocean salt and pine, but the air in Whistler was pine layered with mountain wildflowers, and topped with a hint of the scent of snow, even in June. It was famous as winter sports nirvana, but Chelan liked it even better in the summer.

Whistler was like a hippie who'd won the lottery. In the

mid sixties, she'd been told, it was just a few cabins. Everybody knew everybody. By the 21st century, the average house price was over two million and you could meet people from any corner of the globe, any day of the week. But even though every golf course had every luxurious touch, almost every hotel had every multi-star amenity, and every patio restaurant hosted people in thousand-dollar ski and board clothes, the place still had a funky undercurrent.

Chelan decided to start her search for Bob at the south end and work her way north. She turned at the Creekside gondola base and slowly drove through the parking lot, looking for his car. She cruised the streets of the nearest neighborhood, checking out every driveway.

She doubted she'd spot him here. It was much more likely that he was heading for one of the restaurants in the village. She parked the Mini in one of the lots and walked into the village. The patios were crowded, even though it was still morning. She strolled past every one, straining her eyes to pick out his silver hair or his broad shoulders. She wished she knew what he was wearing.

The buzz in the Longhorn Pub was not quite as hearty as during ski season, but it was close. Chelan cased the dozen or so patrons having a late lunch or an early Happy Hour— no sign of Venice. She trudged from hotel to hotel in the village, checking out each bar and restaurant. She even tried the souvenir and T-shirt shops, just in case. Nada.

Chelan decided to follow the village trail, a paved path that wended through the valley and made the Whistler/Blackcomb area into a walkers' paradise. As she hiked along in the heat of the June afternoon, she seriously contemplated offering one of the kids going by on the River of Golden Dreams five dollars for his inner tube.

The trail carried on past one of the golf courses and she walked into the parking lot. Finding him here was probably a good bet.

Should have staked the farm. There he was, standing behind the open trunk of the Jag, pulling out a set of golf clubs. She knew she should go bounding up to him, like a retriever that had found its quarry, but she held back. What should she say? What if he refused to talk to her?

What if he did? It wouldn't be the end of the world. Really, how could you be an investigative journalist if you gave in to attacks of shyness or self-doubt?

She shook off her hesitation and forged ahead. As she approached, he noticed her and straightened up, his dark eyes sizing her up and his mouth twisting into an expression she couldn't read. She wiped the perspiration from her forehead with the back of her hand, then plastered on the brightest smile she had and stepped forward with what she hoped was confidence. As she came within arms' length of him, she realized how tall he was. She hadn't picked up on that the previous times she'd seen him, across a crowded room at the funeral and the banquet, or seated at his desk in his office.

Tall and large. His forearms were unusually sturdy and his chest, under his pale blue golf shirt, showed the effects of regular weight training.

"Mr. Venice?"

He didn't recognize her. Or pretended not to.

"I'm Chelan Montgomery. We met a while ago in your office."

"From LV-TV." He turned and started to arrange his clubs in the bag, checking the pockets for balls and tees.

After thirty seconds of silence, Chelan got his point. The conversation was over, from his side. But she hadn't driven all this way to be brushed off so easily, especially now that she'd cranked up her courage high enough to actually approach him.

"Mr. Venice, I'm still looking into Keith Papineau's death and I — "

"If you want to talk to me, you'll have to come out on the course. I have a tee time at eleven." He fitted the golf bag to the cart and gave her a charming, almost flirtatious smile. "You can caddy."

THE LION'S SHARE OF THE AIR TIME

A weird turn of events. Still, whatever worked. Chelan grabbed the handle and strode along behind him, pulling the cart with its black and tan leather bag full of clubs.

When they reached the first tee, he pulled a driver from the bag and hit one straight down the fairway. He shielded his eyes from the sun with his hand, watching the ball fly several hundred yards through the air. At least, Chelan supposed he was watching the ball — she couldn't see it at all. Making a sound that was impossible to identify as either satisfied or annoyed, Bob stuffed the wood back into the bag and grabbed the cart handle. He marched off toward the green and Chelan almost had to run to keep up.

By the time they reached the hole, she was puffing. She was pretty sure she was in good shape, so it had to be the heat. He'd walked the whole way about fifteen feet ahead of her and she couldn't talk to him, unless she wanted to shout her questions at his back. When they reached the green, she began a question and he shook his head shortly, then took his time choosing a club and bending over the ball to make a putt. When did people talk during a game of golf?

He noted his score on some sort of electronic device, then set off for the second tee, drawing her along behind him, farther into the rolling green hills of the golf course. She looked around as she did a sort of shuffle-jog to keep up with him. There were no other people anywhere that she could see. Nobody on the other greens, nobody driving motorized carts along the paved paths. If she squinted, she thought she could make out another human a half mile away up on the bluff, on the patio of one of the mansions lining the course. But otherwise, it seemed, it was just her and Bob.

She had a powerful urge to dash for the shrubs and trees at the edges of this open field and take cover. The lush panorama stretched around her on all sides for what seemed like miles and when she glanced up at the sky, it expanded to a massive, vacant space. The sharp sunlight glinted into her eyes, reflecting off something she couldn't see. She was exposed.

She wanted to get this over with. "Mr. Venice, I have to ask you something. Please stop."

He looked at her as if she were insane. "Stop? Now?"

"Yes, please, just for a moment." She inhaled deeply to catch her breath. "I don't want to walk around the entire course with you. I mean, I could, I guess, but you'd probably enjoy your game more if I weren't here, and what I have to ask won't take more than a few moments." He said nothing and she had to take that as a 'yes'. "I know that you loaned Keith a lot of money, but what I don't know is why."

"It's in the past, Ms. Montgomery. Just drop it."

"Was he paying you back?"

"Everybody I lend money pays me back, Ms. Montgomery. Everybody has to pay their debts."

"Or what, Mr. Venice?"

The silence sat between them for several moments and it was clear he wasn't going to move it.

"I found a picture, Mr. Venice. From the eighties. It shows a bunch of people at the airport, going to a swim meet, I think. You, Jason Wheeler, Greg Keene, Keith, Keith's wife, Tony Prinelli, Tony's wife."

"Yeah, what of it?"

"I think somehow there's a link between Keith's death and all these people." She stared into his face to get a read on his reaction, but his sunglasses made it impossible. "What do you think? Is there anything you can tell me about that time, or those people, that might be significant?"

He was staring over her shoulder, off into the distance, and she had to resist the urge to turn around to see if there was something there. "Ms. Montgomery, all of this is really none of your business. You are not a police investigator. You do not work at LV-TV anymore."

Who had told him that? Chelan was not high profile at the station. Her departure hadn't been reported in any of the 'comings and goings' columns in the newspapers or on the station's website and she doubted whether it had even caused comment at the media club.

"I invested with Keith and with Jason and Greg. We won a little, lost a little. That's the way it goes." Bob's head swiveled, just slightly, as he looked at everything in the vicinity except her.

"What about Tony Prinelli? Did you ever do any investing with him? Or was Angela the main thing you had in common?"

He glared at her and she knew she'd crossed a line. Where had that question come from? Impulsiveness was a good thing when you discovered a fabulous handbag, bought it without checking the price, and loved it forever after. It was not so good when you were alone in a vast, manicured park with a man who didn't want to answer any questions, let alone pushy ones.

Nonetheless, she'd bet the farm now, might as well throw in the horse and wagon. "Blair Cunningham, Mr. Venice. Did you know him in the early eighties, too?"

"Back off, Ms. Montgomery. This interview is over." Bob turned and set off toward the second tee.

Ξ

Chelan opened the door on her small apartment and warm air rushed out to greet her. Layla must be away—there was no way anybody could live without windows open in this heat. She tossed her bag on the couch and marched from kitchen to bedroom to bathroom, opening every window. When she finished her circuit, in the living room, she unlocked the balcony door, opened it, and stepped out onto the tiny outdoor space. No breeze. It was days like this that made you wonder why you'd never gone to the landlord and begged him to put in air conditioning. Of course, you'd get nowhere because everybody believes that Vancouver doesn't get any sizzling heat.

Beads of sweat were popping out on Chelan's upper lip. She went to the fridge and opened the door, not expecting to see much of anything. Lo and behold, cold cans of beer lined up in impressive rows on the first and second shelf. She grabbed one and held its chilly side against her face.

Chelan picked up the telephone and punched in Nevada's number. Nothing but voice mail, at home, work and on the cell. She was sitting on the couch, gazing at a blank sheet of paper and wondering what to do next, when Layla came through the door.

"Hey, I see you found the beer." Layla dropped her designer-inspired purse on the counter and captured a can from the fridge.

"Thank you, thank you. It must be about a hundred degrees in here."

"I know." Layla dropped into the only living room chair. Interesting how she could make even drinking a beer seem elegant, Chelan thought.

"What have you been up to?" Small talk wasn't usually part of their deal—in fact, they were rarely in the same room at the same time. But Layla, who usually just passed through, then closed her bedroom door behind her, clearly was showing signs of friendliness. And in Chelan's current state of unemployment, keeping things running smoothly with the roommate was a high priority. Layla was leaning back against the chair, eyes closed, sipping her beer, but her presence seemed to indicate a desire for conversation. Chelan tried again. "Are you just coming in from work?"

"Yeah, we had a financial report that had to go out before the markets open tomorrow morning. The numbers were all screwed up and we had to wait around for the company to answer some questions before we could publish. Then, somebody heard the news about Tess Cunningham on the radio and the whole place stopped for ten minutes while everybody gossiped about that."

"What news about Tess Cunningham?" Chelan pulled herself out of the lounging position on the couch.

"Don't you know?"

She resisted the urge to jump up and give Layla a shake. "No."

THE LION'S SHARE OF THE AIR TIME

"You know, it's amazing. I've gone my whole life without knowing anybody who had anything newsworthy happen to them. Anybody I know personally, I mean. You know. I see stuff in the newspapers all the time about crimes and stuff, but nobody I know. Then in the space of about six weeks, I know tons of people. Jason Wheeler... well, I don't actually know him but it's like I do, seeing him on TV all the time and I see the *Urban Battle* trailers parked around Georgia Street all the time. Gregory Keene—I met him that time you took me to the LV-TV Open House. Keith Papineau, I met that time he dropped you off when the car was in the shop. And now Tess Cunningham. Not that I actually know her, personally, but you do and I room with you, so— "

Chelan's teeth were clenched. "What happened to Tess Cunningham?"

"Where have you been, on Mars?"

"I was driving around. I didn't have the radio on. Well, I did, but I wasn't listening to news." This was stupid—she was imitating Layla's way of drifting off the point, just the way some people can't stop themselves from mimicking others when they hear an accent not their own.

Layla ran a hand through her burgundy hair, leaned forward and gazed into Chelan's eyes. "Tess Cunningham has disappeared."

"Get outa town."

"No, really. Disappeared. Off the face of the earth. Gone. She didn't show up at work this morning. She was out for dinner last night and that's the last time anybody saw her."

Chelan rested her head against the back of the couch and tried to take this in. Layla left the room and Chelan had a brief second of hope that she would now get a little solitude and time for processing this horrendous information. But her roommate returned immediately, two cold beers in hand.

"You want another brew? Oh, you're not finished that

one yet." She flopped back down on the couch. "It's freaky, isn't it? All those other TV people and now her. Of course, they've got that nutbar fan in custody, so maybe the situations aren't connected at all. Maybe she's just gone away, taken a fabulous cruise or something, and she forgot to leave anybody her numbers. Or she might have had an accident or have amnesia or something. There was that man who disappeared in New York last year, do you remember reading about it in the papers? He wandered for about six months, then suddenly remembered who he was. Maybe that'll happen to her." Layla's eyes flashed. "Or maybe she's been kidnapped by somebody. If that's the case, we'll probably hear about some ransom demands or something, soon."

Chelan's cell phone rang and she grabbed it. Just in time. She needed to get out.

Ξ

Nevada had visited Owen many times before at the hospital and she was able to sail past the receptionist with a wave and a smile. She didn't want her arrival announced in advance to him; she wasn't sure how he'd receive it. She had tried calling him, numerous times, and he hadn't returned even one message. One part of her thought she should just leave things alone for now and let him come around, but another part of her had to find out how long he intended to punish her. She poked her head into the doctors' lounge—it was empty. Nobody lounging today.

The cafeteria was full and at first, she couldn't see him, sitting across the room with a table full of other white-coated types. Then, almost like some bad movie, the noise level in the room seemed to drop and she spotted him. He was looking at her, his face unreadable.

She forced herself into forward motion, weaving between the tables until she stood beside him.

"Hi."

THE LION'S SHARE OF THE AIR TIME

He nodded, then directed his attention back to his sub sandwich.

She looked around the table, nodding and nervously smiling at the others. "Owen, could I speak with you privately for a moment?"

He finished his sandwich, brushed his hands off on a napkin, and stood. "I'm sorry, Nevada, but I've got appointments beginning in two minutes and I'm busy right through the afternoon."

As he walked away from the table, she walked along behind him. Hells bells, this was awkward. She'd never known him to be so cold and distant.

"Owen, please," she muttered. "Stop and talk to me."

He sighed, but wouldn't stop walking. "I can't."

She watched his back—his gorgeous, familiar back—disappear through the doors.

23

When Chelan picked up her cell phone, the last voice she expected to hear was Kevin's. And yet somehow, it was the most welcome. He was calling from a pay phone in the West End, he said, and he wondered if she wanted to go for a walk.

She met him in front of one of the apartment buildings at the edge of Stanley Park. "Hey. Do you want to do the seawall? I've got lots of time."

He pulled the headphones from his ears and shook his head. "No, I wanted to walk through the neighborhood. Past Dad's place... his old place."

"It's all good. Are we going to talk or just walk?"

"If you don't mind, just walk." He resettled the earpiece and they headed toward Robson Street. He loped along in time to some piece of music only he could hear. Chelan matched her pace to his.

Although she'd gone to meet him, expecting that it was a shoulder to lean or cry on that he'd sought, she was happy to have the silence and the space to deal with her own thoughts. The news about Tess Cunningham was like a kick in the stomach, knocking the wind out of her. Was it possible that Mrs. Cunningham was the latest victim of some psychopath targeting the Vancouver media? The circumstances were so bizarre. The radio newscast reported that when she failed to turn up at her office, her assistant had gone to her home and found the door ajar, television on, breakfast half eaten and left on the kitchen table. None of her clothes or her luggage were gone. No signs of a struggle or a robbery. It was quite a bit of detail for a radio report, but then Tess Cunningham was a well-known name, and if that information was available it was not surprising that it was used.

Chelan shivered. She was not normally a skittish person. She was careful about locking doors, standing back from strangers, and avoiding deserted streets at night—just basic common sense. But she didn't go through her days, worrying about personal safety, and she didn't spend a lot of time looking over her shoulder. Perhaps it was time to start.

The thing was, though, she didn't really believe it was true. If Tess Cunningham had only been "missing" for a day or so, maybe it could all be explained by a mix-up in schedules or a miscommunication. Add to that a misplaced cell phone, an unexpectedly lengthy meeting, and a spontaneous overnight stay at a hotel, and it could quite easily be that the whole "disappearance" was a misunderstanding.

The story didn't quite explain the weird things going on at her house, though.

"I had my first summer swim meet last weekend," Kevin pulled his headphones off and stuffed his music player in his jeans pocket.

"Your mom mentioned it to me. I heard you did awesome," Chelan was curious about whether he had any destination in mind, but she held off on quizzing him. She'd find out soon enough.

"Did you want to stop in any of the stores?"

"No, Kevin, I don't care. I'm just following you."

"I'd rather walk around the neighborhood, then, if you

don't care. Maybe end up down by English Bay."

They walked for about an hour, then as they came up a tree-lined street west of Denman, Kevin stopped suddenly. The only thing in sight was an old blue beater, parked in a lane just off a dead end. Chelan watched him stare at it for a few moments and then gave it her own full attention. She saw a movement just behind the curbside fender. Slowly, a tiny figure separated from the car and limped away, down the sidewalk. After a few seconds, the limp disappeared and the gait become more fluid. Chelan squinted in the brilliant sunshine, and a second, tinier figure became clear. It was a little dog, attached to the first figure by a leash.

Chelan turned to look at Kevin. "Mrs. Howe."

She took a step forward, planning to catch up or call out her name, but Kevin put a hand on her arm. "Let's just wait. Let her leave."

Chelan's curiosity, about the old car and about Kevin's intentions, held back her instinct to exercise the take-charge position that seniority might have given her in this situation. They watched Mrs. Howe walk a block to the next corner, turn left, and continue out of sight. As soon as she was gone, Kevin leaped forward. Chelan had to hurry to keep up.

"I've been wondering about her for a few weeks now," he said. "A few of the things she said just didn't sound right." He reached the car and peered in through the windows. "This is strange."

Brown towels had been pinned along the interior and it was difficult to see. A piece of thin cardboard had been cut to the shape of the windshield and placed along the dashboard. Chelan circled the car and found a gap between the towel curtains near the back.

"Wow," Kevin stood behind her.

The back seat of the car was covered in books and clothes. A small toiletries bag lay in one corner and a covered coffee mug in another. Shoes and a heavy coat rested on top of what appeared to be a stack of blankets on the floor. In the front seat, on the passenger side, there appeared to be a

THE LION'S SHARE OF THE AIR TIME

flashlight and a pillow.

Kevin backed up a step and Chelan turned to face him. They walked around the side of the car, dropped down on the nearest patch of grass, and prepared for a wait.

Ξ

It was pandemonium at the police station, in a controlled, hierarchical sort of way. Since the missing-person report on Tess Cunningham had been filed, action had been bubbling away below and on the surface. Zack had never seen the chief appear so stressed out. He heard that people were being called back from holidays, a blanket authorization for overtime hours had been issued, and schedules were being massaged and reorganized to put as many hands as possible on this missing person case.

Zack wasn't sure whether it was the woman's status that had given the sudden prod to the department, or whether this was a law enforcement version of the last straw story. Whichever it was, a team of forty police officers and detectives had been assembled and one of the biggest operations in the department's history was underway. The DNA labs and the forensic scientists were on alert; every piece of evidence collected in Tess Cunningham's home and office was to be reexamined. Computer files of thousands of persons known to police were to be pulled up and cross-checked. A public appeal for information on Tess Cunningham's last known whereabouts was being prepared.

Zack phoned home to let them know that he would be late. It was a stroke of good fortune that he got to talk to the voice mail, rather than to Marla.

Ξ

It was dusk when Mrs. Howe and Coaster came trudging wearily back along the sidewalk toward the car. Kevin jumped to his feet.

289

GAIL HULNICK

"Mrs. Howe—hello." He seemed to be a bit freaked out by the haughty look that had settled itself on her face.

"Hello, Kevin. Hello, Chelan. What brings you to this neighborhood?" She stared at them both as if she were a vice-principal who'd caught them smoking in the teachers' lounge.

Chelan got it. Invasion of privacy was the crime here. "Mrs. Howe, we were out for a walk in the neighborhood and we saw you. Is this— "

Kevin blazed ahead while Chelan was still trying to put together the most tactful, respectful way to ask the question. "Is this where you live?"

"Oh, no, dear, what would give you that idea?"

"We saw you getting out of this car. And this car looks like someone lives in it."

Mrs. Howe's chin went up. "All right. I am here. Temporarily. Circumstances arose which, on examination of the options, indicated that residence in a small, inexpensive space would be the best choice." Her twinkle bubbled up. "And it's so portable, too."

Chelan smiled back. "Are you sure you're all right?"

"I'm fine, my dear, really. I have everything I need here, my clothes, my books. I get enough to eat. Coaster keeps me company and makes sure no one bothers me. If someone seems to notice us, we just move along and set up camp somewhere new. I've been all over the West End and Yaletown." Her kindly eyes smiled at Kevin. "Really, I'm all right."

"It's terrible," Kevin exploded. "You can't live in a car! On a street, by yourself, at night… you can't. You should be in a nice apartment, with a big TV, and chairs, and a kitchen, and food, and a radio."

"I have a radio in the car, Kevin, and I get all the entertainment I need. I have plenty of food."

"What about your family, Mrs. Howe, your children?"

Chelan wouldn't have expected it, but Mrs. Howe's repertoire of facial expressions included one that could only

THE LION'S SHARE OF THE AIR TIME

be described as crafty. "They think I have a bachelor suite near downtown, and in a sense, I do. I wouldn't want them to know the details. I'm sure you understand."

Kevin appealed to Chelan. "We should do something about this. She can't be a homeless person. Maybe Mrs. Howe could come and stay with my mom and me for a while."

This proposition clearly horrified Mrs. Howe. She stepped forward and took Kevin by the arm. She might not be large, but she definitely intended to be in charge. "Kevin, I thank you, I really do, and I appreciate your concern. But I'm not homeless. This is my place. And I don't want to stay with anyone. I have my own little home here, my own things. Someone like me, at my age… I don't want to take charity from anyone. I have a little money and I've set myself up to match my needs to my income."

Chelan wondered how this had happened. Too many hours in the casinos? A husband or a boyfriend who drank it all away? Bad habits of her own that sucked up a lifetime of savings? No, she didn't look the type for drugs or alcohol. "Why are you living on the street, Mrs. Howe?"

"You know, it crept up on me bit by bit, not all at once," Mrs. Howe commented, as she opened the front door. Coaster leaped inside and settled himself behind the steering wheel while Mrs. Howe lowered herself into the passenger seat. "I sold my house and gave the proceeds to an advisor to invest for me. He claims I authorized him to take an aggressive approach, try to build up the capital a bit… I don't remember that. Anyway, a big chunk of it was lost. Then the place I was renting here in the West End went up for sale and I couldn't afford the price. I looked around in some of the cheaper areas in the valley but everything was so unfamiliar. Every time I went there I felt overwhelmed, like I was playing that children's game… Pin the Tail on the donkey." She shielded her eyes against the setting sun with a hand and squinted up at Kevin.

"Blindfolded, with people spinning you around and

making you dizzy?"

"That's exactly it, Kevin. I didn't want to go back to Coquitlam, which I'd known for more than thirty years. I'd been there long enough. I wanted to be here. So I rented a smaller place for as long as I could, until the last of the money ran out. For a while, I was staying in the little car I've had since Marv died, but then I sold it to get this bigger one. It's older, but I don't drive very far and it gives me a little extra room to spread out. "

"But what about the government money?" Chelan asked. "The old age pension?"

"Yes, I collect that. It keeps me from starving and I appreciate it."

But it doesn't buy you real estate in Vancouver, Chelan silently added.

Mrs. Howe pulled a light blanket over her knees. "So, everything is all right for me. I'm where I want to be, I have everything I need."

"But are you comfortable? Can you stay healthy, living here?" Chelan wanted to know.

"Yes, I can. Of course, I have some aches and pains. My knees need a little coaxing to start me moving in the morning and my back throbs a bit, but that would be the case even if I were living in a mansion in Shaughnessy."

"But we want to help you," Kevin protested.

"And I will think about your offer to help," Mrs. Howe promised. "Just please don't push me to live the way you think I should live. None of us should do that. We should just live our lives with honesty, let others live theirs, and try to do what's right."

She reached under the seat, pulled out a bag of cookies and offered it to Kevin. Chelan examined her and tried to pin down her own reaction to all this. Mrs. Howe was … what? Brave? Foolish? Absurd? Chelan often spent some of her time, imagining the future, and never once had she pictured herself living in a car. Parking three or four of them in a substantial garage on property that she owned outright, no question. Not living in one. But then, Mrs. Howe probably had never intended to end up like this, either.

But was it really "ending up"? When could any of us say we've "ended up" in a certain situation, except at the very end? Who knew — Mrs. Howe might waltz into a convenience store, buy a two-dollar lottery ticket and find herself in a West Vancouver waterfront mansion by Christmas. Or maybe that lottery ticket could drop into Chelan's hands ...

The reality was, though, that Mrs. Howe didn't have enough money for rent in the community she'd chosen for her home. Chelan had a sudden, blinding flash about the limited number of steps there could be between solvency and surrender to financial pressure. She didn't have a job and if that circumstance continued for long, she would have trouble coming up with her share of the rent on her home, too.

Chelan thought she had a lot of the answers. From an early age, she'd done without the support and love of a mother, thank you very much, and she'd had to share her father's affection with her brother. Actually, she'd had to watch her father obsess over her brother's problems and ignore her concerns, dull as they might have been. With very few fans or interested viewers tuning in her show, she had learned not to listen for applause or advice. She had a plan for her life and the projected curve was upward. Of course, she always had anticipated some setbacks but only in the abstract — she really believed that old saying that 'when one door closes, another one opens'. But with the loss of her job and her new knowledge of Mrs. Howe's situation, she wondered whether she really knew anything about anything at all.

"May I offer you a cookie, dear?"

Chelan snapped to the present and dug her hand into the bag of chocolate chip cookies on offer. The questions about her future and her purpose seemed so limitless, she couldn't even begin to frame them. The questions about

Keith's death and Mrs. Cunningham's disappearance were much more clear-cut. Chelan could face the specific and the immediate, and somehow, she sensed that she had to.

Ξ

Chelan arrived back at her apartment after her encounter with Mrs. Howe and turned on the TV news. The time she had to wait until the late local cast stretched in front of her like the start time for a birthday party to a nine-year-old. She grabbed a notepad and started to make a plan.

Research was the way. She had to use what means she could to find out as much as she could about the last days of each of the victims and the activities of Bob Venice, Conrad Davis, and Tara Carle in those days.

The news began and within seconds, Amanda appeared on the screen, standing in front of a luxury apartment building near Stanley Park. Chelan boosted the volume.

"Police say Tess Cunningham's schedule for today included a keynote speech at a business conference in Whistler. For several hours, it was feared that her car had gone off the highway between Horseshoe Bay and Squamish, but at four o'clock this afternoon it turned up, parked off the road at Function Junction, near Whistler. Anyone with any information about Tess Cunningham's whereabouts is asked to call police at— "

Chelan turned the set off and opened Layla's laptop computer. She started to examine the Internet financial sites, looking for anything she could find on Bob Venice or his companies. She scanned the sports sites for snippets on Conrad Davis, and the broadcasting and 'women of influence' zones for anything on Tess Cunningham.

She called Nevada, who picked up on the first ring. "Yes?"

"Nevada, it's Chelan. I heard about Tess Cunningham—"

"Very weird, isn't it?"

THE LION'S SHARE OF THE AIR TIME

"What do you think happened to her?"

"No idea. Listen, Chelan, I'm glad you called. Let's get together tomorrow, okay? Maybe at the Scribbler? I'm trying to keep this line open tonight. Expecting a call."

" I'm not sure I particularly want to go anywhere near the Scribbler."

"Oh, come on, don't be a baby. Lots of people get fired, downsized, let go, whatever. You gotta get out, let people see you, give them the idea of hiring you."

"I'll think about it. Right now I'm spending my new chunk of free time investigating Keith's death and the other killings."

Nevada sighed. "Why am I not surprised. But listen, whatever you're doing, steer clear of Conrad Davis. I hear he's been going around town saying that you're stalking him."

"What!?"

"Yeah, since that time you showed up at his gym. Tread carefully, Chelan."

"I will. Hey—don't hang up. I need to ask you a couple of questions."

"Shoot."

"Are you still in touch with that television director who told you about Jason Wheeler's visitors the week before he died?"

"What?"

"I'm trying to research the activities of all of the victims in the last weeks before they died—what they were working on, where they went, who they saw, you know. I've got charts for everybody—but with a lot of blanks in them. I don't have much on Jason Wheeler, but I remembered that the director—"

"Josh Dickens."

"Josh Dickens told you that a man and a small, blonde woman in a red dress dropped by to see Jason."

"And?"

"I want to email him pictures of Bob Venice and of

Tess Cunningham."

Silence, as Nevada thought over the implications. "All right, good idea. I've got some newspaper photos I can scan and send to him. You think Bob Venice might be involved?"

"He loaned money to a lot of people and sometimes people use violence, or threats of violence, to get it back." Chelan looked over the notes on her pad. "The other one I'm thinking about is Ted Bougie. About Tess, anyway. When I saw him at the ball game, he told me he knew that Keith had passed his name on to Tess."

"And he thinks that's what's ruined his life."

"Exactly."

"You should stay away from him, too. Make phone calls but don't go meeting anybody alone. In the meantime, I'll see if I can get hold of that TV director by email."

"Can you do it now? Tell him it's urgent."

"Yes, all right, you pushy thing. Just get off my phone so that I can keep this line open. Owen has to call."

"One more thing. The newscast is saying that they found Tess Cunningham's car near Whistler and that she was up there to give a speech. Would she just be up there for the day or would she stay over? Which hotel?"

"At her place, I would imagine. She's kept a cabin there for years."

"Where, exactly?"

"I was there, once, to a party. Let me think. It was February, six feet of fresh powder, Owen was thrilled. We drove to her place after dinner in the Village. This was years before she got to be such a big shot that she only socializes with seven-figure income types."

"Nevada."

"It was… near the Creekside gondola. Yeah. Up the mountainside, just north of the ski-out. A short street, only three or four cabins on it. Not a big cabin, but a three-car garage, of all things."

"Good."

"Good? What do you mean, good?"

THE LION'S SHARE OF THE AIR TIME

"Nothing. Just email that director now, would you?"

"Yeah, okay. I'll call you as soon as I hear from him."

Chelan pulled the telephone book from the shelf near the TV. She flipped through the pages, looking at the listings for Gyms and Fitness Clubs, and found one for the Eagle Gym. It was a long shot, but it had better odds than finding unlisted numbers on short notice.

"Eagle Gym?"

"Urgent phone call for Mr. Conrad Davis," Chelan said, in what she hoped was an official, authoritative tone. "Is he there?"

"Who is calling, please?"

"Security at his apartment building. There's been a break-in."

"Just a moment."

Conrad's personality asserted itself just as powerfully over a phone line as across a sheet of ice. "Who is this? What's going on?"

"Mr. Davis, this is Chelan Montgomery. I've been investigating your brother's death and I think it's connected to Keith Papineau and … some other things." She faltered, then recovered. Was he even still on the line? She had to assume he was, and keep going. "I have to ask you, Mr. Davis—in the eighties, before he died in that hit-and-run accident, was your brother friends with Bob Venice?"

"Bob Venice tried to have my brother thrown off the national team. They weren't friends."

Chelan heard a loud click. The conversation was over.

Her voice mail had picked up a message from Nevada. "Hey, Chelan? Got an answer back from the TV director. Checks out—it was Bob and Tess he saw together that day on set. And it was Keith there earlier in the week. Okay? Call me tomorrow. I have to find Owen tonight."

Chelan's next phone call punctuated an otherwise dull evening for the security guard at LV-TV. "Max, it's Chelan Montgomery. Can you help me with some information?"

"Depends, Ms. Montgomery."

"I know we have a log of people who've visited the station. Could you look up the names of visitors on a particular day?"

"Which day?"

"The day Gregory Keene died."

"Don't have that anymore, Ms. Montgomery. It's evidence. The police came and took that database, along with everything on Mr. Keene's hard drive right after he was killed."

"All right, Max, I understand. Just one more question—the day that Mrs. Cunningham…"

"Disappeared, Ms. Montgomery. That's what her family is saying."

"Okay. At work the day before she disappeared, was there anything unusual going on?"

"No, don't think so. Typical day. A few visitors, a lot fewer since Mr. Keene's show went off the air. Reporters coming and going."

"Did you see Mrs. Cunningham come in?"

"Oh yeah. She was dressed up real nice, as usual. Carrying a big briefcase."

"Did you see her leave at the end of the day?"

"Wasn't really the end of the day, but yeah."

"When was it?"

"Before noon. She came out with two big briefcases. Looked pretty heavy."

"Did you help her to the car with them, Max?"

"No need, she had help."

The pace of this conversation reminded Chelan of the first few interviews she'd had with Detective Esher. "Help from her driver?"

"No, she didn't have the limo, like usual. Or her own little car, either. Fella met her at the door, helped her carry the briefcases, put them in the trunk of his car, then opened the door for her and she got in."

"Was it anyone from the station? Or anyone that you recognized from anywhere?"

THE LION'S SHARE OF THE AIR TIME

"No, sorry."

"That's all right, Max. But you know, if you haven't been asked about this by the police yet, I think you should give them a call and let them know."

"I did talk to them, Ms. Montgomery."

Chelan was already looking down at her list of calls to make when one other thought occurred to her. "What kind of car was it?"

"Jag. Racing green.

24

*I*t was so foggy that night. It often is during the winter here. No one could see more than an arms-length ahead. We were stumbling around the university parking lot, laughing and kidding around. He was telling a lot of jokes. After hours of classes, diving practice, and forty lengths each, most people would be tired and quiet. But these guys insisted we had to go to the bar for just one.

We piled into the car, two in front, three in back. He eased the car out of the parking space. We all stopped talking, giving him a chance to focus his full concentration on driving that ancient Chevy through the fog.

He picked up speed and it seemed like the fog was lifting. The three in the back started to talk and laugh. Everybody was looking forward to a few hours in the Elbow Room: some good music, a brew or two.

Then there was a thump, like bumping through a pothole, and the car swerved left. He put it into 'park', but we all just sat there, no one wanting to make the first move. Then we all climbed out, expecting we had to change a flat tire or try to fix something. Instead, there was a broken body half under the car, face down on the pavement.

One person leaned against the car, trying not to faint. Another ran off to find a telephone and call for help. The funny guy turned away, bent over double, and threw up all over his shoes. That was the driver, the one who hit the guy.

He was the one who would have felt the foot, pressing down on top of his on the accelerator pedal. He was the one who tried to turn the

THE LION'S SHARE OF THE AIR TIME

steering wheel and couldn't. Two hands were gripping it, holding it immobile.

Two hands that seized an opportunity.

I did what I had to do, to pursue the goal and climb to the top. I always do what I have to do, keep on moving, keep on moving higher.

Now, one more jump to make.

Ξ

Tess's Whistler neighborhood was deserted. The only sound came from a blue jay, trying to intimidate any challenger to its claim over an unlucky worm. Chelan drove slowly up and down the streets, trying to search as systematically as possible. Short street, small cabin, three-car garage. Only one other vehicle, a silver four-door of some kind, passed her during what seemed like an hour of hunting.

She was just about to turn right and head higher up the mountain when she saw Bob's car, parked in front of an impressive home with a wraparound cedar deck, floor to ceiling windows, and a river rock chimney. Not huge, that was true, but it was interesting that 'small' was the first word that had come to Nevada's mind in describing it. But maybe her memory was just a bit vague on the details. The three-car garage aspect was correct, and it was the right neighborhood. Chelan wasn't sure whether it was Tess's house or not, but that was definitely Bob's car.

She cruised past, trying to set a speed slow enough to take a look but fast enough to soothe suspicion, if anyone happened to be watching. She parked the Mini, and gathered up her bag. She had no plan, other than taking a walk past the house. She knew that she ought to turn to her mind to prepping her questions, in case she saw Bob or Tess, but every time she tried to form a coherent thought, she was distracted by some detail of the houses she passed.

She looked around for any sign of Tess's sports car or the limo she sometimes used, but saw nothing. The curtains were drawn on all of the windows of the house. What next?

Call the police, maybe? And tell them what? That she'd found a car? For all she knew, the police had already checked out Tess's Whistler cabin—for all she knew, Bob had a perfectly good reason to be there.

She turned around and headed back toward her car. This was insane. She had nothing more than a hunch to go on, just a guess that Tess's absence had something to do with Keith's death and those of the others. She was suspicious of Bob—why? Because dead men had owed him money? Because he'd been seen with Jason Wheeler in the days before his death? To pursue this any further, she would have to snoop around on Tess's property, be prepared to ask Bob a direct question, and run the risk that he'd be so furious he'd dump her name and reputation on a compost heap.

Still, what kind of person would she be if she didn't take action when she was sure something was wrong? Pretty sure, anyway. All she needed to do, wanted to do, today, was find something concrete she could take to Zack Esher, to get him to take her suspicions about Bob Venice seriously. If he was the one who killed Keith, and if Tess needed help, how could she sleep at night if she just did nothing?

She walked back and forth between the Mini and Tess's front door three times before she finally decided she had to make a move. Trying to act like she belonged there, she strolled up the front sidewalk and around to the back of the cabin.

A six-foot fence shielded the deck and the back windows from the neighbors' view. Chelan crept up beside a hot tub that would probably seat twenty and crouched down near a sliding door that opened on a games room. Nobody had bothered to close these blinds.

Chelan fumbled in her bag and pulled out a camera. The telephoto zoom pulled the room closer. A pool table, a widescreen TV, a pinball machine, a computer station, and a serious stereo set-up. An ego wall, with about a dozen framed photographs, dominated the north end of the room.

THE LION'S SHARE OF THE AIR TIME

Chelan leaned as far forward as she could without leaving her cranny between the hot tub and the deck railing, trying to pick up some details on the pictures. Tess with... that one looked like a former prime minister. Tess with a couple of movie stars. Tess with last year's top golfer. A cluster of photos of sports events—thoroughbred racing, hockey, swimming, diving. Two of divers on the platform—one a man, and one a woman. A young woman. Blonde hair, tiny. A young Tess.

Chelan heard a man's voice inside the house, and pulled back as far as she could. From her hiding place, Chelan could see only one corner of the room, and when she tried to swivel to get a wider view, the wooden slats on the outside of the hot tub rubbed against her bare arms. She decided to hold still, watch as much as she could, and snap pictures if possible. She groped in her bag and moved her tape recorder to the top of the pile of stuff.

Someone's back, dressed in a dark suit, crossed her sightline. Odd choice of clothes for a hot day in July. "We're just wasting time here. The authorities may return at any time. We have to make a move."

"We could talk about the accident." A woman's voice.

"The accident was no accident," Bob said. "It was a deliberate, conscious act by a determined, ambitious leader. A leader with a plan. And nobody could be allowed to interfere with that plan. Obstacles had to be pushed aside or avoided. Details had to be organized."

Bob's voice had a rhythmic, hypnotic tone. It was very low and Chelan wanted to lean forward to catch every word. She inched out of her hiding place and closer to the door.

"I need to get away, Bob. You don't really want to keep me back, do you?" Tess's voice. Definitely Tess's voice. Chelan wasn't too late. She wondered whether she should dare to sneak back around to the side of the house, get out her cell phone, and call the RCMP in Whistler.

"I want all this to stop. It's gone on for too many years, Tess. First Cal's death, then Blair killing himself—"

303

"Don't talk about Blair."

"And now all of these others. It's time for you, now, Tess."

"It is my time, Bob. You always said you wanted me to be happy, that I had the brains and the heart to be right up there at the top with you. How could you do this now, if you always wanted me to be happy? I need you on my side, not against me."

The man in the dark suit spoke. "This is taking too long."

Chelan dropped to her hands and knees, then started to crawl forward across the deck toward the corner of the house.

"Just a couple more minutes," Bob said. "A couple of minutes isn't so much, up against so many years. How long have we known each other, Tess? Since 1981? Do you remember those early days, those long evenings in the pub, talking over our dreams for the future? We'd all figured out that hard work and determination were essential. Nothing was going to stop us. I wanted to be a millionaire, you wanted to run a huge company, Blair wanted an Olympic medal. We've fought so hard to get this far. But every battle has its casualties, we both know that. Sacrifices have to be made..."

A shoulder in a blue short-sleeved shirt crashed into the glass of the sliding door above Chelan's head. Bob grabbed for the handle and yanked the door open.

Chelan's eyes met his for an instant and she knew she should use his surprise as an opportunity to get away and to run for help. She seized the edge of the hot tub to pull herself to her feet, turned, and took two steps. She heard a crash, and then an arm gripped her around the middle and pulled her back. On the periphery of her vision, she could see a knife, held near her left cheek.

The arm was clothed in a dark suit jacket. The man spun her around to face the house and marched her through the door.

THE LION'S SHARE OF THE AIR TIME

Bob lay on the floor, rubbing his jaw. Tess sat in a maroon leather armchair, cupping a crystal tumbler full of whiskey in both hands. She moved a finger to point toward the floor and the man pushed Chelan to the carpet.

Chelan recognized him as Dmitri, the driver she'd seen with Tess at the News Awards Banquet. She knew she probably shouldn't open her mouth, but she couldn't help herself. If it was the end, it wouldn't matter anyway.

"Mrs. Cunningham, you've been reported as missing."

"Shut up." Tess didn't look at her, but stared down into her drink as if it were a crystal ball or the answer key to the SATs.

Bob sat up and looked at her. "Ms. Montgomery."

"Mr. Venice. What's going on here?"

"Mrs. Cunningham is not missing, as you can see. She chose to lay low for a few days."

"Shut up, Bob. Dmitri, take Bob upstairs. The ensuite off the master bedroom. I'll watch Ms. Montgomery."

Dmitri hauled Bob to his feet and held the knife near the small of his back as he propelled him toward the staircase. Tess stood up and came to stand in front of Chelan, arms crossed over her breasts, hand still holding the crystal tumbler.

Chelan scanned the room for something she could use. She was on the floor near the wall with the photographs. Nothing was close at hand. The plasma TV, with a screen she might kick in and use, was at least twenty feet away. The desk, with drawers she might grab, was fifteen feet away, near the door to the kitchen.

The desk. Chelan avoided Tess's gaze and stared at the desktop. Could there be a pen or a letter opener? She could see Tess's black leather handbag, partially open. A wallet, hairbrush, cosmetics bag, and a red book spilled out. A familiar red book.

Keith's planner.

"Ms. Montgomery."

It seemed that conversation was compulsory. "Mrs.

305

Cunningham."

"What were you doing skulking on my deck?"

"You've been reported missing." Chelan eased into a position that she hoped would make her appear to be seated. She tried to get the soles of her feet tucked under her, to use as leverage.

"And?"

"I thought you might have been killed. By the same person who killed Keith, and Jason Wheeler and Gregory Keene. And maybe Tony Prinelli, also."

"I see. And did you have a theory about who that person might be?"

"I thought it might be Bob Venice."

"Ah. Not Tara Carle?"

Chelan shook her head. "That never rang true, to me." She tilted her chin, looking Tess full in the face, and the thought was voiced almost as soon as it hit her brain. Maybe a mistake, but too late. "Did you set her up?"

"She did sign the guest book when she came to the station to see Greg's show and she did write some letters to Jason. I wrote a few more, on her behalf..." Was Tess smirking? "... Keith got one and Greg got one. With an address on it. Convenient."

A drumbeat of scuffing footsteps came from upstairs, following by what sounded like a body smashing into a door. Tess was distracted momentarily, but when Chelan rose a few inches she turned on her like a snarling cat. "Sit down!"

Make a plan, make a plan.

"How could you make the police think that Tara Carle had anything to do with Tony's death?" Keep her talking, for a start.

"There was no need. Tony Prinelli was killed during the commission of a robbery at his home."

"And Tess Cunningham?"

She sipped at her drink. "I am still organizing that. Certainly, the body will never be found. It could be that Bob Venice killed her, hid the body, and then committed suicide, in deep remorse over his evil act, born of unrequited passion. Or perhaps he killed her because she uncovered evidence of his role in the deaths of a journalist who owed him money, two TV stars who lost major amounts of his money in a restaurant venture, and an auto mechanic whose first wife left him to pursue an affair with Bob. I can arrange to have the details supported with bits of evidence here and there. And that would let Ms. Carle off the hook, wouldn't it? I haven't quite decided. I haven't decided about you yet, either."

No more sounds came from the second floor. Chelan thought about making a break for the door before Dmitri came back downstairs. She needed to keep Tess talking, distract her somehow.

"Why didn't you take any luggage with you?"

"And leave my house in such a mess? Just to confuse them all. Make it seem odd."

"Why, Mrs. Cunningham?" She had to get her to back off, widen the space between them, and cut the tension between them. "Why have you done all this?"

"I thought you were very close to figuring it out, Ms. Montgomery. I should have had Matthew fire you weeks ago. You found that ancient photograph and you've been waving it around all over town." Tess tipped one foot back on its four-inch heel and wagged the pointed toe of the crimson shoe back and forth. "We all knew each other in the eighties. We had a vision, Blair and I "

"He was your husband, Blair Cunningham, is that right? And he killed himself in the early nineties?"

"Shut up."

They listened for a moment to a muffled sound from upstairs. Might be someone falling, might be furniture being moved.

"Yes, Mrs. Cunningham, I figured out that you all knew one another more than twenty years ago and that all of you had some connection to elite swimming and diving, either as athletes or reporters or team officials," Chelan tried to maintain her voice in a soothing, intelligent tone. "But what I haven't been able to get, is why. Did someone do something terrible to you?"

Tess's face was unreadable. Clearly, her mind was only partially engaged with this moment. She was either drifting back in mental time to some event related to the bloodbath that she had produced in the past two months, or she was speculating about the outcome of the confrontation upstairs. Chelan's curiosity was in overdrive.

Footsteps pounded down the staircase behind Tess. "She did something terrible to a young man named Cal Davis." Bob Venice stood alone, panting at the bottom of the stairs, a bloody knife in his hand. "She made Blair Cunningham run him down and then she persuaded us all to leave him there to die alone in the road. She did it to remove Blair's main competition for a spot on the Canadian Olympic team—the only problem was Blair couldn't swallow it. It ate away at him and finally he dropped out. From everything. Everybody kept it quiet for years because they had a lot to lose, and because you helped them, financially. But Blair couldn't hold it in after a while and he killed himself. Because of you, Tess. You killed him, too."

Tess whirled to face Bob Venice. "Shut up. Where's Dmitri? What happened?"

"Figure it out."

A leap to her feet and a beeline for the door probably would have been the wisest course for Chelan at that point, but she had to get out another question. "Why did she kill four more people now?"

"Keith started sniffing around after he met Conrad Davis, doing the magazine profile on him. He got curious about Cal's death and he confronted Tess about the hit-and-run. But he thought Blair did it, by accident. That it was just a horrible accident that a bunch of scared kids covered up, without thinking through the consequences. It wasn't. She did it, and it was deliberate."

Tess confronted him, fury in every inch of her face and

body. "You can't prove that."

"I was there. I was sitting right beside you, in the front seat, and I saw what you did."

He dodged to her left, and then ran straight at her, his six-foot frame bent over so that his right shoulder hammered into her solar plexus. She fell to one knee, and Bob ran past her, out through the open glass door and into the back yard.

Chelan couldn't believe he was running away and leaving her in a room with this madwoman.

Tess appeared to be stunned for a second, and then she began screaming. "Dmitri! What happened?"

She ran toward the staircase and Chelan tried to make the most of the situation. She probably should have followed Bob right out of the house, but she had just three things she thought she had to do before she made her escape. Groping through her purse, she recognized the shape of the tiny digital camera and pulled it out. She took a quick shot of the room and of Tess, rushing up the stairs. Next was the cell phone: she flipped it open and punched in the numbers. 9-1-1. The last item was Keith's planner, lying half out of Tess's handbag on the desk.

"It's a police emergency," she muttered into the phone, in response to the dispatcher's question, as she sidled over to the desk and seized the agenda book. "555 Water Road. Tess Cunningham."

Chelan heard footsteps on the stair, turned to run, but then thought better of it. She had a lot of space to cover before she reached the door and she had no way of knowing whether Tess was coming down the stairs distraught and incapable of harming anyone, or armed with some deadly weapon she'd found upstairs. She scrunched down in the gap between the desk and the wall.

Tess had calmed herself down in the moments since she'd gone screaming up the stairs. Her face was set, her eyes focused on the sliding door to the backyard, and she seemed to radiate self-control. Self-control and menace. She snatched her purse from the top of the desk and hurried to the door. Chelan jumped up and ran after her. She had no plan, just a nebulous recognition of the fact that if Tess disappeared from this house she might vanish from Vancouver, even from North America, and never face the consequences of her decision to end Keith's life.

She dashed around the side of the house and saw Tess pause in the driveway. Bob's car was gone. Tess started to walk rapidly toward the street, turning south toward the highway. Chelan's Mini was parked a few hundred feet along the road. Pushing herself to her top speed, Chelan let out a loud roar. She was not quite sure why she did—maybe to startle Tess and throw her off guard. The tiny, blonde woman stopped and turned to look at Chelan, which gave her the extra seconds she needed to catch up.

She threw her arms around Tess and shoved her toward the car. Left hand reaching for the handle, Chelan yanked the door open and pushed her down into the front seat. As Tess scrambled across to the other side and tried to pull open the door, Chelan reached into her bag for the remote control key. She punched the 'lock' button and heard the satisfying click of the bolts falling into place. Tess punched the 'unlock' button on the interior of the door—and Chelan relocked the doors from the outside. Tess unlocked the door again—and Chelan relocked it.

Tess's face was panic-stricken and Chelan could tell that most of the words she was screaming were obscene. She drew a deep breath and felt the nausea that had had her in its grip since the moment she'd crept into the house subside. She watched Tess carefully and every time she unlocked the door, Chelan snapped it shut. She kept her trapped in the Mini until the RCMP car rolled into view and two men in uniform took over.

25

Driftwood floated past the Stanley Park seawall in an aimless pattern. It was high tide and from her bench, looking west, Chelan could see a freighter moving toward the bridge. Probably coming in from Japan, on the last few miles of its journey from the teeming East to the edge of British Columbia. Hard to imagine that this ship, now taken into the embrace of a safe harbor, surrounded by buildings, roadways, and people, just yesterday had been rising and falling on the swells of the Pacific Ocean, isolated and autonomous, far from land.

Tourists by the thousands were exploring the park on this sweltering July day, but its verdant gardens, sheltering forests, and open beaches extended wide enough to embrace them all.

Ample room for everyone. Ample space for the thousands of tourists and one young woman, recently out of danger, but now in limbo.

In the week since Tess Cunningham had been arrested, Chelan was more restless than she could remember ever being. Every question that had been answered and laid to rest seemed to spawn a dozen more. Not about the deaths, but about herself. About life.

Her cell phone rang.

"Chelan, are you in town? Come over to the newsroom." Nevada's voice projected more energy than Chelan had heard from her in days.

"What's up?"

"Never mind the questions. Just come. Get the scoop."

Chelan laughed. "Yeah, all right. Fifteen minutes."

When she walked in, she was surprised to see Nevada, Elliot, Wayne, Sam, Amanda, Leonard, Tim, Daniel, and Matthew all standing or leaning on desks in a sort of semi-circle. Chelan wondered whether they'd just finished up a story meeting.

"Chelan, why are you here?" Matthew was the first to see her after she pushed open the door.

"Matthew, please. I asked her to come in." Nevada stepped forward and towered over Chelan's right shoulder.

A curt nod and he was gone.

"Is it just me, or is he even crankier than usual?"

"Don't sweat it, Chelan. He's upset, blames himself that he didn't see Tess for what she really was much earlier in the game."

Elliot picked up a file from the desk he was draped over. "He prides himself on being this savvy news guy and he got fooled, just like the rest of us."

"Elliot has appointed himself Newsroom Shrink," Nevada's smile put a completely surprising spin on the sarcasm of her words.

The group dispersed, but not before everyone, Elliot excepted, took a moment to shake Chelan's hand or touch her shoulder. When they were all gone, she confronted Nevada. "All right, spill."

"Not yet. Do you want coffee?"

"Yeah, sure." Chelan turned toward the glass doors that led to the vending machines down the hall.

"I have a pot brewing. Follow me."

Nevada led the way through the maze of desks in the newsroom toward an open area against the far wall. Bulging file cabinets and a retired wire machine had washed up here

THE LION'S SHARE OF THE AIR TIME

once upon a time, and the area had been storage space ever since. Three carpenters and an electrician were taking measurements and outlining a room in black duct tape.

"Step into my office." Nevada swept an arm from coffeepot to duct tape door.

"Since when?"

"Since whenever it's finished. Matthew's given me the news director job. Leonard's heard the siren call of one of the big American online news sites and he's leaving at the end of the month."

"Nevada, congratulations! At least, I think that's the right thing to say... are you happy about it?"

"Yeah. It'll do." Nevada picked up a mug and poured coffee. Chelan could almost feel waves of satisfaction flowing from her. "Have you heard from the cops lately?"

"Last week. They took my statement and asked me not to go anywhere."

"I just heard that they've issued an apology to Tara Carle and called on all the news outlets in town to do the same. I wondered whether they'd mentioned anything about that to you, when you saw them."

"Not a word."

"Because I would expect," Nevada poured her own cup and flexed her fingers, as if she had to do something with them, even in the absence of a cigarette, "that if you heard something like that, you'd bring it to me, let us get it out first."

"Of course, I would."

"Because I would expect that a full-time reporter at LV-TV would be alert for any tips on breaking news at all times, in all places."

Chelan's phone was ringing, but she ignored it. "Are you offering me a job?"

"I am. Isn't it a kick? That you're getting back on the track? And that I'm in a position to offer somebody a job?" Nevada was obviously thrilled with the situation.

Chelan was not so sure. But she didn't have a clear

window on the source of the discomfort she felt at this moment, and she did have rent to pay. "It's awesome. I'm in."

Nevada held her cup out to tap Chelan's. "Congratulations to us. And to Detective Esher, for putting the Vancouver media murderer behind bars. Do we know yet whether they think they'll be able to convict her?"

"They've got the recording from my cell phone." Chelan raised her mug and grinned at Thomas, who stood on the far side of the newsroom, camera in one hand and tripod in the other. "The sound was pretty muddy, but some genius did magic with a computer and they've got most of it. And they were able to put her at the scene of Keith's and Gregory's murders with her lip prints."

"Her what?"

"I know. I'd never heard of it before either. Apparently, everybody has distinctive lip prints, just like fingerprints. Lip prints aren't quite as useful to the police, because there isn't the oil in them that there is on a fingertip. Not to mention that most people touch things more times in a day than they kiss them. Anyway, Tess Cunningham went to see Keith early that morning, probably because she heard he'd been investigating Cal Davis's death in a hit-and-run accident twenty-some years ago. He offered her coffee, they went out on the balcony, and Keith was pushed off."

The idea was still horrifying, and Chelan felt the nausea in the pit of her stomach that still accompanied every thought of Keith's last day. One of the carpenters began hammering nails into a plank and the noise gave Chelan a good excuse to stop talking for a while.

"Hard to believe that tiny woman could push anybody anywhere," Nevada said. "Maybe she had a secret black belt or something."

"Detective Esher says she had Dmitri with her at the time and that he did it. She's not talking, but Dmitri is out of ICU and he is, apparently."

"Did she do the suicide note at Keith's apartment or

THE LION'S SHARE OF THE AIR TIME

bring it with her?" Nevada asked.

"I guess that will be a significant item for the police to examine in the next few weeks. They'll be able to determine whether it came from Keith's computer, and if it didn't… well, it certainly implies something ugly about premeditation, doesn't it?"

The piercing whine of a power saw interrupted their conversation. As soon as the cut board dropped from the sawhorse to the floor, Nevada motioned to Chelan to follow her into an empty office.

"So Tess didn't think about the coffee mug?"

"Apparently not. She… or Dmitri… somebody… put the cup on the table to hold down the suicide note. No fingerprints, Esher said. Gloves, I guess." Chelan pulled up a chair and sat down. "Keith had a meeting with her the day before and he must have asked her questions that made her decide that he was a threat. I had his planner—the one that had the info he didn't keep on the newsroom intranet—and he had her initials penciled in for a noon meeting. I thought it was Tara Carle, but it was Tess."

"So she took Dmitri and went to see Keith after they'd killed Jason Wheeler the night before?"

"Wheeler was the beginning. Their big cover-up started unraveling with him. Tess found out he'd met with Keith and told him bits of the story. They were all there, you know."

"They who?"

"Jason, Gregory Keene, Tony Prinelli, Bob Venice. They were all there when Cal Davis got run over. They were in the car."

Nevada was on high alert. "Who was driving?"

"Blair Cunningham."

"Wow. Did he tell Tess what happened?"

"Didn't have to. She was in the car, too."

"And wow again." Nevada's gaze was fixed on Chelan." So they agree to keep quiet about it. Blair kills himself ten years later … out of guilt, do you think?"

315

"That's my guess." Chelan agreed.

"But otherwise, it's ancient history. But all of a sudden, Keith is asking questions and then, Jason Wheeler is threatening to tell what happened."

"Or the other way around."

"Yeah. Could be. Do you think the guilt got to Jason, too, eventually?" Nevada asked.

"Yeah. Took a long time to filter through, though, in my opinion."

"No kidding." Nevada wandered in her own thoughts for a few moments, and Chelan pulled out her cell phone and glanced at it. Could she get away with checking her messages right now? What was the etiquette when a friend became a boss?

"And Tess's lip print was found in Gregory Keene's office, too?"

"Also on a coffee cup." Chelan shuddered. "Freakin' amazing … to be that cold. Sitting there, having a coffee, distracting a man while that mountain ape of a driver comes at him from behind."

"Did Dmitri kill Tony Prinelli on her orders, too?"

"So he's saying. He's been very cooperative since he woke up from the stomping Bob Venice gave him in Tess Cunningham's bathroom. He planted the knife in Tara's garden, too."

"Wow. I'm speechless."

"Yeah, it's … incredible. You have to wonder why."

Chelan had been pondering Tess's motivation night and day for a week, and maybe it would be impossible to ever completely get it. She had to admit to some empathy with Matthew's annoyance about not seeing Tess for what she was, and to admiring her for so long. Tess's ambition was toxic, and Chelan had to question whether her own leftover stress was due to a realization that she should never have been inspired by this woman. She liked to think that she was not easy to fool, and yet she had been inspired by a woman who turned out to be a monster.

THE LION'S SHARE OF THE AIR TIME

"You know, we all think the children of wealthy parents have it so easy," Nevada said. "But maybe she thought she had to do anything she could, no matter how evil, just to preserve her status with her parents and her brother?"

"Could be. Or maybe she did it because she couldn't stand for the truth to come out," Chelan said.

"Or maybe she just did it just because she was after the lion's share of the air time. Who knows what goes on in a brain like that?" Nevada ignored the whine of a power saw. "What finally tipped you that it was her?"

"When I saw Keith's planner in her purse, at her house. Only the person who hit me over the head at the station that night would have it. That—and the things she and Bob said. And her diving picture."

Chelan and Nevada stared at one another for a few moments, then a smile teased at the corner of Nevada's mouth.

"What?" Chelan couldn't help but smile in response. "Nevada, I have to say, you seem very cheerful today, in spite of the topic. Is it just the new job?"

Nevada turned to top up her coffee, but not before Chelan saw a full beam flash across her face like a strobe light. It took years off her face. "Owen's back."

"I didn't know he was gone."

"We've been going through a rough stretch for the past few weeks. I thought I might have torpedoed another one, but apparently not. He didn't want ... uh, never mind. I'll spare you the boring details. Is that your phone or am I hearing Handel's Water Music as I go insane?"

"That's my ringtone, sorry." Chelan flipped open the phone and Nevada made her exit with a wave.

"Hello? Kevin. Hey." Chelan moved toward the newsroom door. "Sure, I'll meet you there in half an hour."

Ξ

Kevin sat on the patch of grass where he and Chelan had

waited for Mrs. Howe to return to her car, just a week earlier. He must have been broiling in that dark T-shirt and baggy jeans, but at fourteen, fashion came before comfort. At twenty-four, thirty-four, forty-four, and fifty-four, for that matter. Maybe forever.

"Hey, Kevin, how's it going?" She dropped to the ground beside him.

"Much better, Chelan. Now that we know about my dad." He flicked a quick glance at her face. "Thank you."

Payment enough. More than enough.

"Hey, no problem. We won't ever get over missing him. But at least now we know."

"Now we know." Kevin stared at the street. "Chelan, have you heard from Mrs. Howe?" Chelan shook her head, and took a good look at him, noticing the dark circles under his eyes and his pale skin.

"I haven't seen her for days. I've been walking around Dad's apartment and other places where I used to see her, and nothing."

Chelan stretched her legs out in front of her and leaned back on her elbows. "Kevin, I don't think we should worry. She's made it clear she wants to be left alone. I'll bet she's just set up camp in some other neighborhood."

"I think we should do something."

"What do you think we should do?"

"Call the police." His face was stern, yet anxious. It was so wrong, somehow, that someone so young should be agonizing about something so complicated and so tragic.

"Let's analyze that, Kevin. Pros and cons. On the plus side, they could use their resources to locate her—"

"And we could give her enough money to live on. In a real apartment." Kevin finished her sentence.

"But on the negative side, don't forget that she rejected that idea the first time we put it to her. Maybe she doesn't want to be found, Kevin. Maybe she doesn't want anything from us. Some people are that way. While the rest of us are trying to move forward, they're trying to go somewhere else

THE LION'S SHARE OF THE AIR TIME

entirely. Out of the crowd, away from the current. They have no appetite for it, you know?"

Kevin watched a group of young people walk by, tennis racquets in hand. "But she's homeless!"

"Is she? She doesn't have the home you have or the one I might choose. But she seemed to be at home with herself, in her own skin. That's a lot of more than a lot of us get."

Kevin shook his head. "That's just whack."

"All right." Chelan stood up and straightened her jeans. It was little enough, and maybe it was the right thing to do. "Let's go visit the police station."

Ξ

Zack sat in front of his computer screen, facing the report that he'd been struggling to write since he'd clocked in that morning. The effort on the Wheeler and the other murders had been massive; more than three thousand people were interviewed and reams of notes were taken. It all had to be distilled, put into the record and kept ready for that day, months or even years hence, when they'd all have to stand up in court over it.

It was actually not the part of the job Zack hated most. Unlike most of his fellow officers, he didn't loathe the paperwork part of the process. When he stopped to scrutinize his thoughts about it, which wasn't often, he realized that he considered it as similar to the act of investigation. It was gathering information, pulling it together, and organizing it. In both situations, what appealed to him was the exploration; he liked to follow the threads. But he didn't like drawing the final conclusions. He didn't like having to act, often on incomplete and inconclusive information.

He'd been saved this time, because Tess Cunningham had forced the play. Or maybe it was more accurate to say that Chelan Montgomery had forced the play, by following Venice up to Whistler that day.

But he had to speculate; he always did. Were there

choices he could have made or directions he could have taken that might have solved the case sooner? The woman, with the help of her mercenary of a driver, had covered her traces very carefully, just as she'd helped to cover up that hit-and-run accident so many years earlier. But was there a path he should have taken, right after the first two murders, when he might have found his way to the right answer? If he had had anything, even circumstantial about Tess Cunningham, would he have made a move or would he have hesitated?

He didn't know whether the others dwelt on this stuff in the aftermath of an arrest. Nobody ever talked about it. He might take the opportunity to discuss it with the department psychologist. If he did make the appointment, maybe he'd use it to hammer out an answer to his real question: was he in the right job?

His phone light suspended his reflections and he picked up the receiver. Ninety seconds later, he ushered Chelan Montgomery and Kevin Papineau into his office.

He motioned them to have a seat. "I hope I've made it clear, Ms. Montgomery, how appreciative the department is of all your efforts on this case. And I'd like Kevin to hear it as well. You brought in information at several significant points and in the end, you were the one who hunted down Tess Cunningham. We all owe you."

"Thank you." Chelan tried to smile—the whole conversation made her uncomfortable. "We're actually here today about something else."

"We want to report a missing person." Kevin leaned forward.

"Not technically 'missing'—but we'd like to locate her. We're a bit concerned about her well-being."

Zack was sure there was much more information they could supply him, but it seemed he would have to extract it.

"Would you like to let me know who it is, exactly, we're speaking of?"

"Oh. Of course," Chelan said. "Do you remember Mrs. Howe?"

THE LION'S SHARE OF THE AIR TIME

Once Zack heard the details of Mrs. Howe's living arrangement and her absence from her usual parking spot, the picture was fairly clear.

"Of course, we can put out her description and ask the officers to keep an eye out for her." Zack said. "But technically, she's done nothing wrong, and there's no reason to detain her. If she's not bothering anyone, not breaking any laws, it's not really a matter for us. Aren't there any family members who might get involved?"

"We didn't know her well enough to get their names," Chelan replied.

Ξ

When Chelan returned to her apartment, she found a small parcel wrapped in brown paper on her doorstep. No Layla was draped over the living room couch, so Chelan took that spot and started to pull apart the paper. An envelope fell out.

Dear Chelan,

I think we both know this is a dead end. You haven't had a minute to spare for me since May. I don't really know how or why we were together at all, except that I did like you quite a bit at the beginning. And I thought you liked me. But I need somebody who makes a big place for me in her life. And for family. And somebody who can take things easy, not get all tied up in how things look, or how fast the lane is.

Anyway, it's time to move on, I guess. I'm returning the things you gave me.

I hope you go see Ronnie.

Twain

The box was empty.

Was he right? He'd known her only six months, and in the last two she'd been so caught up in Tess Cunningham's web, she had barely given him any thought. Could someone so recent in her life have anything definitive to say about her? For

321

years her ambition had been driving her, but now, where once had been a yearning, was only emptiness. Maybe Twain was right. How could an empty person give anything?

Wallowing, girl, absolutely wallowing. Chelan gave herself a shake. If it wasn't meant to be, it wasn't meant to be. As Twain wrote, time to move on.

Epilogue

Lillian liked to walk in the tranquility of the morning, before the city awoke. At this time of day, Stanley Park still seemed to be a private place, and her body was still familiar and cooperative. Later in the day, when strangers invaded the paths and her joints were overtaken by obstreperous pain, she would find a place to rest. But the fresh hours were hers and it was a time for movement, for contemplation.

The Rose Garden stretched ahead of her, like some magic forest. But not the forest you might expect, dressed in mossy green and mysterious black, made of strong bone and sinew. Instead it was an enchanted grove of delicate forms in hues of crimson, coral, and lemon. Bright colors and beauty can sometimes clothe secrets, numerous and byzantine.

Not to mention, sources of pain. She stared at the gloriously colored petals and the thorns that marched along the green stems supporting them. A gauntlet, a road of peril, landmines planted in a desert on the road approaching an oasis.

But does the thorn invalidate the flower? If the means are cruel, repugnant, even evil, does that render the end forever disastrous? She didn't think so. The purpose could remain magnificent, even if the interpretation was corrupt.

The Rose Garden was only a short distance from the Park entrance. She walked along West Georgia, toward downtown, in what she hoped did not appear to be a trudge.

She heard a car slow down beside her, pull forward a few yards, and then stop. A man in a natty, blue suit unfolded himself from the driver's seat and approached her.

"Mrs. Howe, I'd like to speak with you. Do you remember me?"

She looked closely at him, and had to admit that he was familiar. From the library perhaps? Or from days gone by in Coquitlam? Then the dime dropped. "Detective Esher, Vancouver PD," she says.

"Yes. Could I speak with you for a few moments? Maybe we could go get a cup of coffee?"

She let him guide her along the street to a tiny Vietnamese restaurant with an outdoor patio. He ordered a plain, black coffee—a ridiculous drink on such a hot, September day. Fall was only a few weeks away; the tourists had departed the city and the school-aged children had been returned to their places behind the closed doors. But even though the calendar and the pace of life in the city indicated that the summer was finished, the weather was inclined to disagree. Her iced tea arrived with a slice of lemon clinging to its rim. Very nice touch. She was conscious of a film of perspiration on her forehead and she wanted to wipe it away with the back of her hand, but she worried about seeming vulgar.

He said nothing, just sat and sipped his coffee, watching the people walk by on the street in much the same way that Coaster gave every passing human his full attention. After a few minutes, she could stand the silence no longer.

"What do you want, Mr. Esher? Why are we here?"

The detective reached into the breast pocket of his suit and pulled out an envelope. "This has been found among Keith Papineau's clothes and personal effects. It has to do with you, and I'd like you to read it."

She took it and reached into her bag for her glasses. The voluminous brown leather tote bag had served her for eight years now, although the shreds of the lining did get in the way on occasions such as this, when she was groping for an item in

THE LION'S SHARE OF THE AIR TIME

the depths. One of these days, she really should just rip it all out.

She unfolded the glasses, put them on, and then unfolded the sheet of white paper.

Dear Heather,

I hope this won't upset you too much but I've set aside a sum of money for a homeless woman that I see every day near my apartment. She wanders around with this little dog and I've been watching them for weeks now, since I moved out and came to live over here. I've asked a few people about her—the guy who has the restaurant on the corner and the guy who delivers the mail—and they say she lives in her car, moving from spot to spot.

I know there isn't a lot of extra money these days, but I just can't get her out of my head and I feel I have to do something.

Lillian's glasses were sliding down her nose. Why on earth didn't she have a handkerchief ready, in that huge purse? Her mother had tried to teach her always to carry a fresh handkerchief and she had ignored every reminder. Just as her own children disregarded many of her pronouncements, no doubt.

"Mrs. Howe? Have you finished reading the letter?"

"No. I'm just… I was just thinking… never mind. I'll read the rest of it now."

There's nothing left over from the LV-TV paycheck, but I'm going to ask Bob for a loan. I won't tell him what it's really for—he'd laugh me out of town. But it'll be my little private joke, knowing fifteen grand of his money is going to help somebody, rather than build another condo or buy another overpriced bottle of wine.

I thought I should let you know, in case he mentions it to you or anyone in the family. He'll probably think I've gambled with it, and let's just let him think that, okay?

I set up a special account at the branch in my neighborhood and I found out her name from her license plate. Lillian Howe. I'm going to talk to her about it today.

"Mrs. Papineau had put off going through all of her ex-husband's things, after he died, and this letter has only just come to light. He wrote it a couple of months ago, just shortly before he died. We've checked with the bank branch and there is an account there with your name on it. A big account."

Lillian's head was spinning and she could barely take in what he was saying. Keith Papineau was going to give her money?

"We've told Mrs. Papineau she should consult with her lawyer about this, of course. But she seemed to think that if her ex-husband wanted you to have this money, then that's the way it should be. Now, that's what she's saying today, and we'll have to sort it all out through the proper legal channels, but it looks as though your ... housing challenges, can we call them?... are about to end, Mrs. Howe." Esher smiled at her — he really was quite a good-looking young man.

"I should tell you that you were on my radar before I got this call from Mrs. Papineau. I believe you know Keith's son, Kevin? And Chelan Montgomery from LV-TV? They were both in my office, very concerned about your lack of permanent residence."

"I didn't want their pity," Lillian said. "I thought it was best just to move along, let them get on with their lives."

Esher stood up and held out a hand to Lillian. "I'd like to go down to the police station, verify your identity and set the wheels in motion for you to gain access to that account. May I give you and ..." He looked down at the dog.

"And Coaster."

"And Coaster a ride?"

Lillian gripped the little dog in her lap as they rode past the high-rise office buildings in the downtown core. Detective Esher glanced at her a few times, but she kept her eyes fixed on the window and the passing parade on the sidewalks outside. She thought she probably appeared to be rather serene, but her mind was churning. Fifteen thousand dollars! It was amazing. She had no delusions that it was a sum that would allow her to buy anything in Vancouver's West End,

THE LION'S SHARE OF THE AIR TIME

but it would certainly allow her to rent something decent for a year or so.

But perhaps it was time to think of migrating somewhere more practical, more realistic for someone in her circumstances. Somewhere she could stretch the money out to cover two or even three years. Or perhaps she could invest it in a way that would let her pay the rent on a place near the ocean?

Clearly, a great deal of thought needed to be given to this new adventure. She decided that her first night of thinking over her new situation would best be spent somewhere with a bed and sheets fit for a queen, a deep bathtub with unlimited hot water, and room service.

As the height of the buildings and the disposable incomes of the people they passed dropped, Lillian realized that they were only a few blocks from the police station. On the stoop of a very cheap hotel on Hastings Street, she saw a silhouette that she recognized.

A young woman bent over a scruffy-looking man who was sitting near the door of the hotel. Tiny woman, huge bag, and as she straightened up and the police car drew nearer, Lillian got a full-face view. It was Chelan, from the TV station.

The disheveled man stood up, unsteadily, and Chelan put a hand under his arm. They swayed there for a dozen seconds while he tried to get his balance, then Chelan opened the door to the hotel and they ventured in together.

Ξ

ABOUT THE AUTHOR

Gail Hulnick is a former reporter, TV broadcaster, and radio show host. She watches the news with her husband David, and divides her time between Vancouver, British Columbia and Savannah, Georgia.

THE LION'S SHARE OF THE AIR TIME

GAIL HULNICK

Made in the USA
Charleston, SC
09 May 2015